WOLF LAKE

A Novel

JOHN VERDON

COUNTERPOINT

Library of Congress Cataloging-in-Publication Data

Names: Verdon, John, author.
Title: Wolf Lake : a novel / John Verdon.
Description: Berkeley : Counterpoint, [2016]
Identifiers: LCCN 2016008988 | ISBN 9781619027336 (hardcover)
Subjects: LCSH: Detectives—New York (State)—New York—Fiction. | Serial murder investigation—Fiction. | Psychologists—Fiction. | GSAFD: Suspense fiction. | Mystery fiction.
Classification: LCC PS3622.E736 W65 2016 | DDC 813/.6—dc23
LC record available at https://lccn.loc.gov/2016008988

Cover design by Kelly Winton
Interior design by Domini Dragoone

COUNTERPOINT
2560 Ninth Street, Suite 318
Berkeley, CA 94710
www.counterpointpress.com

Printed in the United States of America
Distributed by Publishers Group West

10 9 8 7 6 5 4 3 2 1

For Naomi

PART ONE

DEADLY DREAMS

PROLOGUE

She stood shivering in the moonlight between the two giant hemlocks at the end of the frozen lake. She couldn't remember ever feeling so cold, so frightened. The sight of the full moon above the jagged treetops was giving her gooseflesh. The drooping branches were becoming in her mind deformed arms that might reach down and—

No! Stop! She shook her head—her real problem was terrifying enough without letting her imagination run wild.

In the distance she heard the motorcycle approaching—first on the old dirt road, then on the winding trail from the road down to the lake. The closer it came, the tighter the feeling in her chest.

Finally, with a surge of anxiety, she caught sight of the headlight flickering through the woods, then coming across the clearing that separated the pines from the towering black hemlocks.

He stopped in front of her and switched off the engine, planting his feet wide on the ground to balance the heavy bike—his big brother's, which he rode illegally.

She could just make out a few snowflakes in his wind-tousled hair. She wasn't sure whether he looked worried or whether she was imagining it because that was the way she'd expected him to look. Her phone call hadn't been explicit, but she knew her voice had been full of fear and urgency. She was sure, even with his back to the moon, that he was looking at her intently, waiting for her to explain why they were meeting here.

She could hear him breathing, could even hear his heart beating. But that was impossible. Maybe it was her own heart, her own desperate pulse beating in her ears.

She'd prepared what she intended to say, rehearsed it a hundred times that very evening; but now, in this forbidding place, her voice failed her.

"What?" he asked. "What is it?" His voice was sharp, not like she'd ever heard it before.

She bit her lower lip, took a trembling breath, and forced out the words in a barely audible whisper.

She heard him take a deep breath, but he said nothing.

She wondered if he'd heard her—half hoping that he hadn't.

A slow-moving cloud began to creep across the moon.

Sometime after that—she'd lost her sense of time—he restarted the motorcycle, gave the throttle a sudden twist, and accelerated out onto the ice-covered lake, the shriek of the engine slicing through the frigid air, the chrome tailpipe reflecting what was left of the moonlight.

Then, out on the distant center of the lake, the diminishing howl of the engine was broken by a horrifying crack—then another, and another, like a rapid series of muffled gunshots as the ice gave way under the motorcycle's weight. There was a sickening splashing impact . . . the hiss of the hot machine sinking . . . and silence.

The cloud now had obliterated every trace of the moon.

All was darkness. No sound. No light. No thought. No hope. No feeling.

And then, the scream. The scream rising with a feral life of its own, going on and on.

The scream that she came to realize only later had been hers.

CHAPTER 1

The porcupine's behavior was making no sense.

There was something deeply disturbing about its lack of logical purpose—disturbing at least to Dave Gurney.

On that raw morning in early December, he was sitting by the den window, gazing out toward a row of bare trees on the north side of the old pasture. He was fixated on one tree in particular, on one low-lying branch of that tree, as an unusually fat porcupine ambled back and forth along that branch—slowly, repetitively, seemingly pointlessly.

"Which snowshoes are you bringing?" Madeleine was standing in the den doorway, holding a traditional rawhide-on-wood pair in one hand and a contemporary metal-and-plastic pair in the other. Her short dark hair had the especially disarranged look it had when she'd been rooting around in the low-ceilinged attic or the back of a closet.

"I'll decide later."

They were planning to spend a few days at an inn in the Green Mountains of Vermont for some snowshoeing and cross-country skiing. Snow had not yet arrived that year in their own Catskill Mountains, and snow was the part of winter that Madeleine loved.

She nodded toward the den window. "Still obsessed with our little visitor?"

He considered several ways of responding to that, rejecting immediately any mention of the porcupine's resemblance to a shambling, half-senile gangster he'd known in the city. Three years into his retirement from the NYPD he and Madeleine had finally reached a tacit understanding of sorts. Although he was officially no longer the homicide detective he'd been for over twenty years, it had become clear that he wasn't about to morph into the biking, kayaking, all-out nature lover Madeleine had been hoping for. But some accommodation was called for. On his part, he agreed to stop relating how his current experiences in the rural mountains of upstate New York managed to bring to mind past criminal cases. On her part, she agreed to stop trying to convert him into something he wasn't. All this, of course, could lead to some fraught silences.

He looked back out the window. "I'm trying to figure out what he's up to."

She leaned the snowshoes against the wall, came next to him, peered out for several seconds at the bristly animal meandering along the branch. "He's probably just doing some normal porcupine thing. Same thing he was doing yesterday. What's the problem?"

"What he's doing doesn't make any sense."

"Maybe it makes sense to him."

"Not unless he's crazy. Or pretending to be crazy, which is unlikely. Look. Very slowly he makes his way out to the end of that branch. Then, very hesitantly, he turns around. Then he makes his way back the way he came. He's expending energy . . . for what?"

"Does everything have to be explainable?"

"Everything ultimately is explainable. And in this case I'd like to know that the explanation is something other than rabies."

"Rabies? Why would you think such a thing?"

"Rabies causes deranged behavior."

"Do you know for a fact that porcupines get rabies?"

"Yes. I checked. I'm going to put a couple of trail cams out there, find out where he goes, what he does, when he's not bumbling around on that branch."

She made a face, maybe confused, maybe incredulous—he wasn't sure which.

"Trail cams. Outdoor security cameras," he explained. "Motion-activated."

"Security cameras? Good Lord, David, the odds are he's just going about his little porcupine life, and you're treating him like . . . like he's committing a crime." She paused. "Where would you get these cameras anyway?"

"Jack Hardwick. He has a bunch of them."

He didn't remind her that they were left over from an aborted plan he and Hardwick had cooked up during the recent Peter Pan murder case, but, judging from her darkening expression, a reminder was unnecessary. He added, in an effort to pull the discussion back from an abyss of bad memories, "Once I can see how that animal behaves on the ground, I'll have a better idea of what's going on."

"You don't think you're overreacting, just a little?"

"Not if the damn thing has rabies."

She gave him one of those long looks that he could never quite decipher. "We're leaving for Vermont the day after tomorrow."

"So?"

"So when are you planning on doing whatever you're going to do with those camera things?"

"As soon as possible. As soon as I can get them from Hardwick. In fact, I should call him right now."

The indecipherable look changed to obvious concern. "When are you going to pack?"

"Christ, we're only going away for three days."

"Four."

"What's the difference?"

As Gurney left the den in search of his cell phone, Madeleine's voice followed him. "Did it occur to you that the porcupine might be totally harmless and that the reason he's walking back and forth on the branch might be none of your business?"

CHAPTER 2

A half hour later the morning sun was well above the eastern ridge. Its rays slanting through the ice crystals in the dry, frigid air were creating random microscopic sparkles.

Largely oblivious to this phenomenon, Gurney was standing by the French doors in the breakfast nook of their farmhouse kitchen. He was gazing down over the low pasture toward the red barn, the point at which the narrow town road dead-ended into their fifty-acre property—once upon a time a functioning hill farm, a use long since abandoned in the collapse of the upstate dairy industry.

After retiring early from their careers in the city, he and Madeleine had moved to that pastoral part of the western Catskill Mountains because the countryside was breathtakingly beautiful despite its economic depression. Her enthusiasm for the place was obvious from the beginning. Her energetic, unpretentious character; her positive fascination with the natural world; and her visceral delight in simply being outdoors in any season—canoeing, berry-picking, or just wandering along old forest trails—suited her for country life. Adapting to their new environment had been for her an easy, happy process.

He, nearly three years later, was still working on it.

But that sometimes divisive issue was not what was preoccupying him at the moment. He was pondering the disconcerting phone conversation he'd just had with Jack Hardwick.

Hardwick had answered the phone quite pleasantly with none of his customary jibes. He'd sounded so friendly that Gurney had suspected it was a parody of cordiality to be replaced at any moment by some cynical remark. But that didn't happen. Hardwick had responded to Gurney's request for the loan of a couple of trail cams with eagerness—not only to provide them but to deliver them. And not only to deliver them, but to do so immediately.

As Gurney stood by the glass doors mulling over this uncharacteristic rush to be helpful, Madeleine came down from an upstairs room carrying two nylon duffel bags—one blue, one green. She set them down on the floor by his feet.

"Do you have a preference?"

He glanced at the bags and shook his head. "Whichever."

"What's the matter?"

He told her about the phone call.

Her eyes narrowed. "He's coming . . . here? Now?"

"Apparently."

"What's his big hurry?"

"Good question. I assume we'll find out when he arrives."

On cue, from somewhere down the road below the barn, came the throaty rumble of a big V-8 engine. Half a minute later Hardwick's classic muscle car, a red 1970 Pontiac GTO, was making its way up the snow-covered lane through the overgrown pasture.

"He's got someone with him," said Madeleine.

Gurney wasn't fond of surprises. He went out past the mud room to the side door, opened it and watched while Hardwick parked the loud, angular GTO next to his own dusty, anonymous Outback.

Hardwick got out first, his thin-lipped grin exhibiting, as usual, more determination than warmth—the same message conveyed by his ice-blue eyes and aggressively colorless clothes: black jeans, black sweater, black windbreaker.

Gurney's attention, however, was on the person emerging from the passenger side. His first impression was of a different kind of colorlessness—a drab anonymity. A large, plain woman, she was wearing a quilted winter coat and shapeless wool ski hat, perhaps in her early forties.

When she arrived at the door, Gurney offered her a pleasant smile and turned an inquisitive glance toward Hardwick—which seemed to make the man's grin grow brighter.

"You're asking yourself, 'Where's that camera equipment he was supposed to be bringing me?' Am I right?"

Gurney waited, smiled patiently, said nothing.

"As your trusty guardian angel . . ." Hardwick inserted a dramatic pause before proceeding with relish, "I decided to bring you something of far greater value than a fucking trail cam. May we come in?"

Gurney led them into the kitchen end of the long open room that also included a dining area and, at the far end, a sitting area arranged around a fieldstone fireplace.

Madeleine's fraught smile seemed to reflect Gurney's history with his sometime colleague—a difficult man with whom he'd shared a series of near-fatal law enforcement experiences.

Hardwick's grin widened. "Madeleine. You look fantastic."

"Can I take your jackets?"

"Absolutely." He helped the bulky woman beside him remove hers. He did this with a flourish, as if he were unveiling something grand. "Dave, Madeleine, may I introduce . . . Jane Hammond."

Madeleine smiled and said hello. Gurney extended his hand, but the woman shook her head. "Very happy to meet you, but I won't shake your hand, I'm full of germs." She pulled off her knitted cap, revealing a shapeless, low-maintenance hairstyle.

Evidently sensing the absence of any recognition, Hardwick added, "Jane is the sister of Richard Hammond."

Gurney's expression suggested nothing but ongoing curiosity.

"Richard Hammond," repeated Hardwick. "The Richard Hammond—the one in every major newscast for the past month."

Madeleine showed a twinge of concern. "The hypnotist?"

Jane Hammond's reaction was emphatic. "Not hypnotist—hypnotherapist. Any charlatan can call himself a hypnotist, dangle a pendulum, and pretend he's doing something profound. My brother is a Harvard-trained psychologist who utilizes very sophisticated techniques."

Madeleine nodded sympathetically, as though she were dealing with a touchy client at the mental health clinic where she worked. "But isn't 'hypnotist' what they're calling him in the news reports?"

"That's not all they're calling him. The so-called news programs today are nothing but trash! They don't care how unfair they are, how full of lies—" She broke off in a brief fit of coughing. "Allergies," she explained. "I seem to have a different one for every season."

Hardwick spoke up. "Actually, could we sit down?"

Before Gurney could object, Madeleine offered them seats at the round pine table in the breakfast nook—where Hardwick, with a nod of encouragement from Jane Hammond, launched into the story of Richard Hammond's bizarre situation.

CHAPTER 3

"You know about the Adirondack Great Camps, right? Thousand-acre compounds, giant lodges, plenty of room for guests and servants, built about a hundred years ago by the richer-than-God robber barons—Rockefellers, Vanderbilts, et cetera. One of the lower-profile fat cats who built a place up there was a guy named Dalton Gall, a nasty bastard who'd made a fortune in tin mining. There's a peculiar legend involving his untimely death, which I'll come back to."

He paused, as if to give "untimely death" extra emphasis. "Some of the Great Camps, with their huge upkeep costs, started collapsing with the stock market crash. Some became museums celebrating the lives of the greedy scumbags who built them. Some got converted into educational centers where nature fanatics could study the ecology of the frilly-frond fern."

This jab at outdoorsiness provoked a narrow-eyed glance from Madeleine, who was preparing a pot of coffee at the sink island.

Hardwick went on, "Some of the camps continued to be maintained by the descendants of the original owners, usually by turning them into conference centers or upscale inns. Ethan Gall, great-grandson of Dalton, embraced the fancy-inn concept and added a few extras for the bored and restless wealthy. Learn while you're being pampered—that kind of horseshit. French-Vietnamese cooking secrets. Nepalese serenity secrets. Secrets are always in demand. And since even the most privileged have bad habits they'd rather not have, Ethan hired world-renowned psychologist Richard Hammond to provide unique hypnotic solutions. So the place wasn't just any old thousand-dollar-a-day Adirondack inn. It was the one where you got to have a therapeutic chat with none other than Richard Hammond—a chat you could regale your friends with at your next dinner party."

Jane Hammond had been anxiously squeezing her used tissue into a tighter and tighter ball. "I have to say something here. I don't want Mr. Gurney to get the wrong impression of my brother. I can't comment on Ethan Gall's motives. But I can assure you that Richard's motives were pure. His life is his work, and he takes it *very* seriously. Which is another reason why these accusations are so . . . so offensive!" She looked down with dismay at the crushed tissue in her hand.

Hardwick resumed his narration. "So. Whatever Ethan Gall's motives might have been, he gave Dr. Hammond a generous two-year contract, which, among other perks, included the use of a private chalet on the property. All went well until one evening approximately two months ago when Dr. Hammond got a call from a detective in Palm Beach."

"Florida," added Jane.

"Right. A twenty-seven-year-old male by the name of Christopher Wenzel had committed suicide a few days earlier. Cut his wrists sitting in his million-dollar condo on the Intracoastal. No indication of anything requiring special police attention. However, after the suicide was reported in the local news, a minister showed up at Palm Beach PD with an interesting story. Wenzel had come to see him a couple of days before he offed himself, complaining he hadn't been able to sleep right for a whole week. Whenever he'd doze off he'd have this terrible nightmare—same nightmare every time. Said it was making him want to die."

Hardwick paused, as if to let the implications of this sink in.

Gurney felt he was missing something—beyond the question of why this conversation with Jack Hardwick and Jane Hammond was occurring at all. "This information about the suicide was passed along to Dr. Hammond in a phone call by a Palm Beach detective?"

"Right."

"Why?"

"Because Wenzel told the minister that his nightmares had started after he'd been hypnotized by Dr. Richard Hammond to help him stop smoking. So the detective called Hammond, asked if he'd treated the deceased. Richard said that was confidential, HIPAA regulations, blah-blah-blah, but what was the problem? The detective explained the situation, asked if suicides or nightmares were ever side effects of hypnosis. Richard said he'd never heard of such a reaction. And that was pretty much the end of that . . . until a week later. That's when he got another call—this one from a detective in Teaneck, New Jersey."

Gurney said nothing, just waited.

Madeleine's eyes widened.

Hardwick went on. "Another wrist-cutting suicide. Leo Balzac, age twenty-eight. When the Teaneck detective checked the deceased's smartphone calendar, he saw that he'd had an appointment with a local therapist two days before he killed himself. So the detective paid a visit to the therapist, more dancing around the HIPAA bullshit, but eventually he found out Balzac had come to the therapist for a problem he'd been having with nightmares—ever since a certain Dr. Hammond had hypnotized him to help him stop smoking."

Gurney was intrigued. "This second detective got in touch with Hammond to ask about the hypnosis session, the same as the first one did?"

"Right. And Hammond gave him the same answer."

Jane looked up from the table. "It wasn't exactly the same. In addition to insisting that his therapy sessions couldn't cause nightmares, Richard told the second detective about the call he'd gotten from the first detective. It was clear to him that something strange was going on, and he wanted both detectives to have the whole picture. You see how important that is?"

When neither Gurney nor Hardwick responded, she explained. "If Richard hadn't done that—if he hadn't been as helpful as he was—the police in Florida and the police in New Jersey never would have connected the two suicides. It was Richard who innocently volunteered that information. Which proves he had nothing to hide."

Gurney and Hardwick exchanged skeptical glances.

"But," interjected Madeleine, "if I remember the news reports, there was more to the story, wasn't there?"

"A shitload more," said Hardwick. "The really god-awful mess was yet to come."

Before Hardwick could proceed, Madeleine went to the sink island and brought back four mugs of coffee on a tray with spoons, milk, and sugar.

Jane took the mug nearest her and thanked Madeleine for it, then looked her over frankly, as if evaluating her slim, athletic figure—still elegantly sexy at forty-seven—concluding with a smile, "You're so much younger than I'd been picturing on the drive here."

"Younger?"

"Jack told me that Dave was retired from the police department. The word 'retired' conjured up the image of a gray-haired couple puttering in the garden. And you turn out to be . . . well . . . like this. You look about thirty-five, and your husband looks like Daniel Craig."

Madeleine uttered a small laugh. "He may look a bit like Daniel Craig, but it's quite a few years since I was anything close to thirty-five. You're very kind."

Gurney explained, "Most cops qualify for their pensions after twenty-five years on the job. So it's a natural time to get out, you know . . . and . . . and move on to something else." His words trailed off with a descending energy that revealed more about his general feeling of indecision than he'd intended.

"So," said Hardwick, the short syllable functioning like the tap of a gavel to bring them back to the subject at hand. "After Teaneck PD got talking to Palm Beach PD, it was obvious the next step was to pull the New York State Police into the loop, since the common factor between the two suicides, Richard Hammond, resided on NYSP turf. Which is how this bizarre case ended up on the desk of Senior Investigator Gilbert Fenton."

"A real son of a bitch," said Jane.

Hardwick nodded his agreement.

"You know him?" asked Gurney.

"Yeah, I know him. As soon as the situation was dropped in Fenton's in-box, he took a drive out to the Gall estate to interview Dr. Hammond, find out what he could about this hypnosis business, see if the two suicides were caused by anything that would be of interest to law enforcement."

Hardwick leaned forward, his muscular forearms resting on the table. "Fenton's an organization guy, very oriented to hierarchy. So, before talking to Hammond, he wanted to talk to the man in charge— namely, Ethan Gall. But nobody knew where Ethan was. Nobody had seen him for two days. You get where this is going, right?"

Gurney shrugged. "Tell me anyway."

"Four days after Fenton's visit, Ethan's body was found in one of the estate's cabins, about half a mile from the main house. This particular cabin was not very secure. Some animals had gotten in . . ."

Hardwick paused, letting the visual possibilities register. "The ID process took some time. Dental records, then DNA. Enough of the body was intact to determine that at least one wrist had been cut. There was also a knife present with his blood and fingerprints on it."

"How do you know this stuff?"

"I know some people who know some people."

"How did BCI treat the death?"

"The ME's report was inconclusive—apart from noting that the evidence was consistent with a suicide. A lot of the body had been devoured or dragged off. But the wrist cutting—and the common factor of contact with Richard Hammond—convinced Gil Fenton that this was the third in a series of suspicious suicides."

"You mean 'suspicious' as in possible homicides?"

Hardwick looked like he had acid reflux. "Because of their similarities, the three suicides came to be regarded as 'suspicious' in the legally uncharted sense of being brought about by forces other than the independent decisions of self-destructive individuals."

Gurney frowned. "Meaning what?"

"In Fenton's public statements, he keeps suggesting that the suicides were not only influenced by Richard Hammond, but may have been orchestrated by him—in effect, that he may have forced these people to kill themselves."

"Forced them?" Gurney cocked his head incredulously. "How? Through hypnotic suggestion?"

"Hypnotic suggestion . . . and nightmares."

"Are you serious? Hammond is supposed to have given these people nightmares that made them kill themselves?"

"That's Fenton's theory, which he's pushing every time he talks to the press." Hardwick paused, eyeing Gurney speculatively. "What do you think of that?"

"I think it's ridiculous."

Jane Hammond slapped her hand on the table. "Thank you for

saying that! That's what I've been saying myself from the beginning—that it's ridiculous to even think that Richard would do something like that."

Gurney asked, "Was Ethan Gall ever hypnotized by your brother?"

"Yes. In fact, Richard helped him break a lifelong smoking habit."

"And their session was when?"

"Oh, maybe three . . . well, at least two months ago."

"Do you know if Ethan ever complained about nightmares?"

Jane blinked nervously. "There's some confusion about that. Fenton has a handwritten document in which Ethan supposedly described a nightmare he'd been having. But Ethan never said a word about any nightmare to Richard."

"How about the nightmares the other individuals had?" asked Gurney. "Does anyone know the content of those?"

Hardwick shook his head. "The other police departments are keeping whatever details they have under wraps. Which brings me to the final big piece of the puzzle. After a BCI press relations officer disclosed the details surrounding Gall's death, a detective from Floral Park down on Long Island got in touch with BCI to let them know he had a two-week-old suicide on his hands with the same history—a hypnotherapy session with Dr. Hammond followed by bad dreams and sliced wrists. He hadn't bothered to contact Hammond, apparently because he didn't give the hypnosis aspect of the situation much weight. Seems odd he'd overlook that, but odd shit happens all the time. Anyway, his dead guy was a twenty-six-year-old by the name of Steven Pardosa. That's when Fenton went all out with his hypnosis-nightmare-suicide narrative—big press briefing, lots of nasty innuendo, practically accusing Hammond of murder, sending the media hyenas into a feeding frenzy."

"Just a second. How did the Long Island detective know about Pardosa's contact with Hammond, or about his bad dreams?"

"Pardosa told his chiropractor; and when the chiropractor saw Pardosa's obit in *Newsday*, he called the cops."

"So, we've got three males in their mid twenties, plus Ethan Gall. How old was he?"

Hardwick looked at Jane.

She shrugged. "Early to mid thirties? His younger brother, Peyton, is in his late twenties, and there was five years between them."

There was something sour about the way she'd said the brother's name that caught Gurney's attention. He was about to ask about it, but Hardwick started speaking first.

"After the Pardosa thing surfaced, everything clicked into place in Fenton's head. He had four dead people—people he started referring to as 'victims'—who'd all suffered from bad dreams after being treated by Richard Hammond—a doctor known for his experiments in hypnosis. Fenton made Hammond sound like some kind of mad scientist."

"Speaking of which," said Jane, "I have printouts of the horrible news stories that were published after his outrageous press conferences." She stood up and started toward the door. "They're in the car."

Gurney stopped her with a question he felt was overdue. "What does Richard's lawyer have to say about all this?"

"Richard doesn't have a lawyer."

"Even with everything that's going on?"

"That's right." She fell silent for several seconds. "It's a long story. I'm not sure I know how to tell it." She shook her head. "I'll get the file."

"I'll join you," said Madeleine. "I need some air." As she stood up to follow Jane, she gave Gurney a look in which he read a clear message:

This is your chance to find out from Hardwick what on earth is going on here.

CHAPTER 4

The side door closed with a solid thump.
Hardwick looked across the table at Gurney. His pale Malamute eyes, which usually exuded little warmth, showed signs of amusement. "So what do you think, Sherlock? The case does raise a few interesting questions, wouldn't you say?"

"I've got about ten of them on my mind right now."

"For instance?"

"Why the hell doesn't Hammond have a lawyer?"

"He insists the reason he doesn't want a lawyer is because he doesn't need a lawyer. He's so totally innocent that the wild accusations against him will collapse under the weight of their own absurdity."

"That's what he told you?"

"That's what he told the world in his one and only press release. There's a copy in Jane's media file."

"What's your gut feeling about him?"

"Arrogant, brittle, secretive—with an odd vibe that makes me want to kick him in the balls. He also strikes me as a frightened man trying to sound cool. But I have no fucking idea why he doesn't want a lawyer."

"How did you get connected with his sister?"

"She tried to hire a lawyer to represent Richard's interests without him knowing about it. The law firm turned her down, because that kind of arrangement falls somewhere between unethical and impossible. But they did suggest that she might hire a private investigator to look into the case, strictly on her behalf, and she could then do as she saw fit with whatever information was uncovered. Naturally, they recommended me."

"Why would they do that?"

"Obviously because I have a hard-earned reputation for upsetting law enforcement's apple cart, securing justice for the falsely accused, and pissing on authority in general." Hardwick's grin flashed for a split second like the ice crystals in the sunlight.

"Why did you bring this woman—?"

Hardwick broke in. "Why did I bring the desperate Jane Hammond to you? A woman who carries a lifetime of worry in her eyes? A woman whose little brother has always been the rose and the thorn in her life, and who is now in a shitstorm of trouble? A woman who I suspect has no sex life, no peace, no interests of her own? Is that what you were about to ask me?"

"Yes."

He paused, sucked thoughtfully at his teeth before speaking. "There's something particularly odd about this case, and something disturbingly off-center about the good doctor himself. The whole situation seems . . . foggy . . . to me. Almost eerie. And you're better at eerie than I am. So I'd like you to sniff around a bit, get the lay of the land, talk to this guy, find out what you can—especially about that guilty vibe he exudes like last night's garlic—and let me know what you think. Look, nine times out of ten I know what I'm looking at. But this is that one out of ten that I can't figure."

"You're telling me that this is a matter of investigative competence? That you want to pass the baton along to a man with sharper skills than yourself? What kind of bullshit is that?"

"It's the truth. Honest. But . . . to be completely honest . . . it's not the only reason."

"I didn't think so."

"Do you believe in divine providence?"

"Do I believe in what?"

"Serendipity."

"What the hell are you talking about?"

"A grand coincidence. At the very moment that Jane Hammond was sitting in my modest home office describing her brother's desperate situation, describing her desperate need for help, *you* called."

Gurney said nothing.

"So there you are—David Gurney, detective first grade, NYPD Homicide, most decorated officer in the history of the department— planning to surveil a porcupine. A brain fit to confront the greatest criminal minds on earth—focused on a quill ball in a tree. Now tell me, if that isn't fucked up, what is?"

Gurney said nothing.

"So here we are, with a major opportunity that benefits everyone. I get your help in piercing the fog wrapped around this case. Jane gets the investigatory assistance she so badly needs to help her brother. You get to apply your God-given talent to a worthy challenge."

Gurney found the logic of this appeal almost convincing.

The problem was, he knew Hardwick too well.

"Very smooth sales presentation, Jack. I'm almost ready to test-drive the car. There's just one thing missing."

"Missing?"

"The truth. Give me the real reason, and I'll tell you whether I'm interested."

After a few seconds of perfect stillness, Hardwick let out a bark of a laugh.

"Just testing you, Davey. Making sure you still have what it takes. Don't get me wrong. Everything I said was true. But there is one other factor in the equation." He leaned forward and extended his hands, palms up, in a gesture of openness. "Here's the problem. I have a history with Gil Fenton. Seven years ago he did me a favor. Big favor, involving an error on my part. Serious error." Hardwick paused, grimacing. "So Gil has certain facts at his disposal. Under normal circumstances, this would not be a source of great concern. There are reasons he would want to keep these facts to himself. However, if we were to have a head-on collision . . . if he were to see me leading an attack on his handling of the Hammond case . . ."

Gurney gave him a cool, speculative smile. "You want to work quietly in the background while I take your place in the head-on collision?"

"He couldn't damage you the way he could damage me."

"You could just drop the case and refer the lady to another private investigator."

"Sure," said Hardwick, nodding in an unconvincing imitation of agreement. "I could do that. Maybe I should do that. It would probably be the smartest option. Definitely the safest."

He hesitated. "Of course, if we send Jane to someone else, they might fuck up the assignment. And if they fuck up the assignment, we might never find out why all those former clients of Richard Hammond killed themselves."

CHAPTER 5

Gurney heard the side door being opened, followed by the voices of Madeleine and Jane as they hung up their jackets in the mud room.

When the two women entered the kitchen, Madeleine was smiling and shaking ice crystals out of her hair, and Jane was carrying a bulging manila envelope. She brought it to the table and laid it in front of Gurney.

"This is pretty comprehensive. It should give you an idea of what we're up against. I made copies of everything I could find on the Internet. Local coverage of the four suicides. Obituaries. Talk-show transcripts. Interviews with experts in the field of hypnosis."

"Has Richard gotten any support from the academic community?"

"That's a laugh! The so-called 'academic community' is teeming with envious little creeps who resent Richard's success and are probably delighted to see him being attacked."

Gurney eyed the bulging envelope. "Are Gil Fenton's press briefings in there?"

"Every misleading word."

"Did you pull all this together at your brother's request?"

"Not exactly. He's . . . confident that the problem will just go away."

"And you're not?"

"No . . . yes . . . I mean, yes, of course I know it will eventually be resolved. It has to be. I have faith. But you know the old saying, 'God will move the mountain, but you have to bring a shovel.' That's what I'm doing."

Gurney smiled. "Apparently Richard believes that God will move the mountain, so long as Jane brings the shovel."

There was flash of anger in her eyes. "That's not fair. You don't know him."

"So help me understand. Why does he refuse to get a lawyer? Why is it up to you to protect him?"

She gave Gurney a cold stare, then turned away and looked out the window.

"Richard is like no one else on earth. I know people say things like that all the time about people they love, but Richard is truly unique. He always was. I don't mean he's perfect. He's not. But he has a gift."

There was a well-worn reverence in this statement that made it sound as if she'd been making it all her life—as if everything depended on it.

As he studied her profile, the anxious wrinkles radiating from the corner of her eye, the grim set of her mouth, he realized that at the center of this woman's psyche was the belief that things would have to turn out well for her brother because the opposite would be unbearable.

Madeleine asked softly, "Richard's gift—is it for his work as a psychotherapist?"

"Yes. He's . . . amazing. Which makes this awful attack on him so much worse. He does things no other therapist can do."

Madeleine shot a glance at Gurney, a suggestion that he pick up the thread.

"Can you give me an example?"

"Richard has an extraordinary power to change people's behavior virtually overnight. He has an intense sense of empathy. It's a connection that enables him to motivate his patients at the deepest level. He's often able in a single session to free a patient from some habit or addiction he's been struggling with for years. Richard realigns the way people see things. It sounds like magic, but it's totally real."

It occurred to Gurney that if her perception of her brother's talents was anywhere near accurate, the implications could be troubling. If Richard Hammond could so easily persuade people to do things they'd previously been unable or unwilling to do . . .

Perhaps sensing his concern, Jane reiterated her point. "Richard's talent is totally for the benefit of others. He could never use his gift to harm anyone. Never!"

Gurney changed the subject back to one of his unanswered questions. "Jane, I'm still not clear why the effort to extricate Richard from this situation is all up to you. I get the impression he's hardly responding to the problem at all. Am I missing something?"

Her reaction was a pained look. She turned back toward the window, shaking her head slowly.

"I hate talking about this," she said, unfolding a tissue. "It's hard for ordinary people to understand . . . because of Richard's uniqueness." She blew her nose several times, then dabbed at it gingerly. "He has periods of tremendous psychic energy and insight . . . and periods of complete exhaustion. In those periods of achievement, when he does all his best work, he naturally needs someone who can deal with the practical details he doesn't have time for. And when he slows down, when he has to rest . . . well, then he needs someone to . . . to deal with whatever he doesn't have the energy for."

It was beginning to sound to Gurney that Jane Hammond was mired in an unhealthy, enabling relationship with a manic-depressive egomaniac.

Before he could say anything, Madeleine intervened with the sort of understanding smile he imagined was one of her standard tools at the mental health center. "So, you sort of pitch right in and take care of whatever needs to be taken care of?"

"Exactly," said Jane, turning toward her with the eagerness of someone who felt she was finally being understood. "Richard is a genius. That's the most important thing. Naturally, there are things he just can't . . . shouldn't have to . . . deal with."

Madeleine nodded. "And now that he's in some trouble, and also in one of his . . . his low-energy periods . . . it's up to you to do whatever has to be done to deal with the problem."

"Yes! Of course! Because it's so unfair—so unfair that Richard, of all people, is being subjected to this horror!" She looked with a pleading expression from Madeleine to Hardwick to Gurney. "Don't you see? Something has to be done! That's why I'm here. I need your help!"

Gurney said nothing.

Her eyes full of anxiety, she glanced over at Hardwick, then back at Gurney. "Jack told me all about you. About how you solved more homicide cases than anyone else in New York City. And that case where you saved a woman who'd been framed for a murder she didn't commit. You're the perfect person to help Richard!"

"I'm still not understanding something here. You say your brother won't agree to your hiring—"

He was interrupted by the chirpy little melody of a cell phone ringing.

Jane headed directly out to the mud room, speaking as she went. "That's mine. I left it in my jacket pocket." The ring stopped before she was halfway through the hall.

When she returned she was holding her phone in her hand and frowning at the screen.

"Lost the signal?" asked Madeleine.

"I think so."

"The service is tricky around here. You have to pick your spots pretty carefully."

Jane nodded, looking worried, and laid the phone on the sideboard under the window. She watched it expectantly for a few moments before turning her attention back to Gurney. "Sorry. You were saying . . . ?"

"I was saying that I'm confused. Richard won't agree to your hiring a lawyer, but hiring a private investigator would be okay?"

"No, it won't be okay at all. He'll hate the idea. But it needs to be done, and he can't stop me from doing it. I can't legally hire a lawyer to represent him, but I can hire someone to look into the case for me."

"I'm still confused. It doesn't sound to me like he's simply too exhausted or depressed to deal with this situation. His active objection to receiving outside help gives me the feeling there's something more going on here."

Jane came over to the round pine breakfast table and sat down with Madeleine, Hardwick, and Gurney.

"I don't know if I should be telling you this story. But I don't know what else to do." She looked down, addressing herself to her hands folded tightly in her lap.

"Early in his career, which wasn't all that long ago, Richard published a case history that got a lot of attention. It was about a man who was tortured by exaggerated fears. These fears would sometimes dominate him completely, even though in his clearer moments he understood that these horrible things had no factual basis." She paused, biting her lip and glancing nervously around the table before going on.

"One day the man discovered a problem with his car. He'd left it in a parking lot at JFK for a three-day business trip, and when he returned he discovered that he couldn't open the trunk because the key wouldn't turn in the lock. He thought maybe someone had tried to break into the trunk but only succeeded in breaking the lock. So he put his suitcase in the backseat and drove home. But later that night another idea entered his mind—a very peculiar idea, that someone might have hidden a dead body in his trunk. He knew this wasn't a very likely scenario—that a murderer would drive his victim's corpse to an airport parking lot, break into a stranger's trunk, and transfer the corpse from his own trunk to another. That would be an absurd way to get rid of a dead body. But that didn't stop the man from dwelling on it, obsessing about it. The more he thought about it, the more credible it became in his own mind. First of all, there was the JFK airport location—an area in which Mafia-connected bodies had actually been found in the past. And he remembered news stories about mob killings in which the victims were found in abandoned cars."

"Not quite the same thing, is it?" said Hardwick.

"Not at all. But wait—there's more. He couldn't open the trunk himself without destroying it with a crowbar, but he was afraid to have a locksmith open it for him. He was afraid to have anyone else see what might be in the trunk. This fixation would come and go, like the seasons of the year. When the time came two years later to trade in the car, not only was the fixation still with him, he was completely paralyzed by it. He'd think, what if the car dealer or the new owner opens the trunk and finds a dead body or something equally horrible?"

She fell silent, took a slow deep breath, and sat motionless, staring down at her clasped hands.

After a moment Hardwick asked, "So how the hell does this story end?"

"One day the man backed into someone's bumper in a parking lot, and the trunk popped open. Of course, there was nothing in it. He traded the car in, got a new one. That was that. Until the next terror grabbed hold of him."

Hardwick shifted impatiently in his chair. "The point of this story is . . . what?"

"The point is that the man in the case history that Richard published, the man with the periodic paralyzing fears, was Richard himself."

At first no one reacted.

This wasn't, at least in Gurney's case, because of any shock at the revelation. In fact, he'd suspected that's where her narrative was heading from the start.

Hardwick frowned. "So what you're telling us is that your brother is half psychological genius, half nutcase?"

She glared at him. "What I'm telling you is that he has profound ups and downs. The great irony is that this is a man who can help virtually anyone who comes to him, but when it comes to his own demons he's helpless. I believe that's why I've been put on this planet—to take care of a man who can't take care of himself, so he can take care of everyone else."

Gurney couldn't help wondering in exactly what ways Hammond had taken care of the four patients who were now dead. But there was another issue he wanted to address first.

"Does he have that same fear now—that if more people start investigating the deaths of his patients, they may somehow find evidence that implicates him?"

"I think that's it exactly. But you have to understand that his fear is based on nothing. It's just another imaginary body in the trunk."

"Except now we have four bodies," said Hardwick. "And these ones are real."

"What I meant was—"

She was interrupted by her phone chirping on the sideboard where she'd left it. She hurried over to it, looked at the ID screen, then put the phone to her ear. "I'm here," she said. "What? . . . Wait, your voice is breaking up. . . . Who's doing what? . . . I'm losing half of what you're saying. . . . Just a second." She turned toward Madeleine. "It's Richard. Where can I get the best reception?"

"Come over here." Madeleine got up and pointed through the French doors. "Out there, just beyond the patio, between the birdbath and the apple tree."

Madeleine opened one of the doors for her, and Jane walked quickly out over the snow-covered ground, the phone at her ear, seemingly oblivious to the cold. Madeleine closed the door with a little shiver, went to the mud room, and a minute later was out by the apple tree handing Jane her jacket.

Hardwick flashed a fierce grin. "Love that wild trunk bit. So what do you think, Sherlock? Is the doctor a manic-depressive saint with paranoid delusions? Or is everything we just heard a total crock of shit?"

CHAPTER 6

Jane was still out under the apple tree, engaged in a visibly stressful phone conversation, when Madeleine rejoined the two men at the table.

Hardwick eyed her concerned expression. "The hell's going on out there?"

"I'm not sure. I may have misheard what Jane was saying, but I got the impression her brother was telling her that he's being followed."

Gurney's face reflected his discomfort. He spoke as much to himself as to Madeleine and Hardwick. "And his solution to all this is not to hire a lawyer or a private security firm, but just dump it all on his big sister?"

The sky was clouding over. Gusts of wind were pressing Jane's loose-fitting pants against her legs, but she showed no awareness of the cold.

He turned to Hardwick. "What's her real agenda here?"

"Bottom line? She wants you to come to Wolf Lake and find out why those people committed suicide after visiting the lodge. Naturally, she wants you to discover a reason that has nothing to do with the fact that all four of them were hypnotized by her brother."

Madeleine, from whom Gurney expected an immediate objection to this proposed Adirondack diversion from their Vermont getaway, said nothing. She was staring, not out at Jane Hammond in the field, but into her own thoughts, with a troubled look in her eyes. It was a look he didn't immediately recognize. A look that in some subtle way discouraged questioning.

"Problem is, Jack, day after tomorrow Maddie and I are on our way up to northern Vermont. The Tall Pines Inn. It's not something we'd want to cancel or postpone at this point."

"Wouldn't dream of asking you to cancel anything vital to the health and happiness of your marriage." Hardwick winked at Madeleine, who was still in a world of her own. He was speaking in that jokey way of his that drove Gurney up a wall—it created such a sharp echo of the way his own father viewed everything after a few drinks. "I'm sure there's another solution, ace. Think positively and the path will reveal itself."

Gurney was about to tell him to stuff the supercilious tone when he heard the side door open. Jane came through the hallway into the kitchen, still wearing her jacket, her hair windblown. Her obvious distress got Madeleine's attention.

"Jane? Is your brother all right?"

"He's talking about people spying on him, hacking into his computer. I think the police are trying to drive him crazy, make him have a mental breakdown."

Seemingly energized by her brother's problems, she struck Gurney as the classic codependent. He knew that the irony of that sort of relationship is that the "fixer" would be made redundant by any lasting fix. Only by maintaining the long-term weakness of her dependent can she remain relevant. He wondered how closely Jane Hammond fit the model. "Were you getting the sense that these observations of his were . . . realistic?"

"*Realistic?*"

"You told us your brother suffers from exaggerated fears."

"That's different. That's about things he sometimes imagines. This is about things he's actually *seeing*. He isn't psychotic, for God's sake! He doesn't *see* things that aren't there!"

"Of course not," Madeleine intervened. "David is just curious about the *meaning* Richard is giving to what he's seeing."

Jane looked at Gurney. "The *meaning?*"

"A car behind you on the road might be following you," he explained. "On the other hand, it might just be behind you on the road. I'm sure your brother is seeing what he's seeing, I'm just wondering about his interpretation of it."

"I can't answer your question. I don't know enough about what's happening. But that's the whole point, don't you see? That's why I need you. You and Jack. I have no idea why those four people committed suicide. I have no idea what the facts are. I just know they're not what the police say they are. But getting to the truth—that's what you're so good at."

Gurney stole a glance at Madeleine to see how she was reacting to this plea for his involvement, but her expression revealed nothing.

Jane went on. "If you came up to Wolf Lake and met with Richard and asked him the right questions, I bet you could figure out what's real and what isn't. That's what good detectives do, right? And according to Jack, you're the best. Will you do it?"

He sat back in his chair and studied her expression, the hope enlivening her eyes. He answered with a question of his own: "Who actually runs the lodge?"

"That would be Austen Steckle, the general manager. He's in charge of everything up there, especially since Ethan's death, but even before that. Ethan relied on him totally." She paused. "Austen's kind of a tough character, but I have to say he's been very fair to Richard. And he's gone out of his way to protect him from the media vultures. The minute Fenton went public with his crazy accusations, reporters were besieging the place. Austen brought in private security for the first week, had reporters arrested for trespassing and harassment. Word got around, and they stopped trying to sneak onto the estate."

"You mentioned that Ethan has a surviving brother? Is he active in the business?"

"Peyton? He's on the property, but that's about it. He's no use to anyone."

"What's the problem?"

"Who knows? Even the best family can produce a bad seed."

Gurney nodded his vague agreement. "You mentioned Peyton is in his late twenties?"

"Twenty-eight or twenty-nine, I think. Around the same age as Austen. But in terms of energy, focus, and smarts, they're from different planets."

"Any other siblings?"

"None surviving. Ethan and Peyton were originally the oldest and youngest of five children. The three middle ones were killed along with their father when his private plane went down in a thunderstorm. Their mother had a breakdown that led to her suicide two years later. That happened when Ethan was twenty-one and Peyton was in his mid teens. The tragedy just magnified the differences between them. It didn't help that Ethan was appointed Peyton's legal guardian."

"When you mentioned 'bad seed' . . . ?"

"Peyton has been a source of endless problems. As a kid it was stealing, lying, bullying. Then it became an endless succession of crazy girlfriends—hookers, to be brutally honest—disgusting behavior, gambling, drugs, you name it."

"He lives at Wolf Lake?"

"Unfortunately."

Gurney glanced at Hardwick for his reaction, but the man was flipping through screens on his smartphone.

Jane looked at Gurney pleadingly. "Will you at least come and talk to Richard, maybe have a look around?"

"If he's opposed to getting outside help, won't he refuse to see me?"

"Probably, if we ask in advance. But if you've already made the trip, he'll feel compelled to see you."

"You sound sure of that."

"It's part of who he is. When he had his practice in Mill Valley, if someone showed up at his office without an appointment, he could never send them away, no matter how busy he was. If someone was there, he had to meet with them. Let me add, in case you're getting the wrong idea—it had nothing to do with money, with trying to squeeze in another paying customer. Richard never cared about money, only about people."

Gurney thought it odd that a man with no interest in money would have chosen to establish his practice in Mill Valley, California, one of the wealthiest communities in America.

Perhaps sensing his skepticism, Jane continued. "Large organizations have approached Richard in the past with lucrative offers—very lucrative offers—if he would work for them exclusively. But he always turned them down."

"Why?"

"Because Richard has always been devoted to transparency. He would insist on knowing everything about any organization that would want an exclusive right to his research. Not all institutions in the field of psychological research are as independent as they claim to be. No amount of money on earth could persuade Richard to work for any entity whose goals and backing were not 100 percent visible and verifiable. That's the kind of man he is." She leaned toward Gurney. "You will help . . . won't you?"

"We have a timing problem. A short trip we've been planning for quite a while."

She looked wounded. "When?"

"The day after tomorrow. So there's really nothing I can—"

"How long?"

"How long will we be away? Four or five days. Perhaps sometime after that—"

"But things are happening so fast. Isn't there any way—?"

"Yes, matter of fact, there is!" interjected Hardwick triumphantly, holding up his phone with the screen turned outward so everyone could see the travel map it displayed. "The purple route line goes from your house all the way to Tall Pines Inn in northeastern Vermont. Between those two points are approximately two hundred miles of Adirondack mountains. I've found two ways of going around those mountains and two ways of going through them. One of those ways passes within twenty miles of the Gall Wilderness Preserve. All you have to do is start your vacation a day sooner than you planned and spend the first night at the super-exclusive Wolf Lake Lodge."

Jane looked from Gurney to Madeleine, her hands clasped like a praying child's. "You could do that, right? You could stop off there on your way to Vermont, couldn't you?"

Gurney didn't know how to respond without knowing what Madeleine was thinking.

His hesitation prompted Jane to address her directly. "You'll have a beautiful room, and it won't cost you anything."

Madeleine's eyes were still on the map displayed on Hardwick's phone screen.

After a moment, to Gurney's surprise, she nodded.

"We can do that."

CHAPTER 7

After Jane Hammond agreed to meet them the following afternoon at the lodge, she and Hardwick departed.

Madeleine headed for the hallway that led to the bedroom, announcing that she was going to take a shower.

Gurney sensed that she wanted to avoid, at least for the moment, any further discussion of Wolf Lake. He didn't know what to make of that, but he'd learned over the years that pursuing a subject Madeleine wasn't ready to talk about led nowhere. Instead, he decided to take a look into the manila envelope Jane Hammond had left for him.

He brought it into the den and sat down at his desk.

In the envelope were two folders, each bearing a handwritten notation: The notation on the top folder said *First Reports on the Four Deaths.*

Gurney opened it and found the original news items that had appeared on the websites of various local publications. It was odd reading reports written prior to the discovery of all the facts, but he wanted to see how the incidents were initially perceived.

From the *Palm Beach Post*, October 2:

SUICIDE SUSPECTED IN DEATH OF PALM BEACH MAN.

The body of Christopher Wenzel, age 26, was discovered Monday morning in his condominium overlooking the Intracoastal Waterway. A preliminary autopsy report listed the cause of death as possible suicide, with a fatal loss of blood resulting from deep arterial wounds to the wrists. The body was found by an independent cleaning contractor with access to Mr. Wenzel's apartment.

Neighbors said that Mr. Wenzel lived alone but had frequent visitors and noisy parties. No information was available on the deceased's family or employment connections. Building management declined comment.

From the *Bergen Record*, October 10:

TEANECK MAN FOUND DEAD IN HIS CAR.

The body of Leo Balzac, age 27, manager of the Smokers Happiness tobacco shop on Queen Anne Road, was discovered by a neighbor in the parking garage of their apartment complex on DeGraw Avenue. According to police, the deceased was found in the driver's seat of his car. Both wrists had been cut. A knife which appeared to have been used to inflict the wounds was found on the seat next to the body. A police spokesman said that suicide was consistent with the known facts but postponed further comment pending a full autopsy and toxicology report.

A next-door neighbor described Mr. Balzac as "An energetic young man who always seemed to be in a hurry—not the kind of guy you'd ever figure to kill himself."

From *Newsday*, October 26:

FLORAL PARK MAN DEAD, GIRLFRIEND MISSING.

The body of Steven Pardosa was found this past Wednesday in the apartment he occupied in the basement of his parents' home in Floral Park. The discovery was made by Arnold Pardosa, Steven's father, who entered the apartment with a spare key after repeated calls to Steven's cell phone failed to get any response.

A police spokesman characterized the death as a possible suicide, saying only that there were visible wounds to the deceased's wrists and a knife had been found at the scene. The deceased's parents disagreed with the suicide suggestion, insisting that such a possibility was "some kind of cover-up."

Pardosa was 25 years old and had been self-employed for the past
year in a landscape maintenance business. Law enforcement officials
expressed interest in speaking with the deceased's girlfriend, Angela
Castro, who had recently been living with him but whose current where-
abouts are unknown. Ms. Castro has not appeared for the past two days
at the salon where she is employed as a hair stylist. The salon manager,
Eric, who declined to give his last name, said that no calls had been
received from Ms. Castro to explain her absence."

Before going on to the articles covering the death of Ethan Gall,
Gurney jotted down a few facts that caught his attention.

As he'd already mentioned to Hardwick, the similarity of ages was
noteworthy. It could, for example, be the basis for some school-related
or other social contact.

And then there was all that wrist cutting. Despite its high profile in
fiction, and the sky-high number of self-inflicted cutting incidents pro-
pelling young people into ERs each year, successful suicides were rarely
accomplished that way. Men had a strong preference for shooting or
hanging themselves. If just one of those guys had decided to kill himself
by cutting his wrists, that would be unusual enough. All of them making
that same decision was peculiar in the extreme.

And then there was the matter of economics. It was possible that
Christopher Wenzel, the guy with the Palm Beach condo, could afford
a trip to a thousand-dollar-a-day mountain resort to get help with his
smoking problem. But the manager of a small cigarette discount store?
And a lawn-maintenance guy living in his father's basement? On the
face of it, they did not seem like prime candidates for top-shelf therapy
at Wolf Lake Lodge.

And finally, there was the little matter of Steven Pardosa's missing girlfriend. That could mean nothing. Or it could mean everything.
In Gurney's experience, there usually were relevant reasons for people
going missing.

After making a few notes, he picked up the most detailed article on
Ethan Gall.

From the *Albany Times Union*, November 3:

Heir to the Gall Fortune
Found Dead in Mountain Cabin.

A body believed to be that of Ethan Gall has been discovered in an isolated cabin at the Wolf Lake Lodge resort, located within the Gall family's 6,000-acre wilderness preserve, one of the largest privately owned tracts of land in the Adirondacks.

Pending a final autopsy report, police would say only that the condition of the body made an initial assessment difficult and that suicide could not be ruled out.

The Wolf Lake compound includes the main guest lodge—which dates back to the property's origins as a classic Adirondack Great Camp—plus three lakeside chalets and several smaller cabins in the surrounding forest, as well as the Gall family's private residence. These structures were built in the early 1900s by tin-mining baron Dalton Gall, who suffered an unusual death. After having a vivid premonition that he would be attacked by wolves, he was killed by wolves on the lodge property.

Heir to the substantial fortune created by his great-grandfather, Ethan Gall was the founder, president, and chief benefactor of the Gall New Life Foundation—a nonprofit organization dedicated to the education and reform of prisoners for reentry into community life.

The deceased was 34 years old and is survived by his brother Peyton. Lodge manager and family spokesperson Austen Steckle issued the following statement: "This sudden tragedy has created a sense of shock and disbelief here at Wolf Lake. We will have no further comment until we receive an official report from the medical examiner's office."

There were also printouts of similar but shorter articles from the *Burlington Free Press*, the *New York Times*, and the *Washington Post*.

Gurney picked up the phone from his desk and entered Hardwick's number. The man answered immediately. "What's up, Davey?"

"Couple of things. Austen Steckle was described in a news article as the 'family spokesperson.' How many surviving members of the Gall family are there, besides Peyton?"

"Zero."

"The entire family consists of Peyton?"

"As far as Jane knows. I asked her about that."

"Okay. Another question. What's the Gall New Life Foundation all about?"

"Seems legit. Puts parolees through reentry training, education, extensive psych counseling. Actually seems to reduce recidivism. Ethan started it, ran it, put a lot of his own bucks in it."

Gurney made a note to dig deeper into that. "You mentioned this morning there was something weird about Dalton Gall's death, and I saw the same thing in one of the newspaper articles. What's that all about?"

"Who the fuck knows? The story was passed along for a lot of years, maybe got enhanced along the way. Supposedly the old bastard had a dream about getting chewed up and spit out by a pack of wolves, and a few days later that's pretty much what happened to him. Could be a load of crap."

"Kind of an interesting coincidence that our four recently deceased folks also had bad dreams before they ended up dead."

"I agree. But where do you go with that?"

Gurney ignored the question, asked one of his own. "Strike you as odd that a guy who mows lawns for a living would—"

Hardwick finished the thought. "Spring for a grand-a-day stay at an old-fashioned lodge? Beyond odd."

"And what do you make of all that wrist cutting?"

Hardwick responded with a loud bark of a laugh. "I have no goddamn idea what to make of it. See, Davey, all them unanswered questions are precisely why we need your superior intellect."

GURNEY HUNG UP THE PHONE AND OPENED THE SECOND FOLDER Jane had left with him. This one was labeled *Police Press Briefings, Hammond Statement, General Media Coverage.*

The first item was a two-page printout from a media website. Across the top Jane had written, "Sgt. Plant, Bureau of Criminal Investigation, briefing to reporters, November 8." It consisted of the officer's introductory statement followed by a Q&A with unidentified reporters.

Gurney decided to skip that one for the moment and go on to the transcript of the next press briefing.

This briefing was several pages longer than the first. There was, however, a link to the video—an option Gurney preferred. The facial expressions and tones of voice captured on video were a lot more revealing than words on paper. He opened his laptop and entered the link.

As he was waiting for the video to appear, Madeleine came into the den, wearing a bathrobe, her hair wet from her shower.

"Have you decided which pair you want to bring?" she asked.

"Excuse me?"

"Your snowshoes."

He looked over toward the place by the door where he remembered her leaning them that morning—the rawhide-and-wood ones and the plastic ones with the spikes on the bottom. "I guess the spiked ones?"

Her surface smile seemed to be concealing some less-cheerful preoccupation.

"Is something wrong?" he asked.

Her smile broadened unconvincingly. "I was thinking maybe we could get a light for the birds."

"A what?"

"You know, for the henhouse. It gets dark so early this time of year."

"That's what you were thinking about?"

"I just think it would be nice for them."

He knew something else was on her mind, and patience would be the best approach. "It's just a matter of running an electrical line out there, installing a fixture. We can get an electrician to do it, or I can do it myself."

"It will be nice for them to have some light." She took the snowshoes and left the room.

He sat there, staring out the window, wondering what it was she wasn't ready to talk about. His gaze wandered to the trees by the pasture.

The hollow sound of multiple voices and of chairs being moved in a miked room drew his attention to the computer screen. The second police press briefing was about to begin.

The setting was one of those depressing institutional conference rooms that Gurney was all too familiar with from his years in the NYPD. The video perspective, equally familiar, was from a single camera mounted in the back of the room, aimed at the front.

A dozen or so cafeteria-style plastic chairs were occupied half by men and half by women, judging from the backs of their heads. Facing them was a thickly built man at a narrow podium. A blank whiteboard covered the wall behind him.

His body had an egg-shaped stockiness about it. He was wearing the standard uniform of an over-forty detective: dark pants, dull pastel shirt, duller tie, and a gray sport jacket a size too small. Dark hair brushed straight back from a broad creased forehead, along with heavy cheeks and a grim mouth, gave him a startling resemblance to old photos of Jimmy Hoffa.

He checked his watch and opened a loose-leaf binder.

"Okay, folks, let's get started. I'm Senior Investigator Gilbert Fenton, Bureau of Criminal Investigation. There've been some major developments in the past few days relative to Ethan Gall's death. I've got a statement here." As Fenton paused to turn a page in the binder, one of the reporters spoke up.

"You used the general word 'death.' Are you implying that it wasn't suicide?"

"I'm not implying anything. I'm just saying that what we know now leaves the possibility open that his death may not have been 'suicide' in the normal sense of the word. But hold on a minute." He raised his hand in the traffic-cop "stop" gesture. "Let me finish the statement." He looked back down at the binder.

"Our investigation of the Gall death has revealed certain significant facts. The fact that he was hypnotized in the recent past by Dr. Richard Hammond . . . the fact that he experienced a particular nightmare repeatedly in the week preceding his death . . . the fact that the fatal weapon found with his body was similar to a weapon he reported seeing in his nightmare . . . and the fact that details of that nightmare, which he committed to writing, would appear to have been acted out in the taking of his life. These facts alone would be sufficient to justify a fuller investigation. But it has now become apparent that the case is even more extensive."

He turned over a page in the binder, cleared his throat, and continued. "We've learned that three additional individuals took their own lives the same way as Ethan Gall, with a similar pattern of previous experiences. These individuals were also hypnotized by Richard Hammond. They all developed incapacitating nightmares, and all three killed themselves in a manner seemingly consistent with the content of those nightmares."

He closed the binder and looked at his audience. "At this time, I'll take your questions."

Several of the attendees spoke at once.

Again he raised his hand. "One at a time. You, in the first row."

A female voice: "What are you accusing Dr. Hammond of doing?"

"We haven't made any accusations. We're seeking Dr. Hammond's cooperation." He pointed at another reporter.

A male voice: "Are you reclassifying the Gall death as a homicide?"

"It's being classified simply as a suspicious death."

Same male voice: "What possibilities other than suicide are you looking at?"

"We're not currently focused on possibilities other than suicide, but on how and why the suicide occurred."

A female voice: "What did you mean when you said that it might not have been suicide in the 'normal sense' of the term?"

"Well, let's say, just hypothetically, that a powerful form of hypnotic suggestion influenced a person to do something they would not have done of their own accord. That would not be a normal action. It would not be done in the 'normal sense' of that action."

Several voices were raised at once, competing in volume. One astounded male voice predominated: "Are you claiming that Richard Hammond used hypnosis to bring about Gall's suicide, as well as the suicides of three other patients?"

Utterances of surprise and skepticism spread around the room.

Fenton raised his hand. "Let's keep it orderly, okay? I'm not claiming anything. What I'm sharing with you is one hypothesis. There may be others."

His most recent questioner continued, "Are you planning to arrest Dr. Hammond for . . . for what crime?"

"Let's not get ahead of ourselves. We hope to obtain Dr. Hammond's voluntary cooperation. We need to know what, if anything, happened in those hypnosis sessions that could explain the nightmares his patients later experienced and the ritualistic suicides that ensued."

Two female voices at once: "Ritualistic?"

A male voice: "What ritualistic elements were involved? Are we talking satanic?"

Another male voice: "Can you give us the identities of the other three victims?"

A female voice: "Is 'victims' the right term for suicides?"

Fenton raised his voice. "Hey, please, some order here. As for the term 'victims'—I think that's a reasonable term under the circumstances. We've got four people who all killed themselves in pretty much the same way with a weapon they dreamt about after they'd been hypnotized. This is obviously more than a coincidence. Regarding the ritualistic aspect, all I can divulge is that the weapon used in each case was unusual and, according to experts we've consulted, highly significant."

A male voice: "If your theory is correct—that these victims were put under some kind of hypnotic spell that resulted in suicide—what would the criminal charge be? Are we talking about some new kind of murder?"

"The answer to that will be determined as we go along."

The questions went on for half an hour. Fenton showed no impatience with this. If anything, he seemed to be urging the reporters on—an unusual behavior, Gurney thought, for a stolid, conservative-looking cop.

Finally he announced that the briefing was over.

"Okay, ladies and gentlemen, thank you for your cooperation. You can pick up copies of my statement on your way out."

Chairs were pushed back, people began standing, and the video ended.

Gurney sat at his desk for several long minutes, astounded.

He picked up a pen and began jotting down some questions of his own. When he was halfway down the page he remembered that there was still more material in the file Jane had assembled—Richard Hammond's own statement to the press, plus examples of the media coverage that Fenton's briefing had generated.

Gurney opened the folder again, took out a handful of news web-site printouts, and riffled through them. There was no need to read the complete text of any of these more recent articles. The insinuating headlines told the story.

THE DEATH WHISPERER

DID THIS DOCTOR TALK HIS PATIENTS INTO KILLING THEMSELVES?

POLICE LINK CONTROVERSIAL THERAPIST TO RITUAL SUICIDES

COULD A DREAM BE A MURDER WEAPON?

Before he was halfway through the pile of printouts, Gurney put them aside and leaned back in his chair. He found himself fascinated by the underlying facts and baffled by the aggressively public approach being taken by Gil Fenton—which represented not only the embrace of a wild hypothesis but also a departure from NYSP communications policies.

There was one final item in the folder, a single typewritten page with a long heading: *Notice to the Press: Statement by Dr. Richard Hammond Regarding the Investigation into the Deaths of Christopher Wenzel, Leo Balzac, Steven Pardosa, and Ethan Gall.*

Gurney read with increasing interest:

Serious allegations were made recently to the news media by a repre-sentative of New York State law enforcement concerning the deaths of the four individuals named above. These allegations are reckless and misleading.

This statement will be my first, final, and only response. I will not be drawn into the charade being staged by incompetent police investiga-tors. I will not cooperate with them in any way until they cease their malicious campaign of character assassination. Nor will I communicate with representatives of the news media whose embrace of the libelous insinuations of the police are proof of their amoral appetite for sensation.

In short, I will neither participate in, nor publicly debate, nor devote my resources to the obstruction of this farcical investigation and media soap opera. I will hire no attorney, no PR firm, no spokesperson, no defenders of any kind.

Let me be perfectly clear. Suggestions or insinuations that I contributed in any way to the deaths of four individuals are absolutely false. Let me repeat and underscore the simple truth. The deaths of Christopher Wenzel, Leo Balzac, Steven Pardosa, and Ethan Gall were tragic events in which I have played no role whatsoever. They deserve a full and objective investigation, not this degrading circus initiated by malicious police personnel and propagated by a vile news industry.

—Richard Hammond, PhD

Gurney found the statement remarkable for its bravado—especially since it was authored by the same man who had been paralyzed with fear over the highly unlikely possibility of there being a dead body in the trunk of his car.

CHAPTER 8

From Gurney's point of view, the Palm Beach Police Department was just the right size—big enough to have its own detective bureau, small enough to ensure that his contact there would be aware of the key points of any investigation that was underway. Best of all, Lieutenant Bobby Becker owed him a favor. Less than two years earlier, with Gurney's considerable assistance, Becker had managed to put away a vicious serial murderer.

Becker took his call immediately, his gentle drawl fully deployed. "Detective Gurney. What a surprise!" The way he inflected that final word made it sound like it wasn't a surprise at all. "A pleasure to hear from you. I do hope all is well?"

"I'm good. How about you?"

"Can't complain. Or, I should say, I prefer not to complain. Complainin' is a waste of the time we could be better usin' to eliminate the causes of our complaints."

"Christ, Becker, you sound more good ole boy than ever."

"I'm happy to hear that. It is, after all, my native tongue. A Floridian born and bred. We are outnumbered now almost to extinction. Rare birds in our own tree. What can I do for you?"

Gurney hesitated for a moment, searching for the right words. "I've been asked to get involved in a case that has roots in a number of jurisdictions. One of them is Palm Beach."

"Let me take a wild guess. Might you be talking about the 'Deadly Doctor' case? That's what they're calling it down here—when they're not calling it the 'Fatal Dreams' case.

"That's the one. You're not by any chance the CIO on the Wenzel piece of it?"

"No, sir, I'm not. Young fellow at the next desk caught that one, thought everything was cool when the ME signed off on probable suicide. Course that all went to hell once the Reverend Bowman Cox dropped by to tell us it was murder, and the killer was Satan."

"What?"

"You don't know about that?"

"I was told that Wenzel confided to a local minister that he'd been having nightmares ever since he'd seen a Dr. Hammond up in Wolf Lake. And after Wenzel showed up dead, the minister told you guys about it. Then one of you called Hammond, but nothing really came of that conversation, until Hammond called back a week later to tell you he'd just heard from a detective in New Jersey about a second suicide. That's the way I was told the story—no reference to any murder committed by Satan."

"How are you getting your information?"

"In a roundabout way."

"You're not a trusted confidant of Senior Investigator Gilbert Fenton?"

"That's one way of putting it. Tell me more about Satan."

"Well . . . that's not an easy thing for me to do. Our chief of detectives has made a request that details not already reported in the press be kept in the house. I did agree to abide by that request, word of honor. However, Reverend Cox is under no such constraint. I understand he can be reached at the Church of Christian Victory down in Coral Dunes. The reverend is a man of strong convictions, with an equally strong desire to share them."

"Thanks, Bobby. I appreciate this."

"Glad to help. Now, maybe you can answer a question of mine? Actually, it's a question on the minds of many down here."

"Ask it."

"What in the name of holy magnolia is that hog's ass, Fenton, up to?"

That launched them into a long discussion of the unconventional aspects of Fenton's approach to the press. Becker was particularly unhappy with what he perceived to be the BCI investigator's assumption of the role of law enforcement spokesman on all aspects of the case and his grandstanding with the national media, which resulted in the detectives in the other jurisdictions losing control of the flow of information and finding themselves in awkward positions with local reporters.

And then there was the matter of the criminal hypothesis Fenton was promoting, which Becker considered "unprosecutable and sure-as-hell unprovable." Which brought Gurney around to a question that troubled him more than Fenton's actual behavior:

Who in the Bureau of Criminal Investigation—or elsewhere in the New York State Police hierarchy—had signed off on his approach to the case? And why did they?

Someone above him had to be on board. Fenton, after all, exuded the essence of career cop. This dour, close-to-retirement law enforcer would be constitutionally incapable of acting outside a chain of command.

So whose game was this?

And what was the prize for the victor?

For now, all Gurney and Becker had were questions. But the fact that they both were bothered by the same questions provided a measure of reassurance.

Becker ended the call with an afterthought on the Reverend Cox. "To prepare you for any contact you may have with the good minister, I should tell you that he bears a keen resemblance to a large, degenerate bird of prey."

GURNEY'S CALL TO THE PHONE NUMBER ON THE WEBSITE OF THE Coral Dunes Church of Christian Victory resulted in a trip through an automated answering system that led him eventually to the voicemail of Bowman Cox himself.

He left his name and cell number, explaining that he was one of the detectives looking into the quadruple suicide case and was hoping that the reverend might be able to provide some additional insight into Christopher Wenzel's state of mind and perhaps share his own theory of the case.

Less than five minutes after he put down his phone, he got a return call. The voice was all Southern-syrupy. "Detective Gurney, this is Bowman Cox. I just received your message. If your area code is any indication, you are located in upstate New York. Am I correct?"

"Yes, sir, you are. Thank you for calling me back."

"I believe that things happen for a reason. I got your message moments after you left it, because I was about to leave my hotel room and I wanted to check my phone mail first. And where do you think my hotel room is?"

"I have no idea."

"It's where you might least expect it. In the belly of the beast."

"Sir?"

"The belly of the beast—New York City. We are here to defend Christmas from those who hate the very idea of it, who object to its very existence."

"I see."

"Are you a Christian, sir?"

It wasn't a question he would normally answer. But this wasn't a normal situation.

"I am." He didn't add that his own version of Christianity was probably as far from Bowman Cox's as Walnut Crossing was from Coral Dunes.

"That's good to hear. Now, what can I do for you?"

"I'd like to talk to you about Christopher Wenzel."

"And his nightmare?"

"Yes."

"And how all these deaths have come to be?"

"Yes."

"Where exactly are you, Detective, right now, as we speak?"

"In my home in Walnut Crossing in upstate New York."

For several seconds, Cox said nothing. The only sound Gurney could hear over the phone was the soft tapping of fingers on a keyboard. He waited.

"Ah, there you are. Convenient things, these instant maps. Well, now, here's a proposition for you. My feeling is that this conversation is too important for the phone. Why don't we meet, you and I, face-to-face?"

"When and where?"

There was another silence, longer this time, with more keyboard tapping.

"Looks to me like Middletown would be a perfect middle point between us. There's a diner on Route 17 called Halfway There. I feel that the Lord is pointing the way for us. What do you say—shall we accept his suggestion?"

Gurney glanced at his phone screen to check the time. It was 12:13 PM. If he got to the diner at 1:45 and spent an hour with Cox, he could be back home by 4:15. That would leave plenty of time to resolve any open issues regarding the following morning's trip to Wolf Lake.

"Fine, sir, I can meet you there at 1:45."

CHAPTER 9

The drive down through the Catskills to Middletown was familiar and uneventful. The sprawling parking lot of the Halfway There diner was equally familiar. He and Madeleine had pulled in there for coffee many times during the year they'd spent searching for a country house.

Fewer than a third of the tables in the dining area were taken. As Gurney scanned the room, a hostess approached with a menu and an overly lipsticked smile.

"I think I see who I'm meeting here," said Gurney, his eyes on a self-important-looking man sitting by himself in one of the four chairs at a corner table.

She shrugged, handed him the menu, and walked away.

By the time Gurney got to the table, the man was standing, well over six feet tall, with his right hand outstretched. He engaged Gurney in an enthusiastic handshake, while raising his other hand to display an iPad. "I have been doing my research, Detective, and I must tell you that I am mightily impressed." A broad salesman's smile revealed a row of expensively capped teeth.

On the screen of the tablet, Gurney's eye caught part of an old photo of himself next to the word "Supercop"—the pumped-up headline of an article *New York* magazine had run a number of years earlier, featuring the string of arrests and convictions that by some calculations had made him the most successful homicide detective in the history of the NYPD. He'd found the article embarrassing, but sometimes it served a useful function, and he suspected this might be one of those times.

Gurney guessed the reverend was sixty and doing everything he could to look forty.

"I feel privileged to meet you, Detective. Please have a seat."

They sat across from each other. A waitress with a weary smile came over. "You gentlemen know what you want, or you need more time?"

"Maybe just a little time for me to get acquainted with this remarkable man, then we'll be ready to order. That meet with your approval, David? If I may call you David?"

"That's fine."

The Reverend Bowman Cox was wearing a navy-blue jogging suit and a stainless steel Rolex—a model Gurney had seen advertised somewhere for $12,000. His skin was a yellowish tan, unnaturally tight and free of any wrinkles, his hair unnaturally brown and free of any gray. A rapacious hawklike nose and a combative glint in the eyes belied the broad smile.

When the waitress had gone, he leaned toward Gurney. "I thank our Lord for this opportunity to share our thoughts—regarding what I have come to believe is a case of extraordinary evil. May I ask how far you've progressed in your own understanding of it?"

"Well, Reverend, as you—"

"Please, David, no formal titles. Call me Bowman."

"Okay, Bowman. As I see it, the problem in understanding the case is that a number of different jurisdictions are involved due to the location of the suicides. Gilbert Fenton up in the Adirondack region of New York seems to have the closest thing to an overall approach." He was watching the man's expression for hints of how to proceed to trigger the greatest cooperation. He continued, shifting his vocabulary. "But it's the evil dimension of these events that really interests me, the presence of certain inexplicable forces."

"Exactly!"

"The nightmares, for example."

"Exactly!"

"That's an area, Bowman, where I'd love to get your personal perspective. Because of the fragmented way the case is being handled, I know about the nightmares. But I don't know the content of them. The sharing of information among our departments leaves a lot to be desired."

Cox's eyes widened. "But the nightmare is the solution to everything! From the very start, I told them that. I told them the answer was in the nightmare! They have eyes, yet they refuse to see!"

"Perhaps you can explain it to me?"

"Of course." He leaned forward again and spoke with a fevered intensity, his perfect teeth and the surgically tightened skin of his face creating a not-quite-human impression.

"Are you familiar, David, with the phenomenon of men who, having once heard a musical passage, can replay it note for note? Well, I have a similar ability with the spoken word, particularly as it relates to the word of God and man. Do you grasp my meaning?"

"I'm not sure I do."

Cox leaned closer, his reptilian eyes fixed on Gurney's. "In matters of Good and Evil, what I hear is imprinted on my memory—note for note, as it were. I regard this as a gift. So, when I say that I am about to repeat Christopher Wenzel's narration of his nightmare, I mean precisely that. *His* narration. Note for note. Word for word."

"Would you mind if I recorded this?"

A flicker of something in those eyes came and went too quickly to read. "I have been prevailed upon by law enforcement authorities not to share this with the press or the public. But you, as a detective, are obviously in a different category. "

Gurney took out his phone, activated the "record" function, and laid it on the table. Cox stared at it for a few seconds as though weighing risks and rewards. Then with the tiniest nod—the gesture of a blackjack player opting to proceed—he closed his eyes and began speaking. His voice was sharper now, presumably imitating the diction of Christopher Wenzel.

"I'm lying in bed. Starting to fall asleep. But it doesn't feel that good. It doesn't have that easy, letting-go feeling of falling asleep. I'm partly conscious, but I can't move or speak. I know that someone, or something, is in the room with me. I hear a deep, rough breathing—like some kind of animal. Like a low growling. I can't see it, but it's getting closer. Creeping up on me. Now it's pressing me down on the bed. I want to scream but I can't. Then I see hot red eyes. Then I see the animal's teeth, pointed fangs." Cox's own shiny teeth were bared.

"Saliva is dripping from the fangs. Now I know it's a wolf, a wolf as big as a man. The burning red eyes are just inches away from me now. The saliva from the fangs is dripping on my mouth. I want to scream, but nothing will come out. The body of the wolf is hovering over me, getting longer, stretching into the shape of a dagger. I feel the dagger going into me, burning and piercing, again and again. I'm covered with blood. The wolf's growl changes into the voice of a man. I see that the wolf has the hands of a man. Then I know that he *is* a man, but all I can see are his hands. In one hand he has a dagger with a silver wolf's head on the handle, a wolf's head with red eyes. In the other hand he has colored pills. He says, 'Sit up and take these. There's nothing to fear, nothing to remember.' I wake up sweating and shivering. My body aches. I sit on the edge of the bed, too exhausted to stand. I bend over and vomit. That's how it ends. That's what happens. Every night. The idea that it will happen again makes me want to die."

Cox opened his eyes, leaned back in his chair, and looked around the room a little strangely—as if, rather than simply reciting another man's story, he'd been channeling the dead man's spirit.

"So, there you have it, David—the revolting experience related to me by that poor young man on the very eve of his demise." He paused, clearly waiting for a reaction that Gurney was not providing. "Do you not find Christopher's experience utterly appalling?"

"It's certainly strange. But tell me—other than his dream, what else do you know about him?"

Cox looked surprised. "Forgive me, David, but it is plain to me that Christopher's dream is precisely the revelation we need to focus on. The dream that dictated the manner of his death. The dream that exposed the role played by the devil Hammond. *Look ye, saith the Lord, at the Truth that is shown to thee in these events. The Truth of evil is placed before thine eyes.*"

"When you refer to Dr. Hammond as a devil—"

"That term is not idly chosen. I know all about *Doctor* Hammond, with his *Ivy League* psychology degree."

Gurney wondered if Cox's animus toward Hammond was a routine product of the culture wars, or if there might be more to it. But he had another question to pursue first. "Did you know Wenzel in any context outside of the conversation he had with you regarding his dream?"

Cox shook his head impatiently. "I did not."

"Your ministry is located in Coral Dunes?"

"Yes. But our broadcast and Internet outreach is unlimited."

"And Coral Dunes is about an hour's drive from Palm Beach?"

"What is your point?"

"I was wondering why—"

"Why Christopher came all the way to Coral Dunes to unburden his tortured soul? Have you considered the simplest answer of all—that the Lord led him to me?" A beatific smile pulled his tight lips back to reveal that row of perfect white teeth.

"Can you think of any other reason?"

"Perhaps he'd had the opportunity to hear one of our webcast sermons. It is the mission of our ministry to stand with the Lord in the great war consuming our world."

"That war being . . . ?"

Cox looked surprised at the need for such a question. "The war being waged on the divinely ordained order of things. The war waged on the essence of man, woman, marriage, and family. The war waged with all the devil's cunning by the homosexual armies of Satan."

"Are you telling me that Christopher Wenzel drove down to Coral Dunes to tell you about his dream because of your opposition to gay marriage?"

Cox stared at Gurney, his eyes burning with an emotion that might have been fury or a kind of wild excitement. But there was something else in those eyes as well—that special gleam that signals an unshakable belief in a patent absurdity.

His voice rose as he spoke. "What I'm telling you is that he came to me because he was hypnotized, spiritually violated, and about to be murdered by Doctor Richard Hammond. Doctor of degeneracy and debasement."

AFTER SPENDING ANOTHER FIFTEEN MINUTES LISTENING TO BOWMAN Cox—with absolutely no desire to have anything to eat—Gurney left the diner with more questions than he'd arrived with. Questions about Richard Hammond's background, Jane Hammond's honesty and openness, the significance of Wenzel's elaborate dream, and Cox's own fierce hatred of Hammond.

Gurney spent most of the Route 17 segment of his homeward drive arranging in his mind the content and sequence of the phone calls he intended to make: to Hardwick, to Jane, and to Rebecca Holdenfield—a brilliant forensic psychologist with whom he had a complicated history of attraction, alliance, and conflict.

Before he called any of them, however, he decided to email them copies of the audio file. He also wanted to listen to it himself—not so much the dream segment, whose details were vivid in his mind, but the portion of his dialogue with Cox that followed the claim of murder. Regarding that exchange, he wanted to be sure his recollection was precise before discussing it with anyone, especially Rebecca.

After pulling off onto the shoulder, he sent the emails—with brief introductions for Hardwick and Jane and a longer explanation for Rebecca. Then he opened the audio file from the diner, found the point where he wanted to begin, and tapped "Play."

Listening with care to Cox's every word, he pulled back onto the highway and headed into the rolling foothills.

Cox: What I'm telling you is that he came to me because he was hypnotized, spiritually violated, and about to be murdered by Doctor Richard Hammond. Doctor of degeneracy and debasement.

Gurney: Is that what Wenzel told you? That he expected to be murdered?

Cox: He related his nightmare, and his nightmare revealed what he was unable to say.

(Brief silence)

Gurney: You believe that Hammond murdered Wenzel?

Cox: With all my heart and soul.

Gurney: Let me be sure I have the sequence right. You're saying that Hammond hypnotized Wenzel—under the guise of a therapy session that was supposed to help him stop smoking. Then a week later . . . what? Hammond flew down to Palm Beach, hypnotized Wenzel in his condo, and cut the arteries in his wrists—causing him to bleed to death, creating the appearance of a suicide? Is that what you're saying happened?

Cox: You have a blind and dismissive attitude, sir.

Gurney: I want to understand the facts as you see them.

Cox: I see the presence and power of Satan—a reality to which your mind appears closed.

Gurney: My mind can be opened. Just tell me what you believe Richard Hammond actually did to Christopher Wenzel—the specifics, the logistics. Are you saying that Hammond personally traveled to Florida to kill him?

Cox: No, sir, that is not what I'm saying happened. That would be little more than the routine viciousness of mankind, a crime that could have been perpetrated by any common criminal. What actually happened was infinitely worse.

Gurney: I'm confused.

Cox: Hammond had no need to resort to any purely physical action.

Gurney: You're saying now that Hammond did not murder anyone? You're losing me.

Cox: We are dealin' here, sir, with the power of Evil itself.

Gurney: Meaning what, exactly?

Cox: How much do you know about Hammond's background?

Gurney: Not a great deal. I was told that he was famous in his field and that he helped a lot of people stop smoking.

Cox: (Harsh, humorless laugh) Hammond's agenda has nothing to do with smoking or not smoking. That's mere window dressing. Examine his background—his books, his articles. It won't take you long to discover his true agenda, the agenda that was there from the beginning, plain as the fire of hell in the eyes of that wolf. Hammond's agenda, sir, is the twisting of natural minds and the creation of homosexuals.

Gurney: The creation of homosexuals? How does he do that?

Cox: How? The only way it could be done. With the help of the devil.

Gurney: What does the devil actually help him do?

Cox: The answer to that is known only to Hammond and to Satan himself. But my personal opinion is that the man sold his soul in exchange for a terrible power over others—the power to enter their minds and to warp their thinking—to give them dreams of perversion, dreams that drive them either to lives of degenerate behavior or to self-destruction because they cannot endure the curse of such dreams.

Gurney: So, when you say that Hammond "murdered" Wenzel, what you mean is—

Cox: What I mean is that he murdered him in the most evil way imaginable—by planting in his mind a nightmare of perversion he could not bear to live with. A nightmare that drove him to his death. Think of it, Detective. What crueler and more wicked way could you kill a man than make him kill himself?

Gurney ended the audio playback as he was exiting the highway and turning onto the road that would take him through a series of hills and valleys to Walnut Crossing.

Apart from sharpening his memory of Cox's exact words, replaying the conversation hadn't helped. The man's unhinged vision of Wenzel's suicide was more a lightning storm than a source of useful light.

Could Cox be as crazy as he sounded?

Or, if the homophobic ranting was a performance, what was its purpose?

Despite the explanation Cox gave for Wenzel coming to him, Gurney was left wondering if there might have been another reason for that unfortunate man's long drive to Coral Dunes.

CHAPTER 10

When Gurney reached the west end of the Pepacton Reservoir he pulled off onto a gravel turnaround. In an area of spotty cell reception, it was one place where his phone always worked.

He was hoping to find some thread of coherence in the inconsistent pictures of the case presented by Gilbert Fenton, Bowman Cox, and Jane Hammond.

His first call was to Jane.

"I've got a question. Did Richard ever do any work in the area of sexual orientation?"

She hesitated. "Briefly. At the beginning of his career. Why do you ask?"

"I just spoke with a minister who met with one of the young men who committed suicide. He told me your brother provided therapy designed to alter a person's sexual orientation."

"That's ludicrous! It had nothing to do with *altering* anything." She paused, as if reluctant to say more.

Gurney waited.

She sighed. "When he was starting out, Richard saw a number of patients who were conflicted over the fact that they were gay but afraid to let their families know. He helped them face reality, helped them embrace their identities. That's all."

"That's all?"

"Yes. Well . . . there was some controversy—a hate-mail campaign aimed at Richard, generated by a network of fundamentalist ministers. But that was nearly ten years ago. Why is this an issue now?"

"Some people have long memories."

"Some people are just bigots, looking for someone to hate."

Gurney couldn't disagree. On the other hand, he wasn't ready to ascribe Reverend Cox's demonic interpretation of the case to something as simple as plain old bigotry.

His second call, to Hardwick, went to voicemail. He left a message, suggesting that he check his email and listen to the attached audio file. And maybe he could try to get a lead on the missing girlfriend of Steven Pardosa, the suicide case in Floral Park.

His third call was to Rebecca Holdenfield. She picked up on the third ring.

"Hello, David. It's been a long time. What can I do for you?" Her voice, even over the phone, projected a subtle sexuality he'd always found both enticing and cautionary.

"Tell me about Richard Hammond."

"The Richard Hammond who's currently at the center of a tornado?"

"Correct."

"Tremendously bright. Moody. Creative. Likes to work on the cutting edge. You have some specific questions?"

"How much do you know about the tornado?"

"As much as anyone else who listens to the news on their way to work. Four patient suicides in one month."

"You heard the police theory that he caused the suicides through hypnotic suggestion?"

"Yes, I heard that."

"You think it's possible?"

She uttered a derisive little laugh. "Hammond is exceptional, but there are limits."

"Tell me about the limits."

"Hypnosis can't induce behavior that's inconsistent with an individual's core values."

"So hypnotically induced suicide is just flat-out impossible?"

She hesitated before answering. "A hypnotherapist might move a suicidal person closer to suicide, through incompetence or reckless malpractice. But he couldn't create an irresistible urge to die in a person who wanted to live. Nothing remotely like that has ever been documented."

Now it was Gurney's turn to pause for a moment's reflection. "I keep hearing people say that Hammond is unique in his field. And you mentioned a minute ago that he likes to work on the 'cutting edge.' What's that all about?"

"He pushes the boundaries. I saw an abstract of a paper he presented at a meeting of the American Psychiatric Association—all about breaking down the separation between neuropsychology and motivational hypnotherapy. He claimed that intensive hypnotherapy can form new neural pathways, enabling new behavior that was previously difficult or impossible."

Gurney said nothing. He was waiting for her to catch the dissonance between that statement and what she'd said about hypnotherapy's limits.

"But don't get me wrong," she added quickly. "There's no evidence that even the most intensive hypnotherapy could turn a desire to live into a desire to die. And, by the way, there's a whole other aspect to this question of what people are capable or incapable of doing."

Again Gurney waited for her to go on.

"The aspect of character. Character and personality. From what I've seen and heard of Hammond, I'd have to say that morally and temperamentally he's an unlikely candidate for masterminding suicides. He's a perpetual wunderkind, he's neurotic, maybe a bit too much of the tortured genius. But a monster? No."

"That word reminds me, did you get my email?"

"Not if you sent it in the past hour. Been too busy to check. Why?"

"I just met with a Florida preacher who believes that Hammond is very much a monster. I sent you a recording of our conversation."

"Sounds outrageous. Can't listen to it this second, though. I've got a client waiting. But I *will* get to it, and . . . and I *will* get back to you. Okay?"

An unresolved note in her voice told Gurney there was something more she wanted to say. So, once more, he waited.

"You know," she added, "just theoretically speaking . . . if someone could figure out how to do that . . ."

"You mean figure out how to make people kill themselves?"

"Yes. If someone . . . if someone could actually do that . . ." The implications seemed to leave her at a loss for words.

GURNEY SAT GAZING OUT OVER THE RESERVOIR. THE LONGER Rebecca Holdenfield's unfinished comment lingered in his mind, the more convinced he was that he'd heard in it a touch of fear.

He glanced at the dashboard clock. It read 3:23 PM. In a shadowed mountain valley in December, slipping down toward the shortest day of the year, it was nearly dusk.

Gurney's attention began to drift to a series of images. The images were both familiar and disconcerting. Familiar because they'd come to him from time to time—perhaps a dozen times in all, always unexpectedly—ever since he'd had the dream in which they first appeared, shortly after he and Madeleine had moved to the western Catskills and heard the stories about the old farm villages that had been dammed and flooded to create the reservoir.

The villagers had been forced from their homes, dispossessed by eminent domain and New York City's need for water. All the houses and barns, the churches and schools and general stores, everything had been burned to the ground, the charred timbers and stone foundations bulldozed into the earth, and all the bodies exhumed from the valley cemeteries. It was as if the place had never been home to anyone—as if communities that had existed for over a century had never existed at all. The vast reservoir was now the great presence in the valley, the bulldozed relics of human habitation having been long since absorbed into its silty bottom.

But these hard facts, although they seemed to initiate it, were not the final substance of the dream's recurrent images. In his mind's eye he was standing in the dim, blue-green, deadly silent depths of the reservoir. All around him were abandoned homes, bereft of doors and windows. Incongruously, among the inundated farm buildings stood the Bronx apartment house where he'd spent his childhood. It, too, was eerily vacant, its windows nothing but rectangular openings in the murky brick facade. Eellike creatures undulated in and out of the openings. In the lightless interior venomous sea snakes lurked, waiting for their prey to venture in. A slow, freezing current pushed at his back, moving him ever closer to the looming structure with its hideous contents.

So vivid were these images that Gurney's lips drew back in revulsion. He shook his head, took a deep breath, started the car, pulled back onto the county road, and headed for home—resolving never to dwell on that dream again.

The dozen miles of hills and hollows between the reservoir and Walnut Crossing formed a dead zone for his phone. But as he turned onto the narrow road up to his property, he entered the service area of the Walnut Crossing cell tower and his phone rang.

It was Jane Hammond.

"Did you hear?" Her voice was alive with anger.

"Hear what?"

"About Fenton's latest press briefing."

"What happened?"

"He's making everything worse."

"What did he do?"

"He claimed Richard is now his 'primary suspect' in what he's calling four cases of 'intentional homicide.'"

"'Intentional homicide'? That's the term he used?"

"Yes. And when a reporter asked him if that meant that Richard would be arrested and charged with first-degree murder, he didn't say no."

"What *did* he say?"

"That it was being considered, and that the investigation was ongoing."

"Did he say what new evidence prompted this?"

"The same crazy stuff. Richard's refusal to cooperate with the investigation. Of course he refuses to cooperate! You don't cooperate with a lynch mob!"

"His noncooperation is hardly new evidence. Was anything else mentioned?"

"More nonsense about the dreams. Now he's saying that *all four victims had exactly the same nightmare.* Which makes no sense at all."

Gurney pulled over to the edge of the road. One person having the same dream night after night was strange. Four different people having the *same* dream was beyond strange.

"You're sure you heard him right?"

"Oh, I heard him right. He said that they'd each provided a detailed account of the nightmare they'd been suffering from. Wenzel told his minister. Balzac told a therapist. Pardosa told his chiropractor. Ethan wrote his out in a longhand letter to someone. Fenton says the four accounts are substantially the same."

"What point was he trying to make?"

"He said that the fact that *they all had the same dream* after being hypnotized by Richard indicated that Richard was responsible—not only for the dream but for the suicides. And then he added, 'the four suicides we know of *so far*'—like Richard might be a serial killer."

"But Fenton hasn't formally charged him with anything?"

"Formally charged him? No. Viciously slandered him? *Yes.* Destroyed his reputation? *Yes.* Ruined his career? *Yes.* Turned his life completely upside down? *Yes.*"

She went on a bit longer, venting her fury and frustration. Although he normally was uncomfortable with displays of intense emotion, Gurney could sympathize with her reaction to a case that only became more bizarre with each new development.

Four people having the same dream?

How could that be possible?

He continued driving up the road, past his barn, past the pond, up along the pasture lane. As he parked by the mud room door, he caught sight of a red-tailed hawk. It was circling over the field that separated the barn from the house. Its loosely formed circles appeared to be centered over the pen attached to the chicken coop. He got out of the car and watched the unhurried predator make another slow circuit before straightening its flight path and gliding out of sight over the maple thicket that bordered the pasture.

He went into the house and called out to Madeleine, but there was no answer. It was just four o'clock. He was pleased to see that he'd arrived precisely when he said he would and disappointed that Madeleine wasn't present for his rare on-time homecoming.

Where could she be?

She wasn't scheduled to work her shift at the mental health clinic that afternoon. Besides, her car was in its normal spot by the house, so she couldn't be far. It was cold and within an hour it would be dark, so it was unlikely she'd be out on one of the old quarry trails that ran along the bluestone ridges. The cold wouldn't stop her, but the fading light would.

He called her cell number and was startled to hear her phone ring on the sideboard just a few feet from his elbow—where it was serving as a paperweight on a pile of unopened mail.

He went into the den on the off chance that she'd left a note for him on his desk.

There wasn't any note.

The message light on the landline phone was blinking. He pressed the "Play" button.

"Hi, David. Rebecca Holdenfield. I listened to the audio file of your conversation with Cox. 'Bizarre' is too mild a word for it. I have questions. Can we get together? Maybe meet halfway between Walnut Crossing and my office in Albany? Let me know."

He called her back, got her voicemail, and left a message.

"Hi, Rebecca. Dave Gurney. Getting together may be tough. I'm leaving early tomorrow for Wolf Lake in the Adirondacks—to see Hammond, if I can. The following day I go on to northern Vermont for snowshoeing, et cetera. Earliest I'll be back will be five, six days from now. But I do want to hear your opinion of the dream. By the way, the BCI investigator just added an impossible twist to the dream element at a press briefing. Check the story updates on the Internet and get back to me when you can. Thanks."

As he ended the call, the phone rang in his hand. It was Hardwick, who was already speaking when Gurney put the phone to his ear.

" . . . fuck is going on?"

"Excellent question, Jack."

"Are Cox and Fenton competing for Craziest Man on the Planet?"

"You listened to Cox reciting Wenzel's dream?"

"I did. The dream which Fenton now claims all the victims had."

"A claim you find hard to swallow?"

"Horseshit of that magnitude is very hard to swallow."

"Which put us, Jack, in the uncomfortable spot of having to accept either that Fenton is lying with the approval of BCI brass, as part of some grand conspiracy, or that four people did, in fact, have the same dream, and it drove them all to suicide."

"You don't think that's possible, do you?"

"Nothing I've been told about this case seems possible."

"So where do we go from here?"

"We need to search for potential connections. Places where the paths of the four victims may have crossed. Also, any prior contacts they may have had with Richard Hammond. Or with Jane Hammond. Or with Peyton Gall, who Jane mentioned was in his twenties, just like three of the four victims, which may or may not be significant."

"Hell of a job, but I'll start the process."

For some minutes after the call ended Gurney stood at the den window—until the deepening dusk reminded him of Madeleine. He thought he should go out and look for her before it got any darker. But where should he start? It was unlike her to—

"I was down by the pond."

Her voice made him jump, so quietly had she entered the house and come to the den doorway. Once upon a time her comment's uncanny responsiveness to the question on his mind would have disconcerted him, but he'd grown accustomed to the phenomenon.

"The pond? Wasn't it kind of a raw evening for that?"

"Not really. It was just good to be out in the air. Did you see the hawk?"

"You think we ought to do something about it?"

"Other than admire the beauty of it?"

He shrugged, and a silence fell between them.

Madeleine was the first to speak. "Are you going to meet with her?"

He knew instantly that she was talking about Rebecca, that she must have heard the phone message. The question, asked in too casual a tone, put him on edge. "I don't see how. At least not until we get back from Vermont, and even then . . ."

"She'll find a way."

"What does that mean?"

"You must realize she's interested in you."

"Rebecca is interested in her career and in maintaining whatever contacts she thinks might someday be useful."

The half-truth led to another silence—broken this time by Gurney.

"Is something wrong?"

"Wrong?"

"Ever since Jack and Jane were here, seems like you've been in another world."

"I'm sorry. I guess I'm . . . just a little out of sorts." She turned away and headed for the kitchen.

DINNER ENDED UP BEING A BRIEF AFFAIR CONSISTING OF BOILED potatoes, microwaved peas, haddock, and minimal conversation. As they were clearing the table he asked, "Did you let Sara know we'd be leaving a day early?"

"No."

"Are you going to?"

"Yes."

"If we open the chicken coop door in the morning to let them into the pen, someone will have to close it at night."

"Right. I'll call her."

A long silence ensued with her washing and rinsing their dinner plates, the silverware, the haddock pan, and the potato pot, and setting everything in the drainer to dry. This ritual activity at the sink was a task she'd claimed as her own years earlier.

Gurney's peripheral role in the ritual was to sit and watch.

When she was finished, she dried her hands; but instead of getting one of her books and settling into her regular armchair by the wood-stove at the far end of the room, she remained at the sink island, staring into some private mental landscape.

"Maddie, what on earth's the matter?" Even as he was asking the question he knew it was a mistake, driven by irritation rather than concern.

"I told you. I just seem to have a lot on my mind. What time do we have to leave?"

"In the morning? Eight? Eight thirty? Is that all right?"

"I suppose. Are you all packed?"

"I'm not bringing much."

She gazed at him for several long seconds, then turned off the light over the sink island and left the kitchen through the hallway that led to their bedroom.

He looked out through the French doors and saw nothing at all. Dusk had long since turned to solid night, a night with neither moon nor stars.

CHAPTER 11

Sometime after midnight there was a dramatic shift in the weather, with strong winds blowing away the overcast and flooding the maple copse outside their bedroom window with moonlight.

Awakened by the sound of the wind, Gurney got up and went to the bathroom, drank a glass of water, and stood for a while at the window. The moonlight illuminating the winter-faded pasture grass looked like a coating of frost.

He returned to bed, closed his eyes, and tried to empty his mind, hoping to slide naturally back into a comfortable sleep. Instead he found himself helplessly playing host to a succession of unsettling images, bits of the day, baffling questions and half-formed hypotheses—a needle stuck in a groove that went nowhere.

His thoughts were interrupted by a sound—something high-pitched above the wind. Then it stopped. He waited, listening. The sound came again, more distinctly now. The shrill yipping of coyotes. He could picture them, like small wolves, closing in on their prey on the rocky moonlit ridge above the high pasture.

Gurney awoke the next morning exhausted. He forced himself out of bed and into the shower. The hot pelting water worked its customary magic—clearing his mind, bringing him back to life.

Returning to the bedroom, he found the two duffel bags Madeleine had shown him the previous morning. They were resting on the bench at the foot of the bed. Madeleine's was full and zipped shut, his was open and waiting for whatever he intended to bring.

He disliked packing for trips, probably because he disliked taking trips, especially ones he was supposed to enjoy. But he managed to gather and pack what he might need. He carried both bags out through the kitchen to the side door where Madeleine had stacked up their ski pants and jackets, snowshoes and skis. The sight fed his discomfort, as he realized that the only part of the planned excursion that held any interest for him was the brief segment they'd be spending at Wolf Lake.

He took everything out to the car. While he was fitting the bags into the hatchback space, he caught sight of Madeleine, bundled in a heavy coat against the cold morning, making her way up through the pasture from the direction of the pond.

He was back in the kitchen, brewing his coffee, by the time she'd circled back down to the house. When he heard her in the mud room, he called out. "Coffee's on, you want a cup?"

He couldn't make out her muttered answer. He repeated the question when she appeared in the kitchen doorway.

She shook her head.

"Are you okay."

"Sure. Is everything in the car?"

"As far as I know. Duffel bags, ski stuff . . ."

"The GPS?"

"Of course. Why?"

"The detour we're taking. I wouldn't want us to get lost."

"There aren't that many roads up there to get lost on."

She nodded with a touch of that same preoccupation he'd sensed in her the night before. As she was leaving the room, she added with a certain coolness, "There was a phone message while you were in the shower. It's on the landline."

He went into the den to check it, suspecting that it might be Rebecca.

He was right. "Hi, Dave. Four people with the same dream? Meaning what? Generally similar elements? Or precisely identical images? First meaning is a stretch. Second is nuts. Love to delve deeper into this. Listen, I've got a gig every Friday in the psych department at SUNY Plattsburgh. So I'll be there tomorrow. Google says that's just twenty-seven miles from Wolf Lake. Could that work for you? We could meet where I'm staying—the Cold Brook Inn. Coming from Wolf Lake, the inn is just before the campus. Call me."

Gurney stood by his desk trying to sort out the timing and logistics of the proposed meeting, as well as the position it would put him in with Madeleine. Before he called Rebecca back, he'd need to give those issues more thought.

THE FIVE-HOUR DRIVE FROM WALNUT CROSSING INTO THE NORTH-
ern reaches of the Adirondack wilderness offered an alternately beautiful and bleak exposure to the rural landscape of upstate New York.
Many of the little towns were dead or dying—patches of commercial
decay that clung to the state roads like disease growths on tree trunks.
There were whole valleys where the tumble-down condition of everything was so pervasive it seemed the product of a toxic contamination
seeping up out of the earth.

As they traveled farther north, the patches of snow on the sepia
farm fields grew larger, the overcast gradually thickened, and the temperature dropped.

Coming to a village with more signs of life than most, Gurney
pulled into a gas station across from something called the Latte Heaven
Deli-Cafe. After filling the tank, he pulled out of the station and parked
in the first space he found.

He asked if Madeleine wanted coffee. Or maybe something to eat?

"I just want to get out of the car, stretch my legs, get some air."

He crossed the street by himself, entered the little establishment,
and discovered that it wasn't exactly what the name suggested.

The "Deli'" component was a cooler displaying in the light of a dim
bulb the bleak cold cuts of Gurney's Bronx childhood—bologna, boiled
ham, and an orangey American cheese—alongside trays of thickly
mayonnaised potato salad and macaroni salad. The "Cafe" component
consisted of two oilcloth-covered tables, each with four folding chairs.

At one table a pair of wizened women were inclined toward each
other in silence, as though they'd been in the midst of a conversation
during which someone had hit the "Pause" button.

The "Latte Heaven" component consisted of a small espresso
machine that showed no signs of life. There was an intermittent sound
of steam pipes banging and wheezing somewhere beneath the floor. A
fluorescent light fixture on the ceiling was buzzing.

One of the wizened women turned toward Gurney. "You knowin'
what you want?"

"Do you have regular coffee?"

"Coffee we got. Can't say how reg'lar it is. You wantin' somethin'
in it?"

"Black'll be fine."

"Be a minute." She stood slowly, went around behind the cooler, and disappeared.

A few minutes later she reappeared and laid a steaming Styrofoam cup on the counter.

"Dollar fer the coffee, eight cents fer the governor, who ain't worth no eight cents. Damn fool made a law to bring wolves back into the park. Wolves! Can you beat that fer stupid craziness? Park's fer families, kids. Damn fool! You wantin' a top fer that?"

Gurney declined the top, put a dollar fifty on the counter, thanked her, and left.

He spotted Madeleine about two blocks away on the main street, walking toward him. He took a few sips of his coffee to keep it from spilling and went to meet her. As they were ambling together toward their car, a young couple came out of a two-story office building half a block ahead of them. The woman was holding a baby wrapped in a blanket. The man went around to the driver's door of car that was parked in front of the building, then stopped. He was looking over the roof of the car at the woman. Then he started back toward her, moving unsurely.

Gurney was close enough now to see the woman's face—her mouth drawn down in terrible desolation, tears streaming down her cheeks. The man went to her, stood in front of her for a moment with a helpless look, then put his arms around her and the baby.

Gurney and Madeleine noticed the sign on the building and were hit by its significance at the same time. Above the names of three doctors, it read "Pediatric Medical Specialties."

"Oh, God . . ." The words came out of Madeleine like a soft groan.

Gurney would be the first to admit that he had a serious deficiency in the empathy area, that the suffering of others often failed to touch him; but on occasion, as now, without any warning, he was blindsided by a feeling of shared sadness so great his own eyes filled with tears and his heart literally ached.

He took Madeleine's hand and they walked the final block to the car in silence.

CHAPTER 12

B arely a mile out of the village a roadside sign informed them that they were entering the Adirondack Park. "Park" struck Gurney as a term far too modest for this vast tract of forests, lakes, bogs, and pristine wilderness that was larger than the entire state of Vermont.

The terrain around them changed from a succession of down-at-the-heels agricultural communities to something far wilder. Instead of weedy meadows and hilltop thickets, the landscape was dominated by a dark expanse of conifers.

As the road rose mile after mile, tall pines gave way to stunted firs that appeared to have been bent into angry submission by the harsh winter winds. Even open spaces here seemed forlorn and forbidding.

Gurney noted that Madeleine was sharply focused now on everything around her.

"Where are we?" asked Madeleine.

"What do you mean?"

"What are we near?"

"We're not near very much at all. I'm guessing we're seventy or eighty miles from the High Peaks. Maybe a hundred, hundred and twenty miles from Wolf Lake."

There was a frozen mist in the air now, so fine it was drifting sideways rather than falling to the ground. Through this icy filter the wild landscape of hunched trees and gaunt granite outcroppings seemed wrapped in a deepening gloom.

After another two hours, during which he encountered only a handful of other vehicles, all heading in the opposite direction, their GPS announced that they had arrived at their destination. There was, however, no lodge in sight. There was simply a dirt road that met the state route at a right angle, marked by a discreet bronze sign on an iron post:

GALL WILDERNESS PRESERVE

WOLF LAKE LODGE

PRIVATE ROAD——GUESTS ONLY

Gurney drove in. About half a mile into the property he sensed the pitch of the road steepening. The crouching trees began to take on a sinister aspect in the sleety fog, materializing out of nowhere only to disappear seconds later.

Madeleine turned her head suddenly in the direction of something on her side of the car.

Gurney glanced over. "What's the matter?"

"I thought I saw someone."

"Where?"

She pointed. "Back that way. By the trees."

"Are you sure?"

"Yes. I saw someone standing by one of those trees with the twisted branches."

Gurney slowed to a stop.

Madeleine looked alarmed. "What are you doing?"

He backed cautiously down the sloping road. "Let me know when we get to the spot."

She turned back to the window. "There it is, that's the tree. And right there, see, there's the . . . oh . . . I thought the broken-off tree trunk next to the bent one was a person. Sorry." The discovery that it had only been a tree trunk and not a human being lurking in that inhospitable place did little to allay the tension in her voice.

They drove on and soon came to a break in the procession of gnarled firs. The opening provided a passing glimpse of a rugged cabin, as somber and uninviting as the outcropping of icy granite on which it stood. A moment later the cabin disappeared behind the army of misshapen trees closing in again on the road.

The ring of Gurney's phone on the console between them triggered a reflexive jerk of Madeleine's arm away from the sound.

He picked up the phone and saw that it was Hardwick.

"Yes, Jack?"

"Good mawnin' to you, too, Detective Guhney. Just thought I'd call, find out how y'all are doin' on this glorious day the Lawd has provided."

"Is there a point to the Southern accent?"

"Jus' been on the phone with our loo-tenant friend in Palm Beach, and that way o' talkin'—like you was amblin' through molasses—is contagious."

"Bobby Becker?"

Hardwick dropped the drawl. "Right. I wanted to find out if they knew anything down there about Christopher Wenzel, where he came from, how he happened to own that condo."

"And?"

"They don't know much. Except that the driver's license he traded in a couple of years ago for a Florida one put his former residence in Fort Lee, New Jersey."

"Which puts three of our victims in the same metro geography in the not-too-distant past."

"Right."

"From what Jane said about Peyton, he doesn't sound like a guy who'd choose to live in the mountains if his alternative was a townhouse in the big city—unless he's hiding from somebody."

"I raised that point on our way back from your house. Jane thinks he can buy people upstate easier than he can in the city."

"She have any idea who he's buying, or why?"

"No names. But Peyton has a habit of creating trouble. And purchasing the necessary influence to keep consequences to a minimum would require a more modest outlay up in the backwoods than in a city. It's Jane's theory that he's importing his pleasures to the country to keep his misbehaviors in a relatively safe playground."

"Peyton the slimebag."

"You could say that."

"A slimebag who may be about to inherit a fortune."

"Yep."

"From a brother who just died in peculiar circumstances."

"Yep again."

"But, as far as you know, Peyton's not on Fenton's radar?"

"Not even near it." Hardwick's voice broke up into a scattering of unintelligible syllables, ending in silence.

Gurney glanced at his phone screen and saw that the signal strength was zero. Madeleine was watching. "You lost the call?"

"Dead zone."

All his attention was now on the road ahead. The superfine sleet was sticking to the surface, obscuring the position of the road's edges.

"How much farther do we have to go?"

"No idea." He glanced over at her.

Her hands were clenched into fists, her fingers wrapped around her thumbs.

He was focusing now on a ravine about ten feet to the left of where he estimated the left side of the road to be. Then and there, at the worst point for it to occur, the pitch of the road increased by a few degrees. A moment later the tires lost traction.

Gurney dropped down into first gear and tried inching forward, but the rear of the car began slipping sideways toward the ravine. He took his foot off the gas, applied the brake gently. After an unnerving lateral slide, the car came to stop. He put the gear lever in reverse and crept backward down the road and away from the ravine. When he was well below the point at which the pitch steepened, he braked as lightly as he could. Gradually the car came to a halt.

Madeleine was peering out into the surrounding woods. "What do we do now?"

Gurney looked up the road as far as he could see. "I think the crest is about a hundred yards ahead of us. If I can get some momentum . . ."

He eased the car forward. As he tried to accelerate through the spot where the trouble had begun, the rear of the car swung out suddenly, pointing the front end at the ravine. He turned the steering wheel rapidly in the opposite direction—an overcompensation that ended with a jarring thud as the passenger-side tires entered a drainage ditch at the edge of the road.

The engine stalled. In the ensuing silence he could hear the wind picking up and the rapid tick-tick-tick-tick of ice pellets blowing against the windshield.

CHAPTER 13

When his attempts to extricate the car succeeded only in getting it more deeply entrenched, Gurney decided to venture on foot up to the crest of the hill where he hoped he might be able to get either a cell signal or a sense of how much farther it was to the lodge.

He put on his ski cap, turned up his collar, and headed up the road. He'd hardly started when a sound stopped him dead—an eerie howling that seemed to come from everywhere and nowhere in particular. He'd grown used to the yips and howls of coyotes in the hills around Walnut Crossing, but this was different—deeper, with a quavering pitch that produced instant gooseflesh. Then it stopped as suddenly as it began.

He considered moving the Beretta from his ankle holster to his jacket pocket, but he didn't want to ratchet up Madeleine's anxiety; so he just resumed his trudge up the hill.

He'd proceeded no more than a dozen yards when he was stopped again—this time by a cry from the car.

"David!"

He spun around, slipped, and fell hard on his side.

As he scrambled to his feet he caught sight of the cause of her alarm.

A looming gray figure was standing in the icy mist no more than ten feet from the car.

As Gurney moved forward cautiously, he could see more clearly that it was a tall, gaunt man in a long canvas barn coat. A hat of matted fur, seemingly stitched together from parts of animals pelts, covered his head. A sheathed hatchet hung from a rough leather strap around his waist.

With the car between them, Gurney raised his right leg and slipped the Beretta out of its ankle holster and into his jacket pocket, gripping it firmly, thumb on the safety.

There was something almost feral in the man's amber eyes. His discolored teeth had either been broken or filed to jagged points.

"Be warnt." His voice was harsh as a rusted hinge.

Gurney responded evenly. "About what?"

"Evil here."

"Here at Wolf Lake?"

"Aye. Lake's got no bottom."

"No bottom?"

"Nay, none, never was."

"What kind of evil is here?"

"The hawk knows."

"The hawk?"

"The hawk knows the evil. Hawk man knows what the hawk knows. Sets the hawk loose. Into the sun, into the moon."

"What do you do here?"

"Fix what's broke."

"Around the lodge?"

"Aye."

While keeping a close eye on the hatchet, Gurney decided to proceed with the conversation as if it were perfectly normal, to see if it might start to make sense. "My name is Dave Gurney. What's yours?"

There was a flash of something in those strange eyes, a moment of keen attention.

Gurney thought that his name had been recognized. But when the man turned his sharp gaze up the road, it became clear something else had grabbed his attention. Seconds later Gurney heard it—the sound of a vehicle approaching in low gear. He was able to make out a pair of headlights, white disks in the frozen mist, coming over the crest and down the road.

He glanced over to check his visitor's reaction. But he was nowhere in sight.

Getting out of the car, Madeleine pointed. "He ran off into those trees." Gurney listened for footfalls, rustling branches; but all he heard was the wind.

Madeleine looked toward the approaching vehicle. "Thank God for whoever this is."

A vintage Land Rover, the sort in old safari films, came to a stop a little way up the incline from the Outback. The tall, lean man who emerged from it in a country-chic Barbour rain jacket and knee-high Wellington boots created the impression of an English gentleman out for a pheasant shoot on an inclement day. He pulled the jacket hood over his closely cropped gray hair. "Damn rotten weather, eh?"

Gurney agreed.

Madeleine was shivering, burying her hands in her jacket pockets. "Are you from the lodge?"

"From it, yes. But of it, no."

"Excuse me?"

"I did drive here from the lodge. But I'm not an employee of it. Merely a guest. Norris Landon's the name."

Instead of walking across the ice to shake the man's hand, Gurney simply introduced himself. As he was about to introduce Madeleine, Landon spoke first.

"And this would be your lovely wife, Madeleine—am I right?"

Madeleine responded with a surprised smile. "You must be the welcoming committee."

"I'm not exactly that. But I am a man with a winch—which I expect you'll find more useful."

Madeleine looked hopeful. "Do you think it'll get us out of the ditch?"

"It's done the trick before. Wouldn't want to be without it up here. I was talking to Jane Hammond earlier today, and she was anxious about your arrival in this wretched weather. Lodge is short-staffed at the moment. I volunteered to put Jane's mind at ease—check the condition of the road, make sure no trees were down, that sort of thing. Things have a way of changing fast here. Streams turning into whitewater floods, roads collapsing into ravines, rock slides, instant icing—risky on the best of days."

Not quite British or American, his accent was Mid-Atlantic, the diction once adopted by the cultured wealthy in the Northeast and actively nurtured in the Ivy League—until those institutions began to overflow with would-be hedge funders who didn't care how cultured they sounded as long as they got rich fast.

"Do you know where your tow hook is, and can you reach it with the undercarriage in that awkward position?"

Gurney peered under the tilted front end before answering.

"Yes, I think, to both your questions."

"In that case, we'll have you back on the road in no time."

Madeleine looked worried. "Before you arrived on the scene, someone approached us out of the woods."

Landon blinked, appeared disconcerted.

She added, "A strange man with a hatchet strapped to his waist."

"Crazy talk and amber eyes?"

"You know him?" Gurney asked.

"Barlow Tarr. Lives in a cabin out here. Nothing but trouble, in
my opinion."

"Is he dangerous?" asked Madeleine, still shivering.

"Some say he's harmless. I'm not so sure. I've seen him sharpening
that hatchet of his with a damn wild look in his eye. Hunts with it, too.
Saw him cut a rabbit in half at thirty feet."

Madeleine looked appalled.

"What else do you know about him?" asked Gurney.

"Works around the lodge, sort of a handyman. His father worked
here, too. Grandfather before him. All a bit unbalanced, the Tarrs, to
put it gently. Mountain people here from the time of Genesis. Related
to each other in odd ways, if you know what I mean." His mouth curled
in distaste. "Did he say anything intelligible?"

"Depends what you mean by intelligible." Gurney brushed a build-
up of sleet pellets off the shoulders of his jacket. "Perhaps we could hook
up that winch, and talk about the Tarr family later?"

IT TOOK A QUARTER OF AN HOUR TO GET THE LAND ROVER POSI-
tioned at the best angle and the cable set properly on the tow hook. After
that, the winch did its simple work and the trapped car was gradually
freed from the drainage ditch and pulled up to a drivable position on
the road, well above the point at which it had lost traction. Landon
then rewound his winch cable into its housing, turned the Land Rover
around, and proceeded back up the hill with Gurney following.

Once over the crest, the visibility improved considerably and some
of the tension went out of Madeleine's expression.

"Quite a character," she said.

"The country squire or the weird handyman?"

"The country squire. He seems to know a lot."

Madeleine's attention was then drawn to the stark vista appearing before them.

A series of jagged peaks and ridges the color of wine dregs stretched out toward a fog-shrouded horizon. Distance created the illusion of sharp edges—as though those peaks and ridges had been hacked with tin snips out of sheet metal.

The closest peak—perhaps two miles away—was distinctive enough that Gurney recognized it from his quick Internet search of the area before setting out. It was known as Devil's Fang, no doubt because it gave the impression of a monstrous eyetooth turned up against the heavens. Joined to it was Cemetery Ridge. Huge granite blocks arrayed upon it ages ago bore some resemblance to gravestones silhouetted against the sky.

The steep two-mile-long face of Cemetery Ridge formed the west side of Wolf Lake. At the lake's northern extremity, in the long shadow of Devil's Fang, stood the old Adirondack Great Camp known as Wolf Lake Lodge.

CHAPTER 14

As the road descended toward the lake, the forest reverted to fuller and taller pines, temporarily hiding the surrounding mountains from view.

When a final curve of the road brought them abreast of the lake and heading directly toward the imposing stone and timber structure standing at the lake's end, with Cemetery Ridge and Devil's Fang looming over all, the primeval essence of the place struck Gurney again with surprising force.

Ahead of them a massive log-and-shingle portico extended from the front of the lodge. Landon had already parked the Land Rover under it and was waving to Gurney to park behind him. As he and Madeleine emerged from their car, Landon was pocketing his cell phone.

"I was just letting Austen know you're here." He gestured toward the glass-and-timber entrance doors, one of which was being pushed open as he spoke.

Out came a short, solid-looking man with a shaved head and small sharp eyes. As he came toward Gurney he emitted a raw energy, which seemed to be seeping through his bare scalp in the form of sweat.

"Detective Gurney, Mrs. Gurney, welcome to Wolf Lake Lodge. I'm Austen Steckle."

His handshake had the hardness of a professional athlete's. The fingernails, Gurney noticed, were bitten to the quick. His sandpapery voice and urban intonation were as far as they could be from Landon's vaguely upper-class purr of entitlement.

"Can I help with your luggage?"

"Thanks, but there isn't that much." Gurney went around and retrieved the two duffel bags. "Can I leave the car where it is?"

"Sure, no problem. We also have a couple of nice new Jeeps available for the use of our guests. Good off-roaders. If that's your pleasure. Just let me know if you want to use one."

"Okay, Dave," interjected Landon, "looks like you're in good hands." He took a quick look at his watch. "Two forty-two. What say we regroup in the Hearth Room at three for a drink?"

"Fine. See you then."

Landon ambled in through the lodge doors, followed by Steckle, who moved with a quickness and lightness of foot unusual in a stocky man. Gurney and Madeleine entered last.

Inside the big double doors was a pine-paneled, cathedral-ceilinged reception area illuminated by an immense chandelier fashioned from deer antlers. There were sets of antlers mounted on the walls, along with antique guns, swords, knives, fur pelts, and Native American feathered shields.

A stuffed black bear stood erect in a shadowed corner, teeth and claws bared.

When Gurney got to the reception desk, Steckle held up a large, old-fashioned key. "For you, Detective. The Presidential Suite. On the house."

When this produced a questioning look from Gurney, Steckle went on. "Jane told me why you're here—the favor you're doing, looking into the case, and all that. So the least we could do is make you as comfortable as possible. The Presidential Suite used to be the owner's suite, the founder of the lodge, name of Dalton Gall. Very successful man. Owned mines, minerals. Made money like trees make leaves. A few years after the lodge opened, President Warren G. Harding arrived. Of course they gave him the owner's suite. The president loved it so much he stayed for a whole month. After that it became known as the Presidential Suite. I hope you like it. Shall we go up now?"

Gurney picked up the two duffel bags, and Steckle led the way out of the reception area, up a broad pine staircase, and into a corridor with an elaborately figured red rug. It reminded Gurney of the rug in the hotel corridor in *The Shining*.

Steckle stopped at a large wooden door and inserted the big metal key through an old-fashioned keyhole. He turned the tarnished knob and pushed the door open. He went in first, and few seconds later lights came on, revealing a large room furnished in a country-masculine style with leather couches and armchairs, Native American rugs, and rustic floor and table lamps.

Madeleine hung back, letting Gurney go in ahead of her.

"There are no dead animals in there, are there, like that huge thing in the lobby?"

"No, nothing like that."

She came in tentatively. "I hate those things."

Steckle opened the drapes, exposing a row of windows overlooking the lake. A glass door led to a balcony. The wall to Gurney's left was broken by a doorway and a broad archway. The archway led to a room-sized sleeping area with a four-poster bed. The doorway led to a bathroom larger than his den at home—with a separate toilet area, a corner shower stall, an oversized basin, a huge claw-foot tub, and a table piled with bath towels.

The wall to his right was dominated by a portrait of Warren Harding, who presided over America's slide into the lawlessness of the Prohibition era. The portrait was hanging above a stocked bar. Further along the wall was a stone fireplace and an iron rack of split logs.

Steckle pointed to the view through the windows. "Welcome to the wilderness."

NAMED FOR ITS GIGANTIC STONE FIREPLACE, THE HEARTH ROOM was furnished in the same rustic-luxury style as the Gurneys' suite—with leather furniture, tribal art and weaponry, and a bar topped with the scotches, bourbons, gins, ports, sherries, vermouths, crystal glasses, and silver ice buckets of a past generation.

As Gurney and Madeleine entered the room, Norris Landon called to them with a welcoming wave from one of the leather club chairs. "Make yourselves a couple of stiff drinks and come sit by the fire."

Gurney went to the bar and chose a plain club soda. He was surprised to see Madeleine make herself a gin and orange juice.

They took their drinks to the fireplace end of the room and sat on a couch facing Landon, who looked very much at home in the clothes he'd changed into: a yellow cashmere sweater, tan corduroy pants, and shearling-lined moccasins. With a languid smile he raised his glass of what looked like scotch on the rocks. "Here's to the success of your visit."

"Thank you," said Gurney.

Madeleine offered a smile and a nod.

Landon sipped his drink. "Always nice to sit by a fire, eh?"

"Very nice," said Gurney. "Are there any other guests?"

"At present we have the place to ourselves. Mixed blessing that, since staff's been reduced. The Hammonds, of course, are still in residence—bit separate though, over in Richard's chalet. Austen cancelled all the winter reservations after the tragedy. Understandable decision, that. Considering the event itself and then the media explosion. Wise to shut the place down until a satisfactory conclusion is achieved. At least that's my understanding of Austen's decision. Austen and Peyton's decision, I should say."

Gurney nodded, sipped his soda water. "With all the reservations cancelled, your presence must mean you're more than an ordinary guest."

Landon produced an embarrassed laugh. "I'd never claim to be more than ordinary. But I do come here quite often. And since I was already here when it all happened . . . I suppose Austen deemed it fit to let me stay on."

"How long have you been coming here?" asked Madeleine.

"Not all that long, just discovered the place a couple of years ago. But once I discovered it . . . well, there's upland bird season, spring turkey season, fall turkey season, deer season, bear season, small game season, fishing season. And, to be perfectly honest, I simply fell in love with the place. I'm keeping my fingers crossed that the current mess doesn't put an end to it all." He raised his glass again. "Here's to a speedy resolution. For everyone's sake."

The silence that ensued was broken by Gurney. "All those game seasons you mentioned must require quite an arsenal of weapons."

"I would admit to having a nice variety of sporting arms."

"You said something about the lodge having a reduced staff these days. Are there employees besides Austen on site?"

"There's a chef who commutes from Plattsburgh. A kitchen assistant. A housemaid to keep things tidy. Other workers who can be called in when Austen sees the need." He shrugged, almost apologetically. "And then, of course, there's Barlow Tarr."

"Not the typical employee of a thousand-dollar-a-night inn."

"No, certainly not. It was a notion of Ethan's, you see, that all human beings are redeemable. Crock of manure, in my opinion. Whole Tarr clan a perfect case in point. Even Ethan, with all his bloody optimism, was getting close to throwing in the towel with Barlow. Very difficult thing for Ethan to admit that someone was beyond his help. Thing is, Barlow's like the mountain weather. Turn your back for a minute, and you never know what it might turn into. Ethan told him he could stay on, live in his cabin out in the woods—on the condition that he kept away from the guests. But apparently he approached you—a definite violation of the agreement." Landon paused again, apparently weighing the implications.

"Was Ethan in the habit of employing . . . people with problems?"

"Indeed he was. His greatest virtue and greatest flaw."

Gurney paused to consider this pattern, before taking a small sidestep. "How much do you know about the Gall New Life Foundation?"

Landon studied his drink. "Only that it seems to be exactly what one would expect Ethan to have put together. He was a complex man. Determined, stubborn, controlling. An iron will. Absolute faith that his way was the right way. A bulldozer of a businessman. Single-handedly resurrected this place."

"You sound like you see a problem in that."

"Ah. Well. At the heart of the bulldozer there was a missionary. A zealot. A zealot with a belief that anyone can be elevated. Hence the Gall New Life Foundation—dedicated to the reeducation and reentry of serious felons into productive society."

"I've heard that it produced some success stories."

"Indeed it did. Big success stories. Perfect example is Austen himself."

"Austen Steckle is a paroled felon?"

Landon screwed up his face in an expression of chagrin. "May have overstepped myself there, although he's never made a secret of it. . . . Still, not my place. It's his story to tell, not mine." There was a brief silence. "If you have questions about anything else here at Wolf Lake, I'll be happy to share my modest knowledge."

Madeleine spoke up, sounding anxious. "Before, out the road, that Tarr person said something about the lake having no bottom. Do you have any idea what he meant by that?"

"Ah, yes. The bottomless lake. One of the Devil's Twins."

"The what?"

"The Devil's Twins. A peculiarity of the local geology, dramatically enhanced by local superstition. It seems that two lakes in this area, quite a few miles apart on opposite sides of a major ridge line, are actually connected through a series of underground channels and caverns. Wolf Lake is one of the two."

"That's what he meant by 'no bottom'?"

"Yes and no. There's a bit more to the story—the way the connection between the lakes was discovered. Back in the mid nineteen hundreds, two young girls were in a canoe on the other lake. The canoe capsized. One girl made it to shore, the other drowned. They dragged the lake, sent down divers, searched for days, weeks, but couldn't find the body. Great mystery at the time. Lots of theories flying around. Criminal conspiracies, supernatural explanations. Total circus. Journalistic inanity has been with us for a long time."

Madeleine was blinking impatiently. "But then what?"

"Ah. Well. Then. Five years later, a fellow fishing for bullheads snagged his line on what remained of the long-missing body—mostly a skeleton, with some of her clothes still on it. Thing of it is, he was fishing here on Wolf Lake, not on the lake where the girl drowned."

Gurney looked skeptical. "Is there some solid evidence beyond that for the underground connections?"

"Yes. Repeated simultaneous measurements of both lake surfaces show that they always rise and fall precisely in unison, even when a heavy rain storm only impacts one of them directly. So there's no doubt about the existence of the connection, although it's never been adequately explored or mapped." He took another sip from his glass and smiled. "Situations like that can take hold of the ignorant imagination, ever ready to concoct outrageous explanations, especially ones involving evil forces."

Although Gurney couldn't disagree, he found Landon's manner irritating. He decided to change the subject. "You seem able to come and go as you please. Either you're retired or you have a pretty flexible job."

"I'm mostly retired. Bit of consulting here and there. Love being out and about. Love the wilderness. Living the outdoorsman's dream. Time passes, you know. Only live once. You know the old saying: No one on his deathbed ever wishes he'd spent more time in the office. How about you, Dave? Jane tells me that you're partly retired, partly not."

Gurney still found it difficult to describe his status. Madeleine would often comment that the term 'retired' hardly fit a man who'd immersed himself in four major murder cases since his official departure from the job.

"I'm occasionally asked for my opinion of a situation," said Gurney. "And occasionally that leads to some deeper involvements."

Landon smiled, perhaps at the intentional vagueness. "My own feeling regarding careers, particularly ones involving risk, is that there's a time to walk away. Let others do their jobs, grow into their responsibilities. Be a tragedy for a man to lose his life for no reason beyond the desire to keep risking it."

"There could be other reasons for not walking away."

"Ah. Well. Then it becomes more complicated." He studied his drink. "Ego, pride, who we believe we are, satisfactions that give meaning to our lives . . ." His voice trailed off.

After a silence Gurney asked casually, "What sort of consulting work do you do?"

"I advise clients on international business matters. Legal and cultural issues, security concerns. Much rather be in the woods." He turned toward Madeleine. "What about you? You an outdoor sort of woman? I bet you are."

The question appeared to jar her out of a different train of thought. "I do enjoy being outdoors. If I can't get outside, I start to feel—"

Before she could finish, Jane Hammond walked in from the reception area, radiating a mixture of relief and anxiety. Her short, badly dyed hair was sticking out at odd angles. "Dave! Madeleine! You made it! I was afraid with the horrible weather . . . but here you are! So good to see you!" Her voice was hoarse.

"Norris came to our rescue," said Madeleine.

"Rescue? My God! What happened?"

Madeleine glanced over at Gurney.

He shrugged. "Difficult spot on the road, bad maneuver on my part, a slippery ditch . . ."

"Oh no! I was afraid of something like that happening—which is why I asked Norris to check the road. I'm so glad now that I did."

"Everything's fine."

"We did have a scary encounter," added Madeleine.

Jane's eyes widened. "What happened?"

"A strange man came out of the woods."

"Tarr," said Landon.

"Oh. Barlow. He can be scary. Did he say anything . . . threatening?"

"He said something about the evil here at Wolf Lake."

"My God!" Jane looked at Landon, her face a caricature of distress.

"Ah. Well. There's the Tarr family history. Not pretty. Ending up in the local madhouse was a Tarr tradition."

Madeleine's eyes widened. "When you say 'local madhouse,' what exactly—"

Landon answered before she finished. "State Hospital for the Criminally Insane. Not far from here. But not the sort of local attraction the lodge would advertise. When people know about it, it has a way of preying on their minds. You ever heard an Adirondack loon? Even when you know it's just a bird you're hearing, that mournful cry can still give you chills. And if you start thinking that what you're hearing might really be the wailing of a madman wandering in the woods, well . . . that's not conducive to easy sleeping."

Jane stared at him for a moment, then turned to Gurney and Madeleine, who were occupying the end seats on the couch. "I told Richard I invited you for dinner. He wasn't totally thrilled, but he didn't suddenly announce he had to be somewhere else. So we're past the first hurdle. I thought that dinner would be—"

A single, soft musical note, very close by, stopped her in mid-sentence.

Landon shifted in his chair, took a cell phone from his pocket, and peered down at the screen. "Sorry," he said, rising to his feet. Putting the phone to his ear, he left the room.

Jane picked up where she left off. "I thought that dinner would be a natural, relaxed way for you get a feeling for the situation . . . and get to know Richard . . . so you can see for yourself how crazy, how completely crazy, it is for anyone to imagine that he . . ." She shook her head, tears welling in her eyes.

Gurney tended to greet displays of emotion with skepticism, watching for the overly dramatic gesture, listening for the false note. But he concluded that if Jane Hammond was faking her concern for her brother, she was damn good at it.

"So you changed your mind about how to handle this? I thought the idea was that I'd just show up unannounced, and your brother would feel compelled to see me because I'd traveled all this way just to talk to him."

"Yes, but then I thought dinner would be even better—more casual, especially with Madeleine present, a good way for you to get to know who Richard really is."

"He had no objection to that?"

Jane dabbed at her nose with a tissue. "Well . . . I did tell him a small fib."

"How small?"

She took a step closer to the couch and leaned forward in a conspiratorial attitude. "I told him that I'd asked for your help but that you had major reservations about the case, and that you were reluctant to get involved. Since Richard doesn't want you—or anyone else—involved, then naturally he'd be more relaxed with you if he thought you were backing away."

"Then why would I be here now?"

"I told him that you and your wife would be passing through the Adirondacks within a few miles of Wolf Lake on your way to a Vermont ski vacation, and I invited you to stop and have dinner with us."

"So your brother will be happy to have me in his house as long as I'm not interested in the case?"

"As long as you're not *involved* in the case. Some degree of interest would be normal, right?"

"These major reservations I'm supposed to have about getting involved—did he ask you what they were?"

"I said I didn't know. If he asks you, you can just make something up."

This woman wasn't just a caretaker and a fixer, thought Gurney. This was someone with an appetite for manipulation. An arranger of other people's lives who saw herself as a selfless helper.

His natural curiosity about the case was starting to be outweighed by these awkward twists in the process of his involvement. Reluctantly, however, he accepted the new plan—telling himself there would be exit doors if he later changed his mind.

"Dinner—where and what time?"

"At Richard's chalet. Five thirty—is that okay? We eat early in the winter."

He looked at Madeleine.

She nodded. "Fine."

Jane's eyes brightened. "I'll let the chef know. He's limited these days, but I'm sure he'll manage something nice." She sneezed, applied her now-crumpled tissue to her nose. "Richard's chalet is easy to get to. Stay on the lake road. It's just a half mile or so around the tip of the lake, on the forest side of the road. There are three chalets. The first two are unoccupied. Richard's is the third. If you come to the boathouse or to Gall House, where the road ends, you'll know you've gone too far."

"Gall House?"

"The Gall family residence. Of course, the only one living there now is Peyton. Peyton and . . . his guests."

"Guests?"

"His lady friends—although they're not really ladies and not really friends. No matter. None of my business." She sniffled. "It's a huge, depressing stone house, looming up out of the woods, right at the base of Devil's Fang—with a big ugly fence around it. But I really don't think you'll get that far. You can't miss the chalet. I'll make sure the outside lights are on."

"Good," said Gurney, starting to feel restless. Questions were accumulating in his mind that he wasn't comfortable asking just yet.

CHAPTER 15

The drab winter light coming through the suite windows didn't so much illuminate the space as cast an ashen pall over it. Madeleine stood, her arms crossed over her breasts, while Gurney moved from lamp to lamp, switching them on.

"Does that fireplace work?" she asked.

"I imagine so. Would you like me to get a fire going?"

"It would help."

At the hearth Gurney found a neat pile of firewood, some kindling, half a dozen waxy fire-starter bricks, and a long-stemmed butane lighter. He began to arrange the materials on the iron grate in the firebox. He found the task a simple respite from the issues on his mind, which were not simple at all. As he was about to apply the lighter to the kindling, his phone rang. The screen told him it was Rebecca Holdenfield.

To take the call or not to take it—that was the question. He still hadn't reached a decision about their proposed meeting at the Cold Brook Inn; but maybe she had information that could nudge the decision one way or the other.

He took the call.

She told him that she now planned to be in Plattsburgh for at least two days that week—from the following morning until the evening of the day after that.

He promised to get back to her as soon as his schedule became clearer—which could happen later that evening, once he'd met with Hammond—and ended the call.

Madeleine frowned. "What does she want?"

He was taken aback by her tone. He felt his own frustration rising. "What's that supposed to mean?"

Madeleine said nothing, just shook her head.

He paused. "Ever since yesterday morning, there's been something going on with you. Do you want to tell me about it?"

She began rubbing her upper arms with her hands. "I just need to get warm." She turned and walked to the bathroom doorway. "I'm going to soak the cold out of my bones." She went in and closed the door behind her.

After several long seconds, Gurney went to the hearth and lit the kindling. He watched for a few restless minutes as the flames flickered and grew.

When the fire was well established, he went to the bathroom door, knocked and listened, but heard only a heavy stream of water. He knocked again, and again there was no response. He opened the door and saw Madeleine reclining in the huge claw-foot tub as the water gushed down between her feet from a pair of oversized silver faucets. Wisps of steam rose from the surface of the water. A film of condensation was forming on the tile wall next to the tub.

"Did you hear me knock?"

"Yes."

"But you didn't answer."

"No."

"Why not?"

She closed her eyes. "Go out and close the door. Please. The cold air is coming in."

He hesitated, then shut the door, perhaps a bit more firmly than was necessary.

He put on his ski jacket and hat, picked up the big key to the suite, went downstairs through the reception area and out under the portico into the frigid air.

He thrust his hands into his jacket pockets and started walking along the narrow lake road with no destination or purpose in mind beyond a desire to be out of the lodge. Wolf Lake, now the color of deeply tarnished silver in the deepening dusk, stretched into the distance on his left. The spruce forest on his right appeared impenetrable. The lower spaces between the trees were filled with interlocking tangles of spiky branches.

He inhaled long, deep, cold breaths as he walked, in an effort to clear out the toxic jumble. But it wasn't working. There were too many details, too many eccentric personalities, too much emotional confusion. Barely thirty-two hours ago his only concern was an oddly behaving porcupine. Now he was grappling with mysteries buried under impossibilities.

Never had Gurney felt so completely stymied by the basic questions in a case. And he couldn't get Bowman Cox out of his mind—the man leaning forward over the Formica table in the diner, flecks of spittle at the corners of his mouth, insisting on Hammond's responsibility for the death of Christopher Wenzel.

Gurney passed by an extended clearing in the forest with three impressive log-and-glass chalets set comfortably apart from each other. He walked on and soon came to a large structure occupying the space on his left between the road and the water. In the dusky light it took him a minute to identify it as a cedar-shingle boathouse. Given the moneyed history of the estate, he imagined the boathouse might be sheltering a fleet of vintage Chris-Craft runabouts.

As his attention shifted to the jagged prominence of Devil's Fang, black against the gunmetal clouds, a slight movement caught his eye, little more than a speck in the sky. A bird was slowly circling above the desolate peak—perhaps a hawk, but at that distance in the failing light it could as easily have been a vulture or an eagle. He regretted leaving his binoculars in his duffel bag.

Thinking of things he wished he had with him, the flashlight in the glove box—

His train of thought was broken by the sound of an approaching car. It was coming from somewhere on the road behind him, and it was moving fast, faster than made sense on a narrow dirt and gravel surface. He stepped quickly away from the road toward the spruces.

Seconds later a gleaming black Mercedes hurtled past. A hundred yards or so farther along the road it slowed, its headlights illuminating a tall chain-link fence. A motorized gate was in the process of sliding open.

One or more windows of the car must have been rolled down, because Gurney could now hear shrieks of female laughter. A burly man emerged from a small security booth by the gate and waved the car through. He returned to the booth and the gate slid shut. There was a final shriek from the receding car, then nothing.

Nothing but the absolute silence of the wilderness.

CHAPTER 16

By the time he got back to the lodge the grandfather clock in the reception area indicated it was a quarter past five. When he went upstairs to the suite, he half expected that Madeleine would still be soaking in the tub, immersed in the preoccupation she was unwilling to discuss. But he found the bathroom empty, a wet towel draped over the end of the tub.

The lights were on in the main room, just as he'd left them. The fire he'd started was still burning. Warren Harding was still projecting an image of scowling respectability.

He checked the sleeping alcove and its four-poster bed, but the bed was untouched. Madeleine's duffel bag was open on a bench at the foot of it, but there was no sign of Madeleine.

Then the glass door leading out to the balcony opened, and she stepped into the room. She was wearing black jeans, a cream silk blouse, and her ski jacket. She'd even put on a trace of makeup, a rarity for her.

"Time to go?" she asked.

"What were you doing out there?"

She didn't answer. They went downstairs in silence and got in the Outback. They didn't speak again until they arrived at the chalet.

JANE HAMMOND MET THEM AT THE DOOR AND USHERED THEM IN, taking their jackets.

The entrance area of the chalet was formed by three partitions of lustrously varnished honey-colored wood. In addition to creating a kind of foyer, the partitions served as display surfaces for stone tomahawks, deerskin pouches, and other primitive tools. Eyeing the tomahawks, Gurney couldn't help thinking of Barlow Tarr's hatchet.

Jane leaned toward him. "Were you aware of anyone following you?"

"No. But I wasn't checking. Why do you ask?"

"Sometimes there's a big SUV lurking out there on the lake road. Richard is sure he's being followed every time he leaves the house. I think they want him to fall apart. By putting all this pressure on him. Do you think that's what it is?"

He shrugged. "At this point, there's no way of—"

He was interrupted by his phone. He glanced at the screen, saw that the call was from Rebecca Holdenfield, and, despite a strong desire to speak to her, let it go into voicemail.

"Come," said Jane nervously. "We can talk about this later. Let me introduce you."

She led them into the chalet's cathedral-ceilinged great room. A small, slim man with his back to them was fiddling with the logs in a massive fieldstone fireplace. His delicate physique was a surprise. Gurney had been imagining someone larger.

"Richard," said Jane. "These are the people I've been telling you about."

Hammond turned toward them. With a wan smile that could have been an expression of lukewarm welcome or plain weariness, he extended his hand first to Madeleine, then to Gurney. It was small and smooth, a bit on the cool side, the grip unenthusiastic.

His silky blond hair, almost platinum, was parted on the side. In the front it had fallen down in wispy bangs over his forehead, like a little boy's. But there was nothing childlike about his eyes. A disconcertingly luminous aquamarine, they were riveting, almost unnerving.

By contrast, the man's voice was soft and nondescript. Gurney wondered if it was a form of compensation for the uniquely startling eyes. Or a way of reinforcing their dominance.

"My sister told me a lot about you."

"Nothing disturbing, I hope."

"She told me you were the detective who managed to capture Peter Piggert, the incestuous murderer who cut his mother in half. And Jorge Kunzman, who kept his victims' heads in his refrigerator. And the Satanic Santa, who mailed out body parts as Christmas presents. And the demented psychiatrist who sent his patients to a sadist who raped and skinned them before tossing them off the back of his yacht into the ocean. That's quite an accomplished career you've had. Quite a few madmen you've managed to vanquish. And here you are at Wolf Lake. Just passing through. On your way to a romantic inn. Am I right?"

"Yes, that's where we're heading."

"But, for the moment, here you are. In the deep wilderness. Miles from nowhere. Tell me—how do you like it so far?"

"The weather could be better."

Hammond produced a forced little laugh, while his gaze remained steady and observant. "It's more likely to get worse before it gets better."

"Worse?" asked Madeleine.

"Rising winds, falling temperatures, snow squalls, ice pellets."

"When is this supposed to happen?"

"Sometime tomorrow. Or the next day. Forecasts here are always changing. The mountains have unpredictable moods. Our weather is like the mind of a manic-depressive." He smiled slightly at what he seemed to regard as a joke. "Do you know the Adirondacks?"

She hesitated. "Not really."

"These mountains are different from your Catskills. Far more primitive."

"I'm just concerned about getting snowed in."

He gave her a long curious look. "That concerns you?"

"You don't think it should?"

"Jane told me you were driving to Vermont to find snow. Walk in it, ski in it. But perhaps the snow will find you first."

Madeleine said nothing. Gurney noticed a tiny involuntary shudder go through her body.

Hammond licked his lips in a rapid little snakelike movement, his gaze shifting to Gurney. "Wolf Lake has become such an interesting place lately, hasn't it? Irresistible, I would think, for a detective."

Jane, perhaps concerned at her brother's ironic tone, intervened brightly. "Dinner is laid out on the sideboard—salmon canapés, salad, bread, chicken with apricot sauce, wild rice, asparagus, and some nice blueberry tarts for dessert. Plates at the near end of the sideboard; silverware and glasses on the table, along with bottles of chardonnay, merlot, and springwater. Shall we?"

Her tone was as bubbly as her brother's was edgy. But it served the purpose of getting everyone to the food and then to the table. She and Richard seated themselves across from Dave and Madeleine.

Before anyone could say another word the lights went out.

In the sudden near-darkness only the dying fire provided glimmers of illumination.

"It's just the generator," said Jane. "It'll be back on in a few seconds."

When the lights came back on, her hand was on Richard's arm. She withdrew it and turned her attention to Gurney and Madeleine. "We're twenty miles from any kind of civilization, so the lodge compound has its own pair of generators. They switch from one to the other every so often, and we get short blackouts. Austen says it's perfectly normal, nothing to worry about."

"You do have phone service here, right?" asked Madeleine.

"The lodge compound has its own cell tower. But once you pass over the high ridge, there's a dead zone with no reception until you get to Plattsburgh. Of course, the cell tower depends on the generators, so if they go out . . ." Then she quickly added, "But there's virtually no chance of both generators failing at the same time."

Gurney changed the subject. "I gather Ethan Gall was quite a presence in the world."

Richard answered. "Indeed he was. A remarkable man—dynamic, generous, supportive. My work here was his idea."

"Now that he's gone," said Madeleine, "will you be going back to California?"

"My two-year contract was up last month, but shortly before his death Ethan offered to renew it for another year, and I accepted the offer." He hesitated, as if considering how much he wanted to disclose. "Ethan died before the agreement was signed, but Austen was aware of it, and he assured me it would be honored."

Gurney saw an opening for a question he'd been wanting to ask. "I gather that Austen Steckle, despite his background, has become a man of some integrity?"

"Austen has rough edges, but I have no complaints."

"What was his conviction for?"

"I'd prefer that you asked him." He paused. "But I have a question for you. Why did you tell Jane you didn't want to get involved in my situation here?"

Gurney decided to answer as truthfully as he could. "Jane told me that you refused to hire professional help, but that she'd like me to help her gather facts and figure out what's behind these apparent suicides. She certainly has a right to explore the affair for her own peace of mind. But frankly, I'm not comfortable being involved in that."

"Why not?"

"Because you're the key to it all. Somehow, you're at the heart of what's been happening. You may not be at the heart of it the way Gilbert Fenton says you are. But in some way, you've been pulled into the center of it. It would be foolish for me to get involved without your cooperation."

Jane's eyes widened in alarm. This was plainly not the casual approach she wanted him to take.

A silence ensued during which Richard appeared to be imagining dark possibilities.

Gurney decided to take a risk. "Remember, Richard, at the end of the day . . . there was no dead body in the trunk."

If Hammond was shocked that Gurney was aware of the incident, he concealed it well. His only reaction came after a delay of several seconds.

It was an almost imperceptible nod of acknowledgment.

THE RELEVANCE OF THE TRUNK EPISODE SEEMED TO CREATE A SHIFT in Hammond's perspective. It also brought the edgy momentum of the gathering to a kind of resting place.

At Jane's suggestion, they moved from the table to a half circle of armchairs facing the hearth. The glowing coals created a soothing focal point that made the lull in the conversation feel comfortable. Jane served coffee and brought them each a slice of blueberry tart from the sideboard.

The relaxed mood, however, was fragile.

Gurney sensed it ebbing away as they were finishing their coffee and Hammond asked him if he'd read the statement he'd issued to the press.

"I did."

"Then you know that I was absolutely clear on certain points?"

"Yes."

"I said that I would hire no defenders or representatives of any kind."

"True."

"I didn't mean that I myself would hire no defenders, but I'd have my sister do it for me. I wasn't being devious. I meant what I said."

"I'm sure you did."

"But now you want me to reverse that position and bless your employment by my sister."

"Your agreeing to my involvement won't reverse anything. I have no intention of being your defender or representative."

Hammond appeared bewildered, Jane alarmed.

Gurney continued. "The only purpose of my involvement—if I choose to get involved at all—would be to discover how and why those four people died."

"So you're not interested in proving my innocence?"

"Only to the extent that the truth itself proves your innocence. My job is uncovering the facts. I'm a detective, not a lawyer. If I were to get involved in this case, I wouldn't be representing you or your sister. I'd be representing Ethan Gall, Christopher Wenzel, Leo Balzac, and Steven Pardosa. Discovering the truth behind their deaths is something I'd be doing for them. If the truth should end up benefiting you, that would be fine with me. But I'd be representing their interests, not yours."

Throughout this speech Jane looked like she was in a panic to jump in.

Richard's only hint of emotion was a flicker of sadness at the mention of Ethan Gall.

He regarded Gurney for a long moment before asking, "What do you want from me?"

"Any thoughts or suspicions you may have about the four deaths. Anything that could help me make sense of a case that right now makes no sense at all."

"It makes sense to Gilbert Fenton."

"And to Reverend Bowman Cox," Gurney added, wondering what impact the name might have on Hammond.

Judging from his blank look, it had none.

Gurney explained, "Bowman Cox is the Florida minister Wenzel confided his nightmare to. I was curious about the nightmare, so I got in touch with him. He can recite it by heart."

"Why would he do that?"

"He says the nightmare is the key to understanding Wenzel's death, and your role in it."

"My role being . . . ?"

"He told me your therapeutic specialty is the manufacture of homosexuals."

"Not that old nonsense all over again! Did he mention how I do it?"

"You put people in a deep trance. You go through some lurid mumbo jumbo to convince them that they're really homosexual. And when they emerge from the trance, they either dive headfirst into their new lifestyle or become suicidal at the very thought of it."

"That must be a hell of a trance I'm putting them in."

"Yes. Literally. A hell of a trance. Cox claims that your power to destroy people's lives comes from a secret partnership with Satan."

Hammond sighed. "Isn't it remarkable that here in America we treat the mentally ill like dirt—except when they make a religion out of their craziness and hatred, and claim it's Christianity? Then we flock to their churches."

A valid enough observation, thought Gurney, but he didn't want to get off on a tangent. "Let me ask you a clinical question. Could a hypnotherapist implant the details of a dream in a patient's mind and actually cause him to have that dream?"

"Absolutely not. It's a neurological impossibility."

"Okay. Could a hypnotherapist talk a client into committing suicide?"

"Not unless the client was already suffering from a depression severe enough to incline him that way to begin with."

"Did you note that kind of depression in any of the four men who ended up dead?"

"No. They all had positive feelings about the future. That's not a suicidal state of mind."

"Does that lead you to any conclusion?"

"My conclusion is that they were victims of murders staged to resemble suicides."

"Yet Fenton is ignoring that possibility. He's claiming that the unlikelihood of their committing suicide indicates that you caused it. Do you have any idea why he'd take such a strange position?"

Jane broke in, "Because he's a dishonest, lying bastard!" Her fragile china plate with its half-eaten slice of blueberry tart slipped from her lap and shattered on the floor. She stared down at it, muttered a frustrated "Shit!" and began cleaning it up. Madeleine got a sponge and some paper towels from the sink to help.

Hammond answered Gurney's question. "There are two puzzling things about Fenton's position. First, it's based on a clinical impossibility. Secondly, he believes what he's saying."

"How do you know that?"

"That's what I'm good at. Nine times out of ten, I can hear in a person's voice the sound of the truth, the sound of a lie. The way I practice therapy is based a little on technique and a lot on insight into what people really believe and want, regardless of what they tell me."

"And you're convinced that Fenton believes the wild scenario he's hyping to the press?"

"He has no doubt about it. It's in his voice, his eyes, his body language."

"Just when I thought I couldn't be more confused, you've added another twist. A homicide investigator might *briefly consider the possibility* that a hypnotist was behind a string of suicides. But to embrace it as the *only* possible answer seems crazy." He glanced over at Madeleine to see if she had any reaction; but her eyes were on the dying red coals, her mind plainly somewhere else.

Another question occurred to him. "You said you were good at sensing what a person really wants. What do you think Fenton wants?"

"He wants me to confess my involvement in the four deaths. He told me that it's the only way out, and if I don't confess, my life will be over."

"And if you do confess to some yet unnamed felony, what then?"

"He said if I confessed to my part in causing all four suicides, then everything would be all right."

That was the way some investigators talked mentally challenged suspects into confessing, often to crimes they hadn't committed. *If you keep denying it, we'll get mad, and then you'll really be in trouble. Just admit you did it, then everything will be cleared up, and everyone can go home.*

That's the way crimes were hung on people with IQs of eighty.

Why on earth was Fenton taking that approach with a brilliant psychologist?

What goddamn twilight zone was this happening in?

CHAPTER 17

As they sat around the hearth nursing their coffees, Gurney took the opportunity to ask a very basic question. "Richard, I may be assuming I understand hypnosis better than I actually do. Can you give me a simple definition of it?"

Hammond lowered his coffee to the arm of his chair. "A quick story might make it clearer than a definition. When I was in high school in Mill Valley, I played some baseball. I wasn't very good, barely good enough to stay on the team. Then one day I came up to bat five times, and I hit five home runs. I'd never hit a home run before that day. The most remarkable thing was how it felt. The *effortlessness* of it. I wasn't even swinging that hard. I wasn't trying to concentrate. I wasn't trying to hit a home run. I wasn't *trying* to do anything. I was completely relaxed. It seemed that the bat just kept finding the ball and striking it at the perfect angle. Five times in a row."

"And the connection between that and hypnosis is . . . ?"

"Achieving a goal depends less on overcoming external obstacles than on removing internal ones—dysfunctional beliefs, emotional static. Hypnotherapy, as I practice it, is devoted to clearing that internal path."

"How?" That single, sharp word came from Madeleine—who, up to that point, had said almost nothing.

"By uncovering what's in the way. Freeing you from it. Letting you move toward what you really want without being stuck in the underbrush of guilt, confusion, and self-sabotage."

"Isn't that overly dramatic?" she asked.

"I don't think so. We really do get tangled up in some nasty internal thornbushes."

"I thought hypnosis was about concentration."

"Concentrated focus is the aim, but trying to concentrate is the worst way to get there. That's like trying to levitate by pulling up on your ankles. Or like chasing happiness. You can't catch it by chasing it."

She looked unconvinced.

Gurney pursued the issue. "What sort of internal obstacles do you need to clear away with people who want to stop smoking?"

Hammond continued to observe Madeleine for a moment before turning to Gurney. "Two big ones— memories of anxiety being relieved by smoking, and a faulty risk calculation."

"I understand the first. What's the second?"

"The rational individual tends to avoid activities whose costs outweigh their pleasures. The addict tends to avoid activities whose costs precede their pleasures. In a clearly operating mind, the *ultimate balance* decides the matter. Immediate and future effects are both seen as real. In a mind warped by addiction, *sequence* is the crucial factor. Immediate effects are seen as real; future effects are seen as hypothetical."

"So you bring some clarity to that?" asked Gurney.

"I don't *bring* anything. I simply help the person see what they know in their heart to be true. I help them focus on what *they* really want."

"You believe you have a reliable instinct for sensing what people want?"

"Yes."

"Did all four of the victims want to stop smoking?"

Hammond blinked noticeably for the first time. "The desire was strong in Ethan, moderate in Wenzel. In Balzac and Pardosa it was between weak and nonexistent."

"Why would you bother treating someone like that?"

"The truth about the nature and depth of a person's desire becomes clear to me only during the course of the session. They all claimed to have a strong desire at the start."

Gurney looked perplexed.

Hammond went on. "People frequently come at the urging of someone else. Their real desire is to get someone off their back by being compliant. And some people come in the belief that hypnosis will create a desire to stop, even though they have no such desire themselves. Pardosa was the worst—anxious, unfocused, completely scattered—the one who most obviously was doing it at someone else's request. But he wouldn't admit it."

"What about their other desires?"

"Meaning?"

"Did your instinct for sensing people's motives lead you to any other conclusions?"

"Some general ones."

"About Ethan?"

Hammond hesitated, as though considering confidentiality issues. "Ethan wanted everyone in the world to behave better. He wanted to find a proper role for each person and put them in it. A place for everyone, and everyone in their place. He was certain that he knew best. He didn't want recognition. Just obedience."

"I assume he didn't always get the kind of obedience he wanted?"

"He had his successes and his failures."

"How about your sense of Christopher Wenzel? What did he want out of life?"

"Christopher wanted to win. In the worst way, literally. He saw life as a zero-sum game. Not only did he want to win, he wanted someone else to lose."

"What about Leo Balzac?"

"Angry God of the Old Testament. He wanted all the bad guys to be punished. He would have enjoyed standing at a porthole in Noah's ark, watching the sinners drowning."

"And Steven Pardosa?"

"He was the one who lived in his parents' basement. He was desperate for respect. More than anything else, he wanted to be seen as an adult—which is, of course, the universal desire of people who never grow up."

"How about Peyton Gall?"

"Ah, Peyton. Peyton wants to feel good all the time, regardless of the cost to himself or others. Like most drug addicts, he has infantile ideas of happiness. He wants to do whatever he feels like doing, whenever he feels like doing it. He's the prisoner of his own concept of freedom. The enormous inheritance he receives from Ethan's estate will probably kill him."

"How?"

"Unlimited financial resources will remove whatever slight restraint may have been modifying his behavior till now. His disregard of future consequences will take over completely. In Freudian terms, Peyton is pure, 100 percent rampaging id."

All Gurney could think of was the car flying past him on the narrow dirt road and the wild shrieks of laughter. "How did he get along with his brother?"

"There was no 'getting along' at all. They lived in separate wings of the house and had as little to do with each other as possible, apart from Ethan's sporadic efforts to apply whatever pressure he could. If Austen was Ethan's greatest success, Peyton was his greatest failure."

"Do you think Peyton would have been capable of killing Ethan?"

"Morally, yes. Emotionally, yes. Practically, no. I can't see Peyton handling anything that would demand complex thinking, precise logistics, or steadiness under pressure."

"Those are the qualities you believe were required to . . . to engineer the four deaths?"

"They may not have been the only ones, but they're definitely the ones Peyton lacks."

Another question came to mind—a bit of a wild tangent. "Getting back to your ability to sense what people want . . . what about me? What do you think I really want?"

Hammond flashed a chilly smile. "Are you testing me?"

"I'm curious to see how far your instincts take you."

"Fair enough. *What does Dave Gurney really want?* It's an interesting question." He glanced at Madeleine, who was watching him intently, before turning back to Gurney.

"This is only the barest of first impressions, but I'd guess that you have one great imperative in your life. You want to *understand*. You want to connect the dots. Your personality is built around that central desire, a desire you perceive as a *need*. You claimed earlier that you want to represent the victims, to stand up for Ethan Gall, to achieve justice for him and the others. That may or may not be true, but I can see that you believe it. I can see that you're being as open and honest with me as you can be. But you also appear to have a great deal on your mind, issues you're not talking about."

His gaze moved to Madeleine. "You have a great deal on your mind, too."

"Oh?" She reflexively crossed her arms.

"You have something on your mind that's making you uncomfortable. Most of that discomfort comes from keeping it a secret. Your husband knows something is troubling you. He senses that you're afraid to tell him about it. That adds to his own burden. And you can see how your secret is affecting him, but you don't see any simple way out of it, and it's making your situation very painful."

"You can tell all that . . . how? By the way I eat my blueberry tart?"

Hammond smiled softly. "Actually, by the way you *don't* eat it. When Jane first mentioned blueberries, there was a positive flash of anticipation in your eyes, which was quickly overtaken by other thoughts. Your anxiety stole your appetite. You never touched your dessert."

"Amazing. Who knew that failing to eat a tart could be so revealing?"

Her anger had no visible effect on Hammond, whose gentle smile persisted. "A lot is revealed by the way a husband and wife look at each other, particularly the way one looks at the other when the other isn't looking back. So much is written on their faces."

Madeleine returned his smile, but hers was cold. "Do you look in the mirror much?"

"It doesn't work that way, if I understand what you're getting at."

"A man with your insight into facial expressions must gather all sorts of information from his own reflection."

"I wish that were true. In my case, it's not."

"So your psychological dissection skills can only be applied to other people?"

He nodded ruefully. "Sometimes I think of it as my deal with the devil."

Madeleine fell silent, perhaps surprised by the odd reply.

"What do you mean?" asked Gurney.

"I mean I've been given something of value, but there's a related price."

"The thing of value being your insight?"

"My insight into others. The price seems to be a lack of insight into myself. Clarity looking outward, blindness looking inward. I can see your motives plainly. Mine are a mystery to me. The better I get at understanding the actions of others, the less I seem able to understand my own. So there are questions whose answers I can only guess at. You wonder why I don't hire a lawyer, why I don't sue the police for defamation, why I don't sue the tabloids and bloggers for libel, why I don't hire a team of investigators to discredit Gilbert Fenton, why I don't conduct an aggressive public relations campaign in my own defense. You wonder why the hell don't I stand up and fight, launch an all-out war, and bury these bastards in their own lies?"

"It's an excellent question. Is there an answer?"

"Of course there's an answer. But I don't know what it is."

"No idea at all?"

"Oh, I can give you a list of *ideas*. How about a crushing fear of confrontation in general? Or the fear that greater confrontation would bring some dark moment of my past to light? Or a depressive conviction that struggling will only pull me deeper into the quicksand? Or outright paranoia, like my famous fixation on the imaginary body in the trunk of my car? Maybe I'm afraid of hiring an attorney who I'd never be free of, who'd somehow gain control of my life, that I'd be at his mercy forever. Perhaps it's a sublimated terror of my mother, who taught me one thing above all else—never dare to deny whatever she was accusing me of at the moment. Accept the punishment being offered, or face one of her uncontrollable rages."

He let out a sharp, humorless laugh—seemingly at his own speculations. "See what I mean? So many crazy fears to pick and choose from. On the other hand, perhaps I'm motivated by a manic conviction that nothing Fenton says can touch me. Maybe I have a Pollyanna conviction that the truth will prevail and my innocence will speak for itself. Or a foolish pride that tells me not to lower myself to the level of the fools attacking me. Could it be that I crave the satisfaction of seeing Gilbert Fenton's whole case, his whole world, come crashing down without my having to lift a finger?"

He paused, the tip of his tongue darting across his lips. "Perhaps some of these possibilities have occurred to you. They occur to me every day. But I haven't a clue which one is driving my decisions. All I know is that I want to proceed the way I'm proceeding." This was addressed to Madeleine. Now he turned to Gurney. "If you want to seek justice for Ethan and the others, as a matter separate from my defense, that's your business. I won't stand in your way. But let me reiterate: you are not my advocate. Understood?"

"Understood."

No one said anything for a while. The only sound was the faint tick-tick-tick-tick of sleet on the windowpanes.

Then, somewhere out in the forest, the howling began. The same howling that Gurney had heard when their car was stuck in the ditch.

It started with a low wail, like the moaning of wind at an ill-fitting door.

CHAPTER 18

By the time they were getting in their car to head back to the lodge, the howling, distant and mournful, seemed to be coming from every direction—from Cemetery Ridge, from the deep forest in back of Hammond's chalet—even, it seemed, from the dark expanse of the lake itself.

Then it faded into the wind.

As they drove away from the chalet Gurney's thoughts went back to Madeleine's hostile response to Hammond's observations. He felt some resentment that she had hijacked his conversation with Hammond. Admittedly, her approach had generated some revealing responses. But it might not have. It might have shut him down completely.

"You were pretty aggressive back there."

"Was I?"

"The expression on your face seemed to be suggesting that Hammond was lying."

"Only suggesting? I should have been clearer."

"You're sure he's not telling the truth?"

"As sure as you are that he *is*."

"What's that supposed to mean?"

"He has X-ray vision when it comes to other people? But he pays for it with total blindness to his own motives? How convenient! What a perfect way to deflect questions about his decisions. Question: *So, Richard, why did you do such and such?* Answer: *Golly, gee, I don't know. I'm a genius, but I have no idea why I do anything.* Don't you see that he's making a fool of you?"

"How?"

"By tossing out all those 'maybe' reasons for his not hiring a lawyer— making you believe he doesn't have a clue which reason is the real one."

"He didn't make me believe anything. I told you I have an open mind."

"Did your open mind notice that he left out the most likely reason of all?"

"Which is?"

"That a smart lawyer poking around in the case might discover things he doesn't want discovered. Maybe those deaths are just the tip of an iceberg."

"Christ, Maddie, anything is possible. But I still don't see how he's making a fool of me."

"Why are you taking his side?"

"How am I taking his side?"

"Whatever I say, you defend him. You believe everything he says."

"I don't *believe* anything. I'm a homicide detective, not a gullible idiot."

"Then why are you confusing his cleverness with real insight?"

Gurney was at a loss for words. He felt that Madeleine's animus toward Hammond was coming from a vulnerable place in herself, not from an appraisal of the facts.

But what if she was right? What if she was seeing something he was missing? What if his own supposed objectivity wasn't so objective after all?

They arrived back in their suite in a state of strained silence. Madeleine went into the bathroom and turned on the tub water.

He followed her. "Didn't you just take a bath? Like three hours ago?"

"Is there a limit on the number of baths I'm allowed to take?"

"Maddie, what the hell is going on? You've been edgy ever since we agreed to come here. Shouldn't we talk about whatever's bothering you?"

"I'm sorry. I'm just not . . . very comfortable right now." She shut the bathroom door.

All of this was new and unsettling. Madeleine with secrets. Madeleine hunkering down behind a closed door. He went over and sat on the couch. It was several minutes before he noticed that the fire had burned itself out. Only a few small coals remained, glowing weakly through the ashes. His first thought was that he should revive it, give the room some warmth. But his second thought was that he should go to bed. It had been a stressful day, and the following day promised to be the same.

Thinking of the next day reminded him of the call from Holdenfield he'd let go into voicemail. He took out his phone and listened to the message.

"Hi David, Rebecca here. They've added some stuff to my schedule, so I'm going to be tied up most of tomorrow. But I have a suggestion. Breakfast. You don't have to get back to me, because I'll be in the Cold Brook Inn dining room at eight tomorrow morning one way or the other. So come if you can. You can even come earlier if that's better for you. I'll be up at five, working in my room on a paper that's overdue. Okay? Love to hear more about the Hammond case. Drive safely. Hope to see you."

From a practical point of view, the timing, although unusual, might be doable. He recalled that she'd said in her earlier message that it was just twenty-seven miles from Wolf Lake to Plattsburgh. That should take well under an hour, even in bad weather, plus an hour or so with Rebecca. So a total of three hours, max. If he left at seven, he'd be back by ten at the latest. He closed his eyes and began to compile a mental list of questions to ask Rebecca about hypnotism, about Hammond's controversial reputation, and about Wenzel's dream.

His exhaustion overtook him so quickly he was asleep within minutes.

As always happened when he dozed off sitting up, physical discomfort eventually intruded, dragging with it the concerns he'd temporarily anesthetized. He opened his eyes, checked the time on his phone, and discovered he'd slept for almost an hour. He was about to see if Madeleine was still in her bath when he saw her standing at the window. She was wearing one of the lodge's plush white bathrobes.

"Turn off the lights," she said without looking at him.

He switched off the lamps and joined her at the window.

The storm had departed, and the dense overcast had been replaced with a patchwork of clouds making their way across the face of a full moon. He followed Madeleine's line of sight to discover why she'd called him to the window. And then he saw it.

As a cloud moved slowly out of the way of the moon, the effect on the landscape was like a theatrical light coming up on a dark stage. The stage in this case was dominated by an overwhelming presence—Devil's Fang, fierce and gigantic, its jagged edges thrown into dramatic relief. Then another cloud moved in, the moonlight faded, and Devil's Fang disappeared into the night.

Gurney turned away from the window, but Madeleine continued to stare out into the darkness.

"I used to come here." She said it so softly he wondered if he'd heard right.

"You came up here? When?"

"Christmas vacations. I'm sure I mentioned it."

That jogged his memory. Something she'd told him when they were first married. Something about spending a few Christmases with elderly relatives in upstate New York when she was in high school. "With a distant aunt and uncle, or something like that, wasn't it?"

"Uncle George and Aunt Maureen," she said vaguely, still gazing in the direction of Devil's Fang. The second cloud obscuring the moon began to pass, letting the silver light shine down again on that sharp pinnacle.

"You never said much about it."

She didn't respond.

"Maddie?"

"One winter there was a tragic death. A local boy. A drowning."

"At this lake?"

"No, another one."

"And?"

She shook her head.

He waited, thinking she might go on.

But all she finally said was, "I have to get some sleep."

"DAVID!"

There was a frantic tightness in her whisper that woke him immediately.

"There's something in the sitting room."

"Where?" As he whispered the question, he was calculating from memory the rough angle and number of steps to the bag that held his Beretta.

"I saw something pass the window. Could a bat have gotten into the room?"

"Is that what you saw—something flying?"

"I think so."

He relaxed just a little and reached out to the lamp on the night table. He pressed the toggle switch. Nothing happened. He pressed it again. Still nothing.

"Can you reach the lamp on your side of the bed?" he asked.

He heard the futile clicks as she tried it.

He felt around on the night table for his phone. He found it and checked the status icons. There was no cell signal, meaning the lodge's private cell tower was out, meaning there'd been a power interruption.

In the windowless bedroom alcove it was too dark to see anything, but a pale wash of moonlight was faintly illuminating part of the main room, visible through the alcove's broad arch. Gurney lay motionless, searching the darkness for any hint of movement. He saw nothing and heard nothing. Some minutes went by without any return of power.

Then the silence was broken by a slow creaking in the ceiling.

Madeleine grabbed his arm.

They listened together for a long minute.

A small shadow shot past a window in the main room, forcing a cry from Madeleine.

"It's just a bat," he said, as her fingers tightened on his arm. "I'll open the balcony door and let it fly out."

His assurances were cut off by another creak in the ceiling—like a careful footstep on a weak floorboard.

"Someone's up there," whispered Madeleine.

Bringing to mind what he remembered of the front of the lodge, he pictured two regular floors—the ground floor and the floor they were on—plus an attic level. He thought it unlikely that any guest rooms would be in the attic. As he was considering this, there was a faint scraping sound in the ceiling directly above them.

Then nothing. They listened for a long while. But all they heard was the droning of the wind at the balcony door.

What was it about Wolf Lake Lodge, wondered Gurney, that made the sound of a slow footstep, if that's what it was, so disturbing? Was it the power outage that was creating a sense of threat? Surely the same sound in daylight, or even lamplight, would not have the same impact.

Madeleine spoke again in a whisper. "Who do you think is up there?"

"Maybe no one. Maybe it's just the wood contracting with the dropping temperature."

Her concern shifted to the bat. "Will it really fly out if you open the door?"

"I think so."

She relaxed her grip on his arm. He slipped out of bed and felt his way from the alcove to the balcony door and opened it. He guessed the cold front that blew the sleet storm away had lowered the temperature at least fifteen degrees. Unless the bat flew out quickly, the whole suite would soon be freezing.

It occurred to him that a fire would be a good idea—for warmth, light, reassurance.

He stepped away from the open door and began to feel his way toward the fireplace. Shivering in his shorts and tee shirt, he stopped at the chair where his clothes were and put on his pants and shirt. As he turned back toward the fireplace, a sound in the outer corridor stopped him. He stood still and listened. A few seconds later he heard it again.

He got his Beretta out of the bag on the chair. He couldn't help feeling he was overreacting, influenced more by the spooky atmosphere than by any real threat.

"What is it?" whispered Madeleine from the alcove.

"Just someone in the corridor."

He heard a soft thump from the direction of the suite door.

He eased off the Beretta's safety and began moving forward. The moonlight was limited to the area near the windows. In this part of the room the visibility was zero.

There was a second thump, stronger than the first—the sort of dull impact that might be produced by someone bumping a knee, or some other blunt object, against the door.

He felt his way into a position by the side of the door, eased the dead bolt into its open position, then stopped and listened. He heard something that might have been the sound of someone breathing, or maybe it was just the movement of air through the crack under the door.

He grasped the doorknob. He turned it slowly as far as it went, steadied his stance, checked his grip on the Beretta . . . then yanked the door open.

CHAPTER 19

The grotesque apparition in front of him was a shock. A weirdly illuminated face seemed to be suspended in the darkness of the corridor, its features distorted by elongated shadows cast upward by a small yellow flame beneath it.

As Gurney's mind raced to make sense of what he was seeing, he realized that the flame was in a kerosene lamp, that the lamp was being held by a dirty hand with cracked fingernails, and that the jaundiced face in the angled lamplight was one he'd seen before—at the side of the road when his car was stuck in the ditch. The matted fur hat confirmed the identification.

"Tree come down," said Barlow Tarr.

"Yes . . . and . . . ?"

"Smashed the electrics."

"The generators are out?"

"Aye."

Gurney lowered his Beretta. "That's what you came to tell us?"

"Be warnt."

"About what?"

"The evil here."

"What evil?"

"The evil what killed them all."

"Tell me more about the evil."

"The hawk knows. The hawk in the sun, the hawk in the moon."

"What does the hawk know?"

Even as Gurney was asking the question, Tarr was stepping away from the doorway, turning down the wick of the lamp until the flame was extinguished.

A second later he disappeared into the unlit corridor.

Gurney called out, "Barlow? Barlow?"

There was no response. The only sound he could hear was coming from the open balcony door on the far side of the room.

It was the rising and falling rush of the wind in the trees.

AFTER THAT EXPERIENCE, SLEEP SEEMED UNLIKELY.

Convincing himself that the flying bat had departed, Gurney closed the balcony door. He built a large fire in the hearth. He and Madeleine settled down on the couch in front of the blaze.

After speculating about the meaning of Tarr's visit, they agreed the only clear aspect was that the man wanted them to know that Wolf Lake was a dangerous place. Beyond that, his spooky ramblings could mean anything or nothing.

In the end, they fell into a prolonged silence, succumbing to the undulations of the fire.

After a while Gurney found his thoughts returning to Madeleine's connection to the area.

He turned toward her and asked softly, "Are you awake?"

Her eyes were closed, but she nodded yes.

"When you stayed here in the Adirondacks with your aunt and uncle, how old were you?"

She opened her eyes and stared into the fire. "Early teens." She paused. "It's so strange to think that it was me."

"What was so different about you . . . back then?"

"Everything." She blinked, cleared her throat, looked around the room. Her gaze stopped at the kerosene lamp on the small table at Gurney's end of the couch. "What's that?"

"The lamp?"

"The etching on the base."

Gurney looked more closely. He hadn't noticed it before, having set the lamp down on the table before starting the fire, but on the glass base there was a fine-line etching showing an animal crouching, as if preparing to leap at the viewer. Its teeth were bared.

"It appears to be a wolf," he said.

She responded with a shiver. "Too many wolves."

"It's the theme of the place."

"And part of the nightmares those people died from."

"They didn't die from their nightmares. That doesn't happen."

"No? What *did* happen?"

"I don't know yet."

"Then you don't *know* that their dreams didn't kill them."

He was convinced that dreams couldn't kill people, but equally convinced that arguing the point would be fruitless. All he could think was: *None of this makes any sense at all.*

HIGH STRESS AND AN UNSETTLING ENVIRONMENT, FOLLOWED BY THE mesmerizing effects of the fire, left Gurney with no sense of how long they'd been sitting on the couch. He was brought back to the moment by Madeleine's voice.

"What time are you leaving for Plattsburgh?"

"Who said I was going to Plattsburgh?"

"Isn't that what Rebecca's message was about?"

He recalled playing it while Madeleine was in the bathtub. "You heard that?"

"You should turn down the volume if you don't want people hearing your messages."

He hesitated. "She suggested getting together. She's there for an academic commitment."

Madeleine's silence was as questioning as her voice had been.

He shrugged. "I haven't decided."

"Whether to go? Or what time to go?"

"Both."

"You should go."

"Why?"

"Because you want to."

He hesitated. "I think it might be helpful to talk to her. But I'm not comfortable leaving you here alone."

"I've been alone in worse places."

"You could come with me."

"No."

"Why not?"

Now it was her turn to hesitate. "Why do you think I was willing to come here?"

"I have no idea. Your decision surprised me. Shocked me, to be honest. Given a choice between going straight to a snowshoeing weekend or stopping to look into a case of multiple suicides, I never expected you to choose the suicides."

"The suicides had nothing to do with it." She took a deep breath. "When I was in school, going to the Adirondacks for Christmas vacation was absolutely the last thing I wanted to do. The aunt and uncle I mentioned weren't really my aunt and uncle, just distant cousins of my mother. They were isolated, ignorant people. George was depressive. Maureen was manic."

"Why would your parents send you to people like that?"

"Sending me to the Adirondacks in the winter and to music camp in the summer was their strategy for getting closer to each other. One-on-one. Simplify. Communicate. Solve their marriage problems. Of course, it never worked. Like most people, they secretly liked their problems. And liked getting rid of me."

"Are your aunt and uncle, or whatever they are, still alive?"

"George eventually shot himself."

"Jesus."

"Maureen moved to Florida. I have no idea whether she's dead or alive."

"Where up here did they live?"

"In the middle of nowhere. Devil's Fang was actually visible from the end of their road. The nearest real town was Dannemora."

"The town with the prison."

"Yes."

"I still don't think I'm understanding why—"

"Why I wanted to come here? Maybe to see these mountains in a different way . . . in a different period of my life . . . make the memories go away."

"What memories?"

"There was something wrong with George. He'd sit on the porch for hours, staring out into the woods, like he was already dead. Maureen was as sick as George, in the other direction. Always dancing around.

She was wild for collecting rocks—triangular rocks. She insisted they were Iroquois arrowheads. *Ear-a-kwah* arrowheads. She loved the French pronunciation. She said a lot things with a French accent. Other times she'd pretend that she and I were Indian princesses lost in the forest, waiting to be rescued by Hiawatha. When he'd come for us we'd give him our collection of *Ear-a-kwah* arrowheads, and he'd give us furs to keep us warm, and we'd live happily ever after."

"How old was she?"

"Maureen? Maybe fifty. She seemed ancient to me when I was fifteen. She might as well have been ninety."

"Were there any other kids around?"

She blinked and stared at him. "You never answered my question."

"What question?"

"What time are you going to Plattsburgh?"

CHAPTER 20

Gurney placed certain restrictions on his tentative plan to meet
Rebecca at the Cold Brook Inn.

If the power failure continued, he wouldn't go.

If the lodge's cell reception wasn't restored, he wouldn't go.

If the sleet storm started again, he wouldn't go.

But none of those conditions prevailed. The power was restored at
6:22 AM. Cell reception was restored at 6:24 AM. The predawn sky
was spectacularly clear. The air was crisp and still and full of a piney
fragrance. The lodge heating system had come back to life. All in all,
everything was the opposite of the way it had been a few hours earlier.

By 6:55 AM Gurney had washed, shaved, dressed, and was ready
to leave. He entered the still-dark bedroom. He could sense that
Madeleine was awake.

"Be careful," she said.

"I will."

What being careful meant in his own mind was keeping a safe emotional distance from Rebecca, with whom there always seemed to be
possibilities. He wondered if that might have been what Madeleine meant
by it as well.

"When will you be back?"

"I should get to the inn by eight. If I leave there an hour or so later, I
should be back before ten."

"Don't rush. Not on these roads. With the sleet last night, they'll
be slippery."

"You're sure you'll be all right here by yourself?"

"I'll be fine."

"Okay, then. I'm off." He bent down and kissed her.

The crimson-carpeted corridor was now brightly lit, a startling transformation from the previous night's creepy backdrop for Barlow Tarr's lamplit face. As he descended the broad staircase to the reception floor, an aroma of fresh coffee mingled with a woodsy evergreen scent.

Austen Steckle was standing in the doorway of an office behind the reception counter, speaking with some intensity on the phone. He was wearing the kind of chinos that cost five times as much as the Walmart variety. His woodsman's plaid shirt fit his barrel physique so faultlessly Gurney guessed it had been custom tailored.

When Steckle caught Gurney's eye, he ended his call with a statement plainly loud enough for Gurney to hear. "I'll get back to you later. I have an important guest here."

He came out from behind the counter with a toothy smile. "Hey, Detective, beautiful morning, eh? Smell that? That's balsam. From the balsam fir. Aroma of the Adirondacks."

"Very nice."

"So, everything okay with you folks? Suite to your liking?"

"It's fine. Got a bit chilly last night with the power outage."

"Ah, yeah. Part of the wilderness experience."

"We did have a midnight visit from Barlow Tarr."

Steckle's grin faded. "What could he want that time of night?"

"He warned us about the evil here at the lodge."

"What evil?"

"'The evil that killed them all.'"

Steckle's mouth twisted into an expression between disgust and fury. "What else did he say?"

"More of the same. Is this all news to you?"

"What do you mean?"

"Is what I'm telling you new information—this kind of thing with Tarr?"

Steckle rubbed the stubble on his shaved head. "You better come into my office."

Gurney followed him around the reception counter into a room furnished in the same "Adirondack" style as every other space in the lodge. Steckle's desk was a varnished pine slab standing on four upright logs, bark intact. His chair was a rustic bentwood affair with trimmed branches for legs. He motioned Gurney to a similar chair on the opposite side of the desk. When they were both seated, he leaned his thick forearms on the pine slab.

"Hope you don't mind a little privacy, but we may get into some areas here that are not for general consumption. You understand what I'm saying?"

"I'm not sure that I do."

"We got a difficult situation here. You asked me about Barlow. Between you and me? Barlow is a crazy pain in the ass. Delusional. Scares the shit out of people. Talking all the time about wolves, evil, death, all kinds of crap. Delusional crap." He paused. "So you're maybe thinking, why the hell do we put up with crap like that? Why not just kick the fucker out and be done? Or maybe you're thinking the bigger question, why was this crazy fucker Barlow ever allowed to be here to begin with?"

"I was told that someone or other from the Tarr family has been working at the lodge ever since it was built a century ago by Dalton Gall."

"Well, it's true. But that's still no reason to put up with crap. The real problem was Ethan. A great man, Ethan, don't get me wrong. But that *greatness*—and the determination that came along with it? That could be a problem."

"His determination to turn every loser into a productive citizen?"

If that characterization hit a sore spot with Steckle due to his own past, he concealed it well. "Like the Good Book says, every virtue has its vice. But, hey, how can I complain, right? Maybe you heard what Ethan did for me?"

"Tell me."

"I was a thief. An embezzler. I did some time. Luck of the draw, I got chosen for Ethan's rehabilitation program. Suffice it to say, the program worked. Turned me into a new person. I even changed my name. My name for most of my fucked-up life was Alfonz Volk. That was the name of the guy my mother married when she got pregnant. But I found out later he wasn't really my father. My mother had got pregnant by another guy who got killed in a car accident. Guy by the name of Austen Steckle. So she lied to Alfonz Volk so he'd marry her. A very fucked-up

situation. My name should've always been Steckle. That was my genes.
So to change my name to Steckle was the perfect new beginning. When
I graduated from Ethan's program, he hired me to work on the books up
here. Incredible, right? I'll have gratitude to that man till the day I die."

"You're an accountant?"

"I got no credentials, no titles, just a thing about numbers. I'm like
one of them idiot savants, without the idiot part."

"You appear to be a lot more than the lodge's bookkeeper."

"Yeah, well. Time passed. Things changed. Ethan saw that my head
for numbers could be used in a lot of ways. So I progressed to general
manager of Wolf Lake Lodge and financial advisor to the Gall family.
Pretty amazing ride for a small-time thief, right?"

"I'm impressed."

"Right. So how the hell can I criticize Ethan's determination and
faith in people? Yeah, sometimes it means that a Looney Tune like
Barlow Tarr lasts here way beyond the point when he shoulda got the
boot, but it also means that this particular small-time thief you're looking at right here in this chair got lifted out of the gutter and got trusted
to manage not only a thousand-dollar-a-night enterprise but the whole
fucking Gall fortune. Which is like a fairy tale."

"With Ethan gone, what's keeping you from getting rid of Tarr?"

"I ask myself the same thing. Maybe it's superstition."

"Superstition?"

"You know, like I'm only here because of Ethan's decision to put me
here and keep me here. And that's why Tarr's here, too. Maybe I'm afraid
that if I get rid of him, somebody'll get rid of me. Some karma shit. But
that don't really make practical sense. And I'm a practical guy. So I'm
thinking one of these days pretty soon Mr. Loon is out on his crazy ass."

"Speaking of which, I gather you've decided to honor Richard
Hammond's contract for another year."

"What's fair is fair, right?"

"You're keeping an open mind about him?"

"Presumed innocent, right?"

"Even with all that negative media coverage?"

"That's nasty shit, but sometimes we got to live with that kind of
shit, right?"

"So, despite all the bad publicity, you decided to stand by Hammond because of a legal presumption of innocence and a sense of fairness?"

Steckle shrugged. "Also out of respect for Ethan. Before all this shit went down, he agreed to renew Hammond's contract. I want to abide by that decision. Maybe that's just my superstition again, but that's the way it is. Who am I gonna respect if I don't respect Ethan?"

"So you have a presumption of innocence and an oral promise on the one hand. On the other hand, there's the possibility that Hammond might be implicated in the death of Gall himself, as well as three lodge guests. Puts you pretty far out on a limb if Hammond is convicted."

Steckle's eyes narrowed again. "Convicted of what?"

"Some form of felony involvement in all four deaths."

"You avoid the word 'suicide.' There a reason for that?"

Gurney smiled. "It doesn't make sense to me. How about you?"

Steckle didn't answer. He leaned back in his chair and began rubbing his scalp as though his thoughts were giving him a headache.

Gurney continued. "So I'm thinking, considering the big downside possibilities and you being a practical guy, maybe there's another reason you decided to keep Hammond around?"

Steckle stared at him, his mouth slowly stretching into a hard smile. "You want a practical reason? Okay. Simple. If we got rid of Hammond now . . . yeah, that could look like we were dumping garbage overboard, sending a message to the media that we're on the side of the angels. But you gotta consider all the outcomes. And one of them outcomes would be the kind of message it would send to all those people who came here over the past two years to be treated by that man. We dump him now, the message to those guests is that all the shit in the media is true and we put them at the mercy of a monster. Believe me, that's no kinda message to give your paying guests, some of whom are very wealthy people. But if we keep Hammond here, the message is that we have confidence in him and the media stories are horseshit. That practical enough for you?"

"It does help me understand your decision."

Steckle appeared to relax, sinking more comfortably into his chair. "I guess I sound a little cynical. But what can I say? I got to protect the Gall interests here. That's what Ethan trusted me to do. And I owe everything to that man."

GURNEY HAD MORE QUESTIONS FOR AUSTEN STECKLE—QUESTIONS about Ethan and Peyton, about the Gall New Life Foundation, about the three guests who ended up dead.

If he pursued any of that now, though, he'd miss his chance to meet with Rebecca—whose knowledge of Hammond, hypnosis, and dreams could be very helpful.

His solution was to secure Austen's agreement to meet with him again when he returned from Plattsburgh later that morning.

He thanked the man for his time and candor and hurried out to his car.

The air was bracing, the visibility extraordinary. A glass-smooth sheet of ice had formed overnight on the surface of the lake, reflecting an inverted image of Cemetery Ridge.

As Gurney was pulling out from under the timbered portico onto the lake road, his phone was ringing. Seeing that it was Jack Hardwick, he took the call.

"Hey, Sherlock, how's life in the grand lodge so far?"

"It's . . . unusual."

"You sound like you're in your car. Where the hell are you?"

"On my way to Plattsburgh to meet with Holdenfield. She seems to have an interest in the case."

Hardwick uttered his bark of a laugh. "Becky Baby's interest is mainly in you, ace. Where does she want to meet you?"

"I told you—Plattsburgh."

"That's the name of the city. But what I'm asking is—"

Gurney cut him off. "Jack, in a little while I'll be driving out of the range of the lodge's cell tower. Could we cut the crap and get to whatever you called about?"

"Okay, I might have a line on Angela Castro, missing girlfriend of the Floral Park corpse. She has a married brother who lives in Staten Island. I called his number. Young, nervous female voice answered the phone. I told her I was taking a survey for the utility company about appliance usage. She said she couldn't tell me anything because it wasn't her house, I should call back later. I figure I'll pay her a visit. Something tells me this is our Angela. Assuming I'm right, is there anything special you want to know?"

"Beyond the obvious questions about Steven Pardosa's death—what did she see, what did she hear, what does she think, why did she disappear—I'd like to know what he was like before and after his trip to Wolf Lake, his moods, his comments, his nightmares. Why did he go so far away to deal with his smoking habit. How did he know about Richard Hammond?"

"That it?"

"Ask her how Pardosa felt about homosexuals."

"Why?"

"Just a shot in the dark. It was an area of Hammond's practice years ago. There was some controversy about his approach at the time. And this minister, Bowman Cox, is obsessed with the subject, claiming Hammond's focus on it was the cause of Christopher Wenzel's suicide. Speaking of which, I'd like to know whether Wenzel himself had any strong feelings on the subject. Maybe that's what drew him to Cox, what made Cox the man he wanted to discuss his nightmare with. I know this is pretty vague, but we've got to start somewhere."

"I'll look into it."

"You have anything else for me?"

"Some background on Austen Steckle. He's a reformed bad boy, formerly known as Alfonz Volk. "

"He told me that himself. One-time embezzler, magically transformed by Ethan's program into the Gall family's financial advisor and lodge manager."

"Did he mention the drug-dealer chapter in the drama?"

"Steckle—or Volk—was a dealer?"

"Sold coke and other shit to a fancy clientele. A customer who ran an ethically challenged stock brokerage liked his style. Hired him to push crap stocks like he pushed white powder. Turned out he had a talent for it. Made more money on stock scams than he made on coke. But it wasn't enough. That's when the embezzlement started—scumbag employee robbing his scumbag employer. The feds, who had their eye on the firm, pressured yet another scumbag to testify against him. Volk got banged up, did some time, came up for early parole. Enter the Gall New Life Foundation. Alfonz Volk is magically transformed into Austen Steckle, the rest is history. So what's your bottom line on him?"

"I'm not sure. He has a hard edge, which he doesn't try to hide. I need to spend more time with him, maybe ask why he dropped the drug-dealer bit off the resume he shared with me." Gurney checked his phone. "I think I'm about to lose my cell signal, so let me mention a few more issues you might want to look into."

"Pile the shit on, boss. I live to serve."

"Couple of things I'm curious about. These three dead guys who came to Hammond for stop-smoking hypnotherapy—did it work? In that week or so after they went home and before they ended up with sliced wrists, had they stopped smoking or not?"

"You suggesting I drive around Jersey, Queens, and Florida looking for folks who may have checked the dead guys' ashtrays?"

"You worked your magic in the hunt for Angela. I have infinite confidence in you."

"That makes everything so much better."

"Speaking of Angela, maybe we should think twice about making a surprise visit. If you've actually found her, the last thing we want to do is spook her. If she runs you might not find her again, and she's the closest thing we've got to an eyewitness."

"Okay, what's the alternative?"

"Hang back a little. Give her options. Let her feel in control of the situation."

"The fuck are you talking about?"

"You could leave an envelope addressed to her in her brother's mailbox. Include a note explaining who we are, that we have a client who doesn't believe the official suicide theory of Steven's death, that it would be very helpful to us in discovering what really happened—and thus ensuring her own safety—if we could meet with her, or just speak with her, whichever she's comfortable with. Include our cell numbers, our landline numbers, our email addresses, our home addresses. Very important, that last one. The home address thing makes us seem not only reachable on her terms but, in a way, vulnerable. Emphasize that how and when she chooses to get in touch with us—and how much she wants to tell us—is all up to her."

Hardwick was silent for several long seconds. "Sounds like overkill—all those numbers and contact options."

"It's overkill with a purpose. Give someone a bunch of open doors, they feel like they're making a real choice. They may not notice that all the doors lead to the same room."

"Or the same chute into the shitter."

"That's another way of looking at it."

More silence, followed by Hardwick's grunt of agreement. "I'll do it your way. But remember, if it goes south, I piss all over you. Any other requests?"

"I'd very much like to know who in BCI brass approved Fenton's press strategy. Had to be someone high up. It's so far out of the conservative box those guys live in, Fenton would need to have his ass covered. Sooner or later, I'd like to know *why* it was approved—but to begin with I'd be happy knowing the *who* part. And find out what you can about a guy by the name of Norris Landon. Country gentleman type. Partridge hunter, et cetera. Spent a lot of time at Wolf Lake Lodge over the past couple of years."

"Like Hammond."

"Exactly. Be nice to know if there's a connection." Gurney paused. "And one more question in case you find yourself with time on your hands. The big one: What benefit would Hammond get from inducing the deaths of those four people?"

Hardwick was silent so long Gurney thought they'd lost their cell connection. "Jack?"

"I'm thinking about the benefit."

"And?"

"I'm thinking that if some fucker could really do that . . . if he could concoct and implant a fatal nightmare in another person . . . then he might do it . . . just to prove he could do it."

"For the feeling of power?"

"Yeah. For the feeling of absolute godlike power."

CHAPTER 21

By the time Gurney reached the state route that wound down out of the mountains toward Plattsburgh, the sun was up and the color of the sky was shifting from pinkish gray to pure blue.

He was organizing the various conundrums of the case in the order in which he imagined they'd need to be explored and solved. This mental process so thoroughly absorbed him that forty minutes later he nearly drove past the sign for the Cold Brook Inn.

At the front desk a pudgy woman with a welcoming innkeeper's smile answered his inquiry about the location of the dining room with a graceful sweep of her hand in the direction of an open archway at the side of the reception area.

"Black-current scones with clotted cream today," she said in a lowered voice, as though sharing a valuable confidence.

He spotted Rebecca at a table next to a window overlooking Lake Champlain. Next to her coffee cup was a laptop on which she was typing rapidly. Her auburn hair had that look of casual beauty that comes from good genes and good taste. Good genes had also given her a sharp, linear intellect—a quality he found dangerously attractive.

She flipped the laptop shut and smiled a bright, businesslike smile. The warm, sculpted appearance of her lips looked like it had been enhanced with a subtle lipstick, but he knew from interested observation on past occasions that she never wore makeup.

"You're right on time." Her voice was on the low side of the female register.

He nodded at the computer. "Did I interrupt something?"

"Nothing important. Just dashing off a scathing review of an article on the survival value of guilt. The research design was flawed, the conclusions inconclusive, and the interpretation pathetic." Her eyes flashed with the competitive spark that made her such a formidable presence in her field. "So you're working on an incredible case. Everything you've told me about it is nuts. Sit down and tell me more."

He sat across from her, her contagious energy making him feel like he'd had three cups of coffee. "Not a lot more to tell. I met a local lunatic, connected with the lodge, eager to offer me a supernatural view of things."

"Like Dalton Gall's wolf dream and its supposed fulfillment?"

"Did I tell you about that?"

"Found it in an online historical blog—'Strange Tales of the Mountains'—popped up in a 'Gall' Internet search. It's the kind of story stupid people love. Even some smart people."

"Speaking of wolf dreams—"

"What do I think about Wenzel's, as narrated by Cox?" She uttered a derisive little laugh. "A candy store for a Freudian analyst. But I'm not a Freudian analyst. Dreams are useless vehicles for getting to the truth about anything. Dreams are the dust kicked up by the brain as it catalogs the experiences of the day."

"Then why—"

"Why do dreams seem like narrative scenes in weird movies? Because in addition to being a cataloger the brain is a coherence seeker. It's always trying to connect the dots, even when the dots have no natural connection. The brain takes those random dust specks it's stirring up with its right hand, and tries to arrange them in order with its left hand. That's why 'dream interpretation' is total nonsense. You might as well throw a handful of goulash at the wall and pretend it's a map of Hungary."

A young waitress arrived at their table. "Can I get you folks some breakfast?"

"Oatmeal, coffee, whole wheat toast," said Rebecca.

"Same," said Gurney.

The waitress jotted a few words on her order pad and hurried off.

Rebecca continued. "Dreams are as random as raindrops. So, you ask, how could four people have the same one? The answer is, I have no idea. Everything I know tells me it's impossible."

When their breakfasts arrived they ate briefly in silence. At one point, they held each other's gaze long enough that if they'd held it any longer it would have taken on an inescapable significance. Gurney broke the mood with a question.

"You told me on the phone that some of Hammond's work was 'on the cutting edge'—something about his using hypnotherapy to form new neural pathways, changing people's behavior in radical ways?"

"I don't honestly know that much about it. But I've seen the abstracts of technical papers he's published recently that suggest he's exploring areas of behavior modification that are beyond the generally accepted limits of hypnotherapy. It struck me that he wasn't being completely open about his latest achievements."

"That's interesting. Look, I know how busy you are, but—"

She grinned unexpectedly. "If you want to get something done, ask a busy person."

"It's a huge favor, actually. Could you take a closer look at Hammond's published work and see if anything pops out at you?"

"What am I looking for?"

"Anything that might relate to the police theory of the four deaths. Anything that . . . Jesus, Rebecca, I don't even know what questions to ask. I have no idea what's new and scary in that field."

"I love a helpless man." Her grin widened briefly, then disappeared. "There's some potentially disturbing work being done these days in the area of manipulating memories, especially manipulating the emotional tags on certain memories."

"What does that mean?"

"It means that a person's feelings about past events can be changed by altering the neurochemical components of their stored emotions."

"Christ. That's really—"

"Weird-ass, brave-new-world stuff? I agree. But it's happening. Of course, it's positioned in the most positive therapeutic language you can imagine. Ideal way to cure PTSD panic, and so forth. Just separate the specific event from the feeling it generates."

Gurney was quiet for long while.

Rebecca was watching him. "What are you thinking?"

"If the emotional charge on the memory of a past event could be altered, could the same technique be used to change how a person might feel about a hypothetical future event?"

"I have no idea. Why?"

"I'm wondering whether someone who normally would be appalled by the idea of suicide . . . could be made more receptive to it."

CHAPTER 22

W ithin the first few miles of Gurney's drive back up into the Adirondack wilderness, the possibility of artificially altering something as basic as the value a person put on life itself began to seem unlikely, even absurd. On the other hand, it wasn't any more unlikely or absurd than the so-called "facts" of the case.

As he drove farther into the mountains, the excitement he'd felt in his meeting with Rebecca morphed into a kind of uneasiness, which he attributed in part to the overcast that was diluting the blue of the sky and hinting at the approach of another winter storm.

When he arrived at the lodge, Austen Steckle was on the phone behind the reception counter. He ended his call quietly this time.

"Good to see you back. There's a storm warning in effect. Do you know where Mrs. Gurney went?"

"Excuse me?"

"Your wife—she took one of the lodge Jeeps we have for our guests. Said she planned to do some sightseeing."

"*Sightseeing?*"

"Yeah. Lot of people do that. See the mountains. She left right after you."

"Did she say anything about any specific area? Ask you for any directions?"

"Nope. Nothing like that."

Gurney checked his watch. "Did she say when she'd be back?"

Steckle shook his head. "She didn't say much at all."

"Does the vehicle she took have a GPS?"

"Of course. So there's nothing to worry about, right?"

"Right." In fact, he felt he had all sorts of things to worry about. But he made an effort to fasten his attention on something he could actually *do*. Seeing Steckle standing there on front of him brought a possibility to mind.

"If you have a few minutes, I'd like to finish the conversation we were having this morning."

Steckle glanced around quickly. "Okay."

They took the same seats in Steckle's office on opposite sides of the pine-slab desk. "So. What's on your mind?"

Gurney smiled. "I'm confused. About the relationships here."

"What relationships?"

"To start with, the relationship between Ethan and Peyton. I've been told there were problems between them. Can you tell me what kind of problems?"

Steckle leaned back in his chair and rubbed his head thoughtfully. "The kind of problems you'd expect between a super-achiever and a wild-ass addict."

"Ethan didn't approve of Peyton's lifestyle?"

"He sure as hell didn't. Ethan threatened to disinherit him. Tough love."

"Ethan had control of the Gall fortune?"

"Essentially, yeah. Ethan had a lock on the money. Their parents always saw him as the responsible one, so the bulk of the fortune went to him, with the understanding that he'd do the right thing by Peyton. And a little while back he figured the right thing would be to use the threat of disinheritance to get Peyton straight."

"Did he plan to go through with the threat?"

"I think so. The thing is, he gave Peyton a taste of what could happen. In Ethan's original will, the Gall New Life Foundation was supposed to get one third of the estate and Peyton two thirds. Then Ethan revised it, so Peyton would only get one third. He told him he'd change it back if he got off drugs for ninety days."

"How did Peyton react?"

"He actually stayed clean for something like sixty, sixty-one days."

"Then he picked up drugs again?"

"No. Then Ethan committed suicide, or whatever the hell you want to call it."

"While Peyton was still clean?"

"Yeah. He did pick up the shit again, but that was like a few days after Ethan . . . after he ended up dead."

"So even though Peyton was staying clean, Ethan didn't live long enough to change the will back in his favor?"

"Life's unfair, right?"

"So who gets that other third? The foundation?"

"I don't think I have the right to tell you that."

"Why not?"

"All I can say is I'd rather not disclose that information. It could be misinterpreted. I wouldn't want to be the cause of any wrong impression, you understand?"

"But you do know for sure what was specified in the altered will?"

"The Gall family has relied on me, and continues to rely on me, in many ways. Because of that trust, I know a lot. That's all I can say."

Gurney thought it best not to pursue the point. There'd be other ways to get the information. In the meantime, he had more questions.

"Wenzel, Balzac, Pardosa—how well do you remember them?"

Steckle shrugged. "In what way?"

"When you hear each name, what comes to mind?"

"The face. The voice. Clothes. Things like that. What do you want to know?"

"Had any of them been to the lodge before?"

"No."

"You're sure?"

"That's something I'd be aware of."

"How did they know about Richard Hammond?"

"He's famous, right? People know about him."

"Did they strike you as the kind of people who normally come to Wolf Lake Lodge?"

"We get all kinds of people."

"Not many people of limited financial means visit thousand-dollar-a-day resorts."

"I don't think Mr. Wenzel's means were that limited."

"How do you know that?"

"I read about him in the paper—you know, afterward—something about a million-dollar condo in Florida."

"What about the other two?"

"Our guests' private finances are none of my business. They could have money without looking like it. It's not something I ask about."

"What if they can't pay you?"

"We run their credit cards when they arrive. We make sure the full amount is approved. If not, they're required to pay cash up front."

"Did Wenzel, Balzac, and Pardosa pay by cash or credit card?"

"I have no memory of that kind of detail."

"Easy enough to check."

"Now?"

"It could be very helpful."

Steckle appeared to be considering just how cooperative he wanted to be. He turned his chair around to face a computer on a second desk against the wall. After a minute or two he turned back to Gurney looking like he had a bad taste in his mouth. "Wenzel paid with Amex. Balzac paid with a debit card. Pardosa paid cash."

"How unusual is it for someone to pay cash?"

"Cash is unusual, but no big deal. I mean, some people don't like plastic."

Or the trail it leaves, thought Gurney. "How long did they stay?"

With noticeable impatience Steckle consulted his computer again. "Wenzel, two nights. Balzac, one night. Pardosa, one night."

"And Hammond's stop-smoking treatment consisted of just one session?"

"Right. An intensive three-hour session." He pulled back his neatly pressed flannel cuff and frowned at his Rolex. "Are we done?"

"Yes . . . unless you know of anything that happened here that could have resulted in those four deaths."

Steckle shook his head slowly and turned up his empty palms. "I wish I could be more helpful, but . . ." He fell silent, still shaking his head.

"Actually, you've been very helpful." Gurney stood up to leave. "One last thing. Kind of a crazy question. Did any of them make any negative remarks about homosexuals, or gay marriage, or anything like that?"

Steckle looked bewildered and annoyed. "What the hell are you getting at?"

"Just a crazy angle on the case. Probably doesn't mean anything. Thanks for your time. I appreciate it."

CHAPTER 23

Gurney went upstairs, hoping to find a note from Madeleine explaining the nature of her sightseeing excursion—perhaps its route and when he could expect her back.

There was no note.

Although he guessed she'd be somewhere in the large dead zone outside the immediate area of Wolf Lake, he tried calling her anyway.

He was surprised to hear her phone ringing seconds later right there in the suite. He looked around and spotted it on the small table next to the couch.

It wasn't like Madeleine to go out without it, especially if she was driving. Had she been in such a hurry or so preoccupied that she forgot it? But that state of mind was hardly consistent with a sightseeing excursion.

He tried to construct a hypothesis that would explain these facts, as well as her secretive demeanor for the past forty-eight hours, but he couldn't seem to apply the same logical analysis to Madeleine's behavior as he could to a stranger's.

He found himself pacing slowly around the room, a movement that often helped him organize his thoughts. It occurred to him to check for any calls or text messages she might have received before leaving. As he was trying to navigate through the functions of her phone, there was a knock at the door.

It was a louder-than-necessary knock of a type familiar to Gurney. He crossed the room, opened the door, and recognized the flat-faced, heavy-shouldered man standing in front of him as the Jimmy Hoffa look-alike from the press conference video. There was an American flag lapel pin on his ill-fitting sport jacket. He held up his state police credentials.

"Senior Investigator Fenton, BCI. Are you David Gurney?"

"Yes." For a moment he had a terrible thought. "Has something happened to my wife?"

"I don't know anything about your wife. Can I come in?"

Gurney nodded, his anxiety replaced by curiosity. He stepped back from the doorway.

Fenton entered with a cop's watchfulness, glancing around to take everything in, moving to a position from which he could see into the bedroom alcove as well as the bathroom. His gaze lingered for a while on the Warren Harding portrait.

"Very nice," he said in a sour way that implied the opposite. "The Presidential Suite."

"What can I do for you?"

"You like being retired?"

"How do you know I'm retired?"

Fenton produced a smile that was less than friendly. "If someone took an aggressive interest in a major case of yours, showed up on your turf, spent time with a prime suspect, you'd get to know something about them, right?"

Gurney answered with his own question. "To have a prime suspect you must have a definable crime, right?"

"A *definable* crime. Nice term. Plus means, motive, and opportunity. Right out of the textbook." The man walked over to the balcony door and stood with his back to Gurney. "That's why I'm here. Somehow you got yourself pulled into this thing. So we'd like to fill you in on some facts, as a simple courtesy, since you clearly don't know what it is you got yourself pulled into."

"That's very accommodating."

"There's nothing like the facts to get everyone on the same page. Simple courtesy."

"Can't argue with that. But since when do BCI senior investigators fill in outsiders as a simple courtesy?"

Fenton turned back from the window and gave Gurney an appraising look. "You're not just any outsider, are you? You have a reputation. Big one. Very positive career history. Lot of success. So we figured you deserved the courtesy of being fully informed. Could save you time and trouble." He flashed a cold smile.

"What kind of trouble will it save me?"

"The trouble that comes from being on the wrong side of a situation."

"How do you know which side I'm on?"

"An educated guess."

"Based on what?"

There was a tiny twitch at the corner of the man's thin-lipped mouth. "Based on what we know from various sources. What I'm telling you is that this is a serious situation. Involving serious people with serious resources." He paused. "Look, I'm trying to do you a favor here. Put our cards on the table. You got a problem with that?"

"No problem. Just curiosity."

Fenton cocked his head speculatively, as though turning a difficult concept around in his mind. "Curiosity can be a problem when the stuff you don't know is stuff you shouldn't know." He hesitated, his jaw muscles tensing. "If you knew even half the story, you wouldn't be here. You wouldn't be stepping into something over your head. You wouldn't be sitting across a dinner table from Richard Hammond. You wouldn't be anywhere near Wolf Lake."

"But now that I'm here, you want to fill me in on the facts."

"That's what I'm saying." But the distaste with which he said it hinted at some conflict in his mission. Perhaps a career-long antipathy for sharing information outside the boundaries of his law enforcement unit was colliding with an order to do exactly that.

"I'm listening." Gurney sank down into one of the leather chairs by the hearth, gesturing toward another near it. "You want to have a seat?"

Fenton glanced around, selected instead the simplest wooden chair in the room, and brought it to a spot facing Gurney, but not too close. He perched on the edge of the seat as if it were a stool, his hands on his knees. His jaw muscles started moving again. He was staring down at the rug. Whatever was going on in his head narrowed the eyes that were already too small for his slab of a face.

He looked up, met Gurney's inquisitive gaze, and cleared his throat. "*Motive, means, opportunity.* That what you want to hear about?"

"Good place to start."

"Okay. Motive. Would twenty-nine million dollars qualify?"

Gurney frowned, said nothing.

Fenton flashed an ugly smile. "They didn't tell you about that, huh? Little Dick and Jane. They neglected to mention Ethan Gall's will?"

"Tell me about it."

The ugly smile widened. "Ethan had a very simple will—especially for a guy with eighty-seven million dollars, give or take a few million for variations in investment values." He paused, studying Gurney's expression. "One third for the Gall New Life Foundation; one third for little brother Peyton; and one third—that's twenty-nine million bucks—for Doctor Dick."

So that's what Steckle had been talking about. Richard was the legatee whose name he wouldn't disclose.

"Why would Gall leave Hammond that much? Were they that close?"

Fenton made a face between a leer and a sneer. "Maybe closer than anyone knew. But the main reason was to piss off Peyton. Peyton hated the fact that Doctor Dick was Ethan's pet. The whole point was to threaten Peyton. Scare him into being a good boy. "

"How recent was this version of Ethan's will?"

"Very recent. And the thing that puts the nail in Doctor Dick's coffin is that he knew Ethan was about to change it again—give it all back to his little brother. Your dinner companion had a twenty-nine-million-dollar window of opportunity that was about to close. You think that might be a powerful motive for timely action?"

Gurney shrugged. "Maybe a little too powerful and a little too timely."

Fenton stared at him. "Meaning what?"

"Seems too obvious and too neat. But the bigger question is, what *action* are you claiming it motivated?" When Fenton didn't answer right away, Gurney went on. "If you're claiming that Hammond killed Gall in order to grab that twenty-nine million before it disappeared, the real question is *how* did he kill him?"

Fenton looked like he had a mouthful of stomach acid. "I'm not at liberty to discuss the specifics. I'll just say that Hammond developed some motivational techniques that go beyond anything normal, therapeutic, or ethical."

"You're saying that he persuaded Ethan Gall to commit suicide?"

"You find that hard to believe?"

"Very hard."

"His goddamn 'gay emergence therapy' seemed like quite a stretch, too! Think about it." Fenton's eyes flashed with anger. "This is the same son of a bitch who invented a so-called 'therapy' to make normal men believe they were gay!"

"So you figure if Hammond could convince a man he was gay, he could convince him to kill himself?" The logic of that struck Gurney as absurd.

"The technical term for what we're talking about is 'trance-induced suicide.'"

"Whose term is that?"

Fenton blinked, rubbed his hand across his mouth. He seemed to be considering how much more he ought to say. "The people we've consulted. Experts. Best in the world."

If Fenton wanted to identify his experts, he'd volunteer their names. If he didn't want to, there was no point in asking. Gurney sat back in his armchair and steepled his fingers thoughtfully under his chin. "Trance-induced suicide. Interesting. And this can be achieved through a single hypnotherapy session?"

"An intensive three-hour session with a follow-up session on the final day."

"The final day?"

"The suicide day."

"Where did that follow-up meeting occur?"

"With Mr. Gall, right here at Wolf Lake. With the other three, it was done by phone."

"And of course you have a record of Hammond calling each of those three victims on—"

Fenton cut in. "On the day each one cut his wrists." He paused, studying Gurney's face. "You didn't know any of this shit, right? You have no goddamn idea what you're stumbling around in. Blind man in a minefield." He shook his head. "Do you happen to know what subject the famous *Doctor* Hammond wrote his PhD thesis on?"

"Tell me."

"Long title, but maybe you ought to memorize it. 'Hypnotic Elements in the Mechanism of Fatality in Voodoo: How Witch Doctors

Make Their Victims Die.' That's a pretty interesting area of expertise, wouldn't you say?"

Fenton radiated the triumph of a poker player showing a full house, aces high. "Think about it, Gurney. This guy hypnotized four people. They all ended up with the same nightmare. They all talked to him on the last day of their lives. And they all cut their wrists in exactly the same way."

He paused before adding, "Is this really a guy you want to be having dinner with?"

CHAPTER 24

Having written a doctoral thesis examining the psychological levers underlying the practice of voodoo was, at least, suggestive of a past academic interest. It was certainly a provocative coincidence and the sort of thing that would capture the imagination of a jury, but it was hardly, as the lawyers say, dispositive.

The will, however, was another matter. The will nailed down the first third of the motive-means-opportunity triad. The will was a big deal. So big a deal that Gurney felt he had to get to the bottom of it—the precise nature of the provision favoring Hammond to the tune of twenty-nine million dollars, as well as the reason that neither Jane nor Richard had seen fit to mention it—before he could put his mind to any other task.

He took out his phone, called Jack Hardwick, and left a message. "Tell me you didn't know about the twenty-nine-million-dollar motive lurking in the middle of this case. Because if you knew about that little item and chose not to tell me, you and I have a serious problem. Call me ASAP."

He considered calling Jane Hammond next, then decided a personal visit to the chalet, unannounced, to confront Jane and Richard together would be more revealing. He went to his duffle bag, found his notebook, tore out a blank page, and wrote a quick message to Madeleine:

"It's almost 11:00 AM. I got back from Plattsburgh a while ago. Had a visit from Gilbert Fenton. Going over to the Hammonds' place now to sort out a problem. I'll have my phone with me—please call as soon as you get in."

He placed the note next to her phone on the end table. He put on his ski jacket and was already heading for the door when he heard a key turning in the lock. The door swung open, and Madeleine entered the room, her thick wool ski hat pulled down over her forehead and ears, her down jacket zipped up to her chin. She looked cold and tense. She swung the door shut behind her and greeted him with a small "Hi."

"Where were you?" The sharpness in his own voice surprised him.

"I went out for a while."

"Why didn't you leave me a note?"

"I didn't know where I'd be. I didn't expect to be gone that long. The fog and the ice . . ." A visible shiver ran through her body. "I need to take a hot bath."

"Where were you?"

She looked as though she were thinking about a difficult question, then answered. "Someplace that doesn't really exist anymore."

He stared at her.

"I went to the house where George and Maureen used to live. If I didn't know what it was, I wouldn't have recognized it. It was crushed by a tree. Must have been a long time ago. Moss, pine needles, things growing out of it."

"So . . . what did you do?"

"Nothing. Everything was different. The dirt road . . . the old fence . . . everything seemed so much smaller and shabbier."

"How did you find the house?"

"The GPS."

"You remembered the address after all those years?"

"Just the name of the road. But there were only four or five houses." She paused, looked forlorn. "Now there's not much of anything."

"Did you see anyone?"

"No." Another sudden shiver shook her. She clasped her arms tightly to her body. "I'm chilled. I need a hot bath."

The lost look on her face gave him a terrible feeling. Surely it was reflecting something real inside her, yet it was a look utterly alien to the Madeleine he knew. Or believed he knew.

She appeared to notice for the first time that he was wearing his ski jacket. "Where are you going?"

"To see the Hammonds, to get something straight."

"You're driving there?"

"Yes."

"Be careful. The ice . . ."

"I know."

"I have to get into that bath." She turned and walked into the bath-room. He followed her to the door.

"Maddie, you borrowed one of the Jeeps, followed a GPS to some dirt road in the middle of nowhere, stared at an old wrecked house, saw no one, then drove back here in the fog, freezing to death. That's it? That's what you did this morning?"

"Are you interrogating me?"

That's exactly what he was doing, he thought. It was a bad habit, triggered by worry.

She started closing the door. He stopped her with a question. "Does all this have something to do with that kid who drowned?"

"All what?"

"All *this*. This weirdness. This *sightseeing* trip. That dirt road."

"David, I really do want to take my bath."

"What's the big secret? I asked you if it has something to do with the kid who drowned. How did he drown, anyway?"

"He fell through the ice."

"You knew him?"

"Yes. There weren't many kids up here my age, not in the winter, anyway."

"Are any of them still here?"

"Thirty years later? I have no idea. I doubt I'd recognize any of them if they were."

He caught himself nodding understandingly—another ingrained interrogation technique, designed to create the impression of agree-ment, even empathy. He stopped it immediately, embarrassed by the essential dishonesty of the gesture. Keeping his behavior as a detective and his behavior as a husband separate seemed to require endless vigilance. He tried one more question as she was easing the door shut.

"How did he fall through the ice?"

She held the door a few inches ajar. "He raced his motorcycle out onto the frozen lake. The ice cracked."

"How old was he?"

"He told everyone he was sixteen. I heard later that he was barely fifteen."

"Who was there when it happened?"

"Just his girlfriend."

"How well did you know him?"

"Not that well." A sad smile appeared and disappeared.

HER STORY LEFT HIM FEELING UNCOMFORTABLE AND DISTRACTED ON his drive to the chalet. Halfway there a large gray animal darted across the foggy road ahead of him. He jammed on the brakes as it bounded into the darkness of the pine woods and disappeared.

When he arrived it was Jane who came to the door. She greeted him with a high-anxiety smile. "David? Is something wrong?"

"May I come in?"

"Of course." She stepped back, motioning him into the entry area.

"Is Richard here?"

"He's talking a nap. Is there something I can help you with?"

"It might be better if I could speak to both of you."

"If you feel it's important." She hesitated for a moment, then went to get Richard.

She returned a minute later and led Gurney to a seat by the hearth. She perched nervously on the arm of a nearby chair and tugged at a strand of hair by her ear. "Richard will be out in a moment. Has something come up?"

"A couple of questions."

"Such as?"

Before Gurney could answer, Richard entered the room and took a chair. He smiled a bland therapist's smile.

Gurney decided to get right to the point. "Fenton came to see me this morning. He told me something that surprised me."

Jane frowned. "I wouldn't trust anything that man said."

Gurney addressed Hammond. "Fenton told me you're in line for a huge inheritance."

He showed no reaction.

"Is it true?" asked Gurney.

"Yes, it's true."

Anticipating the obvious question, Jane spoke up. "I didn't mention it because I was afraid it would give you the wrong impression."

"How?"

"You're used to dealing with criminals—people who do terrible things for financial gain. I was afraid that Ethan's will would convey the opposite of what it really meant."

"The opposite?"

"Because of the crazy things Fenton has been saying, I was afraid you might see it as something Richard had hypnotized Ethan into doing—even though that's impossible. It was totally Ethan's idea—a nudge to Peyton to straighten out his life."

"A threat, to be honest about it," said Hammond softly. "An attempt to extort improved behavior. The message was simple: 'Shape up, or end up with nothing.' Ethan was determined to reform his brother any way he could."

"The money was never truly intended for Richard," added Jane. "In fact, once the will is probated and the bequest comes to him, he intends to refuse it."

Gurney turned toward Hammond. "Twenty-nine million is a lot to refuse."

Those unblinking blue-green eyes met his gaze. "I've had enough money in my life to understand what it is and what it isn't. When you don't have it, you tend to believe that having it will make a far greater difference than it actually does. It's only by having it that you discover its limitations. My father made a great deal of money, and he never ceased to be a miserable man."

Gurney leaned back in his leather chair and let his gaze settle on the fireless hearth. "Are there any other facts you're keeping from me because they might give me the wrong idea?"

"No," said Jane quickly. "There's nothing else."

"How about the phone calls to the victims?"

"You mean the calls supposedly made to them on the days they died?"

"Yes."

Her lips tightened in anger. "That's all Fenton."

"What do you mean?"

"He claims to have found one of those prepaid phones in the drawer of Richard's night table. But it's a drawer Richard never used, and a phone he'd never seen before."

"You're suggesting that Fenton planted it?"

"He must have, mustn't he?"

"It's one possibility."

"I don't suppose he told you that Richard took a lie detector test—and passed?"

"No, he didn't mention that."

"Of course he didn't! You see what he does? He only mentions things that look bad for Richard, and nothing that proves he's innocent!"

Hammond looked like he'd been through all this before and was getting worn down by it. "Was there anything else you wanted to ask about?"

"He also brought up the subject matter of your doctoral thesis on voodoo."

"Good Lord. What did he have to say about that?"

"He suggested it demonstrated your interest in using mind control to kill people."

Jane threw her hands up in exasperation.

Gurney looked at Hammond. "Is it true your thesis related voodoo curses to hypnotism?"

"It was an objective analysis of the self-destructive mental states witch doctors create in their victims. I can give you a copy of the thesis, but I don't see how it would help you."

"Let's leave the door open on that, in case it might be useful."

"Fine. Anything else for now?"

"Just one last question. Was Ethan Gall gay?"

Hammond hesitated. "How is that relevant?"

"There seems to be a sexuality-related element buried somewhere in this case. I can't say yet whether it's relevant."

"Ethan was too busy for the distractions of love. His energies were devoted entirely to the reformation of the world's misbehaving souls."

There was an edge in his tone that raised a question. Before Gurney had a chance to ask it, Hammond answered it.

"I admit I was interested in Ethan. But he wasn't interested in me. Not in that way."

There was a silence, broken by Jane. "Professionally, Ethan adored Richard. Absolutely adored him."

"Professionally." Hammond's emphasis on the term pointedly underscored its boundaries.

PART TWO

THE
BODY

CHAPTER 25

Gurney parked under the portico. His mind was shuttling back and forth between Hammond and Madeleine. The precise little man with a disconcerting interest in homicidal voodoo and eyes as bright and chilly as sapphires. Madeleine standing alone on a desolate dirt road gazing at the wreckage of a house where she'd spent Christmas vacations more than three decades ago.

He wanted to talk to Peyton Gall but suspected that getting any useful information from him would likely require more than a knock at his security gate. Figuring out the right approach was one more challenge Gurney added to his list as he entered the suite.

Half-imagining that Madeleine might still be in the tub, he was surprised to see her fully dressed, standing by the windows that looked out over the lake. He was equally surprised to see a fire blazing energetically in the hearth.

She turned toward him. "Steckle was here."

"To start the fire?"

"And to ask what we wanted for lunch, and when we might be leaving for Vermont."

"Did he say he wanted us to leave by any particular time?"

"No. But I got the impression he'd like it to be soon."

"What did you tell him about lunch?"

"There were two choices. A cold salmon plate or a Cobb salad. I ordered one of each. You can have whichever you want. I'm not hungry."

"He's bringing it here to the room?"

As if in answer to his question, there was a knock at the door.

He went over and opened it.

Austen Steckle was standing there with a strained smile, holding a room-service tray with a silver dome. "Little late for lunch, folks, but better late than never, right?"

"Thank you." Gurney reached for the tray.

"No, no, let me do it." He stepped past Gurney without waiting for an answer, crossed the room, and set the tray down on the coffee table in front of the hearth. "Fire's going good, eh?"

"Yes."

"Too bad about the weather. Supposed to get a lot worse. Blizzard coming down from Canada."

Madeleine gave him a worried look. "When?"

"Hard to say. That's the thing about these mountains. They've got their beauty, their wild appeal, you know, but then there's the downside, the unknown, you know what I'm saying?"

"I'm not sure we do," said Gurney.

"When it comes to the weather at Wolf Lake, there's always some doubt. I know you folks need to get on to other places. Obviously you wouldn't want to get snowed in for a week."

What was obvious to Gurney was that the man wanted to be rid of them, and the reason probably had nothing to do with the weather. "I have a feeling that Fenton would like me out of here. You have that feeling, too?"

The interesting thing to Gurney about Steckle's reaction was that, for a couple of seconds, he had none. When he did speak, it was in an almost confessional tone. "I didn't want to mention it, since I figured you'd be on your way today, tomorrow at the latest. But I guess I should tell you. Investigator Fenton said that extending the hospitality of the lodge to you at a time when it was closed to regular guests could create the wrong impression."

"What wrong impression?"

"That the Gall family was supporting your efforts to undermine his investigation."

"Interesting."

"He said I should be careful about aiding a person who might be charged with obstruction of justice. He said getting too close to you might not be a good thing for the lodge."

There was thud in the fireplace as one log rolled off another.

Gurney walked over to the hearth, picked up a poker, and started rearranging the logs. He wanted to take a moment to consider the hand he'd just been dealt.

He turned back to Steckle. "Sounds like an uncomfortable spot for you to be in. But the truth is I have no interest at all in undermining his investigation. The more I learn, the more I suspect he's on the right track."

That prompted a curious glance from Madeleine and a frown from Steckle. "Pretty big turnaround. I understood Jane hired you to prove Fenton was wrong."

"That's not the way I work. I just follow the facts."

"Wherever they lead?"

"Absolutely."

Steckle nodded slowly. "And you don't think the facts favor the Hammonds?"

"Frankly, no. But getting back to the pressure you're feeling from Fenton, are you saying I should leave the lodge and drop the case?"

Steckle raised his palms in objection. "Not at all. I'm just being honest with you about the pressure. I just want this shit to be over with."

"I couldn't agree more."

"Good." He looked at Madeleine. "You understand what I'm saying, right?"

"Oh, yes. Perfectly. We all want this to be over with."

"Good. Great." He showed his teeth in something resembling a smile and pointed to the silver dome on the tray. "Enjoy your lunch."

AFTER STECKLE LEFT, GURNEY LOCKED THE DOOR. MADELEINE stood by the fire, looking uneasy.

"Can we check on the weather?" she asked.

"Steckle may be exaggerating the problem to get rid of us."

"Can we check on it anyway?"

"Sure." He took out his phone, went to an Internet weather site, and typed in "Wolf Lake."

When the forecast data appeared, he stared at it. "This is useless."

"What does it say?"

"It says we may get terrible weather but probably won't."

"It doesn't say that. Tell me what it actually—"

"It says there's a 30 percent chance of a major ice storm this evening, with ice-pellet accumulation of two to three inches, resulting in hazardous driving conditions."

"And tomorrow?"

"A 30 percent chance of heavy snow accumulation, up to eighteen inches. Possible four-foot drifts with winds gusting to forty miles per hour."

"So after this afternoon driving will be impossible?"

"It's only 30 percent likely, meaning it's 70 percent unlikely."

She turned back to the window. As she stood gazing out toward Devil's Fang, he could hear her fingernail attacking her cuticle.

He sighed. "If you want, we can leave for Vermont right now."

She didn't answer.

"I mean, if you're worried about bad weather getting in the way—"

She cut him off. "Just . . . wait. I'm trying to make the right decision."

The right decision? About what?

He picked up the poker and set about the rearrangement of the logs. After a while he gave that up and sat down on the couch. Minutes passed before she spoke again—this time so softly he almost couldn't make out the words.

"Will you come with me?"

"Where?"

"I'd like to go back to where I was this morning . . . but have you with me . . . if you'd be willing to come."

He sensed that the important thing was to say yes, which he did, and to put aside the questions that came immediately to mind.

THEY SET OUT IN A FOG THAT THINNED AS THEY DROVE UP TOWARD the ridge that defined the edge of the geological declivity that contained Wolf Lake. Beyond the ridge there was no fog at all, but slippery spots on the road made for slow going.

As they emerged from the Gall Wilderness Preserve, the GPS directed them onto a public road that led even higher into the surrounding mountains.

Twenty-five minutes later, the GPS alerted them to an upcoming turn onto Blackthorn Road. That intersection formed the center of a

ghost town consisting of a few unidentifiable wooden structures in various stages of dilapidation.

"We're almost there," said Madeleine, sitting up straighter.

A minute later the GPS told them to make a right on Hemlock Lane.

"Don't make the right," said Madeleine. "It's rutted and overgrown.
Pull over here."

He did as she said. They stepped out of the car into a cutting wind.
He turned up the collar of his jacket and pulled his woolen ski cap down
over his ears. Whatever it had once been, Hemlock Lane now appeared
to be nothing but a rough dirt path into the woods.

She took his cold hand in hers and led him into the desolate lane.

They proceeded cautiously on the icy surface with the wind in their
faces, climbing over fallen trees. The first structure they came upon
was an abandoned cottage, covered with blotches of black mildew. Half
hidden in the woods behind it were two smaller ones in total disrepair.

Madeleine stopped. "The Carey twins, Michael and Joseph, lived
here with their mother. In the summer she rented out those little cot-
tages in the back, but in the winter it was just them."

As her gaze moved over the scene, Gurney got the impression she
was attempting to see it as it once was.

"Come," she said after a while, leading him along the lane.

Brittle remnants of the summer brambles were leaning in from both
sides, catching at their pants and jacket sleeves. A few hundred yards
farther they came to a second property in worse shape than the first. A
huge fallen hemlock had obliterated at least a third of the main house.
The remains of three small cabins off to the side were covered with
years of decaying pine needles.

"This is it," she said.

"This was the house where you spent your Christmases?"

She tightened her grip on his hand. "It was more than just Christmas
week, though. The last year I came up I was here for six weeks."

"Your holiday vacation was that long?"

"That year it was. My parents had put me in a private school that had
longer winter breaks than public schools and shorter summer breaks."

"What about your sister?"

"When I was fifteen Christine was already twenty-two." She paused.

"They used to call me the surprise baby. That was a euphemism for the shock baby. I'm sure they wished they could wake up one morning and discover I'd just been a bad dream."

Taken aback by this, he said nothing. Rarely had she talked about her parents when they were alive, and never after they died.

She drew him closer to her as they proceeded along the narrowing path. Soon all resemblance to an actual road disappeared. The wind grew more biting. His face was beginning to ache. Just when he was about to question her destination, they emerged into a clearing. Beyond it was a perfectly flat white expanse, which he guessed was a frozen lake.

She led him across the clearing.

At the edge of the white expanse she stopped and spoke with a forced evenness. "This is Grayson Lake."

"Is this the lake where that boy drowned?"

"His name was Colin Bantry." She paused, seemed to reach a painful decision, and took a deep breath. "I was in love with him."

In love . . . with the kid who drowned? "Jesus, Maddie. What . . . what happened?"

She pointed to two enormous hemlocks at the edge of the frozen lake. "One night I asked him to meet me . . . over there. It was so cold. The coldest night of the year."

She fell silent, gazing at the trees.

"I told him I was pregnant."

He waited for her to go on. All he could see, all he could focus on, was the look on her face, a look of desolation he'd never seen there before.

She repeated herself, slowly, as if punishing herself with the words. "I told him I was pregnant."

Again he waited.

"He raced out onto the ice on his motorcycle. All the way out. In the moonlight. Out there." She pointed with a trembling hand. "The ice broke."

"That's how he drowned?"

She nodded.

"What happened with . . . your pregnancy."

"I wasn't pregnant."

"What do you mean?"

"I didn't lie. I really believed that I was. I'd missed my period. Maybe I wanted to be pregnant, wanted to be attached to Colin, wanted a new life, a life where someone wanted me more than my parents did. Oh God, I was so desperate! And I loved him so much!"

"Why do you think he did what he did?"

"The awful thing is, I have no idea. I have no idea, but the thought that tortured me was that he was running away, that he couldn't face me, couldn't face being with me anymore. He didn't say a single word, just . . . just raced off across the ice."

There was a long silence as they stood staring out over the lake.

Eventually Gurney asked, "Was there a police investigation?"

"Of course. Colin's father was a deputy sheriff."

"You told him what happened?"

"I didn't say anything about telling Colin I was pregnant. I said that I didn't know why he rode out onto the ice . . . that maybe he was just showing off, or just felt like doing it. He believed me. Colin was like that. Everyone knew Colin was wild."

There was another silence. Her grip on his hand was almost painfully tight.

He looked into her eyes. "Why are you telling me this now?"

"I don't know. Maybe because we're here."

"You decided to reveal this secret you've been keeping from me all this time—*because we're here?*"

"I didn't see it as keeping a secret from you. I saw it as something I shouldn't inflict on you."

"Who *did* you tell? A friend? A therapist? You must have told someone."

"A therapist, naturally. Around the time we met. When I was doing the training for my clinical certification. I thought therapy would be an ideal way of dealing with it, since in a sense it would allow me to keep it to myself."

"Did it work?"

"I thought at the time that it did."

"But . . . ?"

"But now I think the process gave me the illusion of having dealt with what happened—and the conviction that I never needed to talk about it to anyone ever again. That's what I meant when I said that I didn't think of it as a secret. I just thought of it as a part of the past that belonged in the past, and talking about it in the present would have no purpose."

"What changed your mind?"

"I don't know. All I know is what I felt when Jack held up that Adirondack route map on his phone screen at our kitchen table, and I realized how close we'd be to Grayson Lake."

"You felt some attraction to the place?"

"Oh God, no. The opposite. I felt sick. I almost had to leave the room."

"But you volunteered to come here. You said yes before I did."

"Because at that moment I realized I hadn't dealt with anything. As awful as that moment was, I felt I was being offered an opportunity."

They stood side by side in silence, looking out over the snow-covered lake.

She sighed. "It happened thirty-two years ago. But it never really ended. Maybe because I could never be sure why he did what he did. Maybe because I never came to terms with my guilt. Maybe because they never found his body. Maybe—"

Gurney interrupted, "They never found his body?"

"No. Which revived all the old talk about the evil in the lake. Which is why the people who used to come every summer stopped coming. Which is why the little town eventually died—why it's like the way it is now." She let go of his hand for the first time since they'd gotten out of the car and began rubbing her own hands together.

"What old talk about the evil in the lake?"

"Remember the story Norris Landon told us about the girls in the canoe that capsized long ago—how one of them drowned, and they couldn't find the body?"

"Right—until the skeleton turned up in Wolf Lake five years later."

"Well, that girl drowned right here in Grayson Lake. And when Colin drowned here, too, and they couldn't find his body, it brought the old drowning story back; and people started calling it Graveyard Lake."

"Because of that, people abandoned their houses?"

"Not right away. Graysonville was a marginal sort of place. Never far from poverty. Most people depended on renting rooms or cabins to summer vacationers. I suppose the idea of children drowning and their bodies disappearing took hold of people's imaginations, and they stopped coming. The town, never much to begin with, gradually collapsed."

"The Devil's Twins. Isn't that what Landon called the pair of lakes he claimed were linked through some chain of underground caverns?"

"Yes." A flock of small birds came flying wildly out of the woods and veered out over the lake, swooping and tumbling like autumn leaves in a gale.

She took his hand again in hers. "What are you thinking?"

"I don't know. A jumble of things."

"Do you wish I hadn't told you?"

"Maddie, I want to know whatever you want to tell me. Anything. Everything. I love you."

"No matter what?"

"No matter what."

She nodded, still looking into his eyes, still holding his hand. "We should start back. The snow is coming. I can feel it in the air."

He looked up at the sky. The clouds were thickening and darkening now, and above the frozen lake a hawk was circling unevenly in the rising wind.

CHAPTER 26

When they crested the last ridge before Wolf Lake, the stored-message tone rang on Gurney's phone. Checking the screen, he discovered two messages—one from Jack Hardwick and one from a caller with a blocked ID.

"Look out!" cried Madeleine as a deer bounded out onto the road ahead.

Gurney jammed on the brakes, missing the deer by inches.

"Pay attention to the road and give that to me." She extended her hand for the phone. "Do you want me to play the messages?"

He nodded, and she tapped an icon.

As usual, Hardwick didn't bother to identify himself, but his raspy voice was unmistakable. "Hey, ace, where the fuck are you? We have significant shit to discuss. One—I delivered that letter to the house in Staten Island, slipped it under the front door, with all those contact options. Two—I didn't have a clue about that twenty-nine mil for Hammond. But there's some kind of explanation, right? Three—I got a present for you, nice practical gift. I plan to be passing through the Adirondacks tomorrow, so let's pick a spot to get together. ASAP. Related to that, you know what's on my mind right now? The Baryshansky case. Think about it."

The Baryshansky case? For a moment Gurney was baffled by the reference to the big Russian mob investigation a decade earlier. Then the relevant piece of it lit up like an alarm. That was the case in which the mob had managed to hack the cell phones of two senior investigators in the Organized Crime Task Force. The obvious implication was that Hardwick suspected that the security of their phone conversations had been compromised.

"What is it?" asked Madeleine.

"It sounds to me like Jack has surveillance concerns."

"What does that mean?"

He wanted time to think through the possibilities. "I'll explain later; let me pay attention to the road. Don't want any more deer surprises."

Madeleine asked if he wanted her to play the next message.

"Not right now."

After they'd arrived at the lodge and were standing under the portico, she handed him back his phone. "Are you going to tell me what's going on?"

"I got the impression that Jack thinks he's being bugged."

"That *he's* being bugged? Or that *both* of you are?"

"He wasn't clear about that. But I'm pretty certain my own phone is safe."

She gave him an anxious look. "What about our room here at the lodge?"

"It's possible, but I doubt it."

"Is there a way of finding out for sure?"

"There are detection devices. I'll discuss it with Jack."

"Who would be spying on us?"

"Conceivably Fenton, but I doubt it."

"Who then?"

"Good question. Hardwick knows more than he told me on the phone. I'll set up a face-to-face with him to clarify the situation."

She looked worried. "So what do we do now? Go upstairs to our possibly bugged room? Pretend we're happy little campers?"

"Actually, yes, that's exactly what we need to do."

"What are we supposed to talk about? Or not talk about?"

"The main thing not to talk about is any suspicion that we're being monitored. If our room or phone is bugged—" He stopped in mid-sentence, remembering that he had a message on his phone he hadn't listened to yet. He located it and tapped the icon.

The voice was young, female, and frightened. "Hello. I was hoping you'd answer. The letter said you'd be there. Are you there? Can I give you my number? Maybe it would be safer if I called you back. Okay, so that's what I'll do. I'll call you at . . . exactly . . . umm . . . four o'clock. Okay?"

Gurney checked his watch. It was 3:53. The sun, hidden behind the heavy overcast, would be sinking now behind Cemetery Ridge.

"Is that the girl you wanted to get to?" asked Madeleine.

"I think so."

"Now what?"

"I'm going to stay out here to take her call. You might be more comfortable up in the room."

She made a face. "You really think our room might be bugged?"

"It's *conceivable*. But I really believe that any major surveillance would be aimed at the Hammonds, not us."

"Why?"

"Because the focus of the BCI investigation is on Richard. And Jane is the person trying to protect him. She's also the one who got Hardwick involved, and now he suspects he's being listened in on. I'm thinking it's *her* phone that's been hacked, and that's how the listener might know about his involvement."

"And *your* involvement?"

"Only if she discussed the situation on the phone and used my name in the course of the conversation. But all this is guesswork. I need facts."

After a long silence she took his hand in hers the same way she'd taken it on the forlorn lane in Graysonville. "Are you sure it's all right? What I told you earlier?"

"Of course it's all right . . ." Before he could say anything more, his phone rang. As before, the caller ID had been blocked. He assumed it would be Angela. He looked helplessly at Madeleine and started to apologize.

She cut him off. "Answer it."

He took the call. "This is Dave Gurney."

"I left you a message." It was the same small voice.

"Yes, I got it," he said as gently as he could. The main thing was to not lose her. "I appreciate your willingness to talk to me."

"What do you want from me?"

"It would help me a lot to know whatever you can tell me about Steven."

"Stevie."

"Stevie. Okay. See how little I know? So just about anything you can tell me will be a big help. Did everyone call him Stevie, or just you?"

"His parents called him Steven, which he hated." There was a childish vibe in her voice that made her sound about half the age he assumed she must be.

He decided to play to the vibe. "Parents can be a problem."

"No shit. Especially his parents."

"How about your own parents?"

"I don't talk to them."

"I didn't talk much to mine, either. Tell me, do people call you Angie or Angela?"

"Everybody calls me Angela. Nobody calls me Angie."

"Okay, Angela, let me ask you something. Is there someplace where we could meet and talk about Stevie, someplace you'd feel safe?"

"Why do we have to meet?" There was a skittery edge in her voice.

"We don't *have to*. I just think it might be safer. But it's up to you."

"What do you mean, safer?"

"I don't mean to frighten you, Angela, but you do understand that your situation is dangerous, right?"

She hesitated so long in answering he was afraid he'd lost her. When she did speak, the skittishness had grown to flat-out fear. "I guess so. But why would it be safer to meet?"

"Because our phones might not be secure. If the bad guys have the right equipment, they can hack into just about anything—calls, text messages, emails. You see stuff like that in the news all the time, right?"

"I guess."

"You know the most private way for two people to have a conversation?"

"In the bathroom?"

"Actually, bathrooms are pretty easy to bug."

"Then how?"

"A public area with maybe some background noise or other people talking. That makes it hard for snoopers. That's the kind of situation I think would be the safest for both of us."

"Like a big store?"

"A big store would be perfect. That's good thinking."

"I know a lot of stores. Where are you?"

"I'm up in the Adirondack Mountains."

"At the place where Stevie met with the hypnotism guy?"

"That's exactly where I am. I'm trying to find out what happened to Stevie up here so I can figure out what happened to him later, down at your place in Floral Park."

There was a silence. He waited, leaving the next move in the conversation up to her.

"You don't think he committed suicide, do you?" she asked.

"No. Do you?"

"He couldn't have."

"How do know that?"

"He just wouldn't have done that—not after the promises he made to me. We were going to get married, get our own house. He wouldn't kill himself. That's impossible!"

Gurney had a dozen questions, but he reminded himself that one wrong one could spook her. The goal was to get her committed to a face-to-face meeting—where he'd have more control, plus the opportunity to read the subtleties of facial expressions and body language.

"I understand what you're saying, Angela. I really do. That's why we have to find out what really happened. Or you'll never be safe."

"Don't say that. You're scaring me."

"Sometimes fear is good. Fear of the right things can help us get past fear of the wrong things."

"What do you mean?"

"You're afraid of whoever's behind what happened to Stevie. Am I right?"

"Yes."

"But you're also afraid of me. Because I'm a detective, and you don't really want to talk to detectives, do you?"

Her silence at that point was answer enough.

"It's okay, Angela. I can understand that. But ask yourself this question: Which of those people should you be more afraid of? The person responsible for Stevie's death? Or the person who's trying to get to the bottom of it to make sure no one else gets hurt?"

"I hate this. Why do I have to make these horrible decisions?"

Gurney said nothing, just waited.

"Okay. I can meet you tomorrow. I know a place."

"Tell me where it is and what time you want me to be there."

"You know Lake George Village?"

"Yes."

"Can you be there at ten o'clock tomorrow morning?"

"Yes. Where in Lake George Village?"

"Tabitha's Dollhouse. I'll be up on the second floor by the Barbie Dolls."

STILL STANDING WITH MADELEINE OUT IN FRONT OF THE LODGE, HE accessed the Internet on his phone and typed in "Tabitha's Dollhouse."

It came up immediately—on Woodpecker Road in Lake George Village. The website showed a building designed as an elaborate fantasy cottage. Above the cottage on the web page, arcing like a rainbow across a pure blue sky, were the words, "Home of Fabulous, Lovable, Collectible Dolls."

Madeleine frowned at the screen. "A doll store? That's where she wants to discuss her boyfriend's death?"

"It does seem an odd choice."

"You didn't ask her why?"

"I didn't want to ask anything that might get her off track. She agreed to meet with me, and that's the main thing."

"Do you mind if I come with you?"

"Why would you want to do that?"

"I'd rather not stay here alone."

"You know it's at least a two-hour drive each way?"

"It's better than the alternative."

He shrugged. "I'm going to call Jack from out here, and it may take a while." He pointed at the lodge. "There's smoke coming out of the main chimney, meaning there's a fire in the Hearth Room. Why don't you go in and warm up?"

"I'll go in when you go in."

"Up to you." He returned to the Dollhouse website and pasted its address into Google Maps. He noted the location of a nearby gas station and copied its address to the message area of a blank email. Then he called Hardwick.

The man picked up on the first ring. "Before you say anything, tell me if you understood my reference to the Baryshansky situation."

"I think so."

"Good. Important to keep that in mind. So. How soon can I give you your special gift?"

"Depends on when and how far you're willing to travel."

"Anywhere, anytime. Sooner the better."

"I plan to get together tomorrow with that young lady I've been wanting to meet. Maybe we can cross paths in the same neighborhood."

"Absolutely."

"I have some address information. I'll email it to you."

"I'll watch for it."

Gurney went back into his email program and brought up the one he'd begun with the Lake George gas station location in it. Under the station address he typed in the notation, "Here at 9:00 AM." He addressed the email to Hardwick and sent it.

Madeleine was standing with her arms clutching her body in the frigid air.

He nodded toward the lodge. "Let's go inside and defrost ourselves by the fire."

She followed him to the Hearth Room. Once in front of the crackling blaze she slowly unfolded her arms.

Standing beside her, the radiant heat of the fire seeping into his body, Gurney closed his eyes and let his world contract to the warm orange glow on his eyelids and the tingling of his skin as the deep chill dissipated.

The feeling of peace was broken by the rough edge of Austen Steckle's voice.

"Glad to see you folks finally decided to come in out of the cold. Nasty day, nastier night on the way." Dressed in a dark plaid shirt and khaki pants, he was standing in the center of the broad archway. "Did you hear the wolves?"

"No," said Gurney. "When?"

"Little while ago. Up in the woods in back of the lodge. Horrible sound."

"How often do you see them?"

"Never. Makes it worse. Just hearing them. Monsters creeping around in the forest!"

Steckle's comment created an uncomfortable silence, broken by Madeleine. "You said something about nastier weather tonight?"

"The edge of a storm coming through. Windy as hell, temperature dropping. But that's just a taste of what's around the corner. Weather here jerks you around like a dog killing a rat. Tonight'll be rotten, tomorrow morning'll be sunny, can you believe it? Then, later tomorrow, all hell breaks loose—the big one, coming down from the north."

Madeleine's eyes widened. "The big one?"

"Arctic air mass. Zero-visibility blizzard. A definite road-closer."

Gurney suspected these weather warnings were being employed to encourage their departure. But if Steckle was acting under pressure from Fenton to get them away from Wolf Lake, then perhaps a promised departure could be used as a lever to open another door.

Gurney nodded thoughtfully. "Probably be a good idea for us to get out of here before that storm hits. Otherwise we may never get to Vermont."

Steckle nodded in immediate agreement.

"Problem is," said Gurney, "there's one more person I need to talk to before we can leave."

"Who's that?"

"Peyton Gall."

"Why the hell would you want to talk to him?"

"Ethan's will, and therefore Ethan's death, directly benefits two individuals—Peyton Gall and Richard Hammond, whose bequest Fenton was happy to tell me about. But since Peyton's share is as big as Richard's, he'd have as big a motive. Maybe bigger, since—"

Steckle interrupted. "Yeah, I see how that might look from a distance. But that's miles from reality. You obviously don't know Peyton."

"That's a hole I'm trying to fill."

"Let me fill it for you, before you get stuck in the blizzard of the century for nothing." Steckle joined Gurney and Madeleine in front of the fire. "See, here's the problem with Peyton. It's pretty simple. If Hammond wasn't the brains behind the four deaths—murders, suicides, whatever you want to call them—then somebody else was. But the idea that it could be Peyton is just absurd."

"Why is that?"

Steckle's voice dropped to a harsh whisper. "Because Peyton Gall is a lunatic drug addict whose priorities are limited to coke, pussy, more coke, and more pussy." He glanced at Madeleine. "Excuse my crude language, Mrs. Gurney, but I gotta call a spade a spade. We're talking about a brain-damaged junkie whose social circle consists of the whores he brings in from wherever. Russia, Thailand, Vegas, crack houses in Newburgh—he's gotten to the point where it don't make any difference."

Gurney could see a sheen of sweat on Steckle's shaved head. "As the last surviving member of the Gall family, this lunatic is your new boss?"

"Hah! I have no illusions about my future here. I never had a contract. It was all based on mutual trust with Ethan and shared business goals. You know what it's based on now? Nothing. Be amazed if I'm here in another three months at the rate that fucker is disintegrating."

"I was told he'd straightened out recently, at least for a while."

"True, but little periods of being straight have happened before, and they always end the same way—with him wilder and worse than ever."

"You're telling me he's not only too crazy to have masterminded a complicated crime, he's barely able to function?"

"You got it."

"Then my interview with him will be very brief."

Steckle's frustration was palpable. "He won't want to talk to you."

"I'm hoping you can help me there. Ethically, I can't walk away until I sit down with him and form my own opinion of his capabilities. If what you say about him is true, it shouldn't take long. Tell him I just need fifteen or twenty minutes of his time."

"What if he refuses?"

"He might be persuaded to speak to me if he knows I'll be hanging around until he does—that I'll be keeping an eye on him, maybe taking a close look at his forms of amusement."

Steckle took a deep breath and slowly exhaled. "Fine. Have it your way. I'll pass your request along to him."

"Be great if I could see him tomorrow—before 'the big one' snows us in."

"I'll give it a try." He flashed a mechanical smile and left the room.

Madeleine was studying Gurney's puzzled expression. "What are you thinking?"

"I'm thinking that running an Adirondack lodge is a strange job for a man who hates Adirondack weather."

BACK UPSTAIRS IN THE SUITE GURNEY FELT LIKE HE WAS STUCK IN an area where the signals of two radio stations overlapped. The competing signals were arising from his roles as detective and husband, and the static was growing louder. He couldn't deny that he felt a certain natural attraction to the baffling aspects of the case. He also felt an acute need to be more supportive of Madeleine, especially now; but he wasn't at all sure what action would best provide that support. It occurred to him, not for the first time, that he was more comfortable dealing with murder than with marriage. In the grip of uncertainty, he decided to leave his further involvement in the case up to her.

"If you want me to walk away from this Hammond business, I will. We could leave in the morning, meet up with Hardwick and Angela at Lake George as promised, then go on to Vermont."

"What about Peyton Gall?"

"Hardwick can follow up on that—or not. That's up to him. All I promised Jane was that I'd drop by Wolf Lake for a day or two and take a look. Well, I've taken a look."

"What have you seen?"

"Nothing that isn't contradicted by something else."

"For example?"

"We have a suspect accused of a crime that may not even be possible to commit. We have an unsavory brother of the richest victim, with a huge financial motive for murder—who's not even being considered as a suspect. We have a family legend involving a wolf nightmare that sounds like nonsense—except that a similar nightmare has been involved in four deaths in the past month. And we have a handyman who seems half crazy—except that he also seems to be the only one who believes there's something evil going on at Wolf Lake."

"What about Jane?"

"What do you mean?"

"The saintly little seeker of truth essentially lied to you by failing to mention Richard's position in Ethan's will, which may be the most important fact of all."

"Good point—and one more indication that there nothing's simple about this case. Most of it is bizarre, if not impossible."

"So you're hooked." She produced a fleeting Mona Lisa smile. "Nothing appeals to you more than the bizarre and impossible. You might think you can walk away, but you can't. And even if you could . . . I'd have to stay here myself."

"Why?"

"I have to finish what I came here for."

Before he could respond to that, his phone rang.

The ID on the screen said it was Holdenfield. He looked at Madeleine, and she gestured that he should take the call. He did.

"Rebecca?"

"Hi, David. I'm not sure I have anything of real value for you, but I wanted to get back to you sooner rather than later."

"Thank you. I appreciate it."

Madeleine went into the bathroom and closed the door with a distinct firmness.

"For what it's worth," said Rebecca, "I did a quick look-through of Hammond's journal articles, as well as the media coverage he's gotten from time to time. The general media items were mostly about the controversy over his gay emergence therapy. The antigay crowd may be shrinking these days, but what's left of it is still as virulent as ever."

It brought to mind the hatred in Bowman Cox's eyes. "Any other controversies?"

"Some professional ones. Hammond isn't shy about attacking the pharmaceutical companies for peddling psychotropic poisons. By contrast, he claims hypnotherapy is perfectly safe, and that his own techniques can achieve results that used to be considered impossible."

"Does he spell out those techniques?"

"Ah, well, there's the problem. His clinical success rate has been documented, and it's astounding. With compulsive disorders, phobias, and PTSD symptoms, his rate of achieving total remission is five times higher than the American Psychiatric Association average."

"But . . . ?"

"But when other therapists try to employ the techniques he describes, they don't come close to his results."

"Does that mean he's faking his success stories?"

"No, that's been checked and double-checked. If anything, he's been understating his positive outcomes—a breathtaking fact in itself."

"Then what's the explanation?"

"In my opinion, there's a unique synergy between the method and the man."

"Meaning?"

"Hammond has a uniquely powerful clinical presence."

"You mean he has a talent that enables him to do things other therapists can't do?"

"I'd say that his clinical talent appears to be out of the ballpark. I suspect that other people could learn his techniques, but only by closely observing what he does."

Gurney thought about this for a few moments. "It sounds like Dr. Hammond could put a very high price tag on himself, if he were so inclined."

"That's an understatement." Holdenfield paused. "The odd thing is, he doesn't seem interested in money, or in any of the prestige positions in the field that could be his for the asking."

"One more question before you go. Does the term 'trance-induced suicide' mean anything to you? I heard it used recently, and I was wondering if it had any clinical meaning."

"It's ringing a distant bell. I'll let you know if the context comes to mind. Anything else?"

"Has Hammond ever commented on that new area of research you mentioned—separating thoughts from the emotions they generate?"

"Matter of fact, he has. He suggested in a recent article that it could be achieved through hypnotherapy. He even seemed to be hinting that he might already have done it."

CHAPTER 27

At 6:45 AM the next morning, at the first suggestion of dawn, they were in the Outback, heading for Lake George, heater turned up to the max. By the time they crested the first ridge, Madeleine had fallen asleep.

The secondary roads to the Adirondack Northway were slippery from the night's flurries, and the going was slow. The Northway itself, however, turned out to be free of both snow and traffic, and Gurney was able to make up for lost time.

At 8:56 he entered Lake George Village and a moment later caught sight of the lake—as gray as the cold sky above it. As the road drew closer to the shore, he passed a deserted marina, a closed restaurant, and a lakefront hotel with a nearly empty parking lot.

At 8:59, he pulled into the Sunoco station on Woodpecker Road. He spotted the red GTO parked by the convenience store in back of the gas pumps. Hardwick was pacing along the edge of the parking area smoking a cigarette. He looked grim. The hard set of his jaw, the evident tension in his muscular body, and those ice-blue sled-dog eyes would keep any sane stranger at a prudent distance.

Madeleine stirred in her seat.

"We've arrived," said Gurney, pulling in next to the GTO. "Did you want to walk around a bit?"

She mumbled something and shook her head.

He got out, felt the wind coming off the lake, and zipped up his jacket. As he approached Hardwick, the man dropped his cigarette to the pavement and crushed it underfoot as though it were a wasp that had just stung him. His grimace morphed into an overly broad smile as he came forward, hand extended.

"Davey! Good to see you!" The exuberance of the greeting was as false as the smile.

Gurney shook his hand.

Hardwick maintained the big grin but lowered his voice, "Never know who's watching. Want the gift idea to look credible." He opened the passenger door of the GTO, took out a slim gift-wrapped box, and handed it to him. "Unwrap it and look surprised. And happy."

In the package Gurney found what appeared to be a sleek new smartphone.

"Advanced surveillance scanner," said Hardwick. "Full instructions on the opening screen. Your password is 'Sherlock.' Set it to scan and leave it in your pocket. Automatically maps any space you're in. Locates and identifies audio and video bugs, geo-trackers, recorders, transmitters. Stores the mapping, location, and frequency spectrum data associated with each device for later retrieval. Questions?"

"Where'd you get this thing?"

"Remember the tough little redhead techie on the Mellery case?"

"Sergeant Robin Wigg?"

"Lieutenant Wigg now. Running technology evaluation for the Anti-Terrorism Unit. We stayed in touch. I happened to mention that I had a hostile-surveillance concern. Things like that get her excited. She said I could have this item for three days. Unofficial field test."

"What prompted your surveillance concern?"

"An odd little travel brochure." Hardwick glanced around, up and down the street, then gestured toward the convenience store. "Let's go inside."

Except for a tattooed girl with a green crew cut at the register, there were no other people in the store. Hardwick led the way to a wall of refrigerated drinks. "You want anything?"

"Tell me about the brochure."

He opened one of the glass cooler doors and took out a bottle of springwater. "Chamber of commerce kind of brochure. Harpers Dale. You've heard of it?"

"Hot air balloon rides?"

"Plenty of shit like that. Tourist hot spot at the ass end of one of the Finger Lakes."

"So . . . you got a Harpers Dale travel brochure? And?"

"It came in the mail. Someone had written the word 'Unforgettable' across the front of it. They even fucking underlined it."

"This means what to you?"

"This means a world of shit. You remember why I brought you into this Hammond thing to begin with? I mean, apart from my wanting to save you from wasting your brain on some fucking porcupine."

"You wanted a front man—so Gil Fenton wouldn't know you were personally involved in undermining his case."

"You remember why I didn't want him to know?"

"Because he had some dirt on you from something that went down the wrong way a long time ago. And if he got pissed off enough, he might drop the dime."

"That thing that went down the wrong way? It went down in Harpers Dale."

A teenager with droopy denim pants, an oversized red baseball hat, a fur jacket, and shiny onyx disk earrings came down the aisle, clicking his tongue to a hip-hop beat. He opened the cooler door next to Gurney and took out four cans of a super-caffeinated drink called WHACK.

"Let's get the fuck out of here," growled Hardwick. He paid the green-haired girl for the springwater, and they walked out of the store.

Out by the GTO Hardwick lit a new cigarette and took a couple of fierce drags on it.

"I guess there's no way that Harpers Dale brochure might have been a coincidence?" Gurney asked.

"No reason anyone else would mail me that kind of brochure. And that little addition—'Unforgettable'—no way is that a coincidence. It's a fucking threat. Fenton knows I'm working with the Hammonds. Which means there's a bug somewhere."

"At the chalet?"

"Most likely place."

"Okay. What now?"

Hardwick made an acid-reflux face. "It's a problem I was trying to avoid. But facts need to be faced. Bottom line, whatever Fenton knows or doesn't know at this point makes no fucking difference. I'm in for the duration. If he wants to play the Harpers Dale card, that's his business. But I'll make fucking sure that fucker goes down with me."

He took out another cigarette and lit it.

Gurney shrugged. "It may look like Fenton knows, but it's not a certainty."

Hardwick coughed up some phlegm and spit it on the pavement. "Nothing's a fucking certainty, but it's a good working assumption."

"I'm just saying, in the event that he doesn't know, and the brochure came to you by some other route, you shouldn't advertise your involvement unnecessarily. It's not like he signed his name to it. If you confront him, he could deny being the sender. You'd just be giving him the satisfaction of knowing he'd gotten to you."

"I shouldn't stick my middle finger in his eye?"

"I'd resist the temptation if I were you." Gurney paused, then patted the jacket pocket where he'd stowed the device. "I assume you want me to visit the chalet with this little item to verify your surveillance suspicions?"

"Absolutely. You might want to go over that Presidential Suite of yours, too."

Gurney nodded his agreement, then glanced at the Outback. "Can it identify the presence of a GPS tracker?"

"According to Wigg, it picks up *everything*."

"You checked your own car?"

"Yep. It's clean."

"How about we check mine right now—before I meet with Angela?"

Hardwick took a thoughtful drag on his cigarette. "Good idea."

MADELEINE WAS FULLY AWAKE NOW, EYEING THE SMARTPHONE screen with as much curiosity and concern as Gurney and Hardwick.

A device more advanced than any Gurney had ever seen, the scanner was displaying a clear outline of the vehicle they were sitting in.

Hardwick explained that he had set its "primary range perimeter," one of its breakthrough features, to focus on the area defined by the Outback itself.

Gurney gave him a quizzical look.

Hardwick shrugged from the backseat. "All I can do is repeat what Wigg told me. According to her, this thing incorporates two technologies. One detects and displays transmission frequencies. The other is a new kind of short-range radar—CAM, stands for Close-Area Mapping. It detects and displays the perimeters of any enclosed space. Working together, they give you the precise location of any transmitter."

On the scanner's screen, within a graphic representation of the steel shell of the vehicle, two red lights were blinking—one near the front of the engine compartment, the other near a rear wheel well. Next to each red light were three number sequences and the letters GPT.

Madeleine looked at Hardwick. "What does all that mean?"

"The letters indicate the type of device—GPT for geoposition trackers. The large number next to each is its transmitting frequency. The other two numbers pinpoint the location of the device in vertical inches above the ground and horizontal inches from the car's perimeter."

Gurney looked skeptical. "Two flashing lights indicate the presence of two trackers?"

"The little wizard doesn't lie."

Madeleine's eyes widened. "Those things are telling someone where we are, right now, sitting here in our car?"

"You got it."

"Can you get rid of them?"

"We can, but we need to give some thought to when, where, and how." He looked at Gurney. "Any thoughts on how we should deal with it?"

"That depends on who we think put them there, and why there are two of them."

"Simple redundancy? Or different performance characteristics for different conditions?"

Gurney looked doubtful. "How many times have you found two trackers on one vehicle?"

"Never."

"Maybe the two devices have separate sources?"

Now it was Hardwick's turn to look doubtful. "Like two different investigators? And neither one wants to rely on getting data from the other?"

"Could be separate investigative agencies. And neither one knows about the tracker placed by the other."

"What two agencies are we talking about?"

"I have no idea, just questions. For example, who authorized electronic surveillance on the personal vehicle of a private investigator? Presumably I'm not suspected of committing a crime. If probable-cause warrants were issued for the placement of those trackers, what was the basis? And if no warrants were issued, who was willing to break the law that way? Why do my movements matter that much?"

"You also gotta ask, what's being *done* with the tracking data?"

Madeleine turned in her seat and stared at him. "What do you mean?"

"Location data can be used in a lot of ways. It can be fed directly to an automated drone with hi-res photo capability. Or to the navigation screen of a surveillance team, so they can follow you but stay out of sight."

Gurney checked his watch. "We've got a time issue here. It's almost 9:25, and I need to be half a mile up the road at ten for my meeting with Angela Castro. I'd rather not have that destination fed to anyone. Problem is, disposing of the trackers here would make it obvious that I found them, which would eliminate future options, so we need a different solution."

"Easy," said Hardwick. "Leave the car here, walk to your meeting. No problem."

"No problem—unless we're being photographed from one of those programmed drones you just mentioned. You know how many *thousands* of those things are in operation these days?"

"Jeez!" said Madeleine. "Are you saying something up there in the sky is watching us?"

"I'm saying we should act as though it might be."

Hardwick's acid-reflux expression returned. "Meaning what?"

"Nothing complicated. We just need to keep our actions as far out of sight as possible."

After a pensive silence Madeleine spoke up. "Didn't the hotel we passed have one of those big overhang things out in front, like the lodge? I'm pretty sure I saw one."

Gurney nodded slowly. "I think you're right. And it might solve our problem."

TEN MINUTES LATER, FOLLOWING A HASTILY DEVISED PLAN, THE GTO was parked in the guest lot next to the hotel, and the Outback was parked in a sheltered spot under the front portico. The Outback's position there had been secured, and the valet parking attendant warded off, with a display of Hardwick's PI credentials, a serious-sounding explanation of the need to conduct an emergency vehicle inspection, and an assurance that it would take hardly any time at all.

The plan, such as it was, was that Hardwick would jack up the Outback and undertake an assessment of the planted devices, out of sight of any aerial surveillance, while Gurney would proceed on foot, through the hotel and out a rear entrance, to Tabitha's Dollhouse.

Madeleine entered the lobby with Gurney. They located the hotel gift shop, where he bought an overpriced souvenir sweatshirt and baseball hat. Back in the sitting area of the lobby, he put on the sweatshirt and hat and left his own jacket with Madeleine.

"I should be back within the hour. Stay within sight of the front door in case Jack needs you."

She responded with a tense nod, holding his jacket against her body.

"It'll be okay," he said, a bit too heartily. "I think this Angela Castro meeting will finally get us on the right track." He hugged her, then headed across the lobby into a corridor marked with a red "Exit" sign.

The corridor led to a glass door. He passed through it and emerged onto a paving-stone path that curved around a bed of ornamental grasses, drooping and drained of color. The path led to a wider one along the shore of the lake, which he discovered roughly paralleled Woodpecker Road and provided an intermittent view of its shops and restaurants.

Maintaining a steady jog, he passed a few isolated dog walkers bundled up against the raw gusts coming off the lake. Within a few minutes he caught sight of a building he recognized from its photo on the Internet. Tabitha's Dollhouse looked even stranger now in its mundane surroundings than it had in the soft-focus fantasy of its website.

He walked across a park-like space adjoining the path, and on across Woodpecker Road. He took out his phone, activated the "Record Audio" function, and slipped the phone into the pocket of his sweatshirt. The entrance to the Dollhouse parking lot was through an ornamented archway that bore the legend he recalled from the website: "Home of Fabulous, Lovable, Collectible Dolls." There were four cars in the parking lot. One, Gurney noted, had dealer plates with a New York City prefix. The door to the Dollhouse itself was bracketed by two waist-high garden gnomes.

When he opened the door he was greeted by a sweet aroma that reminded him of the rectangles of bubblegum he hadn't seen or smelled since grammar school. Scores of little doll faces stared at him from a pastel nursery world of soft pinks, blues, and yellows.

A young woman standing behind a central display case was smiling at him with a glazed cordiality. "Welcome to Tabitha's. How can I help you?"

Gurney glanced around at the profusion of dolls on counters, on shelves, in glass cases—all shapes and sizes and styles of dolls, from cherubic infants to weird creatures that might inhabit fairy tales. Or nightmares.

"The stairs to the second floor?" he asked.

She regarded him with increased interest. "Are you here to see Ms. Castro?"

Having a secretive mindset about the meeting, he was surprised to hear her name.

"Yes, I am."

"She's with Tabitha." Her lowered voice suggested that this was in some way special. "I'll show you the way." She led Gurney through a maze of doll displays to a staircase with a pink banister. "You can go right up, sir."

The second floor was much like the first—except that the dolls here were more uniform in appearance, and many were arranged together in social tableaus. Not far from the top of the stairs there was a small sitting area with a bright yellow table and two glossy white chairs. One chair was occupied by a pale, waif-like young woman with a large, overly perfect, blond hairdo. Gurney was struck by its incompatibility with the shy, narrow face it framed—as well as its remarkable similarity to the blond hairdo of a doll in a locked glass cabinet in the corner.

Standing on the other side of the table was a woman different in almost every way from the seated waif. Her large body was draped in a generously pleated maroon maxi dress, embroidered at the neck. Her fingers were covered with shiny rings. Her face was brightly, almost theatrically, made up. And all of this was topped, literally and figuratively, by her hairdo. The seated waif's was eye-catching, but hers was jaw-dropping. An upswept surge of black and silver-streaked waves collided at dramatic angles, bringing to mind a turbulent Turner seascape. This was a woman, thought Gurney, who was fond of making entrances.

She turned toward him with a sweeping gesture of her heavily ringed hand.

"Mr. Gurney, I presume?"

"Yes. And you are . . . ?"

"Tabitha." She made it sound like an incantation. "I was just about to bring Ms. Castro a nice glass of springwater. May I get you something as well? Herbal tea, perhaps?"

"Nothing. Thank you."

"If you change your mind, if you need anything at all, if you have any questions, just tap on the bell." She pointed at a little dome-shaped device in the middle of the table. "It's pure silver. It makes the purest ding you ever heard."

"Thank you."

With a swirl of silky fabric and a waft of flowery perfume, she swept past him down the pink-banistered stairs.

Gurney turned his attention to the young woman at the table. "Angela?"

She responded with a tiny nod.

"May I sit down?"

"Sure."

"First of all, I want to thank you for allowing me to talk to you."

She responded with a wide-eyed stare. "I didn't know what else to do. The letter the other detective left at my brother's house was really scary. What you said on the phone was scary."

"We're just trying to be honest about a situation we need to find out more about."

"Okay."

He looked around at the doll displays. "This is an unusual place you picked for us to get together."

Her mouth opened in alarm. "I thought you said on the phone that a store would be a good idea."

"It *is* a good idea." He smiled and tried to sound reassuring. "I just meant that I've never been in a store like this before."

"Oh, no. Of course not. It's totally unique."

"Tabitha seems very . . . accommodating."

Angela nodded—at first enthusiastically, then with something that looked like embarrassment. She leaned toward Gurney and spoke in an anxious whisper. "She thinks we're going to buy another Barbie."

"Another Barbie?"

"When Stevie and I stayed here, he bought me a Barbie." She smiled with a childish sweetness. "The special one I always wanted."

"You and Stevie . . . stayed here?"

"Well, not right here in the store. At the Dollhouse Inn. Down the road. It's sort of like a motel, but not like any ordinary one. It's totally fantastic. The rooms have *themes*." Her eyes lit up on that word.

"When was this?"

"When he came to see the creepy hypnotist about breaking his smoking habit."

"Did you meet the hypnotist?"

"No, that was Stevie's thing. I stayed at the inn."

"You said the hypnotist was creepy. How did you know that?"

"That's what Stevie said—that he was a really creepy guy."

"Did he say anything else about him?"

She frowned, as if from the strain of trying to remember. "That he was disgusting."

"Did he say what he meant by that?"

She shook her head. "No, he just said it. Creepy and disgusting."

"Did he say anything to you about having nightmares?"

"Yeah, but that was later. Something about a giant wolf sticking a hot knife in him. Stuff like that. A wolf with hot red eyes, on top of him." A visible shiver ran through her body. "God, how gross is that!"

"Did he tell you he had the dream more than once?"

"A lot. I think like every night after he saw the hypnotist. He said it was disgusting."

"The dream was disgusting, like the hypnotist was disgusting?"

"Yeah, I guess."

"Did Stevie use that word a lot?"

The question seemed to make her uncomfortable. "Not really a lot. Just sometimes."

"Can you remember anything about those other times when he used it?"

"No."

The answer came out too quickly to suit Gurney. But he sensed that pursuing the issue would be a mistake. He'd have to find a way to revisit it later.

For the moment, he wanted to lower the level of tension, not raise it. And that meant moving slowly around obstructions rather than trying to break through them. A meandering style of interviewing felt unnatural to his linear mind, but sometimes it was the best way forward.

"How much of a smoking problem did Stevie have?"

"What do you mean?"

"Had he tried to stop before?"

"I guess." She shrugged. "I don't know for sure."

"Did he talk much about wanting to stop?"

"We never talked about smoking."

Gurney nodded, smiled. "I guess most people don't."

"No. I mean, why would they? It's a stupid thing to talk about."

"After his hypnosis session with Dr. Hammond, was Stevie able to stop smoking?"

"No."

"Was he upset by that?"

"I guess. Maybe. I'm not sure. Maybe he didn't really want to stop. Mainly he talked about the horrible dream and how disgusting Hammond was."

"Did he seem angry that the trip had been a waste of time and money?"

"A waste?"

"Well, I'm just wondering, if seeing Hammond didn't help him stop smoking . . . did that make him angry?"

She looked perplexed, as though this were a subject she'd been revisiting in her own mind. "He *said* he was angry, when I asked him about it."

"But . . . ?"

"But when Stevie gets *really* angry . . . I guess I should say when Stevie *got* really angry . . . his eyes would change, like . . . I don't know how to describe it, but . . . but even big guys would back away from him."

"And he didn't look angry that way when you asked about the time and money?"

"No." She fell silent, looking sad and uneasy.

Gurney was pondering the best way to ask his next question when he heard a swish of fabric and out of the corner of his eye caught sight of the formidable Tabitha ascending the staircase with a remarkable lightness of foot.

She came to the table beaming, placing between them a black lacquer tray with a liter of designer water, a fancy bowl of ice cubes, and two glasses. She gave Gurney a coyly apologetic wink. "I brought an extra glass, just in case you change your mind."

"Thank you."

She paused a second or two, then whirled away and down the stairs with a panache that Gurney assumed was her default style.

He noted Angela watching Tabitha's departure with a mixture of anxiety and awe. He waited until she was well out of sight before commenting. "Interesting woman."

"Maybe I shouldn't have told her we might be interested in buying a doll."

"Why did you tell her that?"

"Well, I couldn't tell the truth, right? I couldn't say that I was meeting someone here to talk about my boyfriend's horrible death."

"Who *did* you say you were meeting?"

"You."

"Right. But who did you say I was?"

"Oh. I just said your name and that you were a friend—not that you were a detective or anything like that. I hope it's okay that I said you were a friend?"

"Of course. That was a good idea." He paused. "Was there a special reason you wanted to meet here?"

"I love it here."

He glanced around, trying to put himself in the mind of someone who'd feel at home in such an exotic, fantasy-based environment. "You love it because of all the dolls?"

"Of course. But mainly because this is where Stevie got me my all-time-favorite Barbie."

"Was it a special occasion?"

"No. He just did it. Which made it even more special, you know what I mean?"

"It sounds like he wanted to make you happy."

Her eyes started to well up.

He continued, "So this is a very special place for you. I can understand that."

"And I couldn't stay at my brother's. If Detective Hardwick found me there, then other people could. So my brother lent me some money and a car from one of his used car lots, and I came up here last night. My brother said if I was really afraid of being found, I should pay cash, because cops and other people can track you down through your credit card. Is that true, or is that just on TV?"

"It's true."

"Jeez, it's like someone's always watching you. But that's what I did—paid cash like my brother said. I'm staying in the same room that Stevie and I stayed in."

"Do you plan to stay here for a while?"

"Unless you think that's a bad idea?"

He couldn't think of a better one. And he was doubly glad he'd taken the precaution of leaving his geo-tracked car at the hotel. He reassured her that it might be the best place for her under the circumstances.

"When I'm here, I feel like Stevie is with me." She dabbed at her eyes, making a sad mess of her mascara.

Gurney moved on to a question that had been troubling him from the beginning. "I've been wondering, Angela, did it seem odd to you that Stevie was willing to travel all the way to Wolf Lake Lodge, just to see a hypnotist?"

She sniffled. "Kind of."

"There must be places closer to Floral Park that offer hypnosis sessions."

"I guess."

"Did you ever ask him what he thought was so special about Dr. Hammond?"

She hesitated. "I think maybe he was recommended."

"By who?"

Angela's eyes widened. She seemed to be searching for a way out of a room she'd entered by mistake. "I don't know."

Gurney proceeded gently. He softened his voice. "It's a scary situation for you, isn't it?"

She nodded silently, biting her lip.

"I'm sure Stevie wanted to keep you out of danger."

She continued nodding.

"Are you afraid now because of what happened to him?"

She closed her eyes. "Please don't talk about that."

"Okay. I understand." He waited until she opened her eyes before he continued. "I think you're being very brave."

"No, I'm not."

"Yes, you are. You're here. You're talking to me. You're trying to be honest."

She blinked on that last word. "It's because I'm afraid, not because I'm brave."

"You're trying to do the right thing. You're helping me figure out what really happened." He smiled gently. "Now, about that person who recommended Doctor Hammond—"

She interrupted, "I don't know who that was. I can't even say for sure that that's what the call was about." She hesitated, her eyes on the silver bell in the middle of the table.

The call? What call? Gurney sat back in his chair and waited. He had a feeling that she was trying to get up her courage to go on, and that patience would draw out the facts.

After much hesitation she continued. "All I know is that Stevie got a call from someone; and when I asked him who it was, he got all weirded out and said it was no one. But that was a crazy thing to say, because he was on the phone for a long time. I told him it couldn't be no one, why was he saying that to me? Then he got real quiet. But later that same night he started talking about a special doctor he'd heard about that could help him stop smoking."

"And you put two and two together and figured it was the person on the phone who told him about the doctor?"

"Yeah. That's right. It felt kind of obvious. So I asked him about it. I asked him to his face, was that who told you?"

"What did he say?"

"He just shook his head, sort of like he was denying it. Then he got like pissed off—like nervous pissed off, not really angry pissed off—and said whoever told him about the doctor, that wasn't something I needed to know, it wasn't important who told him, and I had no right to bug him about things like that."

"And after he said that, what did *you* say?"

"I said he should at least tell me who was on the phone."

"And what did he say?"

"At first, nothing. Stevie could get real quiet sometimes. But I kept asking him—because he was being so weird about the whole thing. Finally he said that the call came from someone he knew from way back, that the guy's name wouldn't mean anything to me, it was just someone he'd been at camp with when they were kids."

"Did he say anything else at all about him? Think hard."

"No, nothing." She was biting her lip more intensely now, and her eyes were fixed on the silver bell with what looked to Gurney like incipient panic.

"Take it easy, Angela, it's all right. I'm not going to let anything bad happen to you. Remember what we talked about on the phone?"

She blinked confusedly.

"Remember what I said about fear? Sometimes we have to do something we're afraid of doing—to protect ourselves from a bigger danger. I can see you're afraid to talk about this, but if you tell me everything you know, everything that Stevie said, it will make you safer. Because the more I know, the more I can protect you."

She closed her eyes again and seemed to force out the words. "Okay, so the thing is, it was totally weird. That evening, the way he talked about the phone call was like he was pretending it was nothing, a silly little call that didn't matter, I shouldn't ask about it because it wasn't worth talking about." She paused and took a deep breath.

"Then, at like five o'clock in the morning, like he'd been awake all night thinking about it, he woke me up. He asked me three times am I really awake and am I really listening. And then he told me, real serious like, that I should forget about the call. He said I should never mention it again and I should *never never never* tell anyone else about it—that if anyone else ever found out about it, we could both end up dead."

When she opened her eyes, tears came down her cheeks. "And I never did. I swear. I never said anything about it to anyone. Not one word."

CHAPTER 28

During his jog back to the hotel Gurney was analyzing his meeting with Angela Castro—trying to separate the facts that mattered from the distractions surrounding them.

He wasn't sure in which category to place Tabitha. There was something odd about that physically dominating woman showing such deference to the anxious little Angela.

Then there was the complicated persona projected by Angela herself, with her rigid hairdo and near-anorectic physique. She appeared frightened, childishly romantic, desperate to lose herself in a make-believe world. Yet she was pragmatic enough to have obtained a loan and a car from her brother.

And there was Steven Pardosa's dream, with its now-familiar elements—the wolf, the knife. And his contempt for Richard Hammond, expressed in emotionally charged words like "creepy" and "disgusting."

Gurney felt that the meeting's key element had been Angela's recounting of the mysterious phone call—the effect it had on Pardosa, its possible connection to Hammond, and the extreme demand for secrecy that it generated. Gurney wondered if the potentially fatal result of disclosure had been an explicit threat made by the caller or if that was a conclusion reached by Pardosa as he pondered the implications of the call in the wee hours of the night. The latter version seemed more likely given the way Angela told the story.

And there was something else, an element he couldn't put his finger on. He had a feeling that something Angela had told him wasn't quite right. He tried playing back their encounter in his mind. But the out-of-place piece remained elusive.

When he got back to the hotel, he found Madeleine and Hardwick at opposite ends of a three-cushion couch in the lobby. Madeleine's eyes were closed, but the erect position of her head suggested concentration rather than sleep. Hardwick was talking in a low voice on his phone.

Gurney sat in a chair across from them, separated from the couch by a low glass table.

Madeleine opened her eyes. "Did the young lady show up?"

"As promised."

"What was she like?"

"Odd little creature. Obsessed with dolls. Looks like one herself. Any problems while I was gone?"

She nodded in the direction of Hardwick, who sounded like he was wrapping up his conversation. "He'll tell you."

Hardwick ended his call, tapped a series of icons, scrolled through several graphic images, made some adjustments to the final one, and slid the phone across the table to Gurney. "Take a look at that."

On the screen was a photo of what appeared to be some sort of mechanical framework—which Gurney recognized as the front under-carriage of an automobile.

"My Outback?"

Hardwick nodded. "Zoom in."

Gurney made the motion, and the center portion of the photo expanded to fill the screen.

"Again," said Hardwick.

Gurney repeated the motion. Now the screen was filled by a single structural bar and a man's hand intruding from a shadowy corner of the photo—with the thumb next to what appeared to be the protruding top of a bolt.

"Again."

The final enlargement showed only the thumb and the protruding object. The scale reference of the thumb indicated the object was the size of a stack of four or five nickels.

Gurney shot Hardwick an incredulous glance, not quite able to believe what he suspected he was seeing on the screen.

"Believe it," said Hardwick.

Gurney examined the photo more carefully. "That's maybe one tenth the size of the smallest tracker I've ever seen."

"Agreed."

"You left it in place?"

"Yes. No point in announcing our discovery until we know what we're dealing with."

"The one near the back bumper is the same?"

"Not at all. That's where the situation gets interesting. The other one is a common off-the-shelf item. Not even worth taking a picture of. Same old shit used by BCI. Same old shit that anyone with a few hundred bucks can order from their favorite Internet spy store. So what the fuck's going on here? Any ideas, Sherlock?"

"I'd like to send the photo of the small one to Wigg."

"I already did."

"Good. She knows this stuff inside out. And her new position can only help."

"Agreed. Any thoughts in the meantime?"

"Sure, but that's all they are—thoughts. The two devices being that different from each other suggests that they were placed by separate entities."

Madeleine gave him a look. "*Entities?*"

"I don't know what else to call them at this point. We may be dealing with two agencies, two units within one agency, sanctioned or unsanctioned investigators, et cetera. The only thing that's clear is that there's a technology gap between them."

"In the meantime," said Hardwick, "you want to fill us in on your get-together with Pardosa's girlfriend?"

Gurney spent the next quarter hour recounting the details of the meeting.

Hardwick zeroed in on the phone call Pardosa had received. "Seems like that set the whole thing in motion, or at least set him in motion."

Gurney nodded his agreement. "We need to pursue the 'someone he knew from camp' angle. His parents ought to be able to tell us what camp he attended as a kid and when. They might even know the names of campers he was friendly with. You think you can look into that?"

Hardwick coughed and spit into his handkerchief. "Giant pain in the ass and probably a dead end. But what the fuck else am I—?" He was interrupted by his own phone.

He glanced at the screen, looked surprised. "Christ, that was fast. It's Wigg."

He thanked her for getting back to him, then listened for a minute or so before speaking up again. "Hold on a second, Robin. I've got Gurney here. Let us get to a more private spot so I can put this on speakerphone." He turned to Gurney and Madeleine. "How about we move outside to your car?"

Madeleine looked skeptical. "Our *bugged* car?"

Hardwick assured her that the scanner had detected no audio bugs, just the trackers. They headed out to the car, still parked under the overhang, and took the same seats they'd occupied earlier. Hardwick switched on his phone's speaker. "Okay, Robin. You want to repeat what you started saying a minute ago?"

"I was asking if you're certain the photographed device was gathering geopositioning information and then transmitting it."

Although Gurney hadn't seen Robin Wigg for well over a year, her distinctive contralto voice brought her vividly to mind. A wiry, athletic redhead with an androgynous look and manner, her age might have been anywhere from thirty to forty. She was smart, laconic, professional.

Hardwick answered her question. "According to the scanner you lent me, there's no doubt about it."

"Dave, the device is still affixed your car?"

"Correct. We don't want to remove it yet."

"You just want to know more about it?"

"Right. How advanced it is, et cetera."

"And what that might tell you about the people who placed it?"

"Right. I'm also wondering, have you ever seen anything like it before?"

The question generated a pregnant silence. Sensing that he'd crossed a subtle line, he added, "Whatever you're comfortable telling us would be helpful."

"How much detail do you want on the technical issues involved in this level of miniaturization?"

"Only as much as will help us understand what and who we're dealing with."

"Okay. What you have there is two generations beyond what most law enforcement agencies would consider state of the art. Ninety-nine percent of the surveillance operatives in the world wouldn't even know that such a device exists." She paused. "You getting the picture?"

"Jesus," said Gurney. "What's something like that doing attached to my car?"

"I'm not trying to sound dramatic, but it's pretty clear you've gotten yourself on the radar screen of an adversary with serious resources."

"How much would that little item cost?" asked Hardwick.

"A lot," said Wigg. "But the real barrier isn't money. It's access."

"We're talking about some kind of high-level spook shit?"

There was another silence, as pregnant as the first.

Gurney sensed that Wigg had told them all she was going to, and that pushing it further would be counterproductive. "Thanks, Robin. This has been very helpful. I appreciate it."

"Let me say one last thing. Be *extremely* careful. Anyone deploying that kind of technology is playing in a league way beyond what you're used to."

Wigg's parting comment led Gurney back to the question of who was responsible for BCI's fixation on Richard Hammond—a question he'd been relying on Hardwick to pursue. "Just wondering, Jack . . . any progress in discovering who upstairs might be guiding the way Fenton is handling the case?"

Hardwick leaned forward from his position in the backseat. "That's an amazingly timely question. Fenton's chain of command was the subject of that phone call I was in the middle of when you came into the hotel lobby."

"What did you find out?"

"That Gilbert Fenton's reporting line has become a tad obscure. He's been on 'special assignment' ever since the discovery of Hammond's connection to the apparent suicides."

"Is this 'special assignment' just outside his regular unit, or outside BCI entirely?"

"Nobody seems to know for sure what's going on, even the people who always know everything."

"But . . . ?"

"There's a rumor that he's been taken under the wing of the inter-agency liaison for national security issues."

Madeleine turned in her seat to face Hardwick. *"National security?* What does that mean?"

"Ever since 9/11 its meaning has been expanded to mean whatever the nasty little storm troopers in charge of it want it to mean."

"But in this case . . . ?"

"In this case, who the fuck knows what it means?"

Madeleine made a face. "Are you saying that someone concerned with national security thinks that Richard Hammond is some kind of terrorist? Or spy? That makes no sense!"

Hardwick let out a humorless laugh. "Very little of what they think or do makes sense—until you see it as a way of inflating their own importance. Then it all makes perfect sense."

She stared at him. "You're completely serious, aren't you?"

"Don't get me started. I've run into too many of these self-important, power-mad fuckheads with their self-serving bullshit. The so-called Patriot Act, Homeland Security, and all the corporate pigs sucking on that giant tit have done more damage to this country than Osama bin Laden could ever have dreamt of doing. Bottom line? America has fucked itself up, down, and sideways. Spooks are running the show now—with unlimited access to your personal life."

Gurney waited to let the momentum of Hardwick's anger abate. "Apart from Fenton's reporting-line change, were you able to find out anything else?"

Once again Hardwick hacked up a wad of phlegm and spat it into his soiled handkerchief. "I picked up a few tidbits that might be relevant. For example, prior to joining the state police Fenton did three tours of duty in the army—the final one in army intelligence."

Madeleine appeared incredulous. "Is this turning into a spy drama?"

Hardwick shrugged. "With its hypnotism and behavior-control angles, it's starting to look a lot like *The Manchurian Candidate.*"

"That was a movie," said Gurney, "not something that actually happened."

Hardwick came farther forward in his seat. "There's no reason to believe it couldn't happen. I'd bet anything there are devious little fuckers in the intelligence agencies right now trying to figure out how to exert that kind of mind control."

Gurney felt the need to reel the conversation back into a fact-based framework. "Fenton's tour in army intelligence might be connected to his new reporting line. But we just don't know enough about it yet. Any other discoveries?"

"That's it for now."

"Nothing else on the gay angle?"

"Like what?"

"I don't know. But it's come up in ways that are hard to ignore— Hammond's gay emergence therapy, Bowman's Cox's demonization of it. I'd like to know if there's any evidence of homosexuality or homophobia in the backgrounds of Wenzel and Balzac."

"Bobby Becker down in Palm Beach may be able to give us something on Wenzel. I have no direct line to Teaneck PD, so getting an answer about Balzac is a different deal. I know some people who know some people. But that route can take time. Any more questions?"

"Same ones I've asked before. Are there any red flags in Norris Landon's background? Or in Austen Steckle's—apart from his being a reformed lowlife, drug dealer, and embezzler? And I have one new question. Since Pardosa got a peculiar phone call that apparently directed him to Wolf Lake Lodge, I'm wondering if Wenzel and Balzac got similar calls."

Hardwick sighed. "Be easier to get those questions answered if we had badges to wave around. Full fucking weight of the law can be an advantage."

Gurney flashed a smile to hide his impatience. "I believe we agreed that the next item on your agenda would be a visit to Pardosa's parents?"

"Right. In the hope that they memorized the details of little Stevie's letters from summer camp, including the names of everyone he met there."

"If I didn't know you better, Jack, I'd think you resented the need for a little footwork."

"Fuck you, too, Sherlock."

CHAPTER 29

After Hardwick revved up the GTO and headed south on his long-shot mission to Floral Park, Gurney and Madeleine sat quietly for a while in the parked Outback.

"Are you okay?" he asked.

"No."

"What's wrong?"

"This whole thing is getting darker and more complicated." A gust of wind blew particles of sleet under the hotel portico and they bounced off the windshield. "We better get back to Wolf Lake before the weather gets worse."

He nodded, started the car, and headed onto Woodpecker road in the direction of the Northway. "Maddie, are you absolutely positive we shouldn't just put this situation behind us?"

"I'm positive. And it's not because I like Hammond. I don't. He's a spoiled genius with a sick dependency on his caretaker sister. Judging from that body-in-the-trunk story, he's also a little crazy. But I don't believe he's a mind-controlling murderer. And I know now that walking away from a mess doesn't solve it."

He had the sense that one of the tectonic plates of his life was shifting. Ever since he'd left the NYPD, Madeleine had been predictable in one respect. She'd consistently pressed him to turn his attention away from the world of murder and mayhem and focus on their new life in the country. Never before would she have advised him to stick with a homicide investigation.

The shift was radical and unsettling.

AFTER STOPPING AT A THAI RESTAURANT IN LAKE PLACID FOR A quiet lunch, for which neither of them had much appetite, they arrived back at Wolf Lake a little after four. The dusk was deepening and the temperature was dropping.

As they entered the lodge reception area, Austen Steckle was coming out of the Hearth Room. Past him, Gurney could see the tentative flames of a new fire.

Steckle's smile looked tense and his scalp looked sweaty.

"Hey, just the people I wanted to see." After a nod to Madeleine, he addressed Gurney. "I got you set up like you asked. But the thing is, Peyton's got plans for the evening. For tomorrow, too. And after that, it's hard to tell, you know what I mean?" He pushed back his cuff and glanced down at his gleaming Rolex. "So the thing is, if you want to talk to the man—it's pretty much got to be now."

Gurney looked at Madeleine.

She shrugged.

He looked back at Steckle. "Now is fine. Actually, fifteen minutes from now would be better. I need to go up to our room first. Does he expect me?"

"Yeah, more or less. I'll call and confirm it with him. You know the way, right?"

"I know the way."

"Conversations with Peyton can be difficult. Don't say I didn't warn you."

"I'm used to difficult conversations."

Steckle went into his office.

The Gurneys went up to the suite.

The main room lay mostly in darkness. The wind was whining at the balcony door. He switched on the ceiling fixture in the entry area, then crossed the room and switched on the lamp at the near end of the couch. He thought about lighting the kerosene lamp at the far end, the one with the wolf etching on its base, but decided against it. Better to keep that one in reserve in the event of another power failure.

He took the broad-spectrum surveillance scanner Hardwick had given him out of his jacket pocket and turned it on. The start-up screen mimicked a high-end smartphone.

Madeleine, still bundled up in her jacket, scarf, and ski hat, was watching him. "Are you going to check our room?"

He shot her a warning glance—a reminder that he didn't want anyone who might be bugging the space to discover that they were aware of it.

Following Hardwick's earlier instructions, he navigated through a series of setup options. Less than a minute later the device was fully operational, displaying a schematic diagram of the room he was standing in.

As he walked around, one red dot appeared on the screen, and then a second. Given the graphic delineation of the suite's walls on the screen, the location of each dot and the RF transmitter it represented was clear. The visual indication was supplemented by data on the distance of each transmitter from the nearest horizontal and vertical surfaces (in this case the room's floor and walls), its type, frequency, and signal strength. A line at the bottom of the screen summarized: "DETECTED DEVICES WITHIN SCAN AREA: 2 AUDIO, 0 VIDEO."

He made another circuit of the room to check the consistency of the data. He also wanted to see if any additional bugs might appear, but the scanner found only those two. He switched it off and slipped it back in his pocket. Turning to Madeleine, who'd been observing the process with concern, he pointed silently at the two locations.

The first was the life-size portrait of Warren Harding hanging over the suite's bar. The second was her cell phone on the end table by the couch.

Her expression shifted from concern to anger.

Gurney was eager to inspect the two locations more closely to confirm what the scanner had shown. And, since the two transmission patterns were very different, he was curious to see if the bugs represented the same gap in sophistication as the two trackers on his car. In order to conduct this inspection without passing along the telltale sounds of the transmitters being handled, he'd need to conceal what he was doing with some kind of noise.

He'd been in situations before where a bug needed to be surreptitiously examined. The basic rule was that the audio camouflage needed to be appropriate to the environment. A blender or food processor could mask just about any other sound, but there were very few situations in which they could be employed with any credibility. Ordinary conversation lacked the necessary volume. Percussive music, bursts of laughter, running water—any of those could work in the right setting, but none seemed quite right in the current circumstances.

He was surveying the room for inspiration when a solution was provided by Madeleine in the form of a startling sneeze.

After a moment's consideration he went to his duffle bag, pulled out a small notebook, and opened it to a blank page. He wrote as Madeleine watched: "Follow along with whatever I suggest. Respond naturally. Whenever I nod to you, make a sneezing sound or clear your throat or cough a few times. Start now by sniffling and coughing."

She sniffled loudly and cleared her throat.

He affected a worried tone. "Jesus, sweetheart, I was afraid of that, earlier in the car. That you were coming down with something. Or maybe that your allergies were kicking in."

"It could be an allergy. It feels like that."

"You have any idea what might be causing it?"

"I don't know. Something in the room? The car? The air? All I know is my nose and throat have that itchy feeling."

She spoke with such conviction he almost believed her. "Did you bring anything you can take for it?"

"No."

"Maybe we can find something tomorrow." He waved her closer to him as he approached the Harding portrait. He reached up over the row of bottles on the bar and gave her a nod as he gripped the frame.

When she burst into a fit of sneezing, he lifted the bottom of the frame up and away from the wall and checked under it, paying particular attention to the cable from which the portrait hung. He noted immediately that the ends of the cable were encased in tubular housings, either of which could easily accommodate a device as large as a disposable lighter. The cable itself would be an ideal disguise for an aerial. Nothing about the nature of the hiding place suggested anything but a standard, easily available audio bug. Under cover of another fit of sneezing, he eased the frame back against the wall.

Inspecting Madeleine's phone would be a trickier challenge.

He gestured for her to move toward the end of the couch by her phone. He attempted a worried tone. "Sweetheart, why don't you just settle down for a while and try to relax? Maybe cozy yourself up in a blanket?"

"I'm not really tired. It's just that scratchy, uncomfortable feeling in the back of my throat. You know, kind of raw? Maybe I'm getting a cold after all."

"At least have a seat. You can put your feet up on the hassock. Relaxing can't hurt."

"Okay, fine. It can't make me feel any worse."

She sounded cranky and authentic. In Gurney's experience, an irritated tone always made a faked conversation sound more real.

She sat on the couch, sniffling and repeatedly clearing her throat.

He went to the end table and placed his hand on her phone to check its temperature. It was quite cool, which was not what he'd expected.

The most common violation of a cell phone's integrity was accomplished through hacking into its software in a way that allowed the hacker to remotely manipulate the phone's functions—for example, to turn on its microphone and transmission capabilities, converting the device into an audio bug under the control of the hacker.

But this approach did leave concrete signs—the simplest being the generation of battery heat. Since the scanner had indicated an active transmission from the phone, Gurney had expected it to feel warm. The fact that it didn't meant something odd was happening.

Finding out more would require getting inside the phone itself.

He and Madeleine had the same make and model, so he took his out to make a preliminary assessment of the process. Studying the back panel, it appeared that the first item he'd need would be a very small screwdriver.

Fortunately, among the items that Madeleine packed automatically whenever they went away was a repair kit for her glasses—a kit that included a supply of the tiny screws that hold frames together and the tiny screwdriver needed to tighten them.

The screwdriver appeared to be about the right size.

In order to maintain an appropriate-sounding conversation, he said, "There have to be some differences in the head-cold feeling and the allergy feeling. Can you put your finger on which feeling you're closer to?"

She responded with a rambling, sniffly description of the discomforts associated with each problem. He busied himself meanwhile opening his own phone—so he'd have a visual reference with which to compare hers and note any anomalies.

Once he had his open, he set it on the end table and gingerly picked up Madeleine's. Giving her the signal for more sniffling and coughing, he removed the back panel, then laid the phone with its inner components exposed on the table next to his.

At first glance they appeared identical. As he looked closer, however, he noticed a difference between them in the corner where the microphone was located.

He got their camera out of his duffel bag and took close-up photos from several angles. Then, with Madeleine alternately coughing and complaining hoarsely about the raw feeling in her throat, he replaced the backs of both phones and tightened the screws.

"You might feel better if you took a nap?" he suggested.

"If I sleep now I won't be able to sleep tonight." She sounded so miserable he had to remind himself that it was a performance.

He checked the time. He was due for his appointment with Peyton in less than five minutes. He hurriedly addressed an email to Robin Wigg and attached his photos of the interior of Madeleine's phone. He included the make, model, and serial number; indicated the transmission frequency that had been detected; and added a brief message: "Scanner indicates active transmission. But there's no discernible battery heat or power drain. Possible implanted device in mic area? Need guidance." Then he hit "Send."

CHAPTER 30

A t the end of the lake road the security gate at the imposing Gall residence was already open. A guard, dimly visible in the failing light, pointed to a curving driveway that led toward a looming gray structure.

He followed the driveway several hundred feet to a paved floodlit area in front of a stone porch and a huge wooden door. He got out of the car into a whirling wind.

As he reached the door it swung open into a broad, high-ceilinged, polished-pine entry hall. The design was a grander version of the ubiquitous Adirondack style. The illumination came from a series of three enormous wagon-wheel chandeliers.

From where he stood in the doorway Gurney could see, high on the far wall of the entry hall, a framed portrait of an imperious man in a dark suit—perhaps, he thought, the ill-fated subject of the Gall legend. There was an off-putting chilliness in the cerebral forehead and wide-set eyes. An iron-willed jaw created the impression of a man dedicated to getting his own way.

"You come in, please," called a heavily accented female voice.

Gurney stepped inside.

The door swung slowly shut behind him, revealing to his startled gaze a blonde woman wearing nothing but the bottom half of a thong bikini. She was holding a small remote controller in her hand, perhaps to operate the massive door. Her body, too sumptuous to be entirely the product of nature, was dripping wet. Her gray eyes were as cold as any Gurney had ever seen.

"You follow me now." She turned her glistening, essentially naked back to him and led him along a corridor that branched off the entry hall. At the end of the corridor she opened a glass door into what was evidently an add-on to the original house.

From her attire, or lack of it, Gurney wouldn't have been surprised to find a room with an indoor pool. Instead, he was engulfed in the warm, fragrant air of a tropical conservatory. An undertone of rhythmic, primitive-sounding music created an atmosphere as far removed from the Adirondacks as one could imagine.

Thick leafy plants rose toward a high glass ceiling. Beds of ferns, bordered by mossy logs with orchids sprouting out of them, surrounded a circular area with a floor of polished mahogany. Curving paths of the same mahogany radiated out from it, disappearing behind beds of jungle foliage. Somewhere amid the lush leafy things Gurney could hear the gurgling of a fountain or a small waterfall.

In the center of the open area two high-backed rattan armchairs faced each other with a low rattan table between them. One of the chairs was occupied by a dark-haired man in a luxurious-looking white bathrobe.

The mostly naked woman approached the man and said something to him, the words lost to Gurney in the rhythmic background music.

Responding to her with a loose smile, the man slid his hand slowly between her legs.

Gurney wondered if he was about to witness a live sex show. But a moment later the woman half-laughed, half-purred at something the man said and casually walked away on one of the mahogany paths through the planting beds. Just before she disappeared into the mini jungle she glanced back at Gurney, the pink tip of her tongue moving between her full lips, an image as reptilian as it was seductive.

Once she was out of sight, the man in the bathrobe waved Gurney toward the empty rattan chair. "Have a seat. Have a drink." The voice was a rich baritone, the articulation slow and lazy, as if the man might be drunk or sedated. He pointed invitingly toward the coffee table, on which Gurney noted a bottle of Grey Goose vodka, an ice bucket, and two glasses.

Gurney remained standing where he was. "Mr. Gall?"

The man smiled slowly, then laughed. "Austen told me that a detective by the name of Gurney wanted to talk to me. He said you were Jane Hammond's private dick."

"That's one way of putting it."

"So your job is to prove that her fucking brother didn't kill my fucking brother?"

"Not really."

"If that's your secret mission here, you don't have to deny it, because I don't give a flying fuck one way or the other. Sit down and have a drink."

Gurney accepted the seat offer, which put him close enough now to discern in the languorous, self-indulgent face across from him the same underlying bone structure he'd noted in the fiercely determined face in the entry-hall portrait. It confirmed both the power and the limitations of shared genes.

He sat back in his chair and looked around the big glass-enclosed space. Outside it was dark now, and the interior light—coming from upward-angled halogen spotlights secreted among the plantings—cast queer shadows everywhere. When his gaze reached Peyton Gall, he found the man's dark eyes fixed on him.

Gurney leaned forward. "I'll tell you why I'm here. I want to find out why four people died after seeing Richard Hammond."

"You have doubts about the official version?" Gall said this in an arch tone, as if ridiculing a cliché.

"Of course I have doubts about it. Don't you?"

Gall yawned, refilled his glass with vodka, and took a slow sip. Then he held the glass in front of his face, peering over the top of it. "So you don't think the witch doctor did it?"

"If you mean Dr. Hammond, no, I don't—at least not in any way suggested by the police hypothesis. And frankly, Mr. Gall, you don't seem to think so, either."

Gall was squinting over the top of his glass at Gurney with one eye closed, creating the impression of a man lining up a rifle sight. "Call me Peyton. My sainted brother was *Mister* Gall. I have no aspiration to assume that mantle."

His tone struck Gurney as haughty, sour, and ridiculous. It was the tone of a selfish, imperious drunk—a dangerous child in the body of an adult. This was not a man he'd choose to be in the same room with if he could help it, but there were questions that needed to be asked.

"Tell me something, Peyton. If Richard Hammond wasn't responsible for Ethan's death, who do you think was?"

Gall lowered his vodka glass a few inches and studied it as if it might contain a list of suspects. "I'd advise you to focus on the people who knew him well."

"Why?"

"Because to know Ethan was to hate him."

Despite the theatrical nature of the statement, Gurney sensed real feeling behind it. "What was the most hateful thing about him?"

Anger seemed to cut through Gall's alcoholic fog. "The illusion he created."

"He wasn't what he seemed to be?"

Gall let out a short, bitter laugh. "At a distance, he was fuck-ing godlike. Up close, not so much. So goddamn full of himself in the worst way—the bursting-with-virtue way, the I-know-best way. Fucking control-freak bastard!"

"It must have pissed you off that he changed the terms of his will at your expense."

He was silent for a long moment. "Is that what this is about?"

"Meaning?"

"Meaning, is that what this conversation is about? You thinking that the police have it all wrong . . . that Richard, the faggot hypnotist, is innocent . . . and that I made those fucking people kill themselves? Is that what the fuck you think?"

"I don't think you made anyone kill themselves. That seems impossible."

"Then what the fuck are you getting at?"

"I was wondering if Ethan changed his will just to make you angry."

"Of course he did. Saint Ethan was a puritanical prick who hated the way I enjoyed my life and was always looking for ways to punish me. 'Do what I say, or you'll end up with nothing. Do what I say, or I'll take it all away. Do what I say or I'll give your inheritance to the first little creep who comes along.' Fucking control-freak bastard scumbag! Who put him in charge of the world?"

Gurney nodded. "Life should be easier for you now that he's gone."

Gall smiled. "Yes."

"Even with the change in his will, you still end up with a ton of money. And if the police can prove Hammond was involved in Ethan's death, the bequest to him will revert to you. You'd get fifty-eight million dollars altogether."

Gall yawned for the second time.

Yawning, Gurney knew, was an ambiguous bit of body language, produced as often by anxiety as by boredom. He wondered which feeling was at play. "You have any plans for all that money?"

"Plans bore me. Money bores me. Money has to be watched, managed, massaged. It has to be invested, balanced, leveraged. You have to think about it, talk about it, worry about it. It's a gigantic bore. Life's too fucking short for all that crap. All that *planning*."

"Thank God for Austen, eh?"

"Absolutely. Austen's a boring little fucker himself, but he's a natural planner. Pays attention to money. Takes good care of money. So, yeah, thank God for boring little fuckers like Austen."

"You plan to keep him on, then, managing the Gall assets?"

"Why not? He can watch the bottom line, while I live the way I want to live." He winked at Gurney. A lazy, sly, lascivious wink. "That way everybody gets to be happy."

"Except for the four dead people."

"That's your department, Detective. Austen invests the Gall millions. I fuck the world's most beautiful women. You spend your life worrying about dead people." He winked again. "Everybody's got a specialty. Makes the world go round."

As if on cue, the wet blonde reappeared. The only noticeable difference was that now she was entirely naked.

CHAPTER 31

Gurney found Madeleine in the Hearth Room in an armchair by the fire. Her eyes were closed, but she opened them as he settled into the chair next to hers.

"Your meeting go well?"

"I can't decide whether Peyton is the world's most self-absorbed brat, or just pretending to be."

"Why would he do that?"

"I'm not sure. But I got the impression of someone playing a role in a movie."

"A man who can do whatever he wants?"

"Whatever and whenever."

"Was he alone?"

"Not exactly."

She gazed into the fire. "So what did you learn?"

"That he hated Ethan. That he considered him an intolerable control freak. That he couldn't care less how he died or who might have killed him. That money bores him. That he relies totally on Steckle to deal with the tiresome burden of the Gall fortune. And that all he wants to do with his life is fuck his brains out with a breast-enhanced hooker in a hothouse."

"But you're not sure if you believe him?"

"I don't know if he's as undisciplined as he lets on—a hedonistic leaf in the wind. I think there's a side to him I'm not seeing."

"So . . . what do you do next?"

"Next? We need to check out Hammond's place. Jack thinks it's bugged. He thinks that's how Fenton discovered his involvement. But he wants to be sure."

"You mean now?"

He glanced at his watch. "Good a time as any, unless you want me to do something about getting us some dinner first."

"I'm not hungry." She hesitated. "But I want to come with you. Is that a problem?"

"Not at all." He took out his phone and brought up Jane's cell number.

TWENTY MINUTES LATER HE AND MADELEINE WERE STANDING IN the foyer of the chalet, brushing ice pellets off their clothes.

Wide-eyed with worry, Jane took their jackets and hats and hung them on coat hooks by the door. "Is something wrong?"

"I just want to give you a progress report and ask a few questions, if that's okay."

They followed her into the chalet's main living area, where Richard was tending a modest fire. His expression was as bland as Jane's was apprehensive.

"Sorry to intrude with so little notice," said Gurney, "but I thought it would be useful to bring you up to date."

With a notable lack of enthusiasm, he motioned Gurney and Madeleine toward the couch. When they were seated, he and Jane took chairs opposite them. On the table next to Hammond's chair were two laptop computers, both open.

"So," said Hammond. His unblinking aquamarine eyes were as unsettling as ever.

Gurney gestured toward the computers. "I hope we're not interrupting anything."

"Just a bit of voodoo."

"Beg pardon?"

"On your last visit you questioned my interest in the curses employed by African witch doctors. It reminded me of my last paper on the subject, one I never completed. I decided to finish it now. With my new reputation for magical murder, interest should be high."

"I'd love to hear more about it," said Gurney, "assuming it's not too academic."

"It's a practical description of how the power of a curse can be broken. The key is understanding how the voodoo curse works—how it brings about the victim's death."

Madeleine raised an eyebrow. "Are you saying those curses actually kill people?"

"Yes. In fact, the voodoo curse may be the world's most elegant murder weapon."

"How does it work?" asked Gurney.

"It begins with belief. You grow up in a society where everyone believes the witch doctor has extraordinary powers. You're told that his curses are fatal, and you hear stories that prove it.

"You trust the people who tell you these stories. And eventually you see the proof for yourself. You see a man who has been cursed. You see him wither and die."

Madeleine looked frightened. "But how does that happen?"

"It happens because the victim believes it's happening."

"I don't understand."

"It's not that complicated. Our minds search constantly for cause-and-effect relationships. It's necessary for survival. But sometimes we get it wrong. The man who knows he has been cursed, who believes in the power of the curse, is terrified because he believes the curse has doomed him. In his terror, his appetite decreases. He begins to lose weight. He sees the loss of weight as proof that the process of dying has begun. His terror increases. He loses more weight, gradually weakens, becomes physically ill. This illness—the product of his own fear—he sees as the result of the witch doctor's curse. The more terrified he becomes, the worse the symptoms become that feed his terror. In time, this downward spiral kills him. He dies because he believes he is dying. And his eventual death solidifies the community's belief in the power of the curse."

"I'm impressed," said Gurney. "The killer never touches the victim, the murder mechanism is psychological, and death would essentially be self-inflicted."

"Yes."

"Rather like Fenton's theory of the four suicides."

"Yes."

That led to a fraught silence, broken by Madeleine. "Didn't you start by saying there was a way to break the power of the curse?"

"Yes, but it isn't the way you might imagine. A scientifically minded person might try to persuade the victim that voodoo is nonsense, that it has no real power. The problem with that approach is that it usually fails, and the victim dies."

"Why?" asked Madeleine.

"It underestimates the power of belief. Whenever they collide, facts are no match for beliefs. We may think our beliefs are based on facts, but the truth is that the facts we embrace are based on our beliefs. The great conceit of the rational mind is that facts are ultimately persuasive. But that's a fantasy. People don't die to defend the facts, they die to defend their beliefs."

"So what's the answer? If you see the victim of a curse suffering, actually withering away, what do you do?"

He regarded her for a moment with those unearthly eyes. "The trick is to accept the power, not challenge it."

"Accept it . . . how?"

"When I was in Africa I was once asked to speak to a man who'd been cursed by the local witch doctor and who was, predictably, wasting away. A Western psychiatrist had taken the logical debunking approach, with no positive effect. I took a different route into the man's mind. To make a long story short, I told him that the local witch doctor had in the past so misused the tremendous power of voodoo for his own enrichment that the spirits had taken the power away from him. I explained that to maintain his position, to keep the tribe from realizing he'd been stripped of his magic, the witch doctor had resorted to poisoning his victims. I invented a full narrative, including the details of a recent victim's death. I described a credible process for the poisoning—exactly how it was done, how its symptoms imitated the effects of a legitimate curse. As I was speaking I could see the specifics of the new narrative taking root in his mind. In the end, it worked. It worked because the man could accept it without abandoning his fundamental belief in the power of voodoo."

Madeleine appeared to be struggling with the implications of this.

Gurney asked, "What happened to the witch doctor?"

"Shortly after the rumor spread that he'd lost his mojo, a deadly snake ended up in his hammock." He shrugged. "Witch doctors make so many enemies. And there are so many perils in Africa. So many avenues of revenge."

"Do you feel responsible for his death?"

"Not as responsible as I feel for saving the life of the man he was trying to kill."

As Gurney mulled over the story, he was struck by aspects of Hammond's nature he hadn't seen before—formidability, pragmatic cleverness, willingness to get his hands dirty in a dangerous situation. As he was considering ways to probe these qualities further, his phone rang.

He glanced at the screen. The text message, from a number he didn't recognize, was terse, disquieting, and, for a moment, incomprehensible.

"RESTRICTED TECHNOLOGY. IMMEDIATE RETREAT ADVISED. W."

Then he realized it was a response to the photos he'd sent Wigg of the inside of Madeleine's phone. She was telling him, once again, that the nature of the device indicated the involvement of people he shouldn't be messing with.

He wanted to talk to her, was tempted to call her, but was held back by the message's cryptic tone. However, it occurred to him that he could use the arrival of the message as a natural cover for the bug-scanning procedure that was the real purpose of his visit to the chalet.

He stood up from the couch, looking embarrassed. "Sorry, but something's been dropped in my lap that I need to deal with." As he stepped away, he exchanged his phone for the look-alike scanner in his pocket. He walked slowly toward a far corner of the room, as if for privacy. He turned on the scanner, made his way through the setup steps, and began meandering around the room, his eyes on the screen, as if waiting for an elusive Internet connection.

Jane rose from her chair, meanwhile, to take care of something in the kitchen.

Gurney saw the room's outline take shape on the screen, followed shortly by the appearance of three red dots—dots representing three distinct transmission sources, each operating at its own frequency.

At the same time, he couldn't help overhearing Madeleine's conversation with Hammond.

"So you're saying that you saved the victim's life by making up a story?"

"By giving him an alternative way of understanding his pain."

"But it was a lie."

"And that bothers you? Perhaps you're too much of an idealist."

"Because I value the truth?"

"Perhaps you value it too highly."

"What's the alternative? Believing lies?"

"If I told that obsessed man the truth—that voodoo has no inherent power, that it's nothing but a trick of the mind that suckers the victim into a slow suicide—he wouldn't have believed me. Given his background and culture, he *couldn't* have believed me. He'd have dismissed my truth as heretical nonsense. And he'd have died as a result."

"So the truth is irrelevant?"

"It's not irrelevant. But it's not the most important thing. At best, it helps us function. At worst, it devastates us." Hammond, still in his armchair by the fire, leaned toward Madeleine. "Truth is overrated. What we really need is a way of seeing things that makes life livable."

There was a prolonged silence. When Madeleine eventually spoke, her words remained challenging, but the combative edge was gone from her tone. "Is that what you do as a therapist? Come up with credible falsehoods your clients can live with?"

"Credible *stories*. Ways of understanding the events in their lives, particularly traumatic events. Isn't a narrative that supports a happier life better than a truth you can't live with?"

After another silence she replied softly, "You may be right."

With part of his brain Gurney was struggling to digest what Hammond had said and Madeleine's reaction to it, which he found bewilderingly upsetting. With the other part he was trying to focus on the data the scanner was displaying. That latter effort was interrupted by Hammond's next comment.

"Perhaps there's an event in your own life that you've never managed to integrate into a narrative you can live comfortably with. That's not an uncommon source of pain. But it's a pain that can be relieved."

In the silence that followed, Gurney forced his attention back to the scanner. He made another loose circuit of the space to pinpoint the exact locations of the bugs. He found that they had all been placed more or less centrally—within range of the places where conversations were most likely to occur: the seating area around the hearth, the dining table, and a desk with a landline phone.

The scanner's red dot pattern showed one bug in the base structure of a wooden planter full of philodendrons. It located another, with a similar frequency signature, less than ten feet from the first, in a rustic chandelier. But it was the third that got Gurney's attention. With a transmission frequency in the same super-high range as the micro device in Madeleine's phone, it seemed to be situated inside the delicate finial of an antique floor lamp.

He turned off the scanner and slipped it back in his pocket. He stepped closer to the lamp to examine the little finial, which appeared to have been carved from an opaque gemstone into the shape of a minuscule vase. It was deep green, flecked with irregular bits of bright crimson.

Jane returned from the kitchen. "Were you able to deal with whatever you had to deal with?"

Gurney moved away from the lamp. "That's all taken care of. Sorry about the interruption. I do need to bring you up to date on a few things. And ask you a few questions."

She glanced at her brother. "Did you hear that, Richard?"

He was leaning back in his chair, fingers steepled under his chin. He turned his attention, reluctantly it seemed, from Madeleine to Gurney. "I'm listening."

With active audio surveillance now a certainty, Gurney was calculating how much he should say. One thing was clear—he didn't want to compromise Angela Castro's safety. The rest he'd have to play by ear. It occurred to him that it might be interesting to get Hammond's perspective on the surveillance issue itself.

"Has it ever crossed your mind that your house or car might be bugged?"

Hammond shrugged. "I'd be shocked if they weren't."

"Have you taken any precautions?"

"No. I have nothing to hide."

"Okay. New topic. How crazy is Peyton Gall?"

Hammond produced a fleeting smile. "You've made his acquaintance?"

"Earlier this evening. In his greenhouse. In the company of a naked woman."

"Only one?"

"That sort of thing is common?"

"Oh, yes, quite routine."

"So he wasn't just putting on an act for my benefit?"

"You mean, was he pretending to be a fool so you'd take him off your list of suspects?"

"Something like that."

"I'd say that what you saw is what he is."

"He claimed that money bores him, that he has no interest in it. Truth or bullshit?"

"Truth, to the extent that managing money requires a level of attention and patience he simply doesn't have. Bullshit, to the extent that he has an enormous interest in what it can buy."

"So Peyton gets the coke and hookers, and Austen gets the investment reports?"

"Something like that."

"Okay, on to another subject. I was told by a reliable source that at least one of the victims received a strange phone call a couple of weeks before coming up to Wolf Lake Lodge. The caller may have been advising him to see you."

"What was 'strange' about it?"

"He got the impression he was supposed to keep the call a secret—that he might even be killed if he talked about it."

Hammond looked bewildered. "Killed? If he talked about getting a recommendation to see me?"

"So he said at the time. Does that mean anything to you?"

"Nothing at all."

"Did you ever go to summer camp?"

"What?"

"Summer camp. Did you ever go to one? As a kid, as a counselor? In any capacity at all?"

"No. Why do you ask?"

"It's a long story. But if you've never been to camp, it's irrelevant."

"If you say so." His tone conveyed the petulance of a man accustomed to being the one who decided what was relevant. "Any more questions?"

"Just a comment. I think the case is beginning to open up. I can't say the end is in sight, but I don't think it will look like the picture being painted by Gil Fenton."

Jane, who'd been silently observing the conversation, spoke up. "Thank you! I've never had any doubt about your ability to uncover the truth, but it's good to hear you say it."

"I have a question." Madeleine was addressing Hammond in a tone clearly arising from a private train of thought. "It's about a memory I have of something that happened long ago, not far from here. I thought that coming here would help me deal with it. But it's not working. In fact, it's gotten worse. The memory is out of its box. But I don't know what to do with it. I can't get rid of it. And I can't tolerate it. I don't know what to do."

"And your question is . . . ?" Hammond was smiling, his voice soft.

"Have you ever helped someone with a problem like this?"

"As I started to explain before, I often help people come to terms with past events."

"And you think you could help me?"

Gurney was barely able to restrain an impulse to interrupt, to derail her request.

But he said nothing, fearing the rawness of his emotion. He stood there in stony silence, astounded at her desire to bare her soul to a man who might be implicated in four murders.

Madeleine and Hammond arranged to meet at the chalet at 9:00 AM the following day, and some minutes later they all said their good-nights. Hammond wandered over to the hearth, picked up a poker, and began stirring the crumbling coals. Jane walked with Gurney and Madeleine out onto the chalet's deck-like porch.

The sleet had stopped, but the air was frigid.

"Are you all right?"

So caught up was Gurney in his own rattled thoughts, it took a few seconds for him to realize Jane's question was directed to him.

"Oh . . . yes . . . fine."

Noting disbelief in her eyes, but unwilling to discuss what was really bothering him, Madeleine's proposed meeting with Richard, he searched for another explanation.

"This may seem like a strange question, Jane, but I was intrigued by that green finial on one of your lamps. Do you know the one I mean?"

"The bloodstone? Green with red specks?"

"Yes. That one. Did it come with the lamp, or was it something special you got somewhere else?"

"It was always part of the lamp, as far as I know. Some things here are Richard's, but the lamps and furniture belong to the lodge. Do you have a reason for asking?"

"I've never seen anything quite like it."

"It *is* unusual." She hesitated. "It's funny you should ask about that particular item."

"Why?"

"About a year ago it disappeared. A couple of days later it reappeared."

"You never discovered the reason?"

"No. I asked around, of course. The maintenance people, the cleaning people, no one knew anything. I even mentioned it to Austen. No one had any idea how or why something like that could happen." She looked at Gurney expectantly, as if he might offer a solution.

When he said nothing, she went on. "And now it's happened again."

"What do you mean?"

"Just a month or so ago. I noticed because it's my favorite lamp. I use it every night."

"The same thing happened? The same way?"

"Yes. I noticed one evening it was gone. Two days later it was back."

"This was around the time of the first suicide?"

"Before any of that. Before our world turned upside down."

"You're sure about the timing? That it was *before* the date of the first suicide?"

"Absolutely sure."

"Around the beginning of November, then?"

"Yes."

"And when it happened the first time? You said it was about a year ago. Also at the beginning of November?"

"Yes. It must have been. I remember Austen making some silly joke about poltergeists being stirred up by Halloween."

CHAPTER 32

During their drive back to the lodge, instead of immediately challenging her plan to meet with Hammond, Gurney tried to focus on why it bothered him so much.

Perhaps it was his sense that she was changing. Or the more disturbing possibility that she wasn't changing at all—that the Madeleine in his brain was a fiction, and he was only now seeing the real person. He'd imagined her to be a tower of strength and good judgment. Now she seemed frightened and erratic, willing to put her trust in a therapist who might be a murderer.

As he was parking the Outback under the lodge portico, his bleak musings were cut short by the ringing of his phone.

Jack Hardwick started speaking the instant Gurney picked up.

"Got a hot lead for you—a man you need to meet tomorrow morning. Just down the road in Otterville."

It took Gurney a moment to refocus. "Otterville's a good three hours 'down the road' from here. Who's this man and why does he matter?"

"The man is Moe Blumberg. Former owner and director of Camp Brightwater, which no longer exists. He converted it into some kind of bungalow colony, which he named Brightwater Cabins. But back when it was Camp Brightwater, it was the camp Steven Pardosa attended. Moe's leaving tomorrow afternoon for Israel, where he spends his winters, so it's got to be tomorrow morning, unless you want to track him down in Tel Aviv."

"You don't want to follow up on it yourself?"

"I'd do it with pleasure—but tomorrow morning I'll be down in Teaneck, New Jersey. Friend of a friend set me up with the detective who caught the Leo Balzac suicide case. Man won't talk to me on the phone, so I gotta make the trip. I figure I do him, you do Moe. Fair's fair. What do you say, Sherlock?"

Before he could answer, his attention was diverted by Madeleine getting out of the car.

"I'm freezing," she said. "I'm going inside."

The air coming into the car through the open door was bitterly cold.

She closed the door and walked quickly into the lodge.

Her tone of voice brought back all the negative thoughts he'd been stewing in before Hardwick's call. He got back on the phone and tried to force his mind to the matter at hand. "Have you actually spoken to this Blumberg guy?"

"Briefly. But first I spoke to the Pardosas. Face-to-face in Floral Park. Lot of grief. Lot of fantasy. They're telling themselves that their Steven was finally turning things around. Embarking on a new life. Big prospects for the future. Can't fathom that he'd kill himself. So much to look forward to. Et cetera. I think telling me that was their way of making it seem true. You keep saying something, it starts to sound real. They kept talking, and I kept nodding and shaking my head sadly and smiling at the right moments—all that empathic bullshit."

"Jesus, Jack . . ."

"Anyway, the more I nodded the more they talked. The whole thing took a funny turn, though, when I asked if Steven had ever gone away to summer camp. Conversation got chilly. Obviously not their favorite topic. Seems he only went one year. Thirteen years ago. Some weird shit happened that summer, which they refused to discuss. But with a little nudging—actually, more than a little—they gave me Moe Blumberg's phone number and address, which turned out to be his bungalow colony, which used to be his camp. You following?"

"I'm trying. Keep talking."

"So I called Blumberg, who sounds kinda geriatric on the phone. I told him we were investigating the recent death of one of his former campers and needed some information about the summer he spent at Brightwater. He told me a big fire there a long time ago destroyed the office and all their records—handwritten on index cards in shoeboxes. But when I mentioned the specific year—thirteen years ago—that Steve was there, I got a funny reaction from him, like I got from Stevie's parents. Didn't want to talk about anyone or anything connected with that summer—at least not on the phone. Had to be face-to-face. So I made an appointment for you. Eleven AM. Tomorrow morning. Man leaves at two sharp for JFK."

"What did you tell him about me?"

"That you're a New York detective working on the case."

"A *private* New York detective?"

"I may not have emphasized that specific adjective."

"You told him I'm NYPD?"

"I believe I mentioned that connection."

"In the present or past tense?"

"That's a tough one. Easy to get confused about tenses. Like Bill Clinton said, it all depends on what the meaning of 'is' is."

"If he asks about it, I'm not going to lie to him."

"Naturally. The truth is our friend."

Gurney sighed. "You want to give me his address?"

"Twenty-seven ninety-nine Brightwater Lane, Otterville." He paused, presumably to give Gurney time to write it down, before switching gears. "Let me ask you something. You pretty sure you're speaking from a bug-free environment?"

"Pretty sure, apart from the position trackers. I'm in my car, and my phone is clean, far as I can tell. But Hammond's chalet is another story."

"What did you find?"

"Three audio transmitters."

"No shit! I knew it!"

Taking out the scanner and retrieving the archived scan of the chalet, Gurney gave Hardwick the location, frequency, and signal-strength data that had been gathered. He then recounted Jane's peculiar story regarding the consecutive November disappearances and reappearances of the bloodstone finial that contained one of the bugs.

"Holy fuck." Hardwick whistled softly and zeroed in on the timing issue. "Someone was bugging Hammond at least a year *before* the shit hit the fan? Why?"

"That's an interesting question. If we can answer it, we'll be halfway home."

Gurney ended the call, locked the car, and headed into the lodge.

He spotted Madeleine hunkered down by the fire in the Hearth Room.

Austen Steckle came out of his office. "Mr. Gurney, I need to talk to you." He was glancing around, almost furtively, as if to emphasize the sensitivity of the subject matter. His shaved head was again glistening with sweat.

"Fenton came by looking for you. I gotta say, he didn't look happy. In fact, he looked seriously pissed off. More pissed off than you'd want a man in his position to be. Just letting you know."

"Did he say what his problem was?"

"He was throwing legal terms around. 'Obstruction of justice' was one of them. 'Interfering in the investigation of a felony' was another one. Boil it down, I got the feeling he expected you to be gone by now, and he's pissed off at you still being here. All I'm doing is passing that along. Word to the wise. Man's got the power to throw a hornet's nest at you."

Gurney blinked, almost laughed, at the image. "I appreciate the heads-up. By the way, did Peyton fill you in on our little get-together?"

"Yeah, little while ago. He said it was all cool. No problems. That true?"

Gurney shrugged. "I guess everything is relative. Do you happen to know who the naked woman with him might be?"

Steckle grinned. "Which naked woman? Peyton's got a lot of naked women."

"Then I guess it doesn't matter much."

It was Steckle's turn to shrug. "So, basically, you're saying your interview went okay?"

"I suppose you could say that."

"So, you got any idea when you folks are moving on? When Fenton comes back, I'd like to know what to tell him."

"Soon. Tell him we'll be moving on soon."

They held each other's gaze for a moment. Then Steckle nodded, turned away, and went back to his office.

Gurney went to join Madeleine in the Hearth Room.

He took the chair next to hers, facing the fire. He closed his eyes, searching for the right way to raise the issue that was gnawing at him— when she raised it herself.

"Do you really think it's a bad idea for me to talk to Richard?"

"I certainly think it's a questionable idea."

"At the chalet you looked like you were about to explode."

"To be honest, I was shocked. Your desire to share something intensely private with someone in his situation baffles me. Isn't this the same guy you were furious at yesterday? The guy you told me was a liar because he claimed to have no insight into himself? The guy you told me was trying to manipulate us, make fools of us?"

Madeleine sighed. "I was angry because he hit a raw nerve. I was actually the one who had no insight. I was the one who thought the past had been dealt with. He wasn't the dishonest one, I was." She uttered an ironic little laugh. "Nothing leaves you more vulnerable to your past than the illusion that you've dealt with it."

It struck him that there was a great deal of truth in that. But he still didn't think that her plan to discuss her past with Hammond was a good idea.

As if in response to this silent objection, she looked pleadingly into his eyes. "I have to *do* something. *Now*. Coming here has brought up memories. I can't get them out of my mind."

He wanted to know exactly what memories she was talking about. But he was afraid to ask. He was afraid he might discover that the part of Madeleine he'd never known was the part that mattered the most.

She turned toward him, her hands gripping the padded leather arm of her chair. "If I don't do something I'll fall apart. I can feel it. Please understand. I have no other options. At least seeing Hammond tomorrow morning is *something*."

CHAPTER 33

There was a ringing sound in his dream. The sound morphed into an image of something glittering. The glittering blue-green eyes of Richard Hammond. Glittering. Ringing.

"David, it's your phone." Madeleine was standing next to the bed in a white terry-cloth robe. Her hair was wet. She was extending the phone toward him.

He took it, blinked to focus his vision, saw that the ID had been blocked. The time on the phone was 6:46 AM. He pushed himself up into a sitting position on the side of the bed.

"Gurney here."

"Sorry to wake you, David. It's Robin Wigg."

"No problem. I should have been up already."

"Ever since I sent you that text, I've been debating the need for a follow-up call."

"I gathered from the wording that it's a sensitive area."

"An understatement. By the way, I'm calling unofficially, from out of the office. I'll get to the point. First, regarding that photo of an open phone. The transmitter inserted in the place of the normal microphone is a highly restricted device. I don't mean restricted to the feds in general. I mean restricted to the inner sanctum of national security. Are you hearing what I'm telling you?"

"That I'm on the radar of some dangerous people?"

"Another understatement. Let me be clear, and brief. What's generally known about the FBI, CIA, NSA, and military intelligence operations doesn't scratch the surface of what's really happening. The kind of people who are taking an interest in you have access to records of every website you've ever visited, every phone number you've ever called, every purchase you've ever made with a credit card, every book you've taken out of a library. Unless you've disabled your cell phone GPS, they know every route you've ever driven, every address you've ever stopped at, every friend, every doctor, every lawyer, every therapist. And that's just for starters. If they decide that you might impede an operation that has a national security dimension, they can record your phone calls, bug your home. They can review your bank statements, your tax returns, your high school and college records, your medical history. And they can make you disappear for extended interrogations with no statutory limits, simply by concocting a link between you and some terrorist organization that may not even exist. 'Protecting the homeland' has become a blank check in the hands of some very ruthless people. Any questions?"

"About a hundred. But I don't think I want to hear the answers."

"Good luck, David. And be very, very careful."

He thanked her for taking the personal risk involved in speaking to him. But she'd already ended the call.

Given the picture she'd painted of a shadowy governmental nemesis, it would be easy to construct paranoid scenarios. On the other hand, given the nature of the government's massive intrusion into private lives, could any scenario really be dismissed as paranoid? The advances in data gathering and manipulation were racing far ahead of any ethical consensus regarding their use. Putting such powerful tools in the hands of ambitious, self-righteous bureaucrats was like giving weapons of mass destruction to class bullies.

He realized this ongoing societal train wreck was beyond his control. But he did have control over where to invest his time and effort. Maintaining his focus—or dividing it appropriately between the case issues and Madeleine's issues—would be his main challenge. He could sometimes forget, in his immersion in an investigation, that he was someone's husband.

"Shouldn't you be getting ready to leave?" Madeleine had come back into the bedroom alcove, carrying her iPad, with a loud piece of music playing on it—one of the surveillance-defeating techniques he'd suggested.

"I'll be okay," he said, getting up from the bed. "If I'm out by eight, I can make it to Otterville by eleven. By the way, how were you planning to get to Hammond's place?"

"I could take one of the lodge Jeeps, or even walk, so long as it's not sleeting or snowing. It's less than a mile."

"You're supposed to be there at nine?"

"Richard said I could come earlier and have breakfast with them. Actually, he said we both could come, but I didn't think you'd want to."

The best response he could muster was a tight-lipped nod. He muttered something about showering and shaving, went into the bathroom, and closed the door.

He knew the anger he felt was absurd. But he couldn't deny its reality.

As he was preparing to depart for Otterville, he explained to Madeleine where the scanner had pinpointed the three audio bugs in the chalet, and where she should try to sit with Hammond to limit their effectiveness.

"Keep your back to those transmitter locations, and speak as softly as you can. You could even bring your iPad and have that music playing. You could tell Hammond it helps you relax."

She extended her arms toward him, her eyes filling with tears. She held him tightly—desperately, it seemed.

"What is it?" he asked.

"My decision to come here was a terrible mistake."

"We can leave anytime you want."

"No. The problem is inside me. Running away now won't help." She was silent for a long moment. "You should be on your way. Maybe Mr. Blumberg will have the answer to your Wolf Lake mystery."

Being alone in his car made it easier to focus on the case. He decided to concentrate on identifying the discrepancy he sensed in Angela Castro's answers to his questions at Tabitha's Dollhouse. He took out his phone, located his recording of the interview, and tapped the "Play" icon.

It immediately brought the Dollhouse scene vividly to mind. When he heard Tabitha's voice he was struck again by her strange combination of formidability and deference—and by Angela's explanation that she might be hoping they'd "buy another Barbie."

He wasn't able, however, to pinpoint the discontinuity he was looking for.

So he played the recording again.

It was during the second playing that he heard it. Just one odd word. The word was "later."

It wasn't even the word itself, but the meaning it was given by the way Angela said it.

Gurney asked her what Pardosa had said about Hammond, and she replied that he'd said he was disgusting.

Then Gurney asked if Pardosa had told her about his nightmares.

She replied, "Yeah, but that was later."

What struck Gurney was the way she said "later"—making it sound as though a relatively long interval had elapsed. But she'd also said that Pardosa told her about the nightmare the first time he had it, the night after he met with Hammond.

Presumably the earliest Pardosa could have told her that Hammond was "disgusting" was the afternoon of the day of the hypnosis session. And later that night, or first thing next morning, he told her about his nightmare. So, a gap of perhaps twelve to eighteen hours would have elapsed—hardly a long interval.

Gurney realized that he was getting pretty far out on a speculative branch, based on nothing more than the way a single word struck his ear. Before he proceeded further he needed to know exactly what Angela meant by "later." He knew only one way to find out. He pulled off onto the shoulder of the road, found Angela's cell number in his phone list, and pressed "Call."

She answered in a small frightened voice. "Hello?"

In the background he could hear TV voices, laughter, applause.

"It's Dave Gurney, Angela. Are you all right?"

"I think so. Is something wrong?"

"Nothing's wrong. I'm just curious about something you said, and I thought maybe you could help me. Are you free to talk?"

"What do you mean?"

"Can you speak freely? Are you alone?"

"Who else would be here? I'm in my room."

"At the Dollhouse Inn?"

"Yes."

"Okay. Let me explain what it is that I need help with." He recounted the exchange that had occurred between them, leading up to her use of the word "later" to separate Pardosa's description of his nightmare from his earlier comment that Hammond was disgusting. "I'm wondering how much time passed between those two conversations."

"I don't understand."

"At some point, Stevie told you the hypnotist was disgusting. And then, later, he told you about the nightmare he had. How much later was that?"

"God, I don't know. I mean, I wasn't like counting days or anything."

"It was a number of days, not hours?"

"Oh, no, not hours. Days."

"Okay. Am I remembering right that Stevie told you about the nightmare right after he had it the first time, the night of the same day he had his session with Hammond?"

"Definitely. I know that for sure. Because we were here when he told me."

"At the Dollhouse Inn?"

"Right."

"So that means he must have told you that Hammond was disgusting at least a couple of days before that. You said *days*, right? So that would be before you made the trip to Wolf Lake. He must have told you while you were still down in Floral Park. Is that right?"

There was a silence—except for the sound of the TV.

"Angela?"

"Yeah, I'm here."

"Did you hear my question?"

"I heard it."

Another long moment passed.

"Angela, this is important. How did Stevie know the hypnotist was disgusting before he met him?"

"I guess someone told him."

"The person who called him?"

"I can't say anything about that."

"Because Stevie warned you that you could end up dead if you said anything about it?"

"Why do you keep asking about it?" Her objection came out like a desperate whine.

"Angela, we could all end up dead unless you start trusting me and telling me what you know."

Another silence.

"Angela, when Stevie used the word 'disgusting' to describe a person, what did he usually mean?"

"How could I know that?" She sounded panicky.

"But you *do* know, don't you, Angela? I can hear it in your voice."

Her silence at that point confirmed the truth, so Gurney continued. "You knew what he meant by that word, but it upset you, right?"

Her silence was broken by a sniffle. Then another. Then a swallow. Gurney waited. The dam was breaking.

"Stevie . . . was prejudiced about some things. Some people. You have to understand, he was a good person. But sometimes . . . well, he kind of had a problem sometimes with gay people. Sometimes he would say what they did was disgusting."

"And that they themselves were disgusting?"

"Sometimes he would say that."

"Thank you, Angela. I know it was hard for you to tell me that. Just to make sure I'm not making a mistake, let me ask you one more question. The person who called Stevie on the phone—the person who you figured told him he should go up to Wolf Lake to see Hammond—is that the person who told him that Hammond was gay?"

There was a long silence.

"This is terribly important, Angela. Is that who told Stevie that Hammond was gay?"

"Yes."

"Did you ask Stevie why he was willing to meet with a therapist he knew was gay?"

"Yes, I did."

"What did he say?"

"That I should stop asking questions, that it was dangerous to keep asking questions."

"Did he tell you why it was dangerous?"

"He repeated what he said the night he got the phone call—that we could end up dead."

CHAPTER 34

B y the time Gurney reached the exit sign for Otterville, the cloud cover had thinned and pale winter sunlight was illuminating the landscape.

He debated whether to take the kind of steps he'd taken at Lake George to obscure his destination but decided it wasn't worth the trouble. If the trackers on his car revealed that he was visiting an Otterville bungalow colony, so be it. There were good reasons to keep the whereabouts of Angela Castro a secret, but none of them applied to Moe Blumberg.

He drove through the "hamlet" of Otterville, which consisted of a derelict auto repair shop, a shuttered hot dog stand, and a two-pump gas station. A mile later his GPS directed him onto Brightwater Lane, a dirt road that brought him through the woods to an open area where a dozen or so cabins were spread out along the side of a small lake. In the middle of the clearing was a stone foundation and a few fire-blackened timbers of a building it had once supported. Parked next to it was a well-used Toyota Camry.

Gurney stopped behind the Camry. As he was getting out of his car, he heard a voice calling out. "Over here."

It took him a moment to locate the source—a figure at a window of one of the cabins.

"Come around to the far side. The front door faces the lake."

As Gurney reached the lake side of the cabin and was stepping up onto the covered porch, the door was opened by an old but sturdy-looking white-haired man wearing tan slacks and a blue blazer. The clothes, along with the two suitcases just inside the door, were consistent with the imminent departure Hardwick had mentioned.

"Mr. Blumberg?"

"You see, the lake's the whole point," the man said, as though Gurney had questioned the orientation of the porch. "So it makes sense for the cabins to face that way. You're Detective Gorney, is that right?"

"Gurney."

"Like the cow?"

"I believe that's a Guernsey."

"Right. Come in, come in. You understand I don't have much time?"

"I understand you're off to a warmer climate."

"Fifties, sixties this time of year. Plenty of sun. Beats freezing my *tuchus* off here. Time was when the winters didn't bother me, seemed silly all these old folks running off to Florida, places like that. Doesn't take more than a few years of arthritis, though, before you see the sense in it. If your joints ache here, but they don't ache there, hell, that makes the decision pretty easy, doesn't it? To answer your question, yes, I'm Moe Blumberg. Might be confused about some things but still pretty sure about that."

As they shook hands, Gurney took in the cabin in a few quick glances. The main room, which was all he could see from where he stood, was set up partly as an office, partly as a sitting area centered on an antique iron woodstove. The furnishings were a bit threadbare.

"Have a seat. The other detective wasn't clear on the phone. What's this all about?"

Blumberg made no move to sit, so neither did Gurney.

"A young man by the name of Steven Pardosa died recently in suspicious circumstances. You might have seen something about it on TV?"

"You see a TV here?"

Gurney glanced around again. "You don't have one?"

"Nothing on TV worth the time of anyone with at least half a brain. Noise and nonsense."

"So Detective Hardwick's call was the first you heard of Steven Pardosa's death?"

"He mentioned that name. But I still don't get what this is all about."

"Did he tell you that Steven Pardosa attended your camp thirteen years ago?"

"Something like that."

"But you don't remember the name, or the person?"

"I ran the camp for thirty-eight years, hundred and twenty boys every summer. The last summer was twelve years ago. You think I should remember every camper who came here? You know how old I am, Detective?"

"No, sir, I don't."

"Eighty-two next month. I have trouble remembering my own name. Or what day it is. Or what I came into the kitchen for."

Gurney smiled sympathetically. "You said that the last year the camp was in operation was twelve years ago?"

"That I know for sure."

"And Steven Pardosa was here thirteen years ago. That would be a year before you shut down?"

"That's plain arithmetic."

"It sounds like the camp was successful for many years."

"That's a fact."

"How did you come to the decision to shut it down?"

Blumberg shook his head, sighed. "We lost our customers."

"Why?"

"There was a tragedy. A terrible event. Everything snowballed out of control. Stories, rumors, craziness. Like that phrase—*a perfect storm.* That's what it was. One year we were pure gold. The next year we were shit."

"What happened?"

Blumberg let out an abrupt, bitter laugh. "Answer that and you get the prize."

"I'm not following you."

"Nobody knows what happened."

"You called it 'a perfect storm.' What did you mean?"

"Everything that could go wrong went wrong."

"Can you tell me about it? It could be important."

"*It could be important?* It was important enough to destroy Camp Brightwater—a camp that had been in business, for your information, for fifty years *before* the thirty-eight years I ran it. An institution. A tradition. All destroyed."

Gurney said nothing. He waited, knowing Blumberg would tell the story.

"There was always variability—better years, worse years. I don't mean the business, the financial aspect. That was always solid. I'm talking about the personality mix. The emotional chemistry. The spirit of the group. How the bad apples would affect the rest of the barrel. Some years the spirit was cleaner, brighter, better than other years. To be expected, right? But then, thirteen years ago, that one year everything fell off the wrong end of the chart. The feeling in the air that summer was different. Uglier. Nastier. You could feel the fear. Counselors quit. Some kids wrote to their parents to come and get them. There's a phrase people use nowadays: 'toxic environment.' That's what it was. And all that was before the event itself." Blumberg shook his head again and seemed to get lost in his recollections.

"The event?" prompted Gurney.

"One of the boys disappeared."

"Disappeared . . . permanently?"

"He was present at dinner. He was missing at breakfast. Never seen again."

"Did the police get involved?"

"Sure, they got involved. For a while. They lost interest when it started looking like the kid just ran away. Oh, they searched the woods, put out those missing-person notices, checked the bus stops, put his picture in the local papers. But nothing came out of any of that."

"Why did they think he ran away?"

"Homesick? Hated being here? Maybe was being pushed around a little? You got to understand something. This was thirteen years ago—before all the uproar started about the bullying thing. Don't get me wrong. We discouraged it. But the thing is, bullying was part of growing up back then. A fact of life."

A fact of life, thought Gurney. And, occasionally, a fact of death. "So once the police adopted the theory that he ran away, was that the end of it?"

Blumberg laughed again, more bitterly than before. "I wish to God that was the end of it. That was far from the end of it. A boy disappearing, possibly running away—that was the reality. The camp could have survived that. What the camp couldn't survive was all the crazy bullshit."

"Meaning?"

"The rumors. The whispers."

"Rumors of what?"

"Every kind of evil thing you could imagine. I told you the spirit of the place that summer was nasty even before the disappearance, and it only got worse afterward. The stories some of the boys were spreading, even some of the parents—beyond belief."

"For example?"

"Anything you could imagine, the more horrible the better. That the missing kid had actually been murdered. That he'd been used as a human sacrifice in a satanic ritual. That he was drowned and his body was chopped up and fed to the coyotes. Incredible shit like that. There was even a story that some of the boys, some of the bad apples, got it into their heads that he was a little *fagelah*, and they beat him to death and buried him in the woods."

"Just because he was gay?"

"Gay?" Blumberg shook his head. "What a word for it, eh? Like it was some kind of happy way to be. Better they should call it 'fucking warped'—be more accurate."

Gurney couldn't help feeling a little sick at the thought of the boy's experience at a camp where the ultimate authority viewed him that way.

"Did the police follow up on any of the ugly stories?"

"Nothing came of any of that. So many wild ideas going around that none of them seemed real. Teenage boys have grotesque imaginations. My opinion? I'd have to agree with the police—that he ran away. No real evidence of anything else. Just crazy talk. Unfortunately, crazy talk is like electricity. Lots of dangerous energy."

"The crazy talk killed the camp?"

"Killed it dead. Next summer we filled less than a third of our bunks, and half of those kids left before the season was over. The crazy talk came back, like an infection. The life of the place was dead and gone. Goddamn shame."

"The bad apples—do you remember any names?"

Blumberg shook his head. "Faces, I recognize. Names, I'm not so good. I'm thinking some of them had nicknames. But I can't remember them, either."

"Can you recall the name of the boy who disappeared?"

"That's easy. It came up a thousand times. Scott Fallon."

Gurney made a note of it. "The fire that destroyed the main building with all the records of your campers' names and addresses—was there an investigation?"

"An investigation that went nowhere."

"But despite everything, you stayed here. And reinvented the camp as a bungalow colony. You must be very attached to the location."

"Camp Brightwater was once a magical place. A happy place. I try to remember that."

"Sounds like a good idea. How's the bungalow colony business?"

"It's shit. But it pays the bills."

Gurney smiled and handed Blumberg a card with his cell number on it. "Thank you for your time. If you think of anything else about that bad year, anything that happened, any names, any nicknames, please give me a call."

Blumberg frowned at the card. "Your name is Gurney."

"Right."

"Not like the cow."

"No, not like the cow."

CHAPTER 35

O n the drive back to Wolf Lake, Gurney tried to relate what he'd learned from Moe Blumberg to everything else he knew about the case.

Homophobia seemed to be a common factor—which made him curious to find out if it had surfaced in Hardwick's meeting with the Teaneck detective regarding Leo Balzac's suicide.

He pulled off onto the shoulder, took out his phone, and called Hardwick's number.

The man picked up on the first ring—a good sign.

"What's up, ace?"

"Just wondering if you managed to get to your guy in Teaneck."

"Got to him, sat with him, listened to him. Bottom line, the man is highly pissed off at the politics of the case."

"The politics?"

"Unexplained orders from above. Orders serious enough that they damn well better be followed, but ambiguous enough to be deniable. Only clear thing is that they're descending from the stratosphere where the flick of a finger can send your career into the toilet like a dead fly."

"What does your new detective friend have to do to avoid the fatal flick?"

"Hang back, stay off the minefield, and trust that the situation is in good hands."

"There's that minefield again."

"Huh?"

"Fenton told me I was stumbling around in a minefield."

"Nice when everyone's on the same page."

"Did you ask him if he knew in whose 'good hands' the case now resided?"

"He said he'd been given a hint that their identities couldn't even be hinted at."

"Echoes of Robin Wigg warning us to back away. What do you think's going on?"

"Fuck if I know. Fuck if the guy in Teaneck knows. All he knows is that he's not supposed to know anything, say anything, or do anything. And he finds that very irritating."

"His irritation could make him helpful to us."

"I was thinking the same thing. I mentioned that we'd love to know if Leo Balzac had ever been to Camp Brightwater; or if he'd been known to harbor strong opinions regarding gay men; or if he might have had any past contacts with Gall, Wenzel, or Pardosa."

"And?"

"He said he'd be glad to find out what he could, as long as his involvement would remain a secret. I told him it would—that I'd be delighted to take full personal credit for blasting the case right up the asses of the boys in the stratosphere."

"That must have warmed his heart."

"We'll see what kind of information he actually comes up with. In the meantime, how'd your sit-down go with Moe?"

"He told me that the summer Pardosa was there was pretty awful. One of the campers disappeared. And a nasty rumor circulated afterward was that he might have been killed because he was gay. Problem is, there's no real evidence for it."

"But it does ring that same damn bell one more time."

"Yes. It does."

"Anything else?"

"He kept talking about the 'bad apples' in the barrel. Couldn't remember any names, though. Claimed Pardosa's name meant nothing to him. Maybe I'll give him a call before he gets on his Tel Aviv flight, see if the names Balzac, Wenzel, and Gall stir up any memories."

"Anything else happening? How's Madeleine doing?"

"She's pretty stressed right now. Which reminds me, I need to get going. I've been told there's a record blizzard closing in."

THE FARTHER NORTH GURNEY DROVE, THE DARKER IT GOT. WHEN he reached the crest of the last ridge before Wolf Lake, he stopped at the side of the road. Finally within the coverage area of the lodge cell tower, he called Moe Blumberg's number.

The call went into voicemail. He left a message that included the names of the victims he hadn't mentioned during their Otterville meeting, plus Richard Hammond's for good measure, asking if any of the names triggered memories from that terrible summer thirteen years ago.

As he pulled back onto the road, the sky ahead was the sullen blackish-blue of a bruise, and a few scattered snowflakes were drifting down through the beams of his headlights.

Halfway down the winding road from the ridge to the lake, his headlights swept across a large pine thicket, and he saw something moving. He braked to a stop and switched on his high beams just as the creature, whatever it was, disappeared into the deep woods. He lowered his windows a couple of inches and listened. But the silence was deep and unbroken. He drove on.

By the time he arrived at his parking spot under the lodge portico, Wolf Lake and its surrounding ridges were engulfed in an unnatural darkness, and the snow was falling steadily.

It was 4:30 PM by the grandfather clock in the reception area. He checked the Hearth Room to see if Madeleine might be there, then hurried up the stairs.

Entering the suite he found the main room illuminated only by the kerosene lamp by the couch. His first thought was that there was a problem with the electricity—until Madeleine called out to him. "Don't turn on the lights."

He found her in the bedroom alcove, sitting very still in the center of the four-poster bed with her eyes closed and her pajamaed legs crossed in a lotus position. A second kerosene lamp on the bureau bathed the alcove in an amber glow. A classical guitar piece was playing on her tablet, which was placed on the arm of a chair out near the bugged Harding portrait.

She held up three fingers, which he assumed represented the number of minutes she intended to remain in her yoga pose before speaking to him. He sat in a chair between the bed and bureau and waited. Eventually she opened her eyes.

"Is it all right for us to talk in here?" Her voice sounded less tense than it had for days.

"Yes, here in the alcove, with your music playing out there." He studied her face. "You look . . . relaxed."

"I feel relaxed."

"Why the kerosene lamps?"

"The soft light is calming."

"How did your meeting go with Hammond?"

"Very well."

He stared at her, waiting for more. "That's it?"

"He's good."

"At what?"

"Reducing anxiety."

"How does he do that?"

"It's hard to put it into words."

"You sound like you're on Valium."

She shrugged.

"You're not, are you?"

"Of course not."

"So what did you talk about?"

"Colin Bantry's craziness."

Again he stared at her, waiting for more. "And?"

"My own guilt trip—blaming myself for what he did."

A silence fell between them. Madeleine's gaze seemed to be focused on the lamp.

"What are you thinking?" he asked.

"I'm thinking that Richard is innocent, and you have to help him."

"What about our trip to Vermont?"

"I called this afternoon and cancelled."

"You did what?"

"Don't pretend to be irate. You never wanted to go there anyway." She straightened out her legs slowly from her yoga position and got off the bed. "Maybe you should try to relax. Maybe have a quick nap? I'm going to take a bath before we go to dinner at Richard and Jane's."

"Another bath?"

"You should try it."

She took a small bottle of shampoo out of her duffle bag, went out to the sitting area, took the other kerosene lamp from the end table, and went into the bathroom. He heard her turning on the bath taps and heard the water gushing into the tub.

He took a few deep breaths and tried massaging his neck and shoulders to loosen the tightness in his muscles. He asked himself where his tension was coming from. He didn't like the first explanation that came to mind—that he was jealous and resentful that another man was helping Madeleine in a way he himself had been unable to.

He heard the tub water being turned off. A minute or two later Madeleine returned to the alcove. Standing in the soft light cast by the lamp on the bureau, to all appearances in no hurry, she removed her pajamas and laid them on the bed.

As it always did, the beauty of her body had a powerful effect on him.

She seemed to sense the change in the nature of his attention.

Turning to the bureau, she opened a drawer and took out a bra and panties she'd transferred there from her bag. She laid them on a bench at the foot of the bed. Then she opened a second drawer and took out a sweater and jeans. She laid them on the bench also, moving casually closer to him as she did so.

He reached out, lightly touching the smooth curve of her hip with his fingertips.

She met his gaze with a look that was challenging and irresistible.

Neither of them said a word. She moved her pajamas from the bed, pulled back the covers, and lay down on the sheet. She watched him taking off his clothes.

Their lovemaking was intense, creating for a while a separate world where nothing mattered except what they were doing at that moment.

As he lay next to her in a daze, she leaned over and kissed him on the mouth one more time. Then she got up and left the alcove. A few seconds later he heard the bathroom door close.

Feeling deeply at peace for the first time in days, he let his eyes drift shut.

In retrospect, as he carefully reviewed later what happened, in a search for details that might explain it, he found it hard to recall how much time had elapsed between the closing of the bathroom door and the traumatic horror that changed everything.

Five seconds? Ten seconds? Possibly even thirty seconds?

The high-pitched sound pierced him viscerally, chillingly, struck some primitive part of his brain, before his conscious mind identified it as a scream. It was an excruciating sound of terror, followed by the sound of stumbling and the hard impact of a body hitting the floor.

He jumped from the bed and dashed toward the bathroom, barely noticing that his bare shin collided with a chair along the way, toppling it over backward.

"Madeleine!" he shouted, grabbing the knob of the bathroom door and turning it. "Madeleine!" The door wouldn't open. Something was blocking it. He lowered his shoulder, heaving his weight against the door, pushing as hard as he could.

It slowly gave way, and he squeezed past it.

Inside, he looked around frantically in the dim light of the kerosene lamp. He found Madeleine naked on the floor. She was lying on her side, her arms wrapped around her knees.

"What is it?" he cried, dropping to his knees next to her. "What is it? What happened?"

She tried to say something, but it was lost in a stifled wail.

He held her face between his hands. "Maddie. Tell me. What happened?"

She wasn't looking at him. Her terrified gaze was fastened on something else in the room. He followed her line of sight—to the big claw-foot bathtub. The tub she'd just filled with water.

"What is it? What happened?"

Her response sounded more like a moan than a word.

Only it wasn't just a word. It was a name.

"Colin."

"Colin? Colin Bantry? What about him?"

She answered with a half-stifled cry. "His body."

"What about his body?"

"Look."

"Look?"

"In the tub."

PART THREE

THE WOLF
AND
THE HAWK

CHAPTER 36

When Gurney approached the tub and peered into it, he saw nothing but water and a few wisps of steam. He checked it first in the low lamplight, then switched on the overhead fixture for a better look. He saw nothing out of the ordinary.

He turned his attention back to Madeleine, huddled on the floor, her knees still pulled up against her breasts.

"There's nothing in the tub, Maddie. Just water."

"Under the water!" she cried. "Look!"

"I did look. There's nothing there."

Her eyes were wide with fear.

He tried to speak calmly. "Do you think you can stand up, if I help you?"

She seemed not to understand.

"Maybe I can lift you, carry you, okay? We'll get you off the floor and out of here."

"Look under the water!"

He went to the tub and made a show of inspecting it thoroughly. When he swirled his arm through the water, she uttered a gasp of alarm.

"See, Maddie? Nothing but plain water."

He came back and knelt down beside her. He slipped his arms under her body. His awkward position made lifting her a challenge, and he almost fell on her. In the end, he managed to carry her to the bed.

He switched on both bedside lamps and checked her body once more for broken bones, abrasions, or any other obvious damage. He found only a reddening area on her hip from the fall.

He squatted by the bed, bringing his face even with hers. "Maddie, can you tell me exactly what happened?"

"Colin. In the water. Swollen." She half-turned her head toward the wall that separated the bedroom area from the bathroom. "I saw him!"

A tiny muscle in her cheek was quivering.

"It's all right, Maddie. There's nothing there. It was some kind of optical illusion. The water, the steam, the dim light . . ."

"His body was in the tub—not steam, not dim light! His bloated face, the scar through his eyebrow! The scar from football! Don't you hear what I'm saying?"

Her body began to shake.

"I hear you, Maddie. I really do."

He stood up, reached for the flannel sheet and blanket at the foot of the bed and pulled them over her.

He could see it would be pointless to try to convince her at that moment, petrified and shivering, that imagination, memories, and perhaps the poison of guilt had conspired to create a terrible illusion. She'd dismiss the effort.

He stood watching her until she closed her eyes. There would be an appropriate time, he told himself, to address the experience rationally, perhaps therapeutically. But right now—

His train of thought was broken by a sound coming from the bathroom. A barely audible creaking sound.

Gooseflesh crept up his back.

He slipped into his jeans and a sweater, retrieved the Beretta from the pocket of his jacket, and eased off the safety. After an anxious look at Madeleine, he moved quietly, barefoot, toward the bathroom.

When he got there, he heard the faint creaking again; but now it seemed to be coming from the exterior corridor. In fact, it seemed to be approaching the suite door. He reached the side of the door in a few long strides. The bolt was in its open position. He'd forgotten to slide it shut when he'd come in earlier.

He waited, hardly breathing. He was in the same position he'd been in the night of the power failure—when Barlow Tarr's face had given him such a start.

He grasped the handle tightly, hesitated for a second, then threw the door open.

Seeing Barlow Tarr standing in the corridor once again was not in itself a shock. But there was something in the man's intense stare that gave Gurney a chill.

"What do you want?"

Tarr spoke in a raspy half-whisper. "Be warnt."

"You keep warning me, but I don't understand what the danger is. Can you tell me?"

"Be warnt of the hawk that swoops down like the wolf. Be warnt of the evil here what killed them all."

"Did the evil kill Ethan Gall?"

"Aye, and the wolves ate him, like the old man afore him."

"How did Ethan die?"

"The hawk knows. Into the sun, into the moon—"

"Enough of that! Stop your bloody raving!" An angry voice rang out from the unlit end of the corridor.

Tarr's face jerked as though it had been slapped. He backed away from the suite door. Glancing back along the corridor like a spooked animal, he scuttled down the main staircase.

The source of the command strode into the light. It was Norris Landon, approaching in quick strides, glaring in the direction of Tarr's departure. He stopped at the doorway and turned to Gurney. "Are you all right?"

Gurney nodded. "Yes, thank you."

"Damn fool's not supposed to be in the lodge. Probably silly of me, going at him like that. God knows what he's capable of, especially with a storm coming on."

"Storms agitate him?"

"Oh yes. Well-known phenomenon in psychiatric wards. There's a definite resonance between the primitive side of nature and the unbalanced mind. Things coming undone, I suppose. Thunder and terror. Extremes of emotion. But it wasn't his raving out here in the corridor that started me on my way to your room. I thought I heard a scream." He regarded Gurney questioningly.

"My wife had a bit of a fright. It's all right now."

Landon hesitated, noting the gun Gurney was holding half-concealed at the side of his leg. "I see you're armed."

"Yes."

"Is that a reaction to . . . whatever frightened your wife?"

"Just precautionary. A reflex built into my line of work."

"Ah. And your wife? Is she all right?"

"Perfectly all right."

"Well. This may seem like a crazy question, but . . ."

"But what?"

"I'm just wondering . . . did your wife by any chance . . . see something?"

"What do you mean?"

"Did she see something . . . something that might not have been real?"

"What makes you ask that?"

Landon looked like he was searching for the right words. "The lodge has . . . a strange history . . . a history of what might be called unsavory sightings."

"Sightings?"

"Visions? Spectral presences? Visitations? It all sounds rather silly, I admit, but I've been told that the individuals involved in these . . . incidents . . . were very sensible people, not the kind who usually report these things."

"When did these incidents happen?"

"On various occasions, over the years."

"Did the individuals all report seeing the same thing?"

"No. The way I heard it, each one—"

Gurney broke in. "Heard it from who?"

"From Ethan. It wasn't something he wanted to advertise. The way he told it to me, each woman's vision—they were all women, by the way, who had these experiences—each vision was from someone close to her in life who had died. Or, to be more specific, someone close to her who had drowned."

Gurney showed no reaction beyond normal curiosity. "Did these visions all occur here in the lodge?"

"Well, I did say the lodge, but in the environs as well. In one case, the woman saw a face underwater in the lake. Another claimed she saw her dead brother under a sheet of ice by one of the chalets. The worst incident was an older woman who had a mental breakdown after seeing her first husband—who'd died in a boating accident thirty years earlier—standing in the shower. According to Ethan, she never recovered."

"Water."

"Eh?"

"They all involve water. People who drowned. Drowned people who then 'come back' in circumstances again involving water."

Landon nodded thoughtfully. "True. Water was always involved." He paused. "Well, sorry to take up your time with ghost stories. I'm sure they all have some reasonable explanation. Hearing that scream brought them to mind. Felt I should check on you."

"I appreciate your concern. But I'm curious about one thing. Why are you still here?"

Landon appeared taken aback.

"I mean here at the lodge. After all that's happened. Ethan's death. The deaths of the other guests. The place being essentially shut down. The lurid history and general eeriness of the place. All good reasons not to be here."

Landon smiled. "It's all relative, isn't it? One man's reason to leave is another man's reason to stay. I find the absence of other guests a plus, not a minus."

"And the four unexplained deaths?"

"The fact is, mysteries intrigue me, and those four deaths fascinate me. Which raises an interesting question. I have only myself to be concerned about. But your own situation is more complicated. Another life is involved. You're not subjecting just yourself to those problems you reeled off. If they apply to me, they apply doubly to you. So the real question is, why are *you* here?"

"I was invited here to do a job. I feel I should stay until the job is done."

Landon raised a skeptical eyebrow. "If I had a wife with me, I might not feel that way."

Gurney produced a polite smile. "I appreciate your perspective. Incidentally, if you have any ideas about the four deaths, I hope you'll share them with me." He stepped back, his hand on the door, about to close it.

"What sort of ideas?"

"Ideas about who might be responsible."

Landon shrugged. "I suppose one does have to remain open to the possibility that Richard orchestrated it. Isn't the man famous for pushing the boundaries of hypnotic persuasion?"

There was something playful in Landon's bright, intelligent gaze. And something provocative in his blasé tone. Not to mention the disconnect between his comments and his apparently warm relationship with Jane Hammond.

But Gurney resisted the urge to pursue the issue. He had a more pressing concern.

CHAPTER 37

After locking the door and sliding the bolt in place, he headed for the bedroom to check on Madeleine.

He was startled to find the bed covers thrown back and the bed empty.

His eyes went straight to the balcony, but the door to it was clearly locked. The glass had accumulated a fine layer of snow.

"Maddie," he called out.

He checked the floor on both sides of the bed, then rushed back out into the main room, frantic now, looking everywhere.

The guitar music playing on her tablet had shifted into a dramatic style with florid Spanish rhythms.

He double-checked the bathroom, even though he was sure she wasn't there.

But there she was—standing in a shadowed corner, out of his original line of sight.

She'd wrapped herself in a white blanket. Her hair was disarranged. Her gaze was fixed again on the tub.

She was shaking her head slowly. "I don't understand."

He stepped closer to the tub and peered into it. "What don't you understand?"

"How it could have happened."

"It may be simpler than you think," he suggested.

Seeing her baffled look as a good sign, one open to a reasonable explanation, he launched into an account of how the human mind can "see" things that aren't actually there.

She showed little interest in what he was saying, but he pressed on. "Two eyewitnesses to the same event often give contradictory descriptions. They're both absolutely certain they saw what they saw. The problem is, what they 'saw' occurred mainly in their brain circuits, not in the external world."

"Colin's body was in the tub."

"Maddie, everything we 'see' is a combination of new data coming in through our eyes and old information stored in our brains. It's like what happens on the Internet. You type in the first few letters of a word, and it jumps to a word in its data memory that starts with those letters. But when we're under stress, and our brains are trying to work faster, they sometimes jump to the wrong conclusion. They create the wrong image. We're positive we're seeing it. But it's not really there. We'd swear that it's out there, but it only exists in our brain."

Her gaze was moving around the walls of the bathroom. "You're saying I'm delusional?"

"I'm saying that we're wired to 'see' more than our optic nerves are actually reporting. And sometimes the brain's image factory races ahead of the optical data and turns the rope on the floor into a snake."

She pulled the blanket around her like a cloak. "That wasn't a rope I saw. How could Colin's body . . . get from Grayson Lake . . . into that tub?"

"Maddie, maybe you should put on some clothes?"

"You know, they never found his body. Did I tell you that?"

"Yes. You told me that."

"They never found his body," she repeated slowly, as though that troubling fact could explain what had just happened.

"Maddie? Sweetheart? You had a bad fall. It might be a good idea to lie down."

"They never found his body. Then it was there." She pointed at the tub, letting the blanket slip as she did so. It fell from her body to the floor around her feet.

Gurney wrapped his arms around her. He could feel tremors running through her body. The aftershocks of an earthquake.

He held her tightly for a long time.

LATER, AFTER SHE'D FINALLY COLLAPSED INTO A TROUBLED SLEEP, Gurney sat in front of the cold hearth and tried to figure out what to do next.

The wind was keening softly in the chimney, things at Wolf Lake were making less and less sense, and Madeleine's mental state was undermining his ability to think straight.

Her possible need for psychiatric intervention came to mind, but he pushed the thought aside with a sick feeling. He had no illusions about the dismal state of that art and the practitioners who were too eager to experiment with their mind-altering chemistry sets.

He just wanted her to be all right.

To be herself again.

That train of thought was cut short by the ringing of his phone—and the presence on the screen of an unexpected ID. It was Moe Blumberg, former owner of Camp Brightwater.

"Mr. Gurney?"

"I thought by now you'd be en route to Tel Aviv."

"We're sitting on the plane, still at the gate at JFK. A fucking Hamas madman blew himself up at Ben Gurion airport. So here we sit. Nobody knows nothing."

"Sorry to hear that."

"Me too, along with the three hundred other sardines on this plane. But that's the world we live in now. Get used to it, right?"

"I guess so. What can I do for you?"

"Nothing. Just a thought I had. Your question. Wondering if I recognized any names?"

That got Gurney's attention and triggered his sense of caution. He wanted to get safely out of range of the room's surveillance devices.

"Just a second. My wife's asleep. Let me step into the bathroom so I don't wake her."

Gurney shut the bathroom door behind him. "Okay. You were saying?"

"Sometimes a little corner of my brain lights up when I leave it alone for a while. Things pop up when I stop trying to make them pop up."

"You recall something about the names I mentioned?"

"No, those names don't mean a thing to me. But I'll tell you what I did remember. That summer, there was a secret club. There were four boys. Lion, Spider, Wolf, Weasel."

"I'm not following you."

"Lion, Spider, Wolf, Weasel. Those were their nicknames. They sprayed those four damn words—in red-paint graffiti—on cabins, tents, trees. Even on my goddamn canoe."

"Did you ever find out who they were?"

"No. Sneaky little bastards. Maybe some of the other boys knew who they were, but I think they were scared of them. Nobody would say nothing."

"You think there was some connection between those four boys with the nicknames and the boy who disappeared?"

"Who knows? Your visit just got wheels turning in my head, and that's what popped up—those animal names. So I was thinking I should call you."

"Did the police investigating Scott Fallon's disappearance pursue this 'secret club' angle?"

"Not to my knowledge. Like I said before, to them the Fallon incident was just another runaway situation. And boys are always forming secret clubs. So maybe they were right, and this is a waste of your time."

"Not at all, Mr. Blumberg. This could help a lot. While I have you on the phone, let me ask you something else. Do you recall anything about Scott Fallon's parents—their first names, where they lived?"

"Hah! How could I ever forget? The mother—there was no father, just the mother—she kept coming up to the camp every weekend. Searching. Walking through the woods. Calling his name, even weeks later."

"Do you remember the mother's name?"

"Kimberly. Kimberly Fallon."

"Do you by any chance have an address for her?"

"Sure. Address, email, phone number, everything. After she stopped coming to Brightwater, she'd call me once a week, then once a month, now maybe once a year. But what can I do? I talk to her."

Because of the woman's persistent communication with Blumberg, he had her contact information on his phone. Gurney entered it all on his own phone, thanked Blumberg, and wished him a safe trip. He also made a note of the four nicknames.

Lion. Spider. Wolf. Weasel.

He wondered if the nature of each animal described some characteristic of the boy who chose it. And he couldn't help thinking that the number of boys in the secret club might be significant.

Four.

Four troublemaking boys who were at the camp when Scott Fallon disappeared.

Now, in this strange case, there were four dead men. And at least one of the four, Steven Pardosa, had been at Brightwater that summer.

Gurney still had his phone in his hand when it rang again.

This time it was Jack Hardwick.

"Good news. My buddy in Teaneck is even more ticked off than I thought."

"About the order to back away from the Balzac case?"

"About the order coming from so high up he's not allowed to know where it came from. That really frosted his balls."

"And this is doing us some good?"

"I'd say so. After I saw him this morning he paid another visit to the therapist Balzac shared his weird-ass dream with. He asked her about the gay angle."

"And?"

"First she just repeated that the dream was full of homoerotic imagery, which we already knew. But then she added that it was especially upsetting to Balzac because of his strong anti-homosexual feelings."

Gurney smiled. It was nice to see a corner of the puzzle begin to take shape.

"There's more," added Hardwick.

"From the therapist?"

"From my buddy—who's eager to help in every way he's not supposed to. He told me that Balzac resigned from his job a few hours before he cut his wrists. Sent the owner of the tobacco shop an email. 'Effective immediately, I am resigning from my management position at Smokers Happiness. Respectfully, Leo Balzac.' Short and sweet, eh?"

"That seems an odd gesture."

"So my detective friend thought."

"Did he pursue it?"

"He was told that the details of the case were no longer his concern."

"Because wiser minds up the ladder were taking over?"

"Words to that effect."

"People on the verge of cutting their wrists don't usually spend time writing resignation notes."

"No, they don't."

"People usually resign for one of two reasons. They can't stand what they're doing. Or they've been offered something more attractive."

"So where does that take us?"

"Maybe nowhere." Gurney paused a moment to think about it. "I guess, if he wanted to stop smoking, he could have resigned to get away from tobacco. On the other hand, didn't Steven Pardosa's parents tell you that Steven was on the brink of turning his life around, that great things were just around the corner, something like that?"

"They did, but I wrote that off as bullshit. Like, if only he'd lived, our wonderful son could've cured cancer. Crap like that."

"But suppose Pardosa actually was looking forward to something. And suppose Leo Balzac resigned because he was looking forward to something, too. Makes me curious whether Christopher Wenzel down in Florida had the same happy feeling about his future. Maybe you could call Bobby Becker at Palm Beach PD and ask him if there was any evidence of that."

"What are you trying to prove? That the dead guys were all homophobic shitheads with rosy views of happy times ahead?"

"I'm trying to find puzzle pieces that fit together. And speaking of things fitting together—about ten minutes ago I got an interesting call from Moe Blumberg."

"Anything useful?"

"He remembered four nicknames of the boys who belonged to a secret club at Brightwater the summer Scott Fallon disappeared. They called themselves Lion, Spider, Wolf, and Weasel."

"So what does this mean to you?"

"The specific animal names don't mean much to me, apart from the fact that they're all predators. Of course, there's the 'wolf' echo, but that could be a coincidence. If a kid wanted to pick a vicious nickname, it would be an obvious choice. What strikes me as possibly significant is the fact that there were four of them. And that the other campers were afraid of them. I got the impression from Moe that he wouldn't be surprised if they had something to do with Scott Fallon's disappearance. It's a fact that Steven Pardosa was at Brightwater that summer. We need to find out if our other three 'suicide' victims were there at the same time. Given their ages, it's possible."

"Wasn't Ethan a bit older than the other three?"

"A few years. He could have been there as a counselor."

"Ask Peyton. He ought to know."

"I'll give it a try, but I wouldn't put much faith in anything Peyton says. In the meantime, Blumberg gave me contact information for Scott's mother. If she'll talk to me, maybe I can find out if I'm on the right track."

"Good luck with that, Davey boy. I have a feeling you'll need it."

CHAPTER 38

During his phone conversations with Blumberg and Hardwick, Gurney had been pacing back and forth in the bathroom. With the door closed and his voice low, he'd felt safe from the audio bugs in the outer room. He figured it would also be a good place from which to call Kimberly Fallon.

But first he wanted to go and check on Madeleine.

In the light of the bedside lamp he could see that she was sleeping, but not peacefully. There were tiny movements at the corners of her mouth and eyes. Some of her exhalations were accompanied by small, plaintive sounds. He was tempted to wake her, but then he decided that even restless sleep might do her more good than no sleep at all.

He went back to the bathroom to call Kimberly Fallon.

He was surprised when the phone was answered by a live female voice. "*Tashi delek.*"

"My name is Dave Gurney. I'm trying to reach Kimberly Fallon."

"This is Kimberly."

"I'm sorry, Kimberly, I didn't understand what you said when you picked up."

"*Tashi delek.* Peace and good fortune. It's a Tibetan greeting."

"I see. Well, I wish you the same."

"Thank you."

There was something odd in her tone, an off-center quality he associated with potheads.

"Kimberly, I'm a detective. I'm calling about your son, Scott."

There was silence.

"I'm calling about what happened at Camp Brightwater the summer he disappeared. I was wondering if you'd be willing to help me by answering some questions."

More silence.

"Kimberly?"

"I have to see you."

"Sorry?"

"I can't talk about Scott unless I can see you."

"Are you saying that you want me to come to your home?"

"I just want to see your eyes."

"My eyes?"

"Your eyes are the windows of your soul. Do you have Skype?"

IT TOOK GURNEY ONLY A FEW MINUTES TO GET HIS NOTEBOOK COM-
puter from his duffle bag, move a pile of towels off a low table in the
bathroom, set the computer on it, open the Skype program, and position himself in front of the screen's built-in camera.

At Kimberly Fallon's request he'd given her his Skype address. She
wanted to place the video call from her end. So he got everything ready
and waited.

When he was thinking it wasn't going to happen after all, the call
came through.

On his computer screen he saw a slim woman in her late forties
or early fifties with a druggy smile and large blue eyes. Her hair was
dark brown with streaks of coppery red. Her white peasant blouse and
a string of large colored-glass beads around her neck gave her a retro-
hippy look. There was an oversized painting covering most of the wall
behind her, a swirl of green leaves against a cerulean sky.

With her head inclined slightly to the side, she appeared to be
studying his face.

"You have amazing eyes," she said.

Having no idea how to respond, he thought it best to say nothing.

"There's a lot of sadness in your soul."

Her own eyes had the half-inward look of someone viewing the
world through the lens of some secret knowledge, perhaps psychedeli-
cally inspired.

"Why do you want to know about Scott?"

It was an obvious question for which he should have prepared a
careful answer, but he'd had no time for that. "I think . . . what happened

that summer . . . may have had some delayed effects. There've been some suspicious deaths . . . of people who I believe may have been at Brightwater thirteen years ago, at the same time as Scott. There may be a connection between what's happening now and what happened back then. I realize I'm bringing up painful memories. I'm sorry about that."

She had so little reaction he wondered if she was hearing him.

"Kimberly?"

"There's nothing to be sorry about."

Despite the oddness of her comment, he pressed on. "Moe Blumberg told me that after Scott disappeared you kept coming back to Brightwater to look for him. Is that right?"

She nodded almost imperceptibly. "That was foolish of me."

"Were you able to find any trace of him at all?"

"Of course not."

"Why do you put it that way?"

"I was looking in the wrong place. He'd already crossed over."

"You mean you came to the conclusion that . . . that your son was no longer alive?"

"No, that wasn't it. Life never ends. Scott had simply crossed over to a place of peace and happiness."

Something in her tone prompted his next question. "A happier place than Brightwater?"

Her smile faded. "Brightwater was nothing but torment. Scott hated every minute of it."

"Why did you send him there?"

"That was his father's idea. The sports, having to deal with the roughness and toughness of it—that was supposed to make him a real man. Scott was no good at sports. How does being beaten up and laughed at and called filthy names make you a man? I could have killed him."

"Scott's father?"

"I wanted to kill him. But he left. You know why he left? Because I kept going back to Brightwater to look for Scott. He couldn't stand that. He knew it was all his fault."

"The boys at camp who bullied Scott—was he afraid of anyone in particular?"

She nodded slowly. "The ones with animal names."

"Spider, Lion, Wolf, and Weasel?"

"That's right."

"Did he know any of their real names?"

She shook her head. "He wasn't sure. They wore black hoods over their faces."

"Did he have any guesses?"

"He only told me one name, once, in a phone call home. It was an ugly name. But I can't remember it now. I stay as far away as I can from all that darkness. My spiritual advisor says that we have to put the darkness behind and move toward the light."

"I understand, Kimberly. But please try to remember. It could make a huge difference."

With a reluctant sigh she raised her face toward a light somewhere above her. In its glare the copper highlights in her hair shimmered like little flames. "I think it began with a P . . . or maybe a B."

She turned her hands up to the light, as though hoping that a fuller answer might alight on her palms. Gurney, impatient, was about to prompt her with the names of the four dead men, when she announced her recollection in a voice suddenly hard with hatred.

"Balzac."

CHAPTER 39

After concluding his video conversation with Kimberly Fallon, Gurney checked his phone and discovered voicemail messages from Jack Hardwick and Jane Hammond.

The moment he saw Jane's name he felt a stab of chagrin at what he guessed was the reason for her call.

"Dave? Madeleine? Is everything all right? I was under the impression you were coming here for dinner. Give us a call, okay?"

Another casualty of the evening's stress and confusion. He'd have to apologize, explain. He was about to listen to the message from Hardwick when he was stopped by an odd sound in the bathroom ceiling directly above him.

A faint creaking.

He looked up and saw, or thought he saw, a few tiny specks of plaster dust descend from the edge of the light fixture over the tub. He focused on the spot, waiting for it to happen again. After a few moments, he stepped up onto the rim of the bathtub to get a closer look, balancing himself with one hand against the tile wall.

From there he could see that the decorative medallion around the fixture was imprecisely aligned over the wiring hole in the ceiling, leaving a gap of a millimeter or two along one edge. From the floor the gap appeared to be nothing more than a shadow line.

His first thought was that the opening might provide access for audio or video surveillance. The scanner, however, should have picked up any electronic activity of that nature, and it hadn't. And it certainly wasn't the only poorly centered light-fixture medallion he'd ever seen. He would have dismissed it as a matter of no concern—if it wasn't for that muted creaking sound he'd heard, and that almost-invisible wisp of falling dust.

He went back to the bedroom alcove and put on his shoes. Then he strapped on his ankle holster and inserted the Beretta into it. Listening to Madeleine's breathing, he was relieved that it sounded more regular. But the tic was still active in her cheek. As he was wondering if there was something more he could be doing for her, his phone rang.

It was Hardwick again.

He decided to take the call, but the bathroom no longer seemed a secure place to talk. He got the suite key, went out into the corridor, and locked the door behind him.

He kept his voice low. "What's up?"

"Got some answers back from Palm Beach PD. You asked if there was any evidence that Christopher Wenzel had a bright view of his future. According to Bobby Becker, just before Wenzel headed up to Wolf Lake he put a down payment on a new Audi."

"How does Becker square that with Wenzel's suicide a week later?"

"Becker wasn't the detective who caught the Wenzel case, so this is all kind of secondhand. But it seems that the detective that was on it was taken off it almost immediately. So squaring the purchase with the suicide wasn't a problem anyone down there wrestled with."

"Any explanation for his removal from the case?"

"He was told national security issues were involved. End of story."

"So we have a pattern."

"Of optimistic guys ending up dead?"

"And local investigations being preempted. Anything else from Becker?"

"One big item. You asked if anyone besides Pardosa got an odd phone call before they made their Wolf Lake arrangements. Well, according to Becker, there's a phone record of Wenzel receiving a call from a prepaid cell phone a week before he went up to Wolf Lake. And a record of him calling the lodge reservations number that same day."

"How do we know there's a causal link between the two calls?"

"Let me finish. He got two calls from that prepaid cell number. One on the day he made his reservation, and the second on the day he cut his wrists. The origination point of both calls was the Wolf Lake cell tower. I'd be willing to bet that Balzac and Pardosa got the same pair of calls from that same untraceable phone."

Gurney was quiet for a long moment. "I'm not sure what this particular convergence means. It seems to mean that someone at the lodge—or at least within range of the lodge cell tower—may have persuaded three of the four victims to come and meet with Hammond."

"Right. And called again on the day each of them died."

"That would be the call Fenton claims was a post-hypnotic triggering device—whatever the hell that means." As he was speaking, Gurney was pacing along the corridor outside the suite. The light fixtures on the wall had been turned down, and in the gloom the crimson of the carpet was as dull as dried blood. "This phone call angle could be hugely important, Jack, but I need to let it sink in. Meantime, let me tell you what I found out from Scott Fallon's mother."

"She actually spoke to you?"

"Yes. Definitely on the flakey side, but she gave me some facts and confirmed some assumptions. Her son was gay, constantly bullied, and terrified. But here's the big news. There was a boy her son was especially afraid of. His name was Balzac."

"Goddamn!"

"So now we know that at least two of our current victims were at Brightwater at the same time. Steven Pardosa and Leo Balzac."

"If two of them were there, then I bet all four were. That could be the connection we've been looking for. And that antigay shit sure does keep popping up."

"Yes," said Gurney. "And it keeps getting uglier."

"Are we thinking our four dead guys might have been behind Scott Fallon's disappearance?"

"It's a workable hypothesis."

"In the interest of calling a spade a spade, can we agree that disappearance in this case means death—even though the kid's body was never found?"

The question jarred Gurney back into the world of Madeleine's bathroom breakdown—her traumatic vision of another body that was never found.

Hardwick cleared his throat. "You still there?"

"I'm here."

"When we say Scott Fallon disappeared, we're saying he was killed, right?"

"That's the most likely scenario."

"You all right, ace? You sound a little off."

As Gurney was weighing the pros and cons of discussing Madeleine's experience, his train of thought was derailed by a sound from the attic.

A barely perceptible creaking.

"Sorry, Jack, got to cut this short. I'll get back to you soon as I can."

He ended the call and began searching for a back staircase or other access to the upper floor. Heading along the corridor, he passed eight widely spaced doors that presumably led to guest rooms, four on each side. At the bottom of the last door on the right, a thin line of light was visible, and he heard music playing—something baroque.

With no other guests in residence, he figured it had to be Norris Landon's room.

When he reached what he expected to be the end of the corridor, it made a right-angle turn into an unlit cul-de-sac. This claustrophobic extension terminated in a metal door of the sort one might find on a janitor's closet.

Surprised to find the door unlocked, he opened it to discover the bottom steps of a narrow staircase that lead up to the attic.

He noted odors of dust and mold and something faintly rotten. He located a light switch and flipped it up. A low-wattage bulb came on in a bare porcelain fixture at the top of the stairs.

When he reached the top landing he found that it led to another door.

The door was slightly ajar.

He called out in a loud voice, "Is anyone there?"

Surely it was his imagination, but the silence behind the door seemed to deepen.

He called out again in the authoritarian police cadence that was etched into the circuits of his brain. "If anyone is there, speak up and identify yourself."

There was no response.

He nudged the door open with his foot.

The musty smell grew stronger. The weak bulb in the landing illuminated very little of the attic room in front of him. He groped along the inside wall until he found a switch. The light fixture that came on was attached to a ridge beam high in the peaked ceiling of what appeared to be a vast storage room. A number of large angular objects, perhaps unused pieces of furniture, were draped with sheets. A corroded drip bucket was positioned under a rafter that was glistening with moisture. The air in the room was cold and damp.

Gurney paused to get his bearings. He began to form a picture of how the attic space related to the floor below. He had good spatial instincts and was confident that he'd soon be able to locate the portion of the attic that was above the suite bathroom.

After a few more angle and distance estimations, he made his way cautiously to a door on the far side of the extensive storage space.

Like the previous door, this one was an inch or two ajar. The overall surface bore a thick coating of dust, but the knob was clean.

"Is anyone there?"

The responding silence was so absolute it gave him a touch of gooseflesh—a feeling that was intensified by the high-pitched squeak of a hinge as he pushed the door open.

Reaching around the door jamb to grope for another light switch, he failed to find one. But he heard something that caused him to freeze. A soft sound. The sound of a single exhaled breath.

He stepped forward quickly into the dark room, then sidestepped a few yards along the inside wall. He dropped to one knee and pulled the Beretta from its ankle holster.

Peering fruitlessly into the near-total darkness, he thought he heard another breath, not as close to him as the first.

He remained perfectly still and waited.

A hint of movement caught his eye, so slight he wondered if he'd seen anything at all. Then he felt a movement of air and heard the sound of a door some distance away being eased shut.

Quietly he rose to his feet, holding the Beretta with its muzzle pointing up. After listening intently for at least another minute, he began moving tentatively in the general direction of the door he imagined to be on the opposite side of the room.

He'd taken no more than three or four steps forward when

something touched his face. Startled, he jumped back, his free arm rising automatically into a defensive combat position.

As the seconds passed and his rational mind caught up with his reflexes, it dawned on him that what had touched his face was probably just another form of the switch he'd been looking for.

He reached out and wrapped his hand around a dangling pull cord.

He gave it a gentle yank. A pale light came on high in the timbered ceiling, drawing his attention upward—and delaying for a brief moment the paralyzing impact of what awaited him on the shadowy attic floor.

CHAPTER 40

With gleaming white fangs and glaring amber eyes, rough gray fur bristling and legs flexed for attack, a huge wolf was crouched less than ten feet from Gurney—a distance he knew could be erased instantly in a single leap.

Even with his gaze fixed on the beast, his hand tightening on the Beretta, he realized that the wolf was not alone.

There were four more, spread out in a loose semicircle behind the first, all with bared teeth and malevolent eyes, motionless, as if waiting for a signal.

Gurney absorbed all this as he was lowering his weapon to a firm and steady firing position. And then, as he was sighting down the barrel at the head of the feral monster in front of the pack, his finger settling into position on the trigger, he suddenly understood why the wolves confronting him were motionless.

They were all dead.

Dead, gutted, and preserved.

Their taxidermied bodies set in shockingly vivid attitudes of attack.

Their ferocity strangely undiminished by death.

Whoever had assembled this savage diorama was plainly a master of his peculiar art. But what was the diorama's purpose? And for whom was it arranged?

Weren't wolves a protected species in this part of the world? How long ago had they been killed? Who killed them? And why were they here in the lodge?

Engrossed in the questions raised by the presence of these . . . stuffed cadavers . . . Gurney was brought back to the moment and reminded of his purpose in the attic by the sight of a door on the far side of the room. Surely that was the door he'd sensed opening and closing in the darkness before he found the light pull.

With his weapon still in his hand, but with the safety back on, he stepped gingerly around the wolf pack, its fierce realism keeping him on edge, and headed for the door.

Before he got to it he was stopped by the sound of heavy footsteps approaching.

A moment later the door opened, and Austen Steckle stepped forward wielding a powerful LED flashlight.

The intense beam of light swept back and forth across the room, projecting shadows of the wolves across the floor and attic walls, coming finally to rest on the pistol in Gurney's hand.

"Christ!" He raised the beam to Gurney's face. "What the fuck's happening here?"

Gurney blinked. "Get that out of my eyes!"

He held it in place until Gurney began to move toward him, then quickly lowered it. "Sorry. What's the problem?"

"Did you pass anyone?"

"What?" He seemed honestly confused.

"Someone was in this room and left by that door less than a minute ago. Did you see or hear anyone?"

"Not as I was coming up."

"What do you mean?"

"What I heard from all the way downstairs was someone calling out, 'Is anyone there?' A couple of times. Really loud. Sounded like something was wrong. Nobody's supposed to be up here. This is not a public area."

"That's why I thought it was odd to be hearing footsteps up here."

"What footsteps?"

"Footsteps over our bathroom. Slow, quiet, as though someone was trying not to be heard. You have any idea why someone would be creeping around up here?"

He shook his head, seeming to find the notion outlandish.

"Whoever it was, was just in this room. And left by that door less than a minute before you walked through it. You're sure you didn't see or hear anyone?"

"Not a soul, not a sound. Nothing."

"This area is the part of the attic that would be directly over our suite, is that right?"

Steckle ran his free hand over his shaved scalp, which was sweating as usual, despite the attic chill. "It could be."

"You're not sure?"

"I got no reason to know what's directly over what."

"That door you came through—where does it lead?"

"Back stairwell, fire escape, ground floor, exit door, basement. Lot of places." He paused. "If someone went out that way, that could be why I didn't see him."

Gurney slipped the Beretta into the back pocket of his jeans and gestured toward the crouching wolves, whose shadows continued to shift eerily on the wall with each movement of Steckle's flashlight. "What's the story with the private zoo?"

Steckle produced a harsh, guttural sound—one of the most unpleasant laughs Gurney had ever heard. "It's a joke, is what it is." He aimed his light beam at each of the wolves in a curiously deliberate way. "You heard about the crazy Gall legend?"

"You mean Dalton Gall being killed by wolves after dreaming about them?"

"Right. So Dalton's son inherits the place. Elliman Gall. Big-game hunter. Mountain climber. All that shit. Wolves killed his father, so Elliman sees this as an opportunity to prove something. He kills a shit-load of wolves."

There was a glint in Steckle's eyes that suggested he wouldn't mind killing a shitload of wolves himself. "He has a few of them stuffed. Puts the fucking wolves in the Hearth Room, for everyone to admire. Elliman Gall. Man in control."

"I get the feeling this story has an unhappy ending."

Again Steckle let out that eruptive hacksaw sound that passed for a laugh. "He gets the idea to plant the Gall family crest on the peak of Devil's Fang. Big mountain climber, Elliman tries this in the middle of winter, horrible day like today, slips on the ice, falls eight hundred feet down the rock face, bounces off an outcropping on the way. They never found his head. Actually got ripped off on the way down." Steckle grinned radiantly. "Shit happens, right?"

"Sounds like the man craved admiration."

"He was dying for it." Once more, the awful laugh.

"How did the wolves end up here in the attic?"

"That was my first suggestion to Ethan, when I started working here—to get the goddamn creepy things out of the Hearth Room. There's enough wild shit outdoors; we don't need to have it in our faces indoors."

"You don't sound like much of a nature guy."

"I'm a numbers guy. Nice, predictable numbers. Nature, in my humble opinion, is a fucking horror story."

"An Adirondack lodge seems like an odd place for you to be working."

"You focus on the work, not where you do it."

Gurney realized that Steckle's philosophy wasn't that far from his own way of seeing things. His years in NYPD homicide had repeatedly put him in horrendous places. The thought made him want to change the subject.

"That family crest you mentioned—what was on it?"

"See for yourself." Steckle turned the cold white beam of his flashlight to the far end of the long room. High on the rough pine wall, hanging in the triangular area outlined by the dark rafters, there was a shield-shaped plaque. It bore a relief carving of a man's fist, raised in what could have been a symbol of power or defiance or both. Under the carving were three Latin words:

Virtus. Perseverantia. Dominatus.

Calling on his memory of his high school Latin, Gurney pondered the qualities chosen to represent the family's guiding lights:

Manliness. Determination. Mastery.

He looked at Steckle. "Interesting motto."

"If you say so."

"Those ideals don't impress you?"

"They're just words."

"And words don't mean much?"

"Words don't mean a goddamn thing."

The deeply hostile tone of this seemed rooted in a dangerous part of Steckle's psyche—not an area to be probed when one was alone with the man in a dark attic.

"No matter what anyone tells you, all you got is yourself." His gaze went back to the Gall family crest, high on the far wall. "Everything else is bullshit."

"Like Elliman Gall seeking admiration?" suggested Gurney.

Steckle nodded. "Seeking admiration is the stupidest fucking thing a man could do."

CHAPTER 41

Steckle led Gurney two flights down the dark stairwell to a door that opened into a wide corridor. "This leads out to the reception floor. You'll have to use the main stairs to get back up to your suite."

Gurney replied matter-of-factly, "I may check out the attic one more time tonight before I turn in. Set my mind at rest about those footsteps."

"Didn't you just do that?"

"Is there a problem with my taking another look?"

Steckle hesitated. "It's got nothing to do with me. It's a matter of legal liability."

"Liability for what?"

"Building code problems. It's not a public area. Could be weak floor-boards. Exposed wires. Bad lighting. You shouldn't be up there."

"Don't worry about it. You've told me twice now that it's not a public area. If I sprain my ankle, it'll be my problem for breaking the rules, not yours."

Steckle's expression soured but he said nothing more. When they reached the reception area, he went into his office and closed the door.

Gurney headed for his car.

A bitter wind was blowing snow sideways under the portico. He sprinted from the lodge to the Outback, got his big Maglite out of the glove box and a second smaller flashlight from the emergency kit, and sprinted back inside.

Upstairs in the suite, he was surprised to find Madeleine sitting on the couch in front of the hearth with a small fire burning. Classical guitar music was playing on her tablet. She was wearing one of the lodge's oversized white bathrobes and heavy wool socks. Her hair had been neatened a bit. On the low table between the couch and the hearth were two dinner plates covered by aluminum foil.

She gave him an anxious look. "Where were you?"

He didn't want to unsettle her. "Just having a look around. I'm surprised to see you up. How are you feeling?"

"We forgot about the Hammonds. We were supposed to go there for dinner tonight. Jane came over to see if we were all right. She brought us two plates. She made the fire."

"Caretaker Jane to the rescue." As soon as the words were out, he regretted them.

"She went out of her way to be helpful." Her gaze moved to the two flashlights in his hands. "What are those for?"

"There's a small crack in the plaster in the bathroom. I want to make sure it's not being used for another bug."

Her expression shifted from skeptical to concerned. "Where in the bathroom?"

"The ceiling. A crack by the light fixture."

Her eyes widened. "Check the whole room. There has to be an explanation."

He realized she was talking about Colin's body in the tub. But he knew that no reasonable explanation involving her imagination would be acceptable in her current state of mind.

"Maddie, why don't we get out of here?"

She said nothing, just stared at him.

He persisted. "If I'd seen a ghost . . . this is the last place I'd want to stay. It can't be good for you. Why don't we just go home?"

"That's not true."

"What's not true?"

"That you'd walk away from something like this, if it happened to you."

He tried again. "You know, it's possible to be too close to something to see it for what it is—"

She cut him off. "I saw his body *here*, not at home. The explanation is here."

He sat down on the couch next to her. He found himself staring at the two foil-covered plates on the coffee table. The guitar music from her tablet was building to another crescendo. His gaze shifted to the dying fire.

"Would you like me to add a couple more logs?"

"No. I'm going back to bed. Do we need to keep the music on?"

"I'll turn it off. Then I'll do a quick little check of the attic over the bathroom."

She pulled the bathrobe more snugly around her and closed her eyes.

ON HIS SECOND VISIT THE ATTIC FELT LESS THREATENING. EVEN now, in the same room with those crouching wolves, his sense of purpose seemed to be warding off any eerie imaginings.

Before coming up to the attic he'd set the more powerful of his two flashlights upright on the flat rim of the tub in the bathroom, it's beam aimed at the fissure in the ceiling.

Now he switched off the smaller flashlight he'd used to find his way. For several seconds the darkness was absolute. He became aware of the wind gusting against the angled roof above him, straining against the century-old timbers.

Then, as his eyes adjusted, he caught a glimpse of what he'd hoped to see—a thin line of light between two floorboards perhaps twenty feet from where he was standing. He switched his flashlight back on and made his way around the wolves to where he'd spotted that thin line.

The floor was made of wide pine boards, some of which were loose under his feet, especially at the source of the light. Sticking the back of the flashlight in his mouth, he knelt down and pressed his fingernails into the crack between the boards and slowly tilted one of them up from the joists it rested on. When it was tilted enough to grip it, he lifted it out and put it aside. The next one came up with equal ease.

He'd laid bare a portion of the rough-sawn joist structure that separated the floorboards of the attic from the plaster ceiling of the area below it. Most significantly, he'd laid bare the wiring and support hardware of a light fixture in the ceiling of the room below. He could see that the round medallion designed to cover the opening in the plaster for the fixture wiring didn't quite cover all of it. There was a narrow gap, just a few millimeters wide. A thin line of light from the bathroom below was shining up through it.

He examined the area around the top of the fixture as well as the joist to which it was fastened. He concluded there were no surveillance devices present. There were, however, clear signs that two devices of some sort had been installed and later removed, probably in a hurry.

It appeared that one may have been a fiber-optic video camera with its associated transmitter. There were several short pieces of fresh, sticky duct tape hanging from the side of the joist closest to the opening in the ceiling. There was a small spring clamp taped just above the opening. Gurney guessed it would have held the lens end of the optic cable in place. He figured the pieces of tape would have secured the rest of the cable to the joist to keep it from moving or creating any torquing pressure at the clamp. Cable-like imprints on the tape supported this idea. Two larger pieces of tape at what would have been the far end of the cable had probably supported the camera and transmitter components.

That raised a question. Why hadn't the transmitter come to light when he conducted the surveillance scan of the suite the previous day? Had it been removed by then? Or not yet installed at the time of the scan? If the latter, why was it removed so quickly?

The evidence for the recent presence of a second device was convincing but unenlightening. A small pair of clamps were affixed to the joist above the opening in the plaster, but there was no way of knowing what sort of device they'd held in place.

He checked the widths at which the clamps were set to guesstimate the size of the device they'd held. He concluded it was something roughly the diameter of a lipstick, of unknown length.

Satisfied that he'd discovered as much as there was to be discovered, he eased the floorboards back into place. He stood up and took another look around the cavernous room. In the sweeping beam of his flashlight, the shadows of the wolves lunged wildly across the wall.

He turned his flashlight up toward the Gall crest on the wall.

Virtus. Perseverantia. Dominatus.

He was struck by the coincidence of those stern sentiments being set above the ferocious beasts on the floor. His attention was drawn especially to the culminating term in the series: *Dominatus.*

He recalled that it could be translated in many ways. But common to all those translations was one central concept: Control.

As he thought about it in the context of the case, he began to see it as a recurring theme—from Elliman Gall's obsession with wolf killing, to Ethan Gall's focus on reforming the world by rehabilitating criminal personalities, to Peyton Gall's unbridled self-will.

And it went beyond the Gall family. According to Gilbert Fenton, the essence of the case involved Richard Hammond's *total control* over his four victims.

Fenton's own media strategy, of course, was all about controlling the public perception of the case, controlling its future prosecutorial direction, controlling the fate of Richard Hammond.

The shadowy forces above Fenton were controlling investigatory decisions in four separate jurisdictions.

Going back thirteen years to that infamous summer at Camp Brightwater, Gurney wondered about the anonymous four—Lion, Spider, Wolf, Weasel. Moe Blumberg said their fellow campers were afraid of them. What kind of control had they exercised over those kids? What kind of control had they exercised over Scott Fallon?

That train of thought brought Gurney around to the four recent murders. He was convinced that 'murder' was the only realistic term for what had happened to the four men who bled to death from their severed wrist arteries. Whatever obscure steps had been taken to bring about their deaths, the process must have been orchestrated with their deaths as the goal. In his book, that was the definition of murder.

And murder was the ultimate act of control.

CHAPTER 42

"So what the hell are you saying?" asked Hardwick. "That it was a power struggle? And the dead guys lost? Who the fuck won?"

Gurney was sitting in the Hearth Room. Rather than going directly back to the suite from the attic, he'd stopped there to call Hardwick and bring him up to date on his discoveries and his suspicion that the element of control might be central to the case.

It was that last notion that Hardwick had challenged. He loved the concrete, hated the conceptual, and reacted predictably. "Whatever it's about, Sherlock, I have total faith that you'll figure it out and reveal it to us lesser mortals in your own time. Meanwhile, you want to hear my own Camp Brightwater brainstorm?"

"Nothing I'd like better."

"Okay, then. Leo the Lion."

Gurney thought about it for a moment. "You're saying that Leo Balzac was one of the anonymous four? Because Leo means Lion?"

"It's a direct connection, right? And I'm thinking that Wolf was probably Ethan Gall."

"Because of the family estate at Wolf Lake?"

"Makes sense, doesn't it?"

"Except we have no evidence Ethan was at Brightwater. You have any other linkups?"

"How about Wenzel the Weasel?"

"That's conceivable. There's one more victim and one more nickname. Pardosa and Spider. You see some way they connect?"

"Not yet. But three out of four has to mean something."

"It might mean we're getting desperate for connections. But let's say for argument's sake that our four victims were the four bad seeds at

Brightwater. And that they were responsible for Scott Fallon's death. Is that where you're going with this?"

"Why not? It makes sense." Hardwick sounded excited.

"All right," said Gurney calmly. "But even if that's true, it happened thirteen years ago. What's the connection to the present events?"

"Maybe someone else knew what happened. Or found out about it later. Suppose Richard Hammond found out what happened at Brightwater that summer. Suppose he found out that a gay teenage boy had been beaten to death by Gall, Balzac, Wenzel, and Pardosa." He paused. "Suppose he decided to do something about it."

"Other than pass along what he knew to law enforcement?"

"Seeing how useless law enforcement was the first time around, suppose he decided to avenge Fallon's death himself. Hammond devoted his early career to gay men and boys. How might he react if he discovered the identities of four people who killed a boy just because he was gay? Maybe Hammond took the position at Wolf Lake for easy access to Ethan. Maybe he was the one who made those phone calls that enticed the other three into coming to the lodge. Maybe he even concocted some kind of financial carrot to draw them into the trap."

That struck a chord. It fit with the stories of Wenzel, Balzac, and Pardosa seeming to have improved financial prospects around the time of their meetings with Hammond. But Gurney wasn't convinced.

Hardwick seemed to sense his skepticism. "Look, I'm not trying to sell you this scenario. Truth be told, I hope I'm wrong."

"Why is that?"

"Because if I'm right, Fenton is right. And that's a revolting thought."

"But you aren't pushing the scenario as far as Fenton is. I mean, you aren't buying into the notion of people being hypnotized into committing suicide, right?"

Hardwick didn't answer.

Like a sound effect in a ghost movie, a moan came from the empty hearth at the far end of the room. Gurney told himself it was just the wind passing over the chimney.

CHAPTER 43

He found Madeleine in bed, with one of the bedside lamps still on. He looked to see if the tic in her cheek had subsided, but that side of her face was against the pillow.

To ward off his feeling of helplessness, he tried to focus on Hardwick's theory that Hammond had persuaded Wenzel, Balzac, and Pardosa to come to the lodge. There was some evidence that their financial situations had improved around the time of their visits, but it seemed a leap too far to assume that Hammond was responsible for that.

Thinking about the financial angle brought to mind Angela Castro's comment at the Dollhouse that Tabitha's solicitousness might have arisen from her assumption that they were going to buy another doll. It had never made much sense to Gurney, but he'd never pursued it.

He took his phone into the bathroom, where he found the flashlight still upright on the rim of the tub, still illuminating the ceiling. He switched it off and closed the door quietly.

He called Angela's number.

When she picked up, the first thing he heard was a TV—that same rhythm of voices, laughter, and applause he'd heard in the background of their last phone conversation. He wondered if she ever turned it off.

"Detective Gurney?" Her small voice sounded sleepy.

"Hello, Angela. Sorry if I woke you."

"Is something wrong?"

"Nothing new. Are you still in the same place?"

"What? Oh, yes, the same place."

"When we first met, you mentioned that Tabitha might have been thinking we were going to buy a Barbie. Remember that?"

"Sure."

"Because Stevie had bought you one?"

"I told you that."

"What I'm wondering is . . . do you know how much he paid for it?"

"How could I forget? It was like ten thousand dollars. Plus tax."

"For a Barbie doll?"

"An *original* Barbie doll. From when they first made them. With the original clothes."

"That's a lot of money."

"That's what I told Stevie. But he said he knew it was something I'd always wanted, so I should have it. He said we could have a lot of nice things."

"Did he say where the money was coming from?"

"He said that I shouldn't worry about that, that it was none of my business."

"Like the phone call he got before he went to Wolf Lake was none of your business?"

"I guess."

"So he never told you anything at all about the source of the money?"

"No. But he said the Barbie was just the beginning."

Gurney was stopped by a loud knocking at the suite door. "Angela, I have to go, but I'll call you again soon."

As he left the bathroom, the pounding was repeated, more aggressively.

He adjusted the Beretta in his back pocket to make the grip easily reachable and approached the door.

"Who is it?"

"Police!"

He recognized Fenton's voice and opened the door.

The flat-faced, heavy-shouldered man facing him looked like a worn and wrinkled copy of the Fenton who had visited him less than forty-eight hours earlier. His sport jacket hung open, revealing a shoulder-holstered Glock. He eyed Gurney coldly. "We need to talk."

"You want to come in?"

"No. You need to come downstairs."

"Why is that?"

"You come downstairs or I arrest you right here, now, for obstruction."

"I'll be with you in a minute." Leaving Fenton in the doorway, Gurney went back to the alcove. Madeleine was still in bed, but now her eyes were open.

"Maddie, I have to go downstairs—"

"I heard. Be careful."

He forced a smile. "This shouldn't take long."

THEY SAT IN THE FRONT SEATS OF A WEATHERED FJ CRUISER, PARKED under the outer edge of the lodge portico. Its headlights were reaching out into the snowstorm. Its engine was running, and the heater was on.

Gurney figured it was Fenton's personal vehicle, which meant he was probably off duty.

After a fraught silence during which Fenton stared out at the snow in his headlight beams, he turned to Gurney. "You got your phone on you?"

"Yes."

"Turn it off. Completely off. Then lay it on the console where I can see it."

He did as he was asked. In the dim light cast by the illuminated dashboard gauges, he could see Fenton's jaw muscle tighten.

"I'm confused," said Fenton, but there was more accusation in his tone than confusion. "We just had a nice conversation the other day. I thought I explained that your involvement here was not helpful. In fact, quite harmful. I thought I'd made that clear."

He paused, as if searching for the right words. "Your interference is giving the suspect false hopes. Your interference is prolonging the process by fostering the illusion in the suspect's mind that there's a way out of his difficulties—a way other than an honest, detailed confession. Fostering this illusion is a destructive thing for you to be doing. Extremely destructive. Perhaps I wasn't clear on this point in our last conversation. I hope I'm being clear now."

"Very clear."

"Good. I'm glad to hear you say that." He stared out at the snow. "There's a lot at stake in the outcome of this case. It's not something to be screwing around with."

Gurney knew that provoking this man could be dangerous, but it could also be instructive. "The orders you're getting on how the case should be handled are coming from so high up you figure they must be right? The people who want Hammond to be guilty are so important you figure he must be guilty?"

"Richard Hammond is a homicidal liar. That's a fact. It's not a god-damn order from anybody."

"I heard that he took a polygraph test. And passed it."

"That means absolutely nothing."

"It does seem to be a small point in his favor."

"You don't know your client very well, do you?" Fenton reached down behind the passenger seat and retrieved an open briefcase. He pulled out some papers that were stapled together and tossed them in Gurney's lap. "Reading material, to bring you up to speed."

In the dim dashboard light all he could see was the boldface headline on what appeared to be a copy of a scientific article: "Neuropsychology of Polygraphy: Exploitable Parameters."

Fenton pointed at it. "Lie-detector tests don't mean a thing when the subject is an expert on exploiting their weaknesses."

It struck Gurney that Hammond seemed to be an expert on just about every subject that made him look bad.

Like a trial attorney driving home the final point in his summation, Fenton reached into his briefcase and pulled out a single sheet of paper. "This is a copy of Ethan Gall's handwritten description of his dream, the same dream every one of the victims started having after being hypnotized by Hammond." He handed the sheet to Gurney. "Take it home with you. Read it every morning—to remind yourself of the worst client choice you ever made."

Gurney took it. "Any chance of it being a forgery?"

"Not a snowball's chance in hell. It's been analyzed and reana-lyzed. Pressure patterns, accelerations and decelerations over certain letter combinations, things no forger could duplicate. Besides, who the hell is this hypothetical forger with access to Gall's office? Peyton's generally so fucked up he can barely walk. Hammond himself would just be putting another nail in his own coffin. Ditto his adoring sister. Austen Steckle had his hand in a cast at the time, some carpal tun-nel crap. Who else is there who could have access? Barlow Tarr? I doubt that nutcase can even write. The plain fact is that it's Gall's own description of his own dream in his own writing. And every disgusting thing in it is consistent with the dreams of the other three victims."

He gave Gurney a hard stare. "I'm done explaining this to you. You're one millimeter away from an obstruction charge. You hear what I'm saying?"

"Are we finished here?"

"You better be finished here." Fenton gazed out in silence at the growing storm, then began shaking his head slowly. "I don't get you, Gurney. What are you, some kind of egomaniac who always thinks he's right and the rest of the team is wrong?"

"That would depend on the track record of the team."

Fenton's eyes were fixed on the swirling snow. He was gripping the steering wheel with both hands. "Let me ask you something. Where were you on 9/11?"

Gurney blinked at the abrupt segue. "My wife and I were away when the towers went down, but I got to ground zero that night. Why do you ask?"

"I was in Lower Manhattan that morning. At a joint NYPD-NYSP training session. We got sent to the towers as soon as the first plane hit." The man's knuckles were whitening from the force of his grip on the wheel. "So many years ago, and I still get nightmares. I can still hear the sound."

Gurney knew what "the sound" was. He'd heard versions of this experience from other cops and firemen. While the fires were spreading from floor to floor, people were jumping from the high windows.

"The sound" was the sound of the bodies hitting the pavement.

Gurney said nothing.

Eventually Fenton broke the silence. "You get my point, Gurney? That's what the world is now. That's the new reality. Nobody gets to sit on the fence anymore. It's about the survival of America. This is a war, not a game. You got to be on one side or the other."

Gurney nodded in a vague show of agreement. "Tell me something, Gilbert. Those important, powerful, anonymous people who've taken a special interest in the Hammond case—you sure they're on the side of the angels?"

Fenton turned in his seat, his expression incredulous and furious.

CHAPTER 44

On his way back to the suite, Gurney stopped in the Hearth Room to call Hardwick.

"Things are getting tense. I got another visit from Fenton. The man is under severe pressure to get rid of me."

"Any idea what it is you're doing that's getting them so agitated?"

"They're desperate for Hammond to confess, and they think I'm preventing that."

"These bastards actually believe he hypnotized four men into killing themselves?"

"That would seem to be the case."

"So what do you want me to do?"

"Stay close in case all hell should break loose."

"Anything else I should know about?"

Madeleine's mental state came to mind. But he wasn't ready to discuss that with anyone. "Not right now." He ended the call and went up to the suite. Tucked under his arm were Hammond's article on polygraphy and Gall's description of his nightmare.

He found Madeleine asleep with the bedside lamp on. In the sitting area the foil-covered plates Jane Hammond had brought over remained unopened on the coffee table. He settled down on the couch. The article, he noted, was eleven pages. The dream description was only half a page, so he started with that.

> *Per your request, these are the principal details of the dream I've been*
> *having since our last session. It begins with the illusion that I am*
> *awake, in my own bed. I develop an awareness of another presence*
> *in the room. I feel frightened and want to get up, but I discover I'm*

paralyzed. I want to call for help, but no words will come out. Then
I see, emerging from the darkness, a thing covered with bristling fur.
Somehow I know it's a wolf. I hear it growling. I see its eyes shining,
bright red, in the darkness. Then I feel its weight on me and its hot
breath. The breath has a rotten smell. There's a viscous fluid dripping
from its mouth. Then the wolf is transformed into a dagger. On the
handle there's a wolf's head with glittering ruby eyes. I feel something
going into me. I'm soaked with blood. Then I see a man holding the
dagger, offering me bright little pills. When I wake up I feel terrible. So
terrible that I wish I were dead.

Gurney turned the copy over and discovered on the back a notation written with a different kind of pen in a rougher hand, presumably
Fenton's: "Daggers similar to the one described here found at all four
suicide sites."

He went back to the front of the page and read the dream narrative again.

So many lurid particulars.

Was it conceivable that Hammond had planted this dream in the
minds of four people?

Was it conceivable that the dream had literally killed them?

The concept was astonishing.

So astonishing, Gurney couldn't believe it.

He put the dream description aside and went on to Hammond's
polygraph article.

He started off reading it carefully, then began skimming, seeing no
major revelations. Written years ago when Hammond was a doctoral
candidate, it examined factors that contribute to polygraph errors, both
accidental and induced. Simple factors included tricks such as using a
thumbtack concealed in one's clothing to produce pain at chosen points
in the process to throw off the machine's physiological response read-
ings. At the more complex end of the spectrum were certain mental
states, both meditative and disordered, that blurred the difference
between a subject's honest and deceptive responses.

"What time is it?"

Startled by the sound of Madeleine's voice, Gurney turned to find her standing by the couch, gazing at him with the look of someone emerging from a bad dream.

He checked his phone. "It's a little after nine."

She blinked, hesitated. "David?"

"Yes?"

"Do you think I'm losing my mind?"

"Of course not."

"I saw Colin in the tub. I'm sure of it. But it doesn't make any sense."

"It just means we haven't found the explanation yet. But we will."

"You really think everything is explainable?"

"I don't *think* it is. I *know* it is."

"Is seeing a ghost explainable?"

"You're thinking now that you saw a ghost? Not a physical body?"

"I don't know. I only know it was Colin. But there was something spirit-like about him. A kind of glow, as though I were looking not only at his body but at his soul. Do you believe we continue to exist after our bodies die?"

"I can't answer that, Maddie. I'm not even sure what the question means."

There was a lost look in her eyes. "Nothing like this has ever happened to you, has it?"

"No."

His phone rang.

He let it ring three more times before glancing at the ID screen.

It was Rebecca Holdenfield.

As urgently as he craved any input that might move the Hammond case forward, he didn't feel able to turn away from the look on Madeleine's face. He let the call go to voicemail.

She shivered. "I'm cold. I should go back to bed." She started to turn away from the couch, then stopped. "I forgot to tell you. Jane invited us to breakfast."

Given the situation with Fenton, visiting the Hammonds seemed like a bad idea. On the other hand, he felt it would be good for Madeleine to be out of the lodge, even for an hour.

"That's fine."

She nodded and went into the alcove.

He remained on the couch, trying to calm his racing thoughts. Then, remembering that simple actions often had calming effects, he decided to get up and make a fire.

As he reached the fireplace, he was startled by a thud at the balcony door.

His first thought was that a bird had flown into it. His second thought was that birds don't fly at night in snowstorms.

He went to the door and peered out through the glass panel. A coating of ice made it difficult to see anything. Cautiously, he opened the door.

He saw something lying on the snow that had blown onto the balcony.

He stepped out for a closer look.

It appeared to be an irregularly shaped package, about a foot long and three inches in diameter, clumsily wrapped with newspaper and duct tape.

He took another step to the balcony railing, looking as far as he could see in both directions along the lake road.

He saw no one—heard nothing but the wind.

He picked up the package, judging that it weighed less than a pound.

He took it inside to the coffee table. He pushed the two foil-covered plates out of the way and removed the duct tape that held the package together. Most of the newspaper wrapping came off with the tape.

Two devices lay exposed on the table in front of him.

One he recognized instantly as a fiber-optic surveillance camera.

The other device wasn't familiar at all. It was a matte-black object about the size of a roll of dimes. Along the side was something that appeared to be a serial number. On one end there were eight very small holes, and in each hole a shiny bit of curved glass.

Some sort of lenses? He'd never seen lenses that small. *But what else could they be?* There was one fact, however, about which Gurney became increasingly certain as he studied the dimensions of both devices. These were almost certainly the objects that had been installed in, and then removed from, the joist space he'd inspected in the attic—the space above the bathroom light fixture.

He suddenly noticed what he'd missed in his hurry to examine the devices.

Two words were roughly scribbled in block letters on the inside of one of the newspaper sheets that had been used as wrapping paper.

BE WARNT

CHAPTER 45

The language of the message obviously pointed to Barlow Tarr.
But if it was Tarr, why had he put himself at risk? And what exactly
was the evil Gurney was being "warnt" about—yet again?

And if it wasn't Tarr, why might someone want him to think it was?

Those questions kept him awake till the wee hours of the morning. Then, after sleeping fitfully for a couple of hours, he was awake
again before dawn. Finding himself slipping back into the same loop of
evidence-starved speculation, he decided to get up, take a shower, and
get dressed.

He went to the balcony door to evaluate the weather conditions.
Snow crystals passing through the reach of the lodge floodlights were
sparkling in the dry air. The thermometer mounted on the balcony railing, half-encrusted with ice, looked like it was registering eight below
zero. Gurney took a step out to make sure he was seeing it right.

As he turned to go back inside, something caught his eye. Something
on the road that led down from the ridge to the lodge.

A glint of light.

As he strained his eyes into the darkness he saw a second glint, a
few feet from the first. The two were moving in tandem, like headlights,
only smaller and weaker.

Parking lights, he realized.

He waited, watched, listened.

The lights came closer. Eventually they came close enough that he
could see that they were the parking lights of a pickup truck.

The truck turned onto the lake road, moved slowly past the outer
reach of the lodge floodlights, and on toward . . . toward what?

The boathouse?

One of the chalets?

The Gall mansion?

As the truck faded into the storm, Gurney noted that its disappearance was aided by the absence of any visible taillights.

He went inside and locked the door.

He spent the next half hour on his laptop, scanning through the products offered by suppliers of surveillance and anti-surveillance equipment, hoping to find something that resembled the strange little tubular device that had him baffled.

What he found was a thriving industry. Hundreds of companies, many with the word "Spy" in their names, were marketing sophisticated hardware at affordable prices.

The items fell into two main categories. Devices that purportedly enabled the user to observe and record anything that anyone did or said, just about anywhere. And devices designed to defeat all the capabilities of the first category. The underlying sales pitch seemed to be, "Spy on everyone. Be spied on by no one."

The perfect industry for a paranoid world.

He failed to find anything that looked like the little black gadget with the eight minuscule lenses—if that's what they were.

He examined it again. There seemed to be no way of opening it. He could detect no battery warmth in it. The number etched on the side offered no clue. It did, however, prompt him to try a long shot. He entered the serial number in his Internet search engine.

It produced one result, a website with the obscure address, "www.a1z2b3y4c5x.net."

He went to the site and found nothing there but an otherwise blank page with four data-entry boxes asking for a current ID, previous ID, current password, and previous password.

In a way, it was a dead end. But the wall of security it presented was noteworthy. At the very least, it was a reinforcement of Robin Wigg's warning. And Gilbert Fenton's warning. Not to mention the scribbled warning that arrived in the package.

Thinking of Wigg prompted him to get his phone, take photos of the device from several angles, and email them to her along with the serial number and website URL.

He received a reply less than two minutes later: "Pics inadequate.

Site locked. Send item." He was pleased by her interest but saw no timely way to comply with her request.

"How long have you been up?" Madeleine's voice startled him.

He turned and saw her standing by the bathroom door in her tee shirt and pajama bottoms.

"Maybe an hour or so?"

"We're due at the Hammonds at eight."

She went into the bathroom, leaving the door wide open. She stayed well away from the tub and went straight to the shower stall in the far corner.

Her willingness to use the room at all struck him as a positive sign.

While she was showering, he began thinking about the breakfast they'd be having with Richard and Jane, and how, despite his misgivings about the visit, he might make use of it. There were questions he could ask, reactions he could assess. He could bring up the theory of the four deaths being a form of revenge for a long-ago tragedy. A tragedy involving the disappearance of a gay teenager. It would be interesting to see what Richard had to say about that.

THE WIND GUSTING OVER THE SNOW-COVERED ROAD HAD ONLY partly obscured the tire tracks of the pickup truck that had traveled the same way earlier. Gurney's curiosity was intensified when he saw that the tracks turned off the road toward Richard's chalet and curved around the back of it. The vehicle that made those tracks must still be there. He was tempted to investigate on the spot but changed his mind when he saw how cold Madeleine looked.

Jane, as usual, welcomed them at the front door with an anxious smile. After they hung up their jackets, she led them into the big cathedral-ceilinged living area. "I had the chef at the lodge prepare a few different breakfast items for us—scrambled eggs, sausages, bacon, toast, oatmeal, mixed fruits. He delivered it all himself. The kitchen helper and housemaid stayed home in Bearston today, with the terrible weather, and he's leaving for home himself before it gets any worse. I asked him to put everything downstairs in the rec room, at your friend's suggestion."

"Excuse me?"

A familiar voice intervened. "I said you'd understand, because you're an understanding guy."

Jack Hardwick, grinning brightly, got up from the chair by the hearth. "Actually," he said, glancing significantly at the lamp with the bloodstone finial that Gurney had told him housed one of the bugs, "I thought you might prefer to be downstairs. Closer to the furnace. Feels warmer."

Jane added, "Richard was taking a quick shower. Let me see if he's ready."

As soon as she left the room, Hardwick lowered his voice. "With both of us here, maybe we can double our progress."

"You're not worried about Fenton finding out you're here?"

"I'm done worrying about Fenton. As soon as we get to the truth of this case, his ship sinks. And if he tries to swim, I'll piss in his face."

"Assuming our truth is different from his truth."

"It has to be——"

He was interrupted by Jane calling to them from a doorway on the far side of the stone hearth. "Richard's on his way. Let's go downstairs before the breakfast things get cold."

Once Jane was again out of sight, Madeleine turned to Hardwick. She spoke softly, calmly. "Richard Hammond isn't guilty of anything."

He stared at her for a long moment. "You look pale. You okay?"

"No, I'm not okay. Not at all. But that has nothing to do with Richard."

"Are you sick?"

"Maybe."

Hardwick seemed bewildered by her. He paused. "What makes you say that about Hammond?"

"I just know."

He looked at Gurney, as if seeking a translation.

THE SO-CALLED "REC ROOM" WAS A BIG SQUARE SPACE. THERE WAS an exercise area with a weight machine and a pair of treadmills; a media area with plush seats in front of a wide screen; a conversation area with a couch and armchairs; and an eating area with a sideboard, a dining table, and half a dozen Windsor chairs.

Richard and Jane were sitting across the table from Dave and Madeleine, and Jack was sitting at the end. They'd all gotten what they wanted from the sideboard and had briefly discussed the weather and the dreadful blizzard to come. It quickly became apparent that no one really wanted to talk about it, and the group fell into an edgy silence.

Finally, with her throat sounding painfully raw, Jane spoke up. "I was wondering . . . with all you've been looking into . . . if you might possibly have some good news for us?"

"We do have some 'news,'" said Gurney. "We've discovered that the four deaths may be related to the disappearance of a teenage boy in upstate New York thirteen years ago."

Richard appeared curious, Jane puzzled.

Gurney recounted the story of the tragic summer at Camp Brightwater—in all the detail provided by Moe Blumberg and Kimberly Fallon.

At the mention of Scott Fallon's almost-certain death, Jane's hand went to her heart. "How awful!"

Richard's expression was hard to read. "You're saying that Wenzel, Balzac, and Pardosa were all at Brightwater that summer?"

"It looks that way."

"So what's the connection to Ethan?"

"We're thinking he may have been there as well."

"You must be joking."

"Why is that?"

"Ethan spent his summers from age twelve to twenty-one in Switzerland. Then, when his mother died and he inherited the Wolf Lake estate, he worked here day and night, fifty-two weeks a year, turning the lodge into the going concern it is today."

"What was he doing in Switzerland?"

"Equestrian school, French and German language schools, trap shooting, fly fishing, et cetera. Opportunities to mingle with other young people of good breeding. The notion that Ethan Gall would have been sent to a blue-collar camp in the Catskills is ludicrous." Hammond paused, his faint smile fading. "Wait a second, your question about Brightwater—were you thinking that Ethan could have been involved with those other three in something that rotten, that despicable?"

"It was a possibility I had to consider."

Richard looked accusingly at Hardwick. "You too?"

"My own experience is that any kind of person can be the kind of person you never thought they could be." There was something cold and assessing in Hardwick's eyes.

"I agree, theoretically. But the idea that he could be part of a band of gay-bashing bullies is just so . . . so . . ." His voice trailed off, and he began again. "A couple of years ago, around the time Ethan persuaded me to come to Wolf Lake, he was about to give away everything, all his assets. He intended to transfer ownership of everything to the Gall New Life Foundation in the form of an irrevocable trust—with only a modest annual income from the investment proceeds to continue for himself and Peyton during their lifetimes."

Hardwick reacted with a raised eyebrow.

Gurney smiled encouragingly. "That sounds very generous."

"That's my point. That's who Ethan was. A wealthy man with no love of wealth, except for what good it could accomplish in the world."

Hardwick barked out a loud cough. "You said he was 'about to' do that. Which means he didn't actually do it, right?"

"Austen persuaded him that he could do more good if he retained control of the assets."

Gurney stepped in again. "What sort of 'good' are we talking about?"

"If everything went into an irrevocable trust for the foundation, Ethan would lose what little power he had over Peyton's behavior."

"He couldn't threaten to disinherit him if there was nothing left to be inherited?"

"Exactly. And Austen's final point, the one that really tipped the scales with Ethan, was that the foundation's primary support shouldn't come from the generosity of its founder. It should come from the contributions of the successful 'graduates' of its rehabilitation program. Austen made a strong case for the 'giving back' concept."

"Why was Austen involved?" asked Gurney.

"Austen was involved because money was involved. Of course, Ethan made his own decision. But he always respected Austen's input."

Jane was twisting her napkin. "The three young men you say were at that camp together . . . and came up to see Richard? Were you able to find out anything else about them?"

"Odd things. All three despised gay men. And at least one was informed that you were gay—before he made his appointment to see you. It's possible all three had the same information—since they all got calls from the same cell number before coming here."

Hammond and Jane looked at each other, perplexed.

Jane voiced the obvious question. "Why would someone like that want to see Richard?"

"There's evidence that all three experienced dramatic financial improvements in their lives right around the time of their sessions with Richard."

Hammond looked baffled. "Are you implying someone paid them to meet with me?"

Gurney shrugged. "I'm just telling you what we discovered."

Hardwick gave Hammond an assessing look. "Suppose you learned the identity of three shit-bags who'd beaten a boy to death for the crime of being gay. Suppose you had no doubt about their guilt. But the proof, because of some technicality, would not be allowed in court; so you believed they would escape punishment. What would you do?"

Hammond gazed sadly at Hardwick. "You may have intended that as a trick question. But it's a very painful question."

"And the answer is . . . ?"

"Nothing. I wouldn't do anything. I'd want to kill them, but I wouldn't be able to."

"Why not?"

Tears welled in Hammond's extraordinary blue-green eyes. "I simply wouldn't have the courage."

A silence enveloped the table.

Hardwick nodded thoughtfully, as if the answer made sense to him, as if he now trusted Hammond a little more than he had before.

Gurney felt the same way. He felt that Hammond was probably innocent.

If he wasn't innocent, he was just about the best liar on earth.

CHAPTER 46

Half an hour later, sitting in the Outback in front of the chalet with Madeleine and Hardwick, Gurney pointedly emphasized the need for objectivity.

Hardwick agreed. "I got the impression he was being straight with us. Your gut telling you anything different?"

"My gut is delivering pretty much the same message as yours," said Gurney. "But my brain is telling me my gut shouldn't be the final authority."

Gurney reached into the glove box and took out the small cylindrical device that had arrived in the package on the balcony. He explained his near-certainty that it had been one of two pieces of electronic equipment installed over the bathroom in their suite. He concluded by asking Hardwick if he'd ever seen anything like it.

Hardwick switched on the dome light and studied the device. "Never. You send a photo of it to Wigg?"

"I did. But the thing is, she wants to see the object itself."

Hardwick grimaced. "You suggesting I should hand-deliver it?"

"It's just a quick run down to Albany."

Hardwick put it in his jacket pocket. "Goddamn pain in the ass. You realize this contradicts your request that I hang close by?"

"Your not being here makes me nervous. But not knowing what that thing is makes me more nervous."

"Better not turn out to be a fucking flashlight."

"By the way, that pickup truck in back of the chalet is yours, right?"

"Actually belongs to Esti Moreno, love of my life."

"She's still living with you?"

"You doubt my ability to maintain a stable relationship?"

"Yes."

"I gave her a list of all the key players we know of. She's digging up whatever she can. In fact, she's the one who dug up Steckle's drug-dealing background. She lent me her truck. Hate to leave the GTO at home, but my favorite machine is shit in the snow. Forecast says a ton of that's on the way. Which reminds me of Moe Blumberg."

"Excuse me?"

"The timing. Shouldn't we be worried that a man with a Brightwater background, who probably knows more than he's telling us, just happens to be leaving the country?"

"I hadn't thought to worry about that; but now that you mention it, I probably will."

"And how about the dead kid's mother? When you think about possible motives, wouldn't she have the strongest one of all—to kill the fuckheads who killed her son?"

"From a pure motive point of view, I guess we can keep her in the picture. Problem is, she'd have a credible motive to kill the three who were at Brightwater. But why kill Ethan? And why now? Why not thirteen years ago?"

"That question would apply not just to Kimberly Fallon but to anyone who wanted to get even. The more I think about the old saying, 'Revenge is a dish best served cold,' the less credible it seems as a practical reason to put something off that long. Which makes the revenge motive pretty damn doubtful."

"I don't disagree, Jack. But if revenge has nothing to do with it, then what's the Brightwater connection all about?"

"Fucked if I know. Too many questions in this case. And I'll give you one more. How come Ethan's dream description, which he wrote in the form of a letter, was never mailed?"

"Maybe he intended to deliver it personally to whoever asked him for it."

"You mean, like to some therapist he was secretly seeing in Plattsburgh?"

"Or to Richard—a possibility we seem to be minimizing."

"This conversation is nothing but question marks. If I'm going to get to Albany and back before everything is snowed in, I better leave. I'll let the Hammonds know I'm going."

"Stay in touch."

Hardwick nodded, got out of the car, and headed into the chalet. Gurney pulled out onto the lake road.

WHEN THEY ARRIVED BACK AT THE LODGE, THE GRANDFATHER clock in the reception area was striking the final note of 10:00 AM. There was a deep stillness about the place, an empty feeling. They headed up the stairs. Madeleine's arms were hugging her body tightly. "What are you going to do about the bathroom?"

"There's not a lot to be done."

"You said there was an opening by the light."

"Just a narrow gap between the fixture medallion and the ceiling."

"Can you close it up?"

It was the first thing he did after they went into the suite. All he had to do was nudge the medallion a quarter inch sideways, which he did with a few sharp taps with the handle of his toothbrush.

When he came out of the bathroom he found Madeleine at one of the windows, gazing out toward Devil's Fang. The angle of the light against her cheek was making the tic more noticeable. She was still wearing her jacket and gloves.

"Could you do me a favor and type an email for me to my sister? I don't want to take my gloves off. My fingers are aching with the cold as it is."

"No problem. I'll use my laptop. I hate using the screen keyboard on your tablet."

When he was ready, she dictated the message while still facing the window.

It's been a while since we've spoken. For that I apologize. This may seem a strange way to begin, after so long a silence, but I have a huge request. I need you to look back to the time when I was a teenager— when I was fourteen, fifteen, sixteen. What do you remember about me in those years? What kind of person was I? Were you worried about me? What did I seem to want from you, from Mom and Dad, from my friends . . . from boys? Do you remember what made me angry? Or happy? Or sad? I need to know these things. Please think about them. Please tell me as much as you can. I need to know who I was back then.

She took a deep breath and let out a slow sigh. She wiped her face—seemed to be wiping away tears—with her still-gloved hands.

He felt helpless. After a few moments he asked, "Is there a particular way you want me to sign this for you?"

"No. Just save it, and I'll take care of it before I send it. I had to get those questions written down while they were clear in my mind." She finally turned away from the window. "I'm going to take a hot shower to get the chill out of my bones."

She went into the bathroom, leaving the door open, and turned on the shower taps. She went to the corner of the room farthest from the tub and began taking off her clothes.

He saved the email to her sister and put his laptop to sleep.

He remembered that he'd gotten a call from Rebecca, the call he'd chosen not to take the previous evening in the middle of his conversation with Madeleine. He decided to listen to it now.

"David, when you asked me the other day if I knew anything about the term 'trance-induced suicide,' I said it sounded familiar. I just remembered why. And I looked it up in the New York Times *online archive to refresh my memory. There was a report in the paper almost four years ago concerning one of those government leaker cases.*

"A former CIA employee claimed that a secret directorate with the agency's Field Operations Psychological Research and Support Unit was conducting unauthorized experiments in hypnotic mind control. No big surprise there. However, the purpose of the experiments was to see if an otherwise normal subject could be rendered suicidal. According to the leaker, whose name was Sylvan Marschalk, considerable resources were being applied to the project. I guess the notion of magically persuading people to kill themselves had a lot of appeal. It sounds ridiculous, but probably no more ridiculous than their plot to assassinate Castro with an exploding cigar. Apparently the project was taken seriously enough to generate its own clandestine budget and its own acronym—TIS, for trance-induced suicide.

"A week after he made his revelations he was found dead in Central Park of a massive drug overdose. Naturally, the official line was that there was no secret directorate and no experiments, and Marschalk's claims were the unfortunate ravings of a paranoid drug addict.

"So that's the story, David. If by any chance you're crossing swords with those same folks . . . God help you. Call when you can. Let me know that you're alive. No joke."

Gurney went to his laptop and typed 'Sylvan Marschalk' into his search site. The *New York Times* article popped up first. Actually, a pair of articles. The first focused on "the allegations of a former CIA analyst." The second, dated a week later, focused on the drug overdose. He read both carefully and found nothing in either Rebecca hadn't already mentioned. He checked the other news items that came up in the search, all briefer than the ones in the *Times*. There were no follow-ups.

The story was jarring—not only because of the way it ended, but because the leaker's accusations regarding "induced suicide" research gave more credibility to the concept.

He was still sitting on the couch pondering the implications when Madeleine emerged from the bathroom, wrapped in a towel.

"Can you transfer that email for my sister from your computer to mine?"

"You don't want to send it from mine?"

"No, because when she replies to it, I'd like the reply to come to my own tablet."

He went to the saved email document, entered Madeleine's email address at the top, and hit "Send." Once he saw that the process was completed, he closed down his laptop.

That's when it hit him.

He sat motionless, almost breathless, for several long seconds, considering a startling possibility.

If someone had found the unaddressed document while it was still in his unsent email file, wouldn't they have assumed that he was writing about himself, his own emotional turmoil?

Suppose that was the same incorrect assumption being made about Ethan Gall's handwritten document? Might it not be, in fact, a description of someone else's nightmare—someone who, for reasons yet unknown, dictated their experience in the form of a letter they planned to send to a third party—exactly as Madeleine had done?

This hypothetical scenario took hold of Gurney's mind. Soon he became convinced it was the truth. Someone had gone to Ethan and asked him to write out a letter for him—a letter to the therapist with whom he'd had the "session" that began his series of nightmares. He dictated what he wanted written, and Ethan wrote it down for him.

Ironically, Gurney was so certain that this was the way it must have happened that he began to suspect his own objectivity. He'd learned on a number of occasions that the best way to test an idea he might be loving too much was to expose it to Hardwick's skepticism.

But that was a call he'd want to make with more privacy than the bugged suite permitted. The option of using Madeleine's tablet to drown out his conversation with music—at the same time as she was using it to review the emotionally fraught email she'd be sending to her sister—did not seem feasible. And the speaker volume in his own aging laptop simply wasn't adequate.

He went over to the alcove.

Madeleine was siting on the edge of the bed, studying the wording of her email on her tablet screen, her mouth a tight line of anxiety.

"Maddie?"

"What?"

"I have to go downstairs."

She nodded vaguely.

"I'll be back in a few minutes."

She didn't reply. He took the key, went out, and locked the door behind him.

The Hearth Room still had the cold, empty feeling it had earlier. He settled into a leather armchair against the far wall, a spot from which he could keep an eye on the reception area. Hoping Hardwick would be within range of a cell tower, he made the call.

The man answered immediately, apparently eager to complain.

"Road out of the Wolf Lake estate was a horror. Right now I'm creeping along on the county route behind a monster plow-sander-salter. Impossible to get past him. What's up with you?"

"I wanted to get your opinion on a certain aspect of the case."

"You mean like the totally fucked-up impossibility of the whole thing?"

"Just Ethan's handwritten dream narrative."

There was a pause. Gurney could hear through the phone the heavy rumbling of the plow. When Hardwick spoke again his tone was calmer. "Definitely an odd little item. What are you thinking?"

Gurney explained his new theory of how the written nightmare description could have come to be, and how Madeleine's email dictation had led him to that conclusion.

Hardwick cleared his throat. "It's . . . possible."

Gurney wasn't put off by his apparent lack of enthusiasm. He interpreted it as a sign that he was giving the idea serious thought.

"It's possible," Hardwick repeated. "But if Ethan wasn't writing down his own dream, then whose dream was it? And why were the details later reflected in the way he died?"

"Like the wolf dagger Fenton claims he cut his wrists with? I don't know. I'm not saying the dictation hypothesis is the final answer, but it fits with the idea that Ethan's part in the affair was different from that of the other three victims. He always struck me as the odd man out."

"You're saying we've got three people who had nightmares and ended up dead, and one person who transcribed someone's else's nightmare and ended up dead. But I'm still stuck at the basic question. Could a hypnotist—Richard or anyone else—have caused those nightmares and suicides?"

"Interesting you should bring that up. I just listened to a message from Rebecca Holdenfield about a CIA leaker who claimed that the agency was actively researching that very subject—obviously in the belief that it could be done."

"Of course, they denied it?"

"Of course. But I have to say that all the hints of national security interest in this case could be connected to that kind of program."

Hardwick sighed impatiently. "The problem I have with the fatal-hypnosis thing is that it turns the whole thing back on Hammond and makes Fenton right. As I said before, that is not an acceptable outcome. Hold on a second, ace. Let me put down the phone. I have a chance here to get around the monster plow."

When Hardwick came back on the phone half a minute later, Gurney could hear the rumble of the plow fading into the distance. "So what do you think we actually know, Sherlock?"

"Taking Ethan out of the equation for the moment, we know that three gay-hating men were offered some kind of financial incentive to visit a gay hypnotherapist. We know they all later reported having nightmares, and shortly afterward each one was found dead. And we know that the investigating officer has zeroed in on Richard Hammond as the orchestrator of all this."

"A decision about which we have our doubts?"

"Correct."

"Okay," said Hardwick, beginning to sound exasperated. "Once again we circle back to the key question. If Hammond didn't give them their nightmares, who did? That's the only question that matters. Am I right?"

If Hammond didn't give them their nightmares, who did?

If Hammond didn't give . . .

Holy Christ!

For the second time that morning, Gurney almost stopped breathing. He stared straight ahead but saw nothing. His focus was entirely on the significance of what Hardwick had just said. He repeated it to himself.

If Hammond didn't give them their nightmares, who did?

"Hey, Sherlock, you still there?"

He began to laugh.

"What the hell's so funny?"

"Your question. It only sounds like a question. It's really an answer. In fact, it may be the key to the whole damn case."

CHAPTER 47

Hardwick drove into a cell-service dead zone before Gurney could elaborate on his sudden insight. It gave him an opportunity to test it from different angles to be sure it felt solid.

Twenty minutes later Hardwick called back. "Glad you think I'm so fucking brilliant. But what exactly is this 'key' I gave you?"

"The wording of your original question. You asked, if it wasn't Hammond, then who gave the victims their nightmares."

"So?"

"So that's the solution to the problem we've been banging our heads against from the beginning. The victims were given those nightmares. I mean, they were literally handed to them." Gurney paused, waiting for a reaction.

"Keep talking."

"Okay. Let's leave Ethan out of it for the moment, because something different was going on with him. As for the other three, I believe each one was given a description of the nightmare. They never had the nightmares they complained about, never actually dreamt those things. They just memorized the details they were given and recounted them later as if they'd experienced them."

"Why the hell would they do that?"

"Because that's what they were being paid to do. We already saw evidence that there was some financial benefit connected with their coming to Wolf Lake—that things suddenly appeared to be looking up for all three of them. We didn't know why. But this would explain it. I'm pretty sure that they were paid for coming to the lodge, having a session with Hammond, and then complaining about bizarre dreams. Not only complaining, but reporting the inflammatory details to reliable witnesses—Wenzel to a high-profile evangelical minister, Balzac to a therapist, Pardosa to his chiropractor."

"Sounds like a hell of a scheme. But what was the end game?"

"It could have been a number of things. Maybe they were setting up the basis for taking some kind of bogus legal action against Hammond? A malpractice suit? Phony sexual assault charges? Maybe the whole thing was a plot to destroy his therapy practice? If Bowman Cox's comments were any indication, Hammond stirred up enough animosity in certain circles to make something like that credible. In fact, as I think about it now, I wonder if the Reverend Cox might have played a bigger role than he admits to."

"Christ, Davey, I need a minute to get my head around this. I mean, if nobody dreamt anything, then——"

"Wait—hold on second."

Madeleine, bundled up in ski pants, jacket, scarf, and hat, was heading out through the reception area.

"Jack, I'll call you back in a few minutes."

He caught up with Madeleine at the lodge door.

"What's up?"

"I want to get some air. It stopped snowing."

"You could just step out on our balcony."

She shook her head. "I want to be outside. Really outside. I'm sure the snow is going to start again, so this is my chance."

"Want me to come with you?"

"No. You do what you're doing. I know it's important. And stop looking at me like that."

"Like what?"

"Like I'm going to fall apart. I'll be fine."

He nodded. "I'll be here . . . if you need anything."

"Good." She pushed the heavy door open and stepped out into the frigid air.

With some reluctance Gurney returned to his leather chair by the hearth. He got Hardwick back on the phone. "Sorry for the interruption. So what do you think of the new theory?"

"Part of it I like a lot. I love getting rid of the idea that somebody made somebody else dream something, and the dream made them kill themselves."

"What part don't you like?"

"You're saying there was a carefully worked-out plan involving three gay-hating creeps, possibly the same gay-hating creeps who killed the kid at Brightwater. And they came to Wolf Lake to meet with Hammond so they could later claim that he fucked with their minds, giving them horrible, sickening dreams. And their secret goal was to destroy Hammond's reputation . . . or sue him . . . or build a criminal case against him . . . or maybe blackmail him into paying them to shut up and go away. Am I on track?"

"Better than that, Jack. I think you just hit the bull's-eye. Blackmail. I think that's what it was all about. It's a perfect fit. They'd love the idea of extorting big bucks from a gay doctor, a known aider and abetter of perverts. They could even view their get-rich plan as the work of the Lord. I bet just thinking about it would have given them a power rush."

Hardwick was silent for a long moment. "But here's what I don't get. How come these ruthless, gay-hating bastards are now all dead, while their intended victim is alive and well?"

"An interesting question. Almost as interesting as . . ." Gurney's voice trailed off.

Austen Steckle, in an arctic fur hat and heavy coat, was coming in through the lodge door, pulling a two-wheeled cart full of split logs. He pulled it across the reception area, into the Hearth Room, and over to the log rack near Gurney's chair.

He sniffled and wiped his nose with the back of a heavily gloved hand. "My friend, you need to talk to your wife out there."

"I beg your pardon?"

"Your wife. I warned her about that ice."

Gurney didn't wait to hear the rest. Coatless, he hurried out of the lodge and across the lake road. Although no snow was falling at that moment, gusts of wind were kicking up powdery whirlwinds from the lake surface, making it hard to see very far.

"Maddie!" he called, listening for a reply.

All he heard was the wind.

He shouted her name.

Again there was no reply.

Feeling a touch of panic, he was about to shout her name again when the snowy gusts abated and he saw her—standing still, her back to him, about a hundred yards out on the snow-covered ice.

He called to her again.

She neither moved nor answered.

He stepped out onto the lake surface.

He'd taken only a few steps when a movement in the sky caught his eye.

It was a hawk—presumably the same hawk he'd seen on several occasions circling above the lake, over the sharp peak of Devil's Fang, along the length of Cemetery Ridge. But this time it was circling lower—at an altitude of perhaps two hundred feet.

As he watched, the next circle appeared to be lower.

And the next still lower.

Her face tilted upward, Madeleine was evidently watching it as well.

Gurney was sure now that the bird was gliding in a gradually tightening spiral—the radius shrinking with each successive orbit. It was a behavior he'd observed in raptors above the fields back in Walnut Crossing. In those cases, the purpose of the behavior seemed to be the closer evaluation of prey in preparation for an attack. The iced-over lake, however, seemed an unlikely hunting ground. In fact, with the exception of Madeleine herself, there was nothing visible to Gurney anywhere on the smooth white surface.

Still the hawk circled lower.

It had descended to no more than forty feet above the lake.

Gurney was moving quickly now.

The hawk seemed to hesitate for a moment on its flight path, rocking on its broad wings from side to side, as if assessing the significance of a second figure entering the scene.

Just as Gurney was concluding that his presence had scared it off, it wheeled sharply toward Madeleine, diving at her with startling acceleration.

In an effort to break into a flat-out sprint, Gurney slipped and fell. He scrambled to his knees, pulled out his Beretta, and shouted, "GET DOWN!"

As Madeleine turned in his direction, the plummeting hawk extended its razor talons, and Gurney fired.

The gunshot caused Madeleine to flinch, ducking just enough that the talons flashed by harmlessly over her head.

Amazingly, the hawk came around again in a wide circle, rising thirty or forty feet above her before beginning a second dive.

This time Madeleine ran, sliding, half-falling, out toward the center of the lake. Again the hawk swooped down past her head in a near miss—with Gurney clambering to his feet, running after her, shouting to her to stop, to not go any farther on the ice.

As the hawk, at the far end of yet another circle, turned in toward Madeleine, Gurney spread his feet in a solid shooting stance and steadied his weapon in a two-handed grip. As the bird streaked past him he fired. He caught a glimpse of a tail feather breaking off and twirling around in a passing gust before settling on the ice.

The hawk passed only a few inches over Madeleine's head. Then, instead of circling again, it rose gradually up and away, disappearing finally over the treetops at the end of the lake.

Madeleine had stopped running. She was about fifty feet ahead of him. She looked to be out of breath, or crying, or both.

He called to her. "Are you all right?"

She turned toward him and nodded.

"Come back this way. We need to get off the ice."

She began walking toward him, slowly. When she was ten or twelve feet away, he heard a sound that stopped his breath.

CHAPTER 48

As she shifted her weight onto her forward foot, from directly beneath it came the strained creaking of ice about to break apart.

"Stop! Don't move!" cried Gurney.

She halted like a freeze-frame in a video.

"You'll be all right. Just try not to move."

Gurney searched for solutions, but the only thing that came to mind was a sequence in an action-adventure movie he'd seen as a kid. A Canadian Mountie had pursued a bank robber onto a frozen river. The ice began to crack around the fugitive. The Mountie told him to lie down on the ice to spread his weight. Then he threw him a rope and pulled him to safety.

The scene was silly, but the weight distribution part made sense to Gurney. He persuaded Madeleine to lower herself carefully to the ice, lie flat, and spread out her arms and legs.

Needing something to take the place of a rope, he retreated to the shore, hoping to find a fallen pine branch long enough to do the job. He grabbed the longest one he could find, dragged it out onto the lake, and extended the end of it to Madeleine.

"Grip it with both hands. Don't let go."

It was a painfully slow process. Sitting on the ice to give himself better traction and pushing himself backward with his heels, inch by inch he pulled her out of harm's way.

As they were finally approaching the security of solid ground and getting to their feet, Austen Steckle and Norris Landon came running from the lodge.

Landon had a long tow chain coiled around his arm. "You're safe. Thank God! Sorry it took me so long. Damn door latch was frozen on the Rover."

Steckle looked grim. "What the hell happened out there?"

"Did you see that damn hawk attacking my wife?"

Landon's eyes widened. "Hawk?"

"A big one," said Gurney. "Swooped down on her. She was trying to get away from it. Ended up out there on the middle of the lake. I didn't think hawks attacked humans."

"Normally they don't," said Landon.

"Nothing normal about Wolf Lake," muttered Steckle. "Last summer a goddamn owl attacked a little girl on the shore, ripped her face. And the summer before that a black bear did a pretty good job on a hiker—"

"Those shots we heard?" said Landon. "Was that you shooting at the hawk?"

"That's what scared it off."

Landon turned to Madeleine. "You must be a wreck after all that. Was the ice under you actually starting to give way?"

"I thought I was going to die."

Gurney took Madeleine's arm. With shoulders hunched against the wind, they walked back across the lake road, into the lodge, and on into the Hearth Room, where a fresh fire was blazing. It wasn't until they were standing in front of it that Gurney realized his teeth were chattering.

Landon went straight to the self-service bar. A minute later he joined them at the fire, handing them each a small crystal tumbler half full of an amber liquid. "Cognac. Best medicine for thawing out the bones."

He and Gurney drank. Madeleine sniffed at hers, took a tiny sip, winced at the strength of it, then took another.

Landon downed the last of his drink. "This cognac's not bad at all." He studied the bottom of his empty glass for a long moment. "Making any progress on the crime front?"

"Things are becoming a little clearer."

"That's good to hear. If there's anything at all I can do to help . . ."

"I appreciate that. I'll let you know."

"How's it looking for Richard?"

"Better than it was."

Landon looked surprised. "Care for another cognac?"

"Not now, thanks."

"Right. Well. Stay warm if you can." Raising his hand in a mock salute, he left the room.

Madeleine was holding her palms out toward the fire. Gurney moved closer to her. His tone was gentler than his words. "Maddie, what the hell were you doing out there on the ice?"

"I don't think I can explain it."

"Tell me whatever you can."

"I really did just go out to get some air, like I told you."

"But then you walked out on the ice."

"Yes."

"What were you thinking?"

"I was thinking that in my mind, my memory, I'm always on the shore."

"On the shore of Grayson Lake?"

"Yes."

"So you decided to go walk out on the ice?"

"Yes."

"Was this something Hammond suggested you do?"

"No. There was no plan. I was standing in front of the lodge. I happened to look out at the lake. And suddenly I wanted to be out there."

"Out there like Colin?"

"Maybe. Maybe I wanted to feel what he felt."

CHAPTER 49

Despite the blazing fire, the moaning of the wind in the chimney was creating a mournful atmosphere in the Hearth Room. It made the prospect of retreating to their bugged suite attractive by comparison.

As they were passing through the reception area, Madeleine stopped by the big glass-paneled door. Gurney stopped with her.

Thinking of the two shots he'd fired at the hawk brought to mind the image of the dislodged feather twirling down. "Wait just a minute," he said. "I want to get something."

He opened the door to a blast of frigid air and ran across the road and out onto the lake to the place where he remembered seeing the feather fall. It was still there, sticking up through the new snow just enough to be visible. He grabbed it and hurried back to the lodge, where he examined it briefly—a segment of a russet tail feather with a shattered quill. Then he stuffed it in his pocket, and he and Madeleine headed upstairs.

Just before they entered the suite, he asked her to use the tablet to find an energetic musical selection on YouTube, explaining that he owed Hardwick a callback to finish their interrupted conversation, and he wanted some audio camouflage that would enable him to speak freely.

She chose an atonal piano concerto whose agitato movement could have drowned out a gunfight. Gurney settled down on the couch, switched on the table lamp to brighten the gray light coming in from the windows, and made the call.

Hardwick picked up on the first ring.

"Hey, Jack, how are the roads?"

"Like greased pig shit. Didn't you say you were going to get back to me in a few minutes? You must have some fucking odd concept of the word 'few.'"

Gurney ignored the ritual abuse. "The last thing we were talking about was the odd circumstance of all those bad guys biting the dust while their intended victim remained alive and well. You have any ideas about that?"

"I do. It kinda falls into the counterintuitive box, but it makes sense."

"Okay. So what is it?"

"I'm thinking Jane Hammond may have whacked all four vics. Or at least three of them."

Gurney waited.

"You still there?"

"I'm waiting for the part that makes sense."

"Let's say there was a conspiracy to concoct a creepy-dirty case against Richard—for the purpose of blackmailing him. And suppose Jane found out about it. Or maybe the blackmailers got in touch with her directly. Told her about a big malpractice suit they were planning. Hinted that a generous out-of-court settlement could be in everyone's best interest."

"And then what?"

"And then sweet little Jane went into protective Grizzly Bear mode and decided the only good blackmailers were dead blackmailers. And no crime, no matter how bloody, would really be a crime if it involved saving her precious brother from evil predators."

"You really see Jane doing those murders?"

"Grizzly Bear knows no limits."

Gurney tried to work his way through the scenario. "Theoretically, I get the possible motive. But I'm tripping over issues of means and opportunity. Are you saying that she thought Ethan was part of the conspiracy and killed him, too?"

"I can't say that yet. Ethan's role is still a mystery."

"Why set up the murders to look like the dreams they'd been claiming to have? If she was trying to protect Richard, why do it in a way that would pull him further into it?"

"Maybe she was just trying to create credible suicide scenes. Maybe she was thinking, as long as these guys were dreaming about daggers, it would make sense to have it look like they cut their wrists with daggers?"

"Are you hearing yourself, Jack? Can you really picture Jane

Hammond running around the country—New Jersey, Long Island, Florida—drugging these guys and slicing up their wrists? And if she did all that, why would she be so eager to have you and me rooting around, trying to figure it all out?"

"That last question's easy. She wouldn't have anticipated the way the official investigation would go. Who the fuck would expect a BCI investigator to become obsessed with some exotic trance-induced suicide scenario? So when Fenton turned everything against Richard with that cockamamie concept, what the hell was she going to do? I think she brought us in to dig him out of the hole she put him in. She accepted the risk that she might end up paying the price. It would be better than seeing her brother prosecuted for what she did. That would completely blow her circuits."

"You're making an enthusiastic case, Jack, but—" He was stopped in mid-sentence by the sound, barely audible behind the music, of the shower being turned on.

Again? Jesus! First, an endless succession of baths. Now, showers.

"You there, ace?"

"What? Sure. Just thinking. Going over what you were saying."

"I know it's not all nailed down. Bits and pieces are still bouncing around. The idea just came to me twenty minutes ago. It needs more thought. But my point is, Janie the cuddly caretaker should not be getting a free pass. Just because she talks like a social worker doesn't mean she couldn't slice a few wrists, given the right circumstances."

Gurney had other problems with the Jane-as-killer hypothesis, but he left them unstated. While he had Hardwick on the phone, he wanted to move on to aspects of the case he deemed more promising. But before he had a chance to, the man hit him with an unnervingly timely question:

"How come your wife's so freaked out by all this?"

Gurney wasn't sure how much he should reveal to Hardwick. Or if he wanted to reveal anything at all.

"You think she looks troubled?"

"Looks, sounds, acts. It just seems odd—for a homicide guy's wife who's been through this kind of shit before. So I'm wondering what the deer-in-the-headlights look is all about."

Gurney paused. He hated thinking about it. He looked around the room—maybe for a way out, maybe for an inspiration. He ended up staring at the portrait of Harding. A man who never wanted to deal with anything.

He sighed. "Long story."

Hardwick belched. "Everything's a long story. But every story has a short version, right?"

"Problem is, it's not my story to tell."

"So you're telling me she's not only fucked up, she's fucked up with a secret?"

"Something like that." He looked over his shoulder through the open bathroom door and saw that Madeleine was still in the shower.

"This secret of hers affecting what we're trying to do here?"

Gurney hesitated, then decided to reveal what he could without getting too explicit. "She used to spend her Christmas vacations with relatives here in the Adirondacks. Something bad happened the last year she was here. She's dealing with difficult memories."

"Maybe you should take her home?"

"She wants to get some kind of closure here. And she wants us to 'save' Hammond."

"Why?"

"I think to make up for someone in her life a long time ago who wasn't saved."

"That sounds fucked up."

Gurney hesitated. "She's seeing things."

"What kind of things?"

"A dead body. Or maybe a ghost. She's not sure."

"Where did she see it?"

"In the bathtub."

"Are you fucking kidding me?"

"No."

There was a moment of silence.

"Any particular dead body?"

"Someone from her past. Her Adirondack past."

"Someone connected with the bad thing that happened?"

"Yes."

"And she thinks saving Hammond now will make up for what happened then?"

"I think so."

"Shit. That doesn't sound like the Madeleine I know."

"No. It's not like her at all. She's in the grip of . . . I don't know what."

"What do you want to do?"

"I want to figure out what's going on. Expose the truth. Get her the hell out of here."

He glanced over into the bathroom, saw her still standing in the shower behind the steamy glass door. He told himself this was a good thing. The primal, curative power of warm water.

"So," said Hardwick in an abrupt change of tone, "apart from my delivering the little black tube thing to Wigg, you have a next step in mind?"

"I have a question."

"We already have a shitload of questions."

"Maybe not the right ones. We just wasted five days asking ourselves how four people could have had the same dream. Wrong question. The right question would have been, 'Why did three people say they had the same dream, and why did one person write down the details of that dream?' Because, beyond their own claims, and Gilbert Fenton's endorsement of those claims, there was never any evidence that they actually dreamt anything. We assumed the reports of the nightmares were truthful, and since the men who reported having them were killed, they appeared to be victims, not predators. It never occurred to us that they might be both. I don't want to make a mistake like that again."

"I get your point. We screwed up. So what's your question?"

"My question is . . . are we observing failure or success?"

Over the phone Gurney heard a car horn blowing—followed by Hardwick's truculent, growling voice: "Move it, asshole!"

A moment later, he was back on the phone. "Failure or success? Fuck does that mean?"

"Simple. Your own 'Killer Jane' hypothesis is a failure hypothesis. It assumes that the sessions with Richard, along with the subsequent nightmare claims, were the planned elements of a blackmail conspiracy—but that the deaths weren't part of the plan. In your hypothesis Richard being blamed for the murders was an unintended consequence of Jane killing the bad guys. Bottom line, you're describing a failed conspiracy—with an ironic finale in which the intended victim of the blackmailers becomes the victim of the police. Everyone loses."

"So what?"

"Just for argument's sake—instead of a failure, let's assume we're observing a success. Suppose the staged suicides were the point of the plan from day one."

"Whose plan?"

"The plan of the person who called Wenzel, Balzac, and Pardosa and talked them into meeting with Richard in the first place."

"By selling them the fantasy of a blackmail plan that would make them all rich?"

"Yes."

"While actually setting them up to be killed?"

"Yes."

"But what about the involvement of high-level spook types? The advanced surveillance devices? The warnings from Wigg to back off? What the hell's all that about?"

"I need to understand the four deaths better before I can grapple with that."

"I have my own new idea about those deaths. It still assumes the blackmail plot. But the blackmailers don't approach Jane. They go straight to Richard."

"And?"

"And *he* kills them."

"Ethan too?"

"Ethan too."

"Why?"

"For the money. To get the twenty-nine million bucks before Ethan could change the will back in Peyton's favor. That's one piece I think Fenton might be right about."

Gurney thought about it. "It does seem a little more feasible than your Jane version."

"But?"

"But it contradicts the gut feelings we both had about Richard's innocence, and it leaves big questions unanswered. Who concocted the blackmail scheme? How does Ethan's written dream narrative fit in? Who did he write it for, and why? "

"Far as I can see, your theory doesn't answer those questions, either."

"I think it will—if we pursue it a little further."

"Lead the way, ace. My mind is open."

"First of all, if we view what happened as a well-planned enterprise that turned out exactly as intended, it would mean that Ethan and the other three men were all targets from the start. Targets of the same killer—but probably for different reasons. "

"How do you get to that?"

"Wenzel, Balzac, and Pardosa appear to have been accomplices of the planner—passing along that nightmare story—until they became victims of the planner. Ethan, on the other hand, appears to have been manipulated by someone into hand-writing the nightmare story—probably to make it appear that he was more connected with the other three than he really was, and that he died for the same reason they did."

"I've been thinking about this dictation idea of yours, and there's a problem with it. You gave Madeleine the email she dictated to you, so she could send it to her sister, right? That's what would normally be done. So why would Ethan keep what he wrote?"

"I was wondering about that myself. I came up with two answers."

"Typical of you."

Gurney ignored the comment. "One possibility is that it was dictated over the phone. The other is that Ethan *did* give it to the person who dictated it—who then put it back in his office after killing him."

"Hmm."

"You see a flaw in the logic?"

"No flaw in the logic. You seem to have arranged an impossible pile of shit into a credible sequence of motives and actions. Very logical."

"But you're not sure it's true?"

"All kinds of shit can be logical, but logical doesn't make it real. How do you propose we get from all this logic to the point of nailing the fucker behind it all?"

"Theoretically, there are two ways. There's the long, safe, methodical way. And the short, risky way."

"So we're going to do it the second way. Am I right?"

"Unfortunately, yes. We lack the resources to do it the right way. We can't interview every lodge guest and employee who was on site the day Ethan was killed. We can't go down to West Palm and Teaneck and Floral Park and interview everyone who knew Wenzel and Balzac and Pardosa. We can't find and interview everyone who attended or worked at Camp Brightwater. We can't run a fine-tooth comb through—"

"All right, all right, I get it."

"And the biggest limitation of all is that we lack time. Fenton, and the people pulling his strings, are about to take serious action to get me out of here. And it's not good for Madeleine to be here. In fact, it's very bad for her to be here."

He turned on the couch and looked into the bathroom. She was still in the shower. He tried to tell himself once again that it was a good thing. A restorative thing.

"All right, Davey, I get it. The long, safe way is not an option. So what's the short, risky way?"

"Tossing a rock into the hornet's nest to see what flies out."

"What kind of rock do you have in mind?"

Even as Gurney was listening to the question, the voice on the phone was breaking up.

Hardwick had just driven into another dead zone.

CHAPTER 50

When his mind was full of unanswered questions, Gurney often sought clarity in lists.

As Madeleine was finally emerging from the shower, he got a pad from his duffel bag. He sat down on the couch and started writing down the things he believed he knew about the deaths and the master manipulator behind them.

It included facts provided by Angela Castro, Steven Pardosa's parents, Moe Blumberg, Kimberly Fallon, Senior Investigator Gilbert Fenton, the Reverend Bowman Cox, Lieutenant Bobby Becker of Palm Beach PD, and the Teaneck PD detective contacted by Jack Hardwick— as well as the conclusions he believed those facts supported. Then he created a list of what he considered the major unanswered questions. The second list was longer than the first.

After reviewing everything he'd written, he decided to share it with Hardwick. He opened his laptop, typed the lists into an email, and hit "Send."

As he was taking another look at his handwritten sheets, making sure that he hadn't left out anything important, Madeleine came over to the couch wrapped in a bath towel.

He decided to tell her about his evolving vision of the case—that the reported nightmares weren't dreams that anyone had actually experienced, but elements in a complex plot, and that Ethan's written nightmare narrative was probably dictated to him by someone else.

As she listened to his description of how the puzzle pieces might fit together, what started as a skeptical frown slowly changed to an expression of real interest—and finally to a kind of revulsion.

"Do you think I've got it all wrong?" he asked.

"No. I think you have it right. I'm just wondering what kind of person could devise something that awful. So much lying. Such cruelty."

"I agree." He was momentarily taken aback by the gap between her perception of the situation as something essentially dreadful and his own view of it as a perplexing puzzle to be solved.

She looked down at his two lists on the table. "What's all that?"

"Preparation."

"For what?"

"I need to shake things up a bit. I'm organizing all the things I know and don't know about the case—as a guide for what I can say in a bugged conversation. I want to give whoever is behind all this the impression I know what's going on. But I want to be on solid ground with what I say. If I screw it up, he'll feel safe. I want him to feel threatened."

"But you still have no idea who he is, or what his ultimate motive was."

"The motive part is complicated. From a cui bono financial point of view, the only victim with a significant estate is Ethan, and the only significant beneficiaries are Peyton and Richard—and Jane, of course, to the extent that she's involved in Richard's life."

"I'd say that the extent of her involvement is total, absolute, and unhealthy."

Gurney went on. "A financial motive could explain Ethan's murder, but it doesn't work for the other three. On the other hand, a Brightwater-related motive could explain those three, but it doesn't work for Ethan."

"Maybe whoever killed them had more than one motive."

He nodded. It was a simple enough conclusion. Obvious, in a way. *Different motives for different victims.*

He'd begun to raise that possibility with Hardwick in their last conversation. And the notion was reinforced in his mind now by the memory of a gang-related mass murder he'd been assigned to shortly after his promotion to homicide detective.

At first sight—and a bloody mess of a first sight it was—it appeared to be a typical clash over drug sales territories. A rising gang faction had taken over an abandoned tenement on the border of a rival faction's turf—a provocative encroachment.

One night in July the gang's headquarters in the tenement was occupied by four gang members with submachine guns. A three-man crew from the rival faction, similarly armed, invaded the building and crashed through the apartment door. Less than thirty seconds later, six of the seven combatants were dead. One member of the invading faction escaped on foot.

After giving the wrecked bodies, the blood-soaked floors, and the walls full of bullet holes a cursory once-over, Gurney's partner at the time—a burnt-out detective by the name of Walter Coolidge—decided it was just another lunatic gunfight that everyone lost. Even if somebody had been lucky enough to get away, he'd probably find his sorry ass on the wrong end of an Uzi next time out.

Gurney was conducting the requisite neighborhood interviews that were a routine step at the beginning of every homicide investigation. That night he happened to ring the bell of a wiry little black woman with feisty eyes and sharp ears who insisted she knew exactly what she heard and how she heard it.

She described a burst of machine gun fire that lasted nine or ten seconds—produced, she claimed, by three similar weapons. That was followed by about ten seconds of silence. And that was followed by a second burst, lasting seven or eight seconds. She was certain that the second burst had been produced by a single weapon.

Gurney had been relating all this to Madeleine as she sat on the arm of the couch. Now she blinked in confusion. "How on earth did she know that?"

"I asked her that very question. And she asked me how did I think she could have succeeded as a jazz drummer if she couldn't distinguish between one and three instruments."

"She was a drummer in a jazz band?"

"In her past. At the time I spoke to her she was a church organist."

"But what does this—?"

"Have to do with multiple motives for murder? I'll get to that. The thing is, the sequence of the shots got me thinking. The three-gun burst to start with. The silence. The second one-gun burst. Everybody except one guy ending up dead. I pushed for a thorough crime-scene analysis, trajectory analysis, ballistics analysis, and medical analysis. And I spent a hell of a lot of time talking to local gangbangers. In the end, a new scenario emerged."

Madeleine's eyes lit up. "The guy who escaped at the end shot them all, didn't he?"

"In a way, yes. When the invading crew broke into the apartment, they took the rival crew by surprise. They opened fire with their three Uzi machine pistols, and in no time at all the official job they came to do was done. But one crew member, Devon Santos, had other concerns. Gang life at a certain level is about competition for a seat at the next higher level. And one of his crew brothers had an eye on the same opening he did. So after they wiped out the opposing personnel, Devon walked over to the nearest dead guy, picked up his AK-47, turned around, and blasted away his competitor as well as the crew brother who witnessed what he'd just done. Then he put the gun back in its dead owner's hands and got the hell out of there."

"How could you be sure that's what happened?"

"Ballistics discovered that the two invading crew members who ended up dead had been shot with an AK-47 that was found on a guy who had no powder residue on his hands. Meaning he couldn't have fired the gun. The rest came from an analysis of entry and exit wounds. The final convincer was that odd delay between the two bursts of gunfire—the ten seconds during which Devon made sure the other crew was down for good, and went to pick up the AK-47."

Madeleine gave him a thoughtful look. "So your point is that Devon had more than one motive. He went into the tenement to wipe out the enemy. But also to eliminate the threat of competition from his own side."

"Right. And he shot one of his gang brothers to keep the fact that he'd shot the other one a secret. So he really had three motives, varying according to victim. To Devon's way of thinking, they were all good reasons to kill people."

"And he'd have gotten away with all of it, if it wasn't for you."

"If it wasn't for a sharp witness with an ear for drumbeats."

Madeleine persisted. "But not every cop would have followed up the way you did."

He stared down uneasily at his yellow pad.

Praise had a downside. It increased his fear of failure.

CHAPTER 51

"Greetings, ace. I'm back in live cell country."

"Have you checked your email?"

"If you mean those pithy lists of semi-facts and open questions, I got 'em. I also have a piece of news you might want to add to your fact list."

"Oh?"

"News item on the radio. Kid in some theme park down in Florida died of a spider bite. Not normally that dangerous a spider, but this kid had some kind of allergic reaction to it. Didn't help that the spider was on something the kid was eating. Fucking thing bit the kid's tongue. Throat swelled up. Choked him. Fuck. Don't even want to think about that."

"Me neither, Jack. So what's this got to do with—"

"That nasty little news item gave us an overdue gift from the gods of luck."

"Meaning?"

"Pardosa."

"What are you talking about?"

"That was the species. The name of the spider. It was a Pardosa spider."

Gurney thought about it for a moment. "So you figure that Steven found out that his last name was the name of a spider species, so he adopted 'Spider' as a nickname?"

"Or one of his Brightwater buddies knew it and gave him the label. Or some jerk-off in junior high started calling him Stevie Spider. Who the fuck knows? Point is, it's got to be more than a coincidence."

"Leo the Lion, Wenzel the Weasel, Pardosa the Spider . . ."

"Just one more shithead to go. The Wolf."

"Yes."

"Too bad it's not Ethan. That would've wrapped things up neatly."

"It would have."

"With some luck the Wolf's identity will fall into our lap like the Spider's."

"Maybe."

"Okay, Sherlock, keep your fingers crossed. We might be in line for some more good luck. I'll get back to you after I see Wigg."

Gurney was pleased with the Pardosa discovery. Keeping his fingers crossed, however, was not something he ever did. He didn't like the concept of luck. It was, after all, nothing but a misunderstanding of statistical probability and randomness. Or a silly term one applied to the occurrence of a desired event. And even for the people who believed in it, there was an unpleasant truth about luck.

It inevitably ran out.

DURING GURNEY'S CALL WITH HARDWICK, MADELEINE HAD GOT-ten dressed. Now she came back to the couch so he could hear what she was saying under the music.

"It sounds like you're making real progress."

"We may be getting closer."

"You're not happy about that?"

"I need it to happen faster."

"You said before you want to make the killer feel . . . what, threatened?"

"Yes. By giving him the idea that I know his secrets. That's why I made my lists—to help me decide how much I can say without risking a mistake. A mistake would let him know I'm on the wrong path and kill the whole effect."

She frowned. "Instead of wondering how much you can say, maybe you should be figuring out how little you can say."

"Why?"

"Fear grows in the dark. Why not just open the door a crack? Let him imagine what might be on the other side."

Gurney was no stranger to the what-ifs that thrive in darkness. "I like that."

"Your plan is to let him overhear something through one of the bugs—something that will disturb him?"

"Yes. If someone thinks they're overhearing something you wouldn't want them to hear, it carries enormous credibility. A trick of the mind tells us that anything someone is trying to keep secret from us must be true. That's why I've left the bugs in place. They're the best weapons in the world to use against the bug planter."

"When are you going to do this?"

"As soon as I can. I have a feeling that Fenton is on the verge of arresting me for obstruction of justice."

The tic in her cheek was now plainly visible. "Can he do that?"

"He can. It wouldn't stick, but it would be a giant inconvenience. The only way I can neutralize him now is to prove that his 'fatal nightmare' theory is nonsense. And the only way I can do that is to ID the real killer and his real motive. Or, I should say, motives, plural."

"Like Devon Santos?"

"Very much like Devon Santos."

CHAPTER 52

Gurney was no fan of rapid decisions. He generally preferred to sleep on his ideas and see if they made sense in the light of a new day.

But there was no time for that now.

With the music on Madeleine's tablet playing loudly in the background, he outlined his plan to her, putting it together as he spoke.

Half an hour later they were sitting, bundled in their ski clothes, in the front seats of the Outback—ready to act out and record a prepared scene for later playback in their suite. Gurney put his smartphone in "Record" mode and placed it on the console.

Sounding tired and stressed (at Gurney's suggestion), Madeleine was the first to speak. "Do you want a fire?"

"What?" Gurney sounded preoccupied, annoyed to have his thoughts interrupted.

"A fire."

"Sure. Why not?"

"Well, then. Do you want to get one started?"

"Yes. All right. I will. Just not this second."

"When?"

"For Christ's sake, I've got something else on my mind."

There was a silence. Madeleine again spoke first.

"Do you want me to start the fire?"

"I'll do it, okay? I'm just going over something in my mind . . . making sure I'm right."

"Right about what?"

"The whole motive thing."

"You think you know why they were killed? And who killed them?"

"They were all killed by the same person, but not all for the same reason."

"You know now who's behind it all?"

"I'm pretty sure I do."

"Who?"

"Before I tell you, or anyone else, I need to do one more thing."

"I don't understand. If you know who the killer is, tell me."

"I need to run my logic by Hardwick. Tonight. When he gets back from Albany."

There was another silence.

"David, it's absurd that you're not telling me who it is."

"I need to bounce it off Jack first. I have to be sure the links in my head make sense to him. I'll tell you tonight. Another four or five hours, that's all."

"THIS IS STUPID! IF YOU KNOW, TELL ME NOW!"

"For God's sake, Maddie. Be patient. A few more hours."

"Shouldn't you call the police?"

"That's the last thing I'd want to do. Anything related to the murders would be funneled directly to Fenton. And that's a complicated situation."

"I hate when you do things like this." Her voice was full of quiet anger. "Don't you know how it makes me feel?" She paused. "So what if it's 'a complicated situation'? I think you should call BCI headquarters in Albany right now and tell them everything you know." She paused. "Why don't you do that? Why do these things have to end up with you facing off against the bad guy? We've been through this before, David. God knows we've been through it before. Too damn many times. You always have to turn an investigation into the Gunfight at the OK Corral."

"I don't want the BCI cavalry rolling in here with a fleet of cruisers and helicopters. The truth is I want to take this scumbag down by myself."

Gurney was afraid he might have stepped too far out of character with that last comment, but then he decided it was just right—the sort of braggadocio the argument they were supposedly having might provoke. And it might in turn nudge his opponent into reacting with more emotion than intelligence.

He wondered for a moment if he should mention Brightwater or the Lion, Spider, Wolf, and Weasel nicknames; but he decided to follow

Madeleine's advice and minimize the content of their conversation. To leave whoever might be listening with more questions than answers. To let fear grow in the dark.

As he began thinking about the best way to end their exchange, Madeleine added in an angry voice, "Same old story, again and again. It's always what *you* want—your goals, your commitments, your priorities. It's never about us. What about our life? Does our life occupy any space in your mind at all?"

He was nonplussed for a moment by her tone and choice of words, perhaps because they expressed so harshly the issue that existed in their real lives. The "detective versus husband" dichotomy in his own life. He hoped to God that the fury he just heard was mostly playacting. If it was, it was exactly that kind of spontaneous-sounding emotion that would make their conversation instantly credible to any listener. And it gave him an idea for a good way to conclude the recording.

He sighed, quite audibly. "I don't think I can handle that kind of question . . . that kind of emotion . . . right now."

"No," she said sourly. "Of course not."

After a short pause he concluded. "My nerves are shot, and I didn't get much sleep last night. I'm going to take a couple of your Valiums and close my eyes for a while."

She didn't answer.

He yawned aloud, then switched off the "Record" function.

CHAPTER 53

B ack in the suite they worked quickly. Madeleine's lively cooperation convinced him that the feelings she'd presented during their record-ing session in the Outback were at least partially manufactured for the task at hand. Of course, that might be wishful thinking—but there was no time to dwell on it now.

She took her bugged phone out of the bottom of her shoulder bag, where it had been lying, effectively muffled, under a thick wool scarf in a corner of the suite. At Gurney's suggestion, she placed it on one of the end tables by the couch. It was his belief that the device in it that had been substituted for its original microphone functioned as a transmitter not only of phone calls but of all nearby audio whether or not the phone was in use.

He'd decided to expose their prerecorded conversation to the phone bug as well as the Harding portrait bug. His guess was that one of them had been planted by the bad guy and the other by Fenton or someone in the shadowy hierarchy above him. He saw no downside in "tossing the rock" at both nests. The more hornets making themselves visible the better.

He reloaded the Beretta, replacing the two rounds he'd fired at the hawk, and put the gun in his right-hand jacket pocket. In the left pocket he put the smaller of their two flashlights. He gave the larger one to Madeleine. As he was explaining how it could be employed as a weapon, he was interrupted by his phone's text ring.

The message came from a blocked ID:

xBb770Ae

TellurideMichaelSeventeen

MccC919

LimerickFrancisFifty

It made no sense to him. Beyond the fact that there were certain repeated structural elements, whatever significance the sequences of characters and words might have eluded him. But at least the ring reminded him to put his phone on vibrate.

He emailed the audio file of their Outback conversation to Madeleine's tablet. When it arrived a minute later, he placed the tablet on the coffee table.

He selected the newly arrived audio file and tapped the "Play" icon. He waited until he heard her initial comment, "Do you want a fire?"

He made a small volume adjustment, then gestured to her, and they left the suite. He locked the door as quietly as he could.

He led the way to the far end of the dimly lit corridor and into the dark little cul-de-sac where the door to the attic stairs was located. He opened it.

"We'll stay here by the stairs, out of sight. If and when someone shows up at the suite, I'll deal with it. All you'll need to do is wait here until I've taken care of the situation. I'll come and get you as soon as everything is under control."

After a fraught moment she asked, "That's it?"

"What do you mean?"

"That's it? What you just said? Us hiding in the dark. Waiting for God knows who to approach the suite. Then you go there and . . . what? Confront them? Question them? Arrest them? Play it by ear? That's the plan?"

He didn't immediately reply. As long as he'd been describing the stratagem calmly, it had seemed sensible enough. But the illusion of sensibleness was starting to crumble. He realized there was a desperate, improvised quality to what they were doing—which he was trying to excuse to himself as necessary in the face of diminishing options.

He was saved from the need to respond by the vibration of his phone.

He looked at the screen. It was a message from Hardwick.

"Take a look at this unsigned text I got a few minutes ago—presumably from our techie friend in Albany. 'BAD TIME TO MEET. ASK G FOR KEYS TO THE HOUSE.' Any idea what she's talking about, apart from not being able to meet with me? What keys? What house? What the fuck? I'm on my way back. Hellacious storm rolling in."

For a minute Gurney was as baffled by the text Hardwick had received as by the one he'd received himself.

Then he saw a possible connection—and possible meaning.

He guessed that both texts had come, unsigned for reasons he could easily imagine, from Robin Wigg—the first to him, the second to Hardwick. And the second was probably referring to the first. The "house" would be the locked website he'd asked her about. The "keys" would be the site's IDs and passwords—the alphabetic and numerical character and word sequences she'd sent him.

He opened the text he'd received earlier and looked again at the four lines.

xBb770Ae

TellurideMichaelSeventeen

MccC919

LimerickFrancisFifty

Madeleine, peering at his phone screen, spoke up. "What are you doing?"

Half whispering, he explained his Internet quest to discover what sort of device had been planted above the bathroom ceiling.

She pointed at the message on the screen. "Does that tell you?"

"I think it's the entry data for a website that can tell us."

He brought up a copy of his own email to Wigg with the device serial number and the website address it had led him to. Then he went to the website page with the four data-entry boxes and entered the two alphanumerical IDs and the two passwords. A few seconds later a new page opened on the site, consisting of nothing but a data entry box and three words: ENTER INSTRUMENT CODE.

He got the device serial number from his email to Wigg and entered it.

A new page opened. At the top was a recognizable photo of the device. Below the photo was a dense table of scientific abbreviations, mathematical symbols, and figures that he guessed represented electronic specs and performance parameters. The terms heading the rows and columns were so unfamiliar he couldn't even tell what branch of technology they came from.

He was about to give up any attempt to understand what he was looking at when he spotted a simple word at the lower right corner of the incomprehensible table: "Compare."

He tapped on it.

Another page opened with another dense table. This one appeared to be a comparison of the specifications of several devices. This page had a headline: "Micro-Laser-Enhanced Pseudo Volume Visualization."

Madeleine was staring at the screen as intently as he was. "What does that mean?"

"I have no idea." He copied the headline and pasted it into a new search window.

Nothing came up that matched all the headline terms. Over a million hits matched at least one of the terms—a useless pile of data under the pressure of the moment.

He saved the web page's headline and began composing a reply to Hardwick's text. He included the website address, the IDs and passwords, and the headline—along with a request for Hardwick to do some research on it. He concluded with a brief description of the activity he and Madeleine were engaged in at the moment.

He read through the message and sent it.

Madeleine put her hand on his arm. "Are you sure . . . this is the way we should be handling this?"

Her question amplified his uncertainty. "Right now, it may be the only way."

He opened the door to the attic stairs and checked the dusty stairwell once again with his flashlight. He saw nothing unusual and heard nothing but an eerie, empty silence. They sat down gingerly on one of the lower steps—and waited, side by side, in the dark, listening.

CHAPTER 54

In darkness and silence, Gurney's mind often drifted toward unanswered questions.

That afternoon, sitting next to Madeleine in the silent gloom of the attic staircase, he was considering a question that had been lurking at the edge of his consciousness ever since he'd examined the joist space over the bathroom.

Might the unidentified little device that had been installed there, and was now in Hardwick's possession, be some sort of miniaturized projector?

Discounting the significant size problem, it would make sense. The reflective inner surface of the tub would make a serviceable screen. The subtle distortion created by the concavity of the tub bottom, by the water itself, and by the rising wisps of steam might actually enhance the "reality" of a projected image. More credibility would be added by the specific physical environment—i.e., people were accustomed to seeing bodies (live ones) in tubs. The mind would tend to accept such an illusion as real.

But what would be the purpose of such a cruel trick? To push Madeleine into an emotional breakdown? Gurney wondered if Fenton could be that obsessively determined to get rid of him. Who besides Fenton might find it worth the trouble? The killer? One of Fenton's anonymous overlords? How would they know about Colin Bantry? How would they know that Madeleine would be so vulnerable to that issue at that time?

Then a truly uncomfortable personal question occurred to Gurney: Which explanation would he prefer to be true? That Madeleine's experience had been assembled in the smoke and mirrors of her own mind? Or that it had been the product of sophisticated technology?

He wondered if he'd been focusing on the first possibility because the second had about it such a strong whiff of paranoia. Or perhaps because it brought so many additional complications to a case that he feared might be already be beyond his abilities.

He felt anger rising in him.

Anger at his own apparent inadequacy.

Anger at the endless accumulation of questions.

Anger at the possibility of someone damaging Madeleine's mental balance.

Her voice broke into his private purgatory. "Are you okay?"

"I was thinking about what you saw in the tub. I was thinking it might—"

His comment was cut short by the sound of heavy footsteps hurrying up the front staircase from the reception area.

"This could be what we've been waiting for. Stay here. Don't make a sound." Gurney quietly left the stairwell, moving out to a point from which he could see down the length of the corridor. He checked his watch. He could barely make out the time, but he judged that the recording he'd set to play back in the suite would have ended just a few minutes earlier.

A short, thickset figure, breathing heavily, approached the suite door and knocked. "Mr. Gurney?" The voice was Steckle's. He knocked a second time.

Gurney waited and watched.

Steckle knocked a third time, waited, then opened the door with a key. He called out, "Hello? Anybody here?" After a brief hesitation, he went inside and closed the door behind him.

Gurney returned to Madeleine. "It's Austen Steckle. In our suite."

"What's he doing in there?"

"I'll find out. But I'd like you to be a little further out of sight. Maybe at the top of these stairs? He took out his flashlight and pointed at the attic door on the top landing. "See that? If you hear any commotion down here, just step into the attic and shut the door behind you."

"What are you going to do?"

"Find out if Steckle is one of our hornets." He pointed up the stairwell again with his flashlight.

She headed up the stairs. When she reached the top, he went out into the corridor and moved quickly to the suite door.

It wasn't locked. He eased it open and stepped inside.

In the cold, gray light Steckle was moving across the sitting room. There was something in his hand.

Gurney gripped the Beretta in his jacket pocket. "You looking for me?"

Steckle spun around, his eyes widening. "Mr. Gurney. I thought . . . I mean . . . are you all right?"

"Fine. What are you doing?"

"I came to warn you." He held out the object in his hand. "Look at this."

"Do me a favor. Turn on that lamp by the couch."

"Right. Sure."

The lamplight illuminated a brightly honed hatchet.

"Tarr was chopping the battery cables on your Outback. Just finished doing the same to the Jeeps. And Norris's Land Rover. When I went out to stop him, he threw this damn thing at me. Could have taken my head off. Son of a bitch ran off into the storm. Christ! I wanted to make sure you and Mrs. Gurney were all right."

"We're fine."

Steckle glanced toward the alcove. "I knew we shouldn't have kept that son of a bitch around."

"Any idea where he went?"

"Who the hell knows? He ran into the snow, into the woods, like an animal." He held up the hatchet. "Lay it on the coffee table."

"Why?"

"I want to look at it, but I don't want to touch it."

He laid it next to Madeleine's tablet. "That's some goddamn weapon, eh?"

Gurney took a few steps closer, his hand still on the Beretta in his pocket. "You said he was chopping my battery cables?"

"Was giving them a whack just as I came out."

"Why on earth would he do that?"

"How the hell would I know what goes on in that lunatic's head?"

More interesting to Gurney than Steckle's story about the severing of the battery cables was the unlikelihood of it having occurred the way he claimed. And it seemed inconceivable that Barlow Tarr was the hornet aroused by the bugged conversation, much less the mastermind of the most complex murder plot Gurney had ever encountered.

"You're the detective. What do you think's going on?" asked Steckle.

"Let's take a minute and talk about that. Maybe we can figure it out together. I have some questions I think you can help me with. Have a seat."

Steckle hesitated, seemed about to object, then sat down with obvious reluctance.

Gurney perched on the arm of the couch opposite him. "First, before I forget . . . what kind of name is Alfonz Volk?"

"That's not my name. Volk was the guy my mother married."

"So you told me. But what nationality was he?"

"I don't know. Slovenian maybe. Something like that. Why do you want to know?"

"Just curiosity." In Gurney's long experience with interrogation, jarring changes of subject often produced good results. "So what do you really think that business with Tarr was all about—assuming he's not just a lunatic doing things that make no sense at all."

"I don't know. You cut battery cables, cars don't run. Maybe he doesn't want any of us to leave."

"What do you think his reason would be for keeping us here?"

Steckle shook his head. "I don't know."

"You think he might have killed Ethan?"

"I guess it's possible, right?"

"Why would he have done it?"

"Maybe he figured Ethan was finally going to get rid of him."

"You think he killed him to keep from being fired?"

"It's possible."

"Except Tarr was never at Camp Brightwater. And the killer was."

For a split second Steckle's expression froze.

"Where Scott Fallon was killed. Where this whole mess began."

Steckle shifted his weight closer to the edge of the chair. "You lost me."

Gurney took the minute to consider how Steckle could fit into the shoes of the killer. He *could* have been the fourth bully at Brightwater, the boy known as Wolf. He *could* have invited his three old camp pals to the lodge. He *could* have sold them on the notion of the blackmail scheme. He *could* have killed them after they'd carried out their instructions to spread the nightmare fiction. And, of course, he *could* have killed Ethan. Means and opportunity would be available.

The big question would be motive.

Gurney recalled the conversation he'd had with Steckle in the attic, the conversation about the Gall crest and the Gall history. The conversation about power and control. And he considered the practical consequences of the four deaths.

The more he thought about it, the clearer the puzzle became. And there was this final, simple convincer. He'd tossed the rock into the hornet's nest, and Austen Steckle had flown out.

Every fact was now explainable.

But not a single thing was provable.

As he was pondering the best way forward, he heard the soft buzzing sound his phone made on a wooden surface in vibrate mode. He reached from his chair over to the end table and, keeping a careful eye on Steckle, picked it up.

It was a text from Hardwick.

"*Shitty roads. Pulled off and researched the tech terms on the mystery site. That thing may be a micro version of a classified hi-def image projector used by the military.*"

Steckle moved uneasily on the edge of his chair.

Gurney looked up from his phone. "What made you so sure we were in our room?"

"What do you mean? Why wouldn't you be?"

"Because most of the time we haven't been. We've been in and out, downstairs, out by the lake, in the Hearth Room, the Hammonds' chalet, other places. And you knocked. Three times. You even called out to us. And you got no response. None at all. I'm surprised you didn't conclude we were out."

"Why are you making a big deal out of this?"

"You looked so surprised to see me coming into the room behind you—more than surprised, absolutely baffled—as if you couldn't understand how it could be happening."

"The hell are you talking about?"

Gurney withdrew the Beretta from his pocket and made a point of confirming the presence of a round in the chamber.

Steckle's eyes widened. "What the fuck . . . ?"

Gurney smiled. "It's almost funny, isn't it? All that planning, all that elaborate deception. Then you trip over a pebble. The wrong look at the wrong moment. And it all collapses. You were positive we were here in our suite, because our conversation came to you through the bug that you planted here. Audio surveillance is such a reliable tool. Except when it isn't. Problem is, it has a big limitation. It can't distinguish between live voices and recorded voices."

Steckle's face was as pale as the gray light from the windows. "This is completely nuts."

"Save your breath, Alfonz."

"Austen. My name is Austen."

"No it isn't. Austen was the name of the rehabilitated man, the good man. But that man never existed. Inside, you were always Alfonz Volk. Embezzler, manipulator, and general piece of shit. You're a bad man who killed good people. And that's a real problem." Gurney rose from the arm of the couch.

He stepped over to the row of windows and ripped the cords out of two venetian blinds, then picked up an iron poker from the hearth. He tossed one of the long cords in Steckle's lap.

"What's this?"

Gurney adopted an attitude of creepy calmness. "The cord? The cord is the easy way."

"Easy way . . . to do what?"

"The easy way to make sure you don't run away." He glanced vaguely at the poker but said nothing about it. The hard way was easy enough to imagine—and more frightening in the imagination than words could make it.

Gurney smiled. "Please tie your ankles together—nice and tight."

Steckle stared at the cord. "I don't know what you think I did, but I guarantee you got it wrong."

"You need to tie your ankles together right now." Gurney's hand tightened visibly on the poker.

Steckle was shaking his head but did as he was told.

"Tighter," said Gurney.

Again he did as he was told. His scalp was glistening with sweat.

When his ankles were firmly bound together, Gurney told him to put his hands behind him. When he complied, Gurney used the second venetian blind cord to tie his wrists, running the end of the long cord under the seat of the chair and knotting it to the ankle cord.

Steckle was breathing heavily. "This is all a bad dream, right?"

Gurney came around in front of the chair to face Steckle. "Like the dream you dictated to Ethan?"

"What? Why the hell would I do that?"

"Why is obvious. What I didn't understand at first was why Ethan would do it for you. Then I remembered something Fenton told me—to prove you couldn't have forged the letter. He told me that up until last week you had a cast on your hand. He figured that exonerated you. But that turned out to be the answer to my question. You got Ethan to write out the dream narrative for you because of that cast."

"Gurney, this is crazy talk. Where's the evidence?"

Gurney smiled. "Evidence is only required by courts."

Steckle's jaw muscles tightened.

Gurney's voice now was hard as ice. "The legal system doesn't work. It's a game. Smart guys win, dumb guys lose. Harmless idiots get jammed up for having a few street pills in their pockets, and really bad guys—the guys who kill good people—dance through the system with fancy lawyers."

He pointed the Beretta at Steckle's right eye, then at his left eye, then at his throat, his heart, his stomach, his groin. Steckle flinched. Gurney continued. "The bad guys who kill good people—those are the ones who really bother me. Those are the ones I can't ignore, the ones I can't trust the courts to punish."

"What do you want from me?"

"Nothing, Alfonz. You have nothing to trade. You have nothing I want."

"I don't understand."

"It's simple. It's not a negotiation. It's an execution."

"I didn't kill anybody."

Gurney appeared not to hear him. "When bad people kill good people, I have to step in and do what the courts fail to do. Bad people don't get to kill good people and walk away. Not on my watch. That's my purpose in life. Do you have a purpose in your life?"

Gurney raised the Beretta in a sudden movement, aiming it between Steckle's eyes.

"Wait! Christ! Wait a second! Who the hell are these good people you're talking about?"

Gurney did his best to conceal a sense of victory. He had Steckle believing he might be able to escape vigilante justice by proving his victims unworthy of any justice at all. It was a path on which the man was likely to incriminate himself in the belief that he was saving himself.

"The good people I'm talking about are Ethan Gall and your buddies from Brightwater. But especially Ethan. That man was a saint."

"Okay, just a second. You want to know the truth?"

Gurney said nothing.

"Let me tell you about Ethan, the fucking saint."

Steckle launched into an excoriation of Gall as a maniacal control freak, obsessed with manipulating the lives of everyone around him—a tyrant who used the Gall New Life Foundation as a prison where his whims were law.

"Every day, every minute, he tried to humiliate us, rip us into little pieces that he could glue back together, whatever way he wanted to—like we were goddamn toys. The great god Ethan. The great god Ethan was a disgusting monster. The whole world should be grateful he's dead!"

Gurney frowned as if absorbing significant new information. He lowered the gun, just a little. It was a tiny gesture with great meaning. It suggested that he could be persuaded. "What about Wenzel, Balzac, and Pardosa? You going to tell me they were control freaks, too?"

Now Steckle's eyes were full of calculation—the process of deciding how much to say without irrevocably incriminating himself. "No. I wouldn't say that. My honest impression of them? From what I saw of them here at the lodge? Ants at the picnic. Petty criminal types. No loss to anyone. Trust me."

Gurney nodded slightly. A man learning sad truths. "No one would miss them?"

Steckle produced an approving little click with his tongue. "In a nutshell."

"What about Hammond?"

"What about him?"

"A lot of damage has been done to him with that nightmare nonsense."

"Yeah? Well, how about all the damage that bright-eyed little faggot did—screwing up people's lives with his great-to-be-gay crap?"

"So you're saying he deserved to be framed for four murders you committed?"

"Whoa! All I'm saying is what goes around comes around. You're saying good people got killed. I'm just setting you straight. Those people were scumbags."

Gurney lowered the gun a little further, creating the impression that Steckle's argument might indeed be softening his determination to execute him. Then he frowned and steadied the gun, as though he'd come upon a final decision point.

"What about Scott Fallon? You telling me he was a scumbag, too?" He aimed the Beretta directly at Steckle's heart.

"I had nothing to do with that!" The denial came out in a burst of panic—the denial and, in its wording, the implicit admission of his presence at Brightwater.

Gurney raised a skeptical eyebrow. "The Lion, the Spider, and the Weasel . . . but not the Wolf?"

Steckle seemed to realize that he was stepping into quicksand to escape from the fire.

Steckle shook his head. "They were crazy. All three of them."

"Your buddies in the secret club were crazy?"

"I didn't realize how crazy. Fucking horrible. Horrible pointless shit they would do."

"Like what they did to Scott?"

Steckle was staring at the floor. Maybe wondering how deep the quicksand was.

Gurney repeated his question.

Steckle took a deep breath.

"They dragged him out to the lake one night."

"And?"

"They said they were going to teach him to swim."

Gurney felt himself recoiling inwardly from the scenario that was unfolding in his mind. He forced himself back to the moment. "I heard that the police dragged the lake but never found a body."

"They fished him out and buried him in the woods."

"They being Wenzel, Pardosa, and Balzac?"

Steckle nodded. "Crazy fucking bastards. Hated homos. I mean really hated them."

"Which made them the ideal recruits for . . . your project."

"What I'm saying is that they were worthless fucking brain-dead assholes."

Now Gurney nodded. "Not good people. So killing them wouldn't—"

He was stopped by something that sounded like a faint scream. It seemed to have come from another part of the lodge—somewhere above him.

He left Steckle tied to the chair and ran out of the suite, down the corridor, and into the dark attic staircase where he'd left Madeleine.

CHAPTER 55

S he wasn't on the stairs where he'd last seen her.

He called to her. There was no answer. He remembered there was a switch on the wall of the stairwell. He felt for it, flipped it up, and the bare-bulb light came on in the ceiling over the top landing. He bounded up the stairs, two at a time, the Beretta still in his hand.

He opened the attic door and felt for the wall switch he knew was there. The fixture high in the peaked roof came on. In the dusty light, the sheet-covered objects in the room—excess furniture, he assumed—appeared as before.

He made his way quickly through this large storage area toward the door at the opposite end.

He called out Madeleine's name again.

A strained voice came from somewhere beyond the far door. "In here."

He ran to the door and pushed it open.

At first all he could see were the wolves—crouching in the unsteady beam of a flashlight—and their distorted shadows moving jerkily on the wall behind them.

Then he saw Madeleine, backed into a corner, flashlight in hand, and he immediately regretted his decision not to mention the wolf tableau when he told her about his attic exploration—for fear that it would only raise her already high anxiety level.

He located the cord dangling down from the roof-beam fixture and gave it a yank. The huge cave-like space was filled with a dim, dirty-looking light.

He went to Madeleine. "Are you okay?"

She pointed with the flashlight. "What are they?"

"Wolves. Killed by Ethan's grandfather. Part of the weird family history." He paused. "How did you end up in here?"

"I was at the top of the stairs. I thought I heard someone in the corridor near the foot of the stairs, so I went into that first room, the one with the sheets over everything. Then I was sure I heard the stairs creaking, so I came over into this room. At first I didn't see the wolves. But then—my God, what a shock! But what about you? What happened in the suite?"

Gurney related the key points of the confrontation as quickly as he could—everything from Tarr's alleged chopping of the battery cables to Steckle's panicked admission of prior contact with Wenzel, Balzac, and Pardosa; his knowledge of Scott Fallon's death; and his hatred of Ethan Gall—all to Madeleine's increasing astonishment.

"Steckle's down there now? In our room? My God, what do we do now?"

"I don't know. The main thing is, he's out of commission. But I am curious about those battery cables. Let's go down and take a look."

THE SCENE THAT GREETED THEM IN FRONT OF THE LODGE WAS exactly as Steckle had described it. The hoods of the Outback, the Land Rover, and the three Jeeps were raised, the cables on all five batteries had been severed, and the battery casings had been penetrated by powerful blows from a very sharp hatchet or other axe-like implement.

"Looks like he was telling the truth," said Madeleine, zipping her jacket up to her chin against the sleety wind.

"About what was done, yes. But who did it is still an open question."

"And you're thinking Steckle did it to implicate Tarr?"

"He could have."

"But . . . ?"

"But he might have had another reason, too. To keep us here."

"You mean, to keep us from getting away from him?"

"Yes."

He realized that they might be able to snowshoe out, but the nearest civilization was at least fifteen miles away—and in sub-zero storm conditions that were getting worse by the hour such an endeavor could be extremely dangerous, if not fatal.

"God, I'm freezing to death," said Madeleine. "Can we go back inside?"

Before Gurney could answer, all the lights in the lodge went out.

The background hum of the generator died.

And the only sound was the icy wind gusting through the pines.

CHAPTER 56

With the help of their flashlights they made their way back into the lodge.

In the reception area, Gurney went behind the main desk to the old-fashioned pigeonhole compartments built into the wall and took the key from the compartment labeled "Universal"—which he hoped would open all the guest-room doors. The idea of keeping Steckle in their suite with them overnight did not appeal to him. He was thinking the best solution would be to keep the man securely immobilized in a neighboring room.

In the upstairs corridor, instead of going directly to the suite, Gurney stopped at the door next to it and tried the key. It worked. He explained his plan to Madeleine, and they went into the room to look it over.

In the beam of his flashlight Gurney spotted two kerosene lamps on the fireplace mantle along with a propane igniter—which he used to light both lamps, turning up the wicks for as much brightness as they could offer. Although the room was smaller than the suite, it had similar features and furnishings.

With the central heating out of commission with the failed generator system, there was already a noticeable chill in the room—which prompted Gurney to set about building a fire. He wasn't particularly concerned about Steckle's comfort, but letting the man freeze to death overnight would create unnecessary problems.

Madeleine watched anxiously as he bent over the hearth, arranging a pyramid of split logs over a bed of kindling. "Shouldn't you be calling someone? The state police? The sheriff's department?"

"I can't. The generator powers the cell tower."

"Aren't there any landlines?"

"The nearest would be in Bearston. Might as well be on the moon."

"What are you going to do about Tarr?"

"There's not much I can do—not at the moment."

"What about everyone else?"

"What do you mean?"

"Norris? Richard? Jane? Shouldn't you tell them about Steckle? And warn them to be on the lookout for Tarr—in case he's the one who wants to trap us all here?"

The overload was starting to get the best of him. "I should. Of course. He straightened up from his fire-making and took a deep breath. "But there's something important I need to tell you first. Something we discovered with the help of Robin Wigg. I got a text from Jack while I was with Steckle. It's about what you saw in the tub."

She stood very still.

"What you saw may have been a projected image—projected into the tub from the space above the ceiling."

She blinked in bewilderment.

"Wigg gave us access to a password-protected website. There was a picture there of one of the devices that I believe was in the attic, over our bathroom—a very high-tech projector."

Madeleine blinked, looked stunned.

"There's a good chance that what appeared to be an actual body was a manipulated image. Probably an old photograph of Colin Bantry that had been digitized, sharpened, colorized . . . then altered in ways consistent with the effects of drowning."

"But what I saw didn't look anything like a photograph."

"It wouldn't have. It would have looked very real. Very convincing."

Her appalled gaze seemed fixed not on him but on her memory of what she'd seen. "My God, who would do such a thing?"

"Someone hell-bent to get what he wants at any cost."

"Someone? You mean someone other than Austen Steckle?"

"Steckle is certainly clever and ruthless and willing to kill to get what he wants—but this projection thing has a different feel to it. Maybe it's the restricted technology angle, maybe it's the fact that it doesn't quite fit with the other things he's done. Steckle is a practical man, and I don't see a practical relationship between the trouble he'd have setting that up and any benefit to him. And there's the knowledge question—how could he possibly know about you and Colin Bantry?"

Madeleine nodded. "Okay. I see that. But where does that take you?"

"In the direction of a hidden manipulator. One with unlimited resources. Someone willing to use those resources to get us to leave Wolf Lake immediately."

"By terrorizing me?"

"Yes. By creating that godawful bathtub illusion."

She shook her head, seemingly at a loss for words.

"I'm sorry I didn't get to the truth of it sooner."

"But you're sure now? You're sure that's what it was?"

"Yes."

"My God, I'm so . . . so . . . I don't know what. Confused? Furious? Relieved?" She let out a small nervous laugh. "So I'm not crazy after all, am I?"

"No, Maddie, you're perfectly sane."

"We have to get him. We have to get that rotten bastard."

"We have to. And we will."

She nodded, her eyes alive with a new focus.

WITH THE BLAZE IN THE FIREPLACE WELL ESTABLISHED AND BANKED with enough logs to keep it going through the night, Gurney decided it was time to move Steckle in there from the suite.

He was stopped by the slam of a door at the far end of the corridor, followed by the sound of approaching footsteps. The footsteps came to a halt some distance away, and there was a sharp rapping at what he guessed to be the suite door.

Gurney stepped out into the corridor. In the rising beam of his flashlight, he registered a now-familiar pair of Wellington boots, Barbour storm coat, and tartan scarf.

Norris Landon had a flashlight in one hand and a rifle in the other. "Gurney? What the hell?"

"Long story. What are you doing?"

"Our vehicles were sabotaged. Batteries whacked out of commission with an axe or some such thing. I tried to find Austen, but he's nowhere to be found. I did find some footprints leading away from the destruction—which I intend to follow to get some answers. I figured a bit of armament might be in order." He nodded toward his rifle. "Thought I'd knock on your door before I headed out, see what you knew about the state of things."

Gurney saw no reason to conceal the facts. He gave Landon a somewhat abbreviated but largely accurate version of the interview in which Steckle had all but admitted his guilt. He included Steckle's own account of his encounter with Barlow Tarr and the hatchet. He added that, while Tarr may indeed have been the culprit, it was possible that Steckle himself had done the damage. He concluded by explaining that Steckle was currently under restraint in the suite, in a kind of emergency custody, and would remain so until appropriate authorities could be brought into the picture.

Landon appeared dumbfounded. "Bloody hell. Austen. The whole nightmare business was just a ploy, then?"

"It would seem so."

"Christ, you're saying he took Fenton in completely? Made an absolute fool of him? The press conferences, news reports—they were all wrong?"

"Apparently."

"Devilishly clever."

"Yes."

He paused, shaking his head. "What now?"

"Depends on how soon there's a break in the weather. Speaking of which, are you really serious about going out to follow footprints? In the dark? In a snowstorm?"

"I'm a hunter, Mr. Gurney. I'd like to get to the bottom of the mess someone made of those vehicles. You say it might've been Steckle. But my money'd be on Tarr—just from the appearance of things. Gut feeling. The chaos down there. The wreckage. Work of a madman." He paused. "I'd also like to take a look at the generators. Might just've been snow in the ventilation intakes that triggered a shutdown."

"Be careful. You might be running into a man with a very sharp hatchet."

Landon smiled. "Have you ever hunted wild boar in the underbrush at dusk?"

Gurney said nothing, waited for the punch line.

"I have. So, believe me, I can handle Barlow Tarr." The smile disappeared, and the man turned away into the dark corridor.

Gurney left the door ajar until he'd heard Landon descend the staircase to the reception area and go out into the storm.

"Quite a character," said Madeleine.

Gurney went to the room's row of windows that looked out over a balcony similar to the suite's. Through the swirling snow he soon caught sight of Landon's flashlight beam emerging from under the portico, then dimly moving away from the lodge, presumably as the man followed whatever footprints the wind had not yet erased.

"Okay," he said, "let's get back to the job at hand."

Flashlight in hand, he led the way out of the room and through the dark corridor to the suite door. He unlocked it and went in, followed by Madeleine. The air inside was cold.

He swept the beam of light around. Everything seemed in order. Although a large floor lamp was partially blocking his view of Steckle, he could see enough of the man's arms tied behind the back of the narrow wooden chair he'd left him in to be reassured that no progress had been made toward escaping.

"It's freezing in here," said Madeleine.

The room, Gurney realized, was colder than it should have been, even considering the lack of central heating for the past half hour.

He pointed the flashlight at each of the windows. They were all closed, as was the door to the balcony. But then he noticed with instant concern the source of the frigid air. In the balcony door's large glass panel there was a jagged hole next to the locking mechanism.

Someone had broken in, or tried to break in. He swept the light around the room again.

With a sick feeling he stepped around the obstructing floor lamp and started moving toward the figure bound in the chair, not sure if he was seeing what he thought he was seeing.

"Steckle!" he cried.

There was no answer.

As what he was looking at became clearer, a sick feeling nearly overwhelmed him. He tried to turn Madeleine away as she came up beside him. But it was too late.

She saw exactly what he saw. Half gagging, half groaning, she grabbed his arm.

The bulky physique and the recognizable clothes made it fairly certain that the body in the chair was Austen Steckle's.

The lack of absolute certainty arose from the fact that the head had been severed from the torso and lay on the floor, chopped into pieces.

CHAPTER 57

G urney tried to persuade Madeleine to return to the room next door, but she refused.

Trembling and tight-lipped, she insisted on staying right there with him—watching as he checked the sitting area, bedroom alcove, bathroom, and balcony to ensure that the killer was no longer present. She continued to watch—although with evident difficulty and revulsion—as he proceeded with a general inspection of the disfigured corpse.

The sight was as awful as any he'd encountered in all his years as a homicide detective.

He took out his smartphone and made a photographic record of the body, particularly the grotesque damage done to it, from multiple angles. Although there was no cell service and no access to the Internet, the phone's batteries could still power its other functions.

He also photographed the area around the body, the broken glass panel in the balcony door, and as much of the balcony itself as he could without stepping outside and compromising any footprints or other trace evidence.

There was no point in trying to check the body for lividity, temperature decrease, or the signs of rigor mortis that could establish an approximate time of death. The murder had obviously occurred during Gurney's relatively brief absence from the suite.

With the help of his flashlight, he took a closer look at the remnants of the head. The final opinion would, of course, be the medical examiner's, but he had no doubt that he was looking at the result of multiple blows from something with a sharp, heavy, axe-like blade.

Something like Barlow Tarr's hatchet.

The hatchet that Austen Steckle had brought to the suite with him.

The hatchet that was now gone.

In the interest of crime-scene preservation, they left the body in place exactly as they'd found it—and left everything else as undisturbed as possible. They weren't about to occupy the room any longer than necessary, so they did have to remove their things.

Gurney took a fresh blanket from one of the bureaus and laid it on the bed. He put their bags, loose clothing, bathroom articles, laptop, and tablet on the sheet. He gathered up the corners, creating a kind of catch-all sack with which they could take what they needed in a single trip; and they moved it all to the room where they'd been planning to take Steckle. The solution wasn't in perfect compliance with crime-scene protocol, but he felt it was the best they could do under the circumstances.

AS THE SHOCK AND HORROR OF THEIR DISCOVERY BEGAN TO ABATE, and they guardedly occupied their new quarters, Gurney felt increasingly pressured—and stymied. It seemed that none of the things that cried out for immediate action could be acted on.

A madman with a hatchet had to be corralled. Law enforcement had to be alerted to the radically changed situation. The Hammonds had to be warned. Yet none of these things seemed possible with phone service dead, night falling, roads obstructed by snowdrifts, vehicles crippled.

He felt obligated to get word to Richard and Jane, but how? He wasn't going to leave Madeleine alone in the lodge with an axe murderer loose. And he wasn't about to ask her to come with him on a mile-long trek through a sub-zero blizzard.

As frustrating as it was, he knew he had to resign himself to the limitations of the situation—and focus on what he could do.

At least the fire he'd started was gaining strength and beginning to warm the room. He checked the supply of kerosene for the lamps and judged that it would be adequate for a few days. He went into the bathroom, turned on the tub taps, and managed to capture a few gallons of water before the residual tank pressure was exhausted.

He pulled the heavy drapes across the row of icy windows to conserve heat, locked the doors to the balcony and to the outer corridor, and tipped chairbacks under the knobs as makeshift braces.

As he was adjusting the draft in the fireplace flue to maximize the burn time of the logs, Madeleine was standing by the bed, looking down at the blanket full of things he'd brought in from the suite. She picked up what he'd retrieved earlier from the lake—what he'd assumed at the time was one of the hawk's tail feathers.

"Is this what flew off that thing when you shot at it?"

He glanced over from the fireplace. "Yes. Tail feather, I think."

"It may have come from the tail, but it doesn't feel like a feather."

"What do you mean?"

"Just that. Feel it."

The texture was hard and rather plastic-like. But he knew nothing about feathers. Madeleine, on the other hand, knew a great deal. Every time she found a new one on their property in Walnut Crossing, she brought it back to the house and researched it on the Internet. She'd accumulated a collection of turkey, grouse, crow, blue jay, and cardinal feathers; even a few hawk and owl feathers.

"How's it supposed to feel?"

"Not like that. And there's another thing. What happened to me out there on the lake? I really don't think that's something a hawk would do, unless its nest was being threatened."

He recalled something Barlow Tarr had said. Something about "the hawk man" setting the hawk loose. Setting it loose "into the sun, into the moon." It sounded like gibberish at the time. Since hawks didn't fly at night, setting one loose "into the moon" made no sense.

Unless, as Madeleine was now suggesting, it wasn't a hawk at all.

Configuring a miniature drone to look and move like a bird would be an enormous technical challenge. For clandestine operations, however, a drone that passed for a bird would offer huge advantages— advantages that might be worth the development cost, especially if no one else believed such a device was feasible.

Madeleine frowned. "There was a hawk circling over us at Grayson Lake."

"I know. And over that little lane down to the lake. And here, every day, over this lake."

"Watching us?"

"Possibly."

"So we're being observed from the air, listened to in our room, and tracked in our car."

"Apparently."

"By the same person who . . . who projected that image of Colin?"

"Probably."

"Good God, David, who's doing this to us?"

"Someone who's extremely worried about us being here. Someone with tremendous resources. Someone Gilbert Fenton is willing to take orders from."

"Someone who wants Richard to be tried and convicted for those four deaths?"

He almost agreed. But then he remembered the strange thing that Hammond told them during their dinner at the chalet. He told them that what Fenton wanted more than anything was for him to *confess*—and Fenton had promised that once he confessed, *everything would be all right.*

It had struck Gurney at the time as the sort of deceptive inducement to confession that anyone with half a brain could see through, and he was surprised that Fenton would try to pull a ruse like that on a man as sophisticated as Hammond; but the really strange part was that Hammond was positive that Fenton was being honest and that he actually believed a confession would be the end of Hammond's problems.

What would it mean if confession was the real goal, not conviction?

"David?"

"Sorry?"

"I was asking who you thought was behind all this spooky surveillance stuff."

"I may get to the answer when I figure out why a confession is so important to them."

She looked confused.

He reminded her what Hammond had told them at dinner. He added something else he remembered as he was speaking—Fenton's angry complaint that Gurney's efforts were giving Hammond false hope, essentially prolonging the agony, and that the man's only way out was a complete confession.

"So that's why they want us out of here? Because you're standing in the way of a confession?"

"I think so. But to get to the bottom of the whole case, I need to figure out the significance of that confession."

"In the meantime," she said, "we really need to warn the Hammonds."

"I wish we could. But the only way would be to make the trek there. And I can't leave you alone here. Not after what happened to Steckle."

"Then I'll come with you."

"In that blizzard?"

"We did bring our ski clothes. And ski masks. And snowshoes."

"It's dark."

"We have flashlights."

He recognized in her tone a depth of determination that would make further argument a waste of time. Ten minutes later, against his better judgment, they were down in the reception area, strapping their snowshoes onto their insulated boots. With their ski pants over their jeans and their hooded down jackets over their sweaters and their ski masks over their faces, they headed out onto the lake road.

In the pools of light formed by their flashlights Gurney could see the windblown outlines of footprints. As they progressed along the snow-covered road and passed the far end of the lodge itself, the faint suggestion of footprints veered off toward the side of the building in the direction of the generators. It reminded him that Landon had said something about checking them as he headed out in his pursuit of Tarr.

On the off chance that the man might be there now, perhaps attempting some repair, Gurney persuaded Madeleine to take the short detour with him.

They made their way around the building through the drifts. At the edge of a clearing that separated the lodge from the surrounding forest, the beam of his flashlight revealed two large rectangular objects. Approaching closer, he could see the ventilation slots, heavy-duty cables, and propane tanks that identified the rectangular objects as generators. He could also see that a carport-like structure—a slanted metal roof on high posts—intended to keep the generators from being buried in snow, had been partially crushed, apparently from the tree that had fallen on it during the earlier blackout.

Madeleine uttered a gasp at the sharp crack of a branch giving way under the pressure of snow and wind somewhere in the nearby forest.

Seeing no sign of Landon and realizing that closer examination of the generators was unlikely to give him any useful information, Gurney made one last sweep of the area with his flashlight.

"What's that?" asked Madeleine.

He looked where she was pointing.

At first he saw nothing.

Then he saw something dark on the ground, sticking out from behind the nearer of the two generators.

It looked like a gloved hand.

"Stay here." He made a cautiously wide approach for a better perspective on the generator's hidden side.

As his angle of view changed, the situation became clearer.

There was indeed a gloved hand in the snow. The hand was attached to an arm attached to a body that was lying facedown. Snow had blown against one side of the body, half covering it. But the parts that were exposed were familiar. In particular, the knee-high Wellington boots. The chic Barbour storm coat. The tartan scarf.

As he got closer, he moved the beam of his flashlight along the body, up past the scarf.

Then he flinched.

The head had been chopped into at least half a dozen bloody pieces.

"What is it?" called Madeleine, starting toward him.

"Stay back." It was his reflexive cop's voice, a voice of command. Then he added in a more human tone, "You don't want to see this."

"What is it?"

"A repeat of what we saw in the suite."

"Oh God. Who . . . ?"

"It looks like Tarr found Landon before Landon found Tarr."

He forced himself to make a closer inspection of the butchered head. It appeared to have been hacked apart in the same manner as Steckle's, likely with the same weapon. A ring of blood had spread out into the snow around the gruesome mess, forming an outlandish halo of red ice.

As he swept his flashlight back and forth over the body, he saw on the side covered with snow part of a rifle barrel. He bent over and brushed the snow away. It was a custom Weatherby with a hand-tooled claro-walnut stock. He tried to pick it up to see if it had been fired, but it was frozen to the ground.

It occurred to him that the body itself, including the dismembered head, would almost certainly be frozen to the ground as well.

Whatever sharp-toothed scavengers might be abroad in the forest that night, and however helpful it might be to the medical examiner to keep the remains intact, moving that body indoors by himself was not an option he was willing to consider.

He went back to Madeleine. "We need to get inside."

"We still have to warn Richard and Jane."

He shook his head. "Not after what I just saw. I'm not going to risk something happening to you, just to lower the risk of something happening to them. Before we can help anyone else, we need to establish a secure position for ourselves."

"A secure position . . ." She repeated the words as though she were trying to absorb a measure of confidence from them. She nodded, gazing over at Landon's rifle—frozen to the ground and now barely visible through the swirling snow. "Do you think he might have some other guns in his room?"

"There's a good chance he does. I ought to get hold of them for our own defense—and to keep Tarr or anyone else from getting them."

"*Anyone else?*"

"It seems pretty likely that Tarr killed Landon and Steckle, but we don't know that for sure. There's always Peyton, or someone working for Peyton. These two new murders aren't making much sense to me yet."

CHAPTER 58

In addition to locating and retrieving any other guns Landon may have brought to the lodge, Gurney was hoping he might find among the man's things some clue to the reason for his death—and possibly for Steckle's death as well.

The timing of the murders suggested that the killer may have had access to the transmissions of one of the audio bugs and was aware not only of what Steckle had admitted to, but of Gurney's temporary absence from the suite. That made Gurney wonder if they'd been grossly underestimating Tarr all along.

To his surprise, Madeleine insisted on remaining in their new room while he conducted the search of Landon's possessions.

Before going down the hall, he made a final security check of their windows and balcony. Two differences from the suite—positive differences, under the circumstances—were that the balcony door in this room was solid wood with no glass panel, and the windows were significantly smaller. Breaking in here would be a lot more difficult.

He checked the Beretta to confirm there was a round in the chamber and that the magazine was filled to its fifteen-round capacity. He considered putting the pistol down in his ankle holster, then decided to keep it in his jacket pocket—a bit closer to hand.

He picked up the large Maglite and the master room key and stepped out into the dark corridor. He waited until he heard Madeleine double-lock the door behind him, then proceeded to Landon's room.

He tried the door. It was locked, as he expected it would be. He inserted the key, turned it, and the door opened.

He stepped inside and swept his flashlight beam around the space, which appeared to be a smaller version of the suite, similar to the room they were now occupying. The same kinds of furnishings were arranged in the same way. He saw a kerosene lamp at each end of the fireplace mantle. There was a propane igniter on the log rack, and he used it to light the lamps.

On the coffee table between the couch and the hearth there were three laptops, three smartphones, a scanner, and a locked metal file box—unusual equipment for a vacationing hunter.

He explored the bedroom alcove. The bed was neatly made. There was a closet full of expensive-looking sports clothes. Behind the hanging shirts and jackets was a portable walnut gun cabinet with a combination lock. The overall impression was very refined, very upscale.

Except for the smell.

It was faint but repulsive.

Like sour sweat. With a hint of decay.

Mindful of his reason for being there, he removed the gun cabinet from the closet and brought it out into the main room. He laid it on the floor and got an iron poker from the hearth. As he was about to pry the lock off, one of the laptops on the coffee table caught his eye. A small pulsing light indicated it hadn't been shut down, only closed and put to sleep.

He lifted the lid. The screen lit up. There were twenty or so folders as well as dozens of document icons—mostly photo and video files.

Before clicking on any of them, he opened the other two laptops and pressed their power buttons. After a few seconds each displayed a screen asking for an ID and a password. Within a few seconds of his failure to enter anything, both screens went blank and both computers shut down completely. He was unable to restart them.

That level of security was interesting, to say the least.

He went back to the first laptop. He wondered if it was more accessible than the other two because its files didn't matter, or because Landon had left the room in such a hurry he'd neglected to shut it down properly. Hoping it was the latter reason, he began opening the photo files.

The first nine were aerial images of rural roads. Examining the images closely, he saw that there was a common factor among them. The presence of his Outback.

The next half dozen showed the Outback in various locations at Wolf Lake: emerging from under the lodge portico, on the lake road going toward the chalet, parked at the chalet, returning from the chalet.

As he was about to go to the next image, the date on one of the other folders caught his eye. It was that very day. He opened the folder and in it was one audio file. He opened it and clicked on the "Play" icon. He immediately recognized his own voice and Steckle's—the confrontation they'd had in the suite. Steckle's self-incriminating statements. His Brightwater admissions. His history with Wenzel, Pardosa, and Balzac. All bugged and recorded by Landon.

Gurney went back to the remaining icons on the screen and began opening them. There were three aerial videos he could see were taken at Grayson Lake: he and Madeleine emerging from the Outback, then standing in front of a tumbledown house, then standing by the lake itself.

Next was an aerial video that appeared to have been taken from the perspective of a rapidly moving, swooping camera—a video of Madeleine, turning, running, terrified out on the middle of Wolf Lake. Plus a quick passing shot of himself, Beretta pointing at the camera.

Lastly, there was a folder containing a series of Photoshopped images of a young man with a crooked smile and a scar through one eyebrow, wearing a leather jacket. The series started with an image that might have appeared in a school yearbook and, step by digital step, ended with an image that looked very much like a bloated corpse.

Gurney's jaw muscles tightened as he gazed in quiet anger at this final proof.

Proof that it was Norris Landon who was responsible for the sophisticated surveillance. Proof that it was Norris Landon who had inflicted all that pain on Madeleine. He wished that the man could be brought back to life—so he could have the pleasure of killing him.

So he could wield that fatal hatchet himself.

Then, when his visceral reaction to what Landon had done subsided sufficiently for him to think clearly, a more complicated thought process took over. He began to wonder about Landon's overall role in the affair.

What was his relationship with the other players? With Steckle? With Fenton? With Hammond? With the four dead men?

What, ultimately, was the game that involved them all?

And then a more immediate question intruded into Gurney's consciousness: What the hell was that odor?

Its source was proving elusive. It seemed to be everywhere. He checked the closet, the drawers in the bureau, the bed, the chairs, the couch, the end tables, the wet bar, the bathroom, the shower stall—even the floors, the walls, the windows.

He looked under the bed, under the armchairs, under the couch, under the coffee table, under the throw rugs. Unable to locate the source, he focused on trying to identify the smell itself. It was acrid, faintly rotten . . . and slightly familiar. Like an elusive word or name, it was more likely to come to him once he stopped chasing it. To change his focus, he sat on the couch in front of Landon's laptops and once again went through the accessible photo and video files.

They only confirmed Gurney's growing certainty that Landon was a representative of the anonymous "national security" interests that Fenton and Wigg had alluded to. If so, then he may well have been the force endorsing Fenton's view of the case and promoting the importance of securing a confession from Hammond.

It reminded Gurney of the *New York Times* story about the CIA leaker, Sylvan Marschalk, and his claim that a clandestine group at the agency was researching ways of inducing suicide through hypnosis. Marschalk's nasty demise within days of making his allegations gave them a disturbing credibility.

Other bits of information began stirring in Gurney's memory. The fact that Richard had been at Wolf Lake Lodge for two years, and that Landon had been making visits to the lodge for the same two years. The fact that Richard had written papers that pushed the boundaries of hypnotic technique. The fact of his expertise in the fatal psychology of voodoo. Jane's mention that Richard had been approached several times by research entities whose structure and goals were less than transparent.

Those little dots were certainly not conclusive individually, but they could be connected in a way that suggested Richard's expertise had for some time been on the radar screen of a clandestine group not unlike the one Sylvan Marschalk had tried to expose. Landon would fit into that scenario as their undercover representative on the scene, the man whose original purpose would have been to monitor Richard's "cutting edge" progress in hypnotherapy and ultimately to draw him into their orbit.

As Gurney sat there on Landon's couch, his mind racing through the possibilities, he began to see how the case elements arose from two wholly separate interests. Steckle's interest in the Gall fortune. And the government's interest in Richard Hammond.

Those interests might never have intersected—if only Austen Steckle hadn't made it seem that Hammond was responsible for four suicides, and if only Norris Landon had been less eager to believe it.

Gurney was confident that he understood what Steckle had done, and why. The man had been remarkably clever and successful, up to a point. What he couldn't have anticipated, however, was the intense interest the "fatal nightmare" aspect of the case would attract in that shadowy corner of the government represented by Landon. And how that interest would influence the investigation.

Something else occurred to him there on the couch with the coffee table and laptops in front of him. The room's unpleasant odor seemed to be the strongest in that very area.

He stood up and removed the cushions. As he was examining them individually, he heard something behind him that sounded like a drop of water striking a hard surface. He turned toward the fireplace.

When he was about to attribute it to his imagination, he heard it again.

He stepped over to the hearth, aiming his flashlight into the big sooty firebox, then down at the iron grate designed to support the logs. There was a dark shiny spot on one of the dusty bars in the grate. As he bent over for a better look, another drop descended onto that same spot.

He assumed the chimney was leaking. A bit of melting ice, perhaps.

But when he moved the flashlight closer to the dark spot for a final check, he discovered that the liquid on the grate was actually dark red. He touched it lightly with his forefinger.

It had the unmistakable stickiness of blood.

He lowered himself to his knees, and, with gritted teeth, pointed the beam of the Maglite up into the flue.

It was hard to tell what he looking at. It appeared to be something with matted hair. In the midst of the hair there was an irregular splotch of wet blood.

The first chilling thought that came to mind was that he was look-ing at the top of a human head—which would mean that someone's head or, improbably, their entire body had been jammed upside down into the chimney.

That seemed impossible.

As he leaned in for a closer examination, the odor became more repellant.

Reluctantly he lay down on the hearthstone in front of the firebox for the best viewing angle and aimed the flashlight directly up at the hairy, bloody thing.

It was plainly larger than a human head. Perhaps it was an animal. If so, it was a large one. The matted hair was gray.

Could it be a gray timber wolf?

Wolves had been circling around the case from the beginning.

He retrieved a pair of tongs from the iron stand by the log rack and used them to get a solid grip on the object.

When he pulled down sharply, it came loose, dropping down into the firebox and seeming for a moment to be alive and expanding. Gurney recoiled, then realized what he was staring at was a rolled-up pile of rough winter clothing—a stained fur hat, a dirty canvas coat, battered leather boots. With the help of the tongs he dragged the fur hat from the ashy firebox out onto the floor. The back half of the hat was saturated with half-congealed blood.

Next he pulled out the canvas coat and the boots.

It didn't take long for him to conclude that these were the garments worn by Barlow Tarr.

So why the hell were they hidden in Norris Landon's fireplace?

And where was Tarr?

Had he been killed, too?

The amount of blood on the hat would make it more than a possibility.

But who could have killed him?

Gurney recalled his own comment to Madeleine: *I think Tarr found Landon before Landon found Tarr.*

But suppose it was the other way around.

Suppose that bloody scene by the generator wasn't what it appeared to be.

As the new scenario dawned on Gurney, bringing with it a surge of fear for Madeleine's safety, there was a small sound behind him—the tiniest squeaking of a hinge. Gurney stood quickly, turning toward the suite door.

Half in the darkness of the corridor, half in the low amber light cast by the kerosene lamps, the face of Norris Landon was just barely discernible.

The man took a step forward into the doorway. He had a sleek small-caliber pistol in his hand with a miniature suppressor, an up-close assassin's gun—light, quiet, easily concealable. His gaze moved slowly from Gurney to the open laptop on the coffee table, then to the bloodied coyote-pelt hat on the floor, then back to Gurney.

His eyes were full of cold hatred.

Gurney met his gaze. He said nothing. He needed to get a clearer sense of the moment before deciding on the best approach to save his life.

Landon spoke. "In an ideal world, I'd have you prosecuted for treason."

"For solving four murders and saving an innocent man?"

"Hell, Gurney, you have no idea what problems you're causing—the wreckage I'm trying to fix. You have no idea what's at stake. You're worse than that lunatic, Tarr."

"The lunatic who gave me your projector?"

Landon paused, giving Gurney a long appraising look. "People like Tarr are sand in the gears. It's people like you that create real problems."

Gurney picked that moment to cast a split-second glance down at his right ankle, then blinked a few times as if in an effort to hide the movement of his eyes. He wanted to convey the impression of a man thinking about a gun in his ankle holster.

The Beretta was at that moment in Gurney's jacket pocket, a fact he didn't want Landon to suspect. He hoped the slight downward glance had been seen as something not intended to be seen. It was a subtle game.

"What do you mean, people like me?"

"People wearing blinders," said Landon. "People who refuse to see the reality of the world we live in."

Echoes of Fenton, thought Gurney. Or Fenton echoing Landon.

"It's a war, Gurney, the largest and deadliest war of all time. Our enemy is determined, obsessed, driven by the hope of destroying us. We need every advantage we can lay our hands on."

"Like TIS?" As Gurney spoke, he moved his right ankle ever so slightly forward. He saw the movement register in Landon's eyes just before he blinked at the mention of the acronym for the CIA's suicide-research program.

Landon raised his pistol, pointing it at the center of Gurney's chest. "Sit down."

"Where?"

"On the floor. Facing me. Next to the coffee table. Keep your hands above your waist. Well above your waist. I hate firing a gun in an enclosed space. It leaves a ringing in my ears."

Gurney complied.

"Now extend your legs straight out in front of you."

Again Gurney complied. The movement revealed the bottom half inch of the ankle holster. He expected Landon to approach him to remove the gun he would believe was there. Instead, Landon told him to drag the heavy coffee table across his extended legs and place his hands on top of the table. He did so, discovering that the position was an effective way of making it impossible for him to reach the holster.

Landon looked pleased, then adopted a quizzical expression. "What were those initials you mentioned?"

"TIS. Trance-induced suicide. The program Sylvan Marschalk leaked to the press. The leak that got him assassinated."

"That druggie traitor a hero of yours?"

"Never met the man."

"But you think his death was a great loss to the world? Let me set you straight. When a little shit like Sylvan Marschalk imperils a program that could save thousands of American lives, he forfeits his own. There's no right under God or the Constitution to recklessly weaken our defenses in a time of war. Let me make this perfectly clear. We are at war."

"And Barlow Tarr was the enemy?"

"Tarr was a distraction."

"And my wife? Is she the enemy?"

"You and your wife chose to support the wrong side."

"You mean we were delaying Richard Hammond's confession?"

"You were getting between your country and an individual who was a potential strategic asset. You were warned. More than once."

"I assume Hammond was identified as a potential strategic asset because you believed he could induce suicide, a technique you and your friends would kill for."

Landon said nothing. His expression was distant and emotionless.

"So when you heard that someone hypnotized by Hammond later complained about nightmares that made him want to kill himself, and then he actually did kill himself—and when that happened not once but four times—you assumed the TIS problem had been solved. Now, if only you could get Hammond to explain how he'd done it. You didn't give a damn about getting him to confess *that* he'd done it. It was all about getting him to confess *how* he'd done it. Too bad he had nothing to confess. Too bad you were wrong. Too bad you have to clean up the mess. You wouldn't want anyone back at the agency to find out what a godawful error you'd made—that you'd mistaken Steckle's con job for the real thing."

Gurney made this speech in a relaxed, confident, almost amused voice. He knew he was treading a perilous line between provoking rage and planting a seed of uncertainty. But perilous lines were part of the game.

Landon's expression betrayed nothing.

Gurney extemporized. "Speaking of con jobs—you might want to look at some photos I have."

Madeleine's advice came to mind. *Just open the door a crack.*

"Where are these photos?"

"On a USB drive."

"Where?"

"In my pocket."

Gurney pointed to his right jacket pocket, which, in his seated position on the floor, was just above the edge of the coffee table.

Landon gave him a long appraising look.

"Shall I toss it to you?" asked Gurney. "Or do you want to come and get it yourself?"

Landon hesitated. Then he took a step closer and aimed his pistol at Gurney's throat. "Slowly remove the drive from your pocket. *Very slowly.*"

Looking as anxious and defenseless as he could, Gurney reached slowly into his pocket.

In a single smooth movement he gripped the Beretta and, without removing it from his jacket, pointed it in the direction of Landon and began firing.

He wasn't sure which round hit the man or where it hit him; but in the midst of the six-shot burst the man emitted a feral yowl and lurched backward into the corridor. By the time Gurney managed to heave the weighty coffee table off his legs, get to his feet, and stumble to the door with the Beretta in one hand and the Maglite in the other, the dark corridor was silent. He swept the light back and forth, but there was no sign of Landon.

He switched off the flashlight to avoid becoming an easy target and felt his way along the corridor to his own door. He unlocked and opened it.

Just inside, in the faint kerosene lamplight, he found Madeleine— wide-eyed, teeth clenched, with an iron poker drawn back like a base-ball bat, ready to swing. She stared at him for a good five seconds before taking a breath and relaxing enough to lower the poker.

After telling her as quickly as he could what had happened, he went back to Landon's room and retrieved the man's laptops, smartphones, and gun cabinet.

Then he reloaded the Beretta's magazine, barricaded their door, and rebuilt the fire.

The wind was howling fiercely now, the blizzard had finally arrived in full force, and there was nothing more they could do until daylight came.

CHAPTER 59

S leep was impossible. There was too much to worry about, think about, plan for.

In a way, from an intellectual point of view, the case was over. The most perplexing questions had been answered, the major deceptions had been exposed. The puzzle had been solved. But a god-awful mess had been created along the way.

Bureaucratic and career imperatives were likely to make the mess bigger before it got smaller. The likelihood of obtaining any clarity or accountability from the forces associated with Norris Landon was in the neighborhood of zero. If those forces were indeed part of the CIA, zero would be an optimistic estimate. And BCI's appetite would be minimal for any re-investigation that would make their first approach to the case appear fanciful at best.

From an emotional point of view, things were perhaps the least settled. Through the whole restless night he and Madeleine huddled together on the couch in their ski clothes facing the fire. The groaning and creaking of the old building kept Gurney on edge, kept him speculating on the condition, whereabouts, and intentions of Landon.

The speculation was circular and endless. As were his thoughts about Colin Bantry's place in Madeleine's life, about her ability to recover from the shock of the things she'd seen, about the greed and ruthlessness of Austen Steckle, about the twisted history of the Galls, and about the delusional obsessions of those who hated America and those who claimed to love it.

A thought he'd had many times before came to him now with renewed power: *God save us from our saviors.*

From time to time he added a log to the fire. From time to time Madeleine sat up and stretched into one of her yoga positions.

Oddly, with so much to discuss, they spoke hardly at all.

At the first light of dawn they both began to doze.

Moments later they were awakened by a heavy mechanical rumbling.

Trying to place it, Gurney realized it was coming from outside the lodge. He slipped into his boots, removed the chair he'd jammed under the knob of the balcony door, and stepped out into the icy wind.

The sound was getting louder. The source, he discovered, was a big yellow truck that was just turning onto the lake road in the direction of the lodge. Mounted on the front of the truck was the largest industrial snow blower he'd ever seen—with an intake opening at least ten feet wide and five feet high. The massive rotating blades that pulled the ice and snow into that giant maw were rotating fast enough to create a blur. The secondary impeller blades must have been operating at an even greater speed judging from the energy with which the expelled material, converted to a powder, was rising from the disposal chute.

At a height of forty or fifty feet a strong crosswind was catching that geyser of finely pulverized ice and snow and blowing it far into the pine forest. When the roaring machine came abreast of the clearing in front of the lodge where the wind was strongest, the frozen output was carried hundreds of feet out over the lake.

As Gurney watched, the truck moved on past the lodge in the direction of the chalet and Gall House, effortlessly clearing four-foot-high ice-impacted drifts from the road surface.

Madeleine came out onto the balcony next to him. "Shouldn't you stop him and give him a message for the police?"

"That road dead-ends at the Gall mansion. He has to come back the same way. I'll stop him then."

She looked toward the brightening eastern ridge. "Thank God the snow stopped. But it's freezing out here. We should go back inside."

"Right."

They went in, shut the door tight, and stood at the window.

Madeleine produced a fragile smile. "It looks like the sky might actually be blue today."

"Right."

She gave him a curious look. "What are you thinking?"

"I'm wondering why a county truck is clearing a private road."

She stared at him. "Isn't that something to be happy about?"

"You can be happy. I'll do the worrying."

"That seems to be your regular job." She paused. "I think I'm ready to leave this place. What about you?"

"I'm ready. But once we get word to the police, we'll need to make statements. About everything that's happened here. That could take some time. Then we'll be able to leave."

She looked anxiously out at the road. "Maybe you should go downstairs now so you don't miss him on his way by."

"Lock the door after me."

As a precaution against being caught off guard by Landon, he removed the Beretta from his pocket and held it in his hand, muzzle down.

He went downstairs and waited outside the main door, turning up his collar against the cutting wind. Within a couple of minutes the huge machine reappeared. To Gurney's puzzlement, it turned off the road and in toward the lodge. With its snow blower shut down, it proceeded toward him, moved slowly under the portico, and stopped. The big diesel engine idled noisily for a few seconds before falling silent.

The operator stepped down out of the high cab, removing the wool hat and thick scarf that together had been covering most of his face.

"Jesus, it's cold. How the fuck do people live here?"

"Jack?"

"No, your fairy godmother."

Gurney pointed at the truck. "Where . . . how . . . did you . . . ?"

"Borrowed it. Couldn't get in here without it. Adirondacks, my ass. This is fucking Siberia."

"You *borrowed* that thing?"

"Kinda borrowed, kinda commandeered. You know, police emergency, et cetera."

"But you're not the police."

"No time to split hairs. Is there any special reason you have that gun in your hand?"

"Long story. The short version is that Austen Steckle is dead, Barlow Tarr is dead, and I shot a CIA agent, who may or may not be dead."

Gurney filled Hardwick in on Steckle's plot to gain control

of the Gall fortune—and the toxic interaction between his fatal-nightmare stratagem and the mind-control ambitions of Landon's group at the CIA.

"So you figure at the end Landon was trying to save his career by wiping out the evidence of his mistake?"

"Something like that."

"Including you and Madeleine?"

"Most likely."

"Holy fuck. Hard to tell who was worse, Steckle or Landon."

Gurney responded without hesitation. "Landon."

"How so?"

"Steckle was a devil. Landon was a devil who thought he was an angel. The ones who think they're angels are the worst of all."

"You might have a point there."

"So what's this very interesting news you have for me?"

"Hardly seems to matter now, considering the fact that Steckle's dead. But Esti looked a little deeper into Steckle's earlier life as Alfonz Volk. Any idea what Volk means in Slovenian?"

Gurney smiled. The news was a little too late to be useful. But it was pleasant to have one's suspicions confirmed. "Wolf?"

"Precisely. Now, can we please go inside before my balls turn into ice cubes?"

HAVING CHOSEN THE HEARTH ROOM—WITH ITS SINGLE DOORWAY, lack of windows, and open view of the reception area—as the best place for them to sit down and work out their next steps, Hardwick went about building a fire.

Gurney went upstairs to get Madeleine.

He found her standing at the basin, wearing jeans and a sweater, brushing her teeth. She stopped and gave him an odd little smile. "I'm just trying to feel normal."

Her told her about Hardwick's appropriation of the monster snow blower and about Esti Moreno's discovery linking Steckle to Brightwater.

Neither event seemed to surprise her. "What do we do now?"

"We need to find Landon, check on the Hammonds, check on Peyton, check on the status of the generators, get word out to the county sheriff's department and to BCI. There's a hell of a lot more that'll have to be taken care of after that, but not by us."

She smiled and nodded. "You did it."

"Did what?"

"You saved Richard."

He knew it was pointless to repeat that saving Richard hadn't been the goal. And there was also the small matter of not knowing for sure if the man was still alive.

"Right now we need to sit down with Jack, figure out who's going to do what."

They made their way along the dark corridor to the main staircase, illuminated now by the morning light coming up from the reception-area windows and glass-paneled doors. As they were descending the stairs, Gurney heard voices in the Hearth Room.

"Sounds like Richard and Jane," said Madeleine with a relieved smile.

The Hammonds were plainly alive and well. Jane was engaged in an intense conversation with Hardwick while Richard stood a bit to the side, listening.

When Jane saw Gurney coming into the room with Madeleine, she stopped in mid-sentence and turned to him, her eyes widening with hope. "Is it true? Is it really all over?"

"As far as the case against Richard is concerned, I'd say that's over. It's clear that he was just the fifth victim of a complicated plot. There were no trances, no suicides. The deaths were all murders. The crime was complex, but the motives were simple—greed and control."

For her benefit and Richard's, he repeated the summary of the situation that he'd already given to Hardwick.

Jane's mouth fell open. "My God! We didn't know anything. Nothing at all. When the snow blower came by the chalet, and we could finally use the car, we thought we should come over to the lodge—to make sure you and Madeleine were all right, and to ask Austen about the generators. When we walked in, we found Jack and, well, here we all are."

Richard stepped forward and extended his hand. "Thank you, David." That was all he said, but he said it with such a palpable sincer-ity that nothing more seemed necessary.

Jane nodded enthusiastically. "Thank you. Thank you so much." She came over to Gurney and hugged him, tears welling in her eyes. She went over to Hardwick and hugged him. "Thank you both. You've saved our lives."

Hardwick looked eager to shift the conversation in a less emotional direction. "If you have any interest in pursuing a lawsuit against the state police or against Fenton personally—"

Richard cut him off. "No. To have it over and done with is good enough for me. From what you're telling me, Fenton's case has completely collapsed. Let that be the end of it."

He'd hardly finished when the lodge door opened and Fenton himself walked into the reception area, followed by a uniformed trooper. The trooper took up a position at the door as Fenton strode over to the Hearth Room, stopping in the archway entrance.

His gaze moved from face to face, then came to rest on Hardwick's. His mouth twisted into a smirk. "Well, well. I'd heard a nasty rumor that my old buddy Jack was trying to screw up an important case of mine. And then, just this morning, I get a call from the Highway Department about someone who claimed to be from BCI commandeering a major piece of highway equipment. I thought I ought to look into it myself. And look who I find in possession of that stolen equipment. Sorry to say, it appears to me that everyone in this room may be implicated."

The smirk stretched into a sadistic grin. "This is a serious matter. I'm afraid I can't let a past friendship get in the way of my present duty."

Hardwick smiled. His voice was cordial. "You know, Gil, you never did have much of a brain. But right now you're setting a new record for shitheadedness."

Perhaps because of the disconnect between the tone and the words, it took a moment for the comment to register. When it did, Fenton started moving toward Hardwick, and the trooper by the outer door started moving toward the Hearth Room with his hand on his holstered Glock.

Seeing disaster seconds away, Gurney intervened the only way he was sure would work. He said, loud and clear, "Austen Steckle is dead. Norris Landon killed him."

Fenton's forward movement ceased.

The trooper came to a halt in the middle of the reception area.

Both looked as bewildered as if Gurney had announced the arrival of space aliens.

FOR THE NEXT TEN MINUTES FENTON LISTENED STONE-FACED—except for an occasional twitch at the corner of his eye—to a detailed narrative of Austen Steckle's diabolical plot with its core illusion of induced suicides; the reverberations of that notion in a dark corner of the national security world; and Landon's desperate cover-up attempt.

At length Fenton muttered a single-word question. "Steckle?"

Gurney nodded. "A very intelligent man. Maybe the only murderer in history clever enough to persuade his intended victims to publicly announce they were feeling suicidal."

"And you shot Landon?"

"I had to. He was in the process of trying to kill everyone here, including me, who could reveal his misinterpretation of the suicides. In his world, gullibility is an unforgivable sin."

Fenton nodded like a man suffering from a concussion. The silence ended a few seconds later with a commotion in the reception area—which he seemed hardly to notice.

A burly man in a leather jacket had burst in through the front door and was speaking to the trooper in a loud voice—demanding a police escort to the regional hospital in Plattsburgh.

Gurney's first thought was that it might have something to do with Landon. But when the trooper questioned the man further, he explained that he had Peyton Gall "and a lady" in Gall's Mercedes, and that Peyton and the lady might or might not be frozen to death, having "dozed off after a few drinks" in a hot tub that turned into a container of ice water during the blackout. That, in Gurney's opinion, was just outlandish enough to be true.

When the trooper came to ask how Fenton wanted it handled, he stared at him uncomprehendingly and muttered, "Do whatever you want."

The trooper went back and told the man—who Gurney now recognized as the unfriendly guard at Peyton's gate—to get his frozen passengers to Plattsburgh as best he could. The man complained loudly, swore, and left.

Gurney suggested to the trooper that he call for reinforcements to begin the search for Landon, for a crime-scene team to deal with the body out by the generators and the one tied to a chair upstairs in the suite, for an electrician to restore power, and for another BCI senior investigator to provide whatever assistance might be needed under the circumstances. He made these suggestions clearly enough for everyone to hear them—so the trooper could interpret the lack of objection from Fenton as approval to proceed.

Explaining that his radio was more reliable on the ridge than in the lodge, the trooper headed out on his communications mission. Fenton followed him from the lodge to the cruiser, but didn't get in. When the cruiser departed, Fenton remained under the portico, gazing after it.

"He's completely fucked," said Hardwick.

"Yes."

Hardwick coughed into a filthy handkerchief. "I better return the borrowed snow blower to the Highway Department yard and put that bullshit stolen-equipment issue to rest."

"Good idea."

"I left Esti's truck there when I took the snow blower, so I'll get that and come back."

"When you're out there passing through live cell country, get the word to our contacts in Palm Beach, Teaneck, and New Jersey. Tell Esti. Tell Robin Wigg. Tell anyone you feel like telling. I want to be sure there's no way anyone can roll this up and make it disappear."

Hardwick zipped up his jacket and headed out to the giant machine.

Neither he nor Fenton acknowledged the other.

CHAPTER 60

Shortly after Hardwick departed, the Hammonds announced their
intention to return to the chalet and begin the process of sorting
and packing their belongings. Although nothing was certain and the
timing was yet to be determined, they imagined they would be returning soon to Mill Valley.

In addition to his share of the estate's liquid assets, Peyton's inheritance would include the lodge, the lake, and a few thousand acres of
Adirondack wilderness. There was no way of knowing what his plans
for it might be; but if Richard was sure of anything, it would be that he
personally would have no place—nor would he want one—under the
new regime.

By the time the Hammonds were pulling out onto the lake road, the
sun had risen well above the eastern ridge, turning the ice crystals in
the air into shimmering points of light. Madeleine was eager to get out
of the gloom of the lodge into the brightness of the day. Gurney got their
heavy jackets, scarves, gloves, and hats from the room. They bundled
themselves up and stepped outside into the cold, clear air.

Evidently wanting to avoid any personal contact, Fenton moved
away from the portico and began trudging slowly along the lake road in
the direction opposite the one the Hammonds had taken.

"I suppose I should feel sorry for him," said Madeleine. "But when
I think of what he did to Richard . . ." She shook her head. "What a
horror it all was."

"It was all wishful thinking."

"On Fenton's part?"

"On everyone's part. Ethan wanted to believe that his rehabilitation program had transformed the sociopathic Alfonz Volk into the
straight-arrow Austen Steckle. Landon wanted to believe that the secret

mind-control technique he'd been pursuing for years was finally within his grasp, if only he could force Hammond to divulge it. Fenton wanted to believe that he was a good soldier on the right side of a just war."

"And Steckle?"

"Steckle wanted to believe that achieving total control of everything, and eliminating anyone who might take it away, would finally make him perfectly happy."

"And what about me?"

"You?"

"I was no slouch at wishful thinking. I really did believe that I'd dealt with that terrible teenage mess—just because I'd told a therapist about it. I wanted to believe I'd put it all aside. And I think she wanted to believe that her therapeutic skills had worked wonders. God, it's not the lies people tell us that do the real damage. It's the lies we tell ourselves—the ones we're desperate to believe."

"It's amazing how we can be so wrong about so many things."

She smiled at him. "Can we walk over by the lake?"

"Sure."

As they were crossing the road, a speck of color on the thin layer of packed snow the snow blower had left behind caught Gurney's eye.

It was the color of blood.

A few feet farther on, there was a similar red speck.

They reached the far side of the road without his seeing any more.

Madeleine turned in the direction of the ridge road—the same way Fenton had gone. As she and Gurney ambled along, she took his arm. "Why did Landon have to kill Barlow Tarr?"

Gurney was thinking about those spots in the snow—almost certainly blood. It took a moment for her question to register.

"Maybe he was afraid Tarr knew something. Or maybe he just hated Tarr's interference, hated that he had the temerity to remove those devices from the attic. I remember him complaining about Tarr's fondness for chaos. That could have been motive enough for a control freak like Landon."

"Why go to the trouble of putting his own coat and boots on the body?"

"Improvisation. Might have seemed like a useful idea at the time—create confusion, keep us off balance. I'm not sure he had time to think it through. Landon was under tremendous pressure at the end. His life, his career—everything was on the line. He did not work for a forgiving agency. He was trying to dodge the consequences of his own mistakes. I think he was making up his exit plan as he went along."

"What an awful way to live."

"Yes."

As they walked on in silence, with no sight of Fenton on the road ahead, an unnerving thought occurred to Gurney—perhaps the result of his own mention of an exit plan—the thought that Fenton, in the light of his huge miscalculation, might be desperate enough to shoot himself.

He shared that fear with Madeleine.

She shook her head. "I doubt it. He strikes me as the kind of man who makes a lot of mistakes, creates trouble and pain in the lives of other people, but always finds a way to rationalize what he's done and blame it on someone else. He's not a nice man."

Gurney couldn't disagree with that.

"I'm starting to get cold," she said. "Can we go back to the lodge?"

"Of course."

"I'm looking forward to going home."

He paused. "Do you feel that coming here has been of any help in dealing with the past?"

"I think so. I'm not hoping for a magic eraser anymore. And I seem to be able to think about Colin now without being chewed up by what happened. How about you?"

"Me?"

"Your murder case—how do you feel about the way it ended?"

He thought about the drops of blood in the snow and wondered if it had ended.

She looked at him curiously.

He was searching for a way to answer her question without frightening her all over again—when he was distracted by a vehicle coming down the ridge road.

It turned out to be Jack Hardwick in Esti Moreno's pickup.

When he came abreast of them, he stopped and pointed backward with his thumb. "Saw Gilbert Asshole back there. Looked like he was pondering the prospect of a totally fucked-up career. You know what I say? I say fuck him." He produced a glittering grin. "I made some calls. So did that trooper who came with Fenton. Cavalry's on the way. Any sign of Norris?"

"Not at the moment," said Gurney.

"Shoot the fucker on sight," said Hardwick cheerily. "See you at the lodge." He rolled up his window and proceeded the final hundred yards or so to the portico. He got out of the truck, lit a cigarette, and leaned against the rear fender.

When Gurney and Madeleine got to the area where he'd seen the red stains in the snow, he told her he wanted to take a quick look around before the police vehicles started rolling in, which was not entirely untrue. After giving him that appraising look of hers that said she knew he was leaving something out, she walked over and waited by the truck with Hardwick.

Gurney meanwhile laid out a mental grid, roughly forty feet by forty feet, surrounding the red spots. Then he paced slowly back and forth within the grid, moving gradually in the direction of the lake.

When he'd progressed almost to the road's edge, he saw an exposed bit of something black and metallic embedded in the snow that had been packed down against the road surface by the weight of the snow blower. He scraped just enough of the snow aside with the tip of his boot to recognize the object. It was a compact suppressor, and it was attached to the barrel of a small-caliber pistol. He'd last seen that pistol in Landon's hand.

His next realization brought him close to vomiting.

He recalled looking out the window that morning in the early dawn light . . . hearing the mammoth snow blower approaching . . . watching it rip effortlessly through the waist-high drifts that buried much of the road. He could picture the tower of pulverized ice and snow erupting from the spinning impeller blades, shooting up into the wind and swirling out over the lake.

Gritting his teeth now against the sickness rising in his throat, he forced himself to walk out on the frozen surface. At first he saw nothing but snow—snow gusting and eddying over the ice. He walked farther out, almost to the middle of the lake. Then he saw what he was looking for—what he'd hoped he wouldn't see. There, in the blowing snow, was a tiny shred of fabric. And then another. As he walked on, he glimpsed a scrap of something that might be flesh. And farther on, a sliver of something that might be bone.

He turned back, moving with all the calmness he could muster, eventually joining Madeleine and Hardwick by the truck.

She regarded him questioningly at first, then with concern. "Should we go inside?"

He nodded.

As they were starting toward the lodge door, Hardwick looked down the road, cupping his hand to his ear. He began humming the theme from *The Lone Ranger* as a stream of police vehicles came into sight.

For a while, Gurney and Madeleine had the Hearth Room to themselves. He got a bottle of springwater from the cabinet under the guest bar and drank it down.

After a long silence Madeleine said, "Do you want to tell me about it?"

He stalled, giving his stomach more time to settle. And his mind to clear. He could think of no gentle way to say it. "I saw what's left of Norris Landon."

Her eyes widened in dawning horror.

"Apparently he didn't get very far after I shot him. It looks like he collapsed on the road. And the snow covered him."

"Covered him . . . and then this morning . . . Jack . . . Oh God."

After all he'd seen in his homicide career, even after the horrors he'd seen just the night before, he was shocked by Landon's fate—the grinding of his body into thousands of little fragments. Maybe there was a deep and bleak reminder in the man's utter obliteration.

Dust to dust. With a vengeance.

A numb exhaustion began to overtake him.

Madeleine took his hand. "Come, sit on the couch."

He allowed himself to be led to it. She sat next to him, holding his arm tightly against her.

He lost track of time.

After a while she said, "At least now it's over."

"Yes."

"What will you tell them?"

"Only what I know for sure. That I shot Norris Landon and he disappeared in the dark corridor." He paused. "The rest is up to them."

He was thinking that winter had just begun.

The snow would fall, and keep falling.

The wind would blow down from Cemetery Ridge and Devil's Fang.

And in the end Wolf Lake would keep its final gory secret to itself.

He put his head on Madeleine's shoulder.

The warmth of her body flowed into him.

As he drifted out of consciousness, he wondered idly where the hawk had gone.

And where it would circle next.